# Bloodstone

# Bloodstone

## Nate Kenyon

Best wishes,

Five Star • Waterville, Maine

First Edition
First Printing: January 2006

Published in 2006 in conjunction with Tekno Books and Ed Gorman.

Set in 11 pt. Plantin.

Printed in the United States on permanent paper.

**Library of Congress Cataloging-in-Publication Data**

Kenyon, Nate.
Bloodstone / by Nate Kenyon.—1st ed.
p. cm.
ISBN 1-59414-438-9 (hc : alk. paper)
1. New England—Fiction. I. Title.
PS3611.E677B58 2006
813′.6—dc22 2005027048

For my grandfather Edward,
a man of patience, love and eternal good humor.

Rest in peace, old friend.

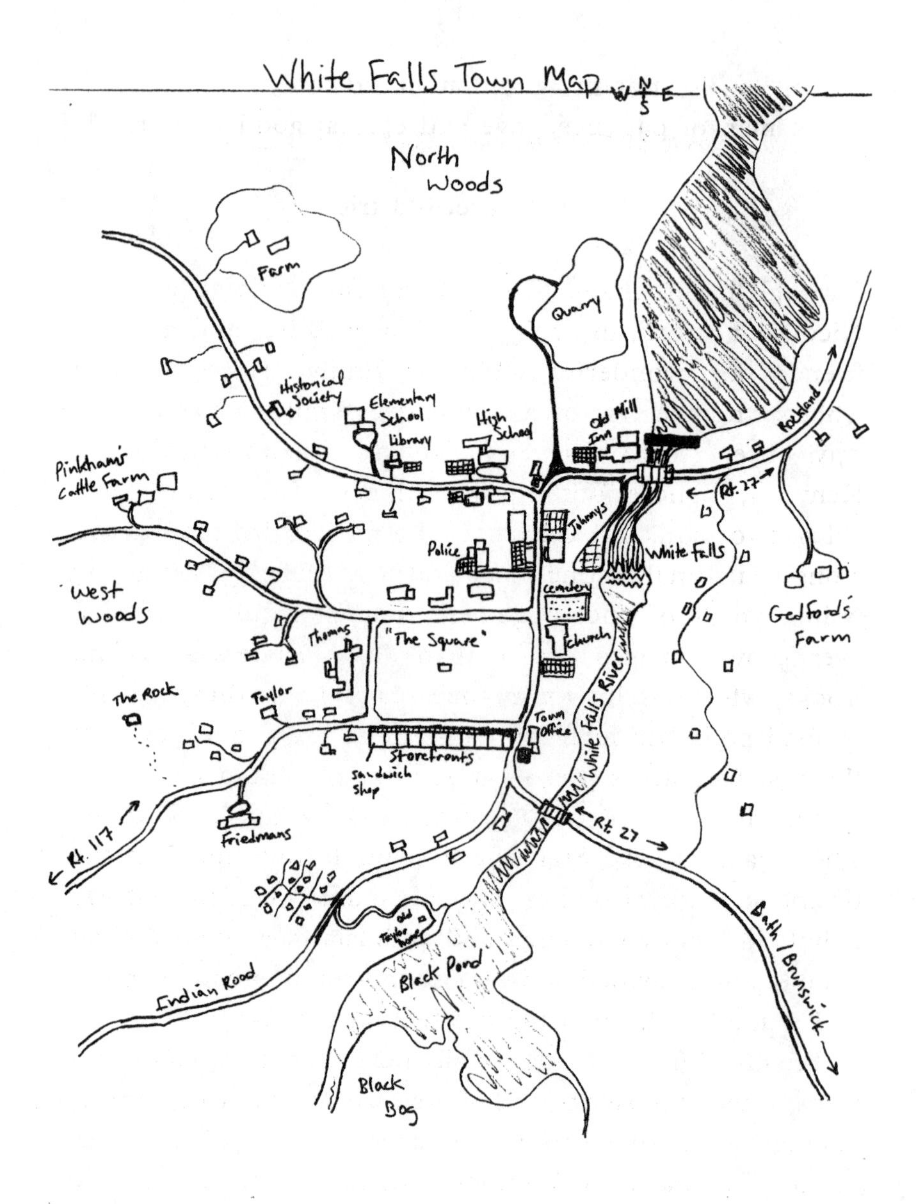

White Falls Town Map
N
W
E
S
North Woods
Farm
Quarry
Historical Society
Elementary School
Library
High School
Old Mill Inn
Rockland
Rt. 27
Pinkham's Cattle Farm
Police
Johnnys
White Falls
West Woods
cemetery
Gedfords' Farm
Thomas
"The Square"
church
The Rock
Taylor
Town Office
White Falls River
Storefronts
Sandwich Shop
Friedmans
Rt. 117
Rt. 27
Old Taylor Home
Black Pond
Indian Road
Bath / Brunswick
Black Bog

# Acknowledgments

I would like to thank, first and foremost, my lovely wife Nicole—my rock, my editor, my cheerleader, and my best friend; our wonderful children, Emily, Harrison, and Abbey; and the rest of my extended family, who have always been there for me. Browns, Beales, Bowmans, Kenyons, Clancys. Without them this book would not exist. I'd like to thank Ed Gorman, who passed this manuscript along to its final resting place and who offered a struggling writer words of encouragement more valuable than he'll ever know. I'd also like to thank John Helfers at Tekno Books, who took his sweet time reading this thing but remained polite through my constant nagging, and gave me the best Christmas present a guy like me could get.

Big thanks to Patricia Estrada, my editor, and to the whole gang at Five Star, the best publishing house in the business; and an extra special thank you to Tiffany Schofield, who has energy and enthusiasm enough for ten people, and provided constant support and encouragement as I stumbled through the production process.

Finally, I'd like to thank all those who read early versions of the manuscript and offered words of advice and encouragement. All errors or stretches of the truth (such as the old Thomaston Prison, left operational through artistic license) are my own.

# Acknowledgments

# Prologue

On a cloudless night in April an ancient gray Volkswagen drifted through the outskirts of a town called Holy Hill, South Carolina, before pulling into the Sleepy Inn parking lot. The two people inside the car had seen many such towns over the past few days, and many such motels. They parked near the manager's office.

"I'll just get us a room," the man said to the woman driving, pretty and thin but too pale. "Remember," he said, "I'll be able to see you from the window. Don't try anything stupid. I don't want to cuff you again."

The woman nodded. She knew enough about that. Last time the handcuffs were too tight and had cut cruelly into her flesh. She rubbed her wrist absently, touching the dark-blue bruises that marked their passage.

The man opened the passenger door and got out, flakes of rust fluttering to the ground, then reached back in and pulled the keys from the ignition. Then he closed the door with a *thunk* and walked quickly to the office.

He was such a tall man, *almost as thin as me,* the woman thought. She could see his head and shoulders through the grime-smeared window, and she could see the top half of another man's head. He had thick, white hair and looked like someone's grandfather.

She started to shiver uncontrollably. *Help me,* she pleaded silently to the old man. *Oh please, help . . .*

★ ★ ★ ★ ★

". . . a room for me and my wife," the man was saying. He stood at the counter facing the manager of the motel. The manager had a deeply lined country face and his hands were large and chapped, and he cupped them together on the counter like two lifeless birds.

"Just the one night?"

"We'll be leaving early."

"We got single rooms with twin beds. You can push 'em together if you want."

"That's fine," the man said. He stole a quick glance out the window. "Twin beds are just fine."

The manager reached for a key from the rack behind his head and then opened the dog-eared register on the counter. A brand-new computer monitor and keyboard sat nearby gathering dust. "Sign in here. Out by ten tomorrow or you'll be paying for another night whether you stay or not. There's a breakfast place down the road where you can get a cup of joe. Opens up early."

The man took up a pen, hesitated just a moment and signed, *Mr. and Mrs. Claude Barnes.*

"Okay, Mr. Barnes," the manager said. "Room twenty-three, just two doors down—"

"Do you have anything toward the end of the motel?" the man said. Then, seeing the look on the manager's face, he continued, "My wife is a light sleeper. If there's anything farther away from the road . . ."

The manager nodded. "Sure. I'll put you in room four." He took another key down from the rack.

The man took the key and left the office, his palms sweaty and his blood thumping. He could see as he stepped back into the parking lot that the woman hadn't moved from the driver's seat. He slid a hand in his coat pocket and fingered the handcuffs, feeling their weight, their substance. The metal was cool and slippery. He couldn't possibly watch the woman all the time. He would have to begin to trust her eventually. He was tired, so very tired. They had been on the road for two days straight, driving through the night.

He walked around the car and opened the driver's side door. The woman looked up at him like a dog that had been kicked. It made him sick to see her looking at him like that. "Get out," he said roughly, and stepped back. She obeyed, but he couldn't help noticing her flinch as he reached out to close the door. He knew he would have to cuff her later, and it made him angry. He didn't like getting angry but couldn't seem to help it. He'd never been good with women, had never been able to understand them. She was scared and there was nothing he could do to change that now.

A cold wind had come up, the kind that brings tears. It ruffled their hair and tore at their clothes as they walked quickly across the mostly empty parking lot, and brought a smell of leaves and cold mud, dead things lying in watery ground.

The man fumbled the key into the door lock and turned it. The motel room was dark and hot. He felt around on the wall until he found the light switch, and then he closed the door quickly behind them. The room looked like it had last been remodeled sometime in the 1960s; water-stained wallpaper, lamps with pale-green shades, landscape prints in chipped frames and faded pastel colors. He smelled pine-scented cleaner and stale sweat, a room that cried out to be opened up to the wind and stripped to the bare boards.

He sat down heavily on the nearest bed, feeling it sag under him. The springs poked at him like little bony fingers. He wanted a hot shower but didn't dare take one yet.

She was staring at the twin beds. "Will you handcuff me again tonight?"

"Damn it," he said softly, the fight slipping away from him at once. "Don't talk to me about that. Not now."

The woman had turned her eyes on him. "I won't run. I promise."

"Yes you will," he said. "I would."

"I didn't run away just now. I saw you in there through the window. I could have gotten away any time. I could have screamed for help. That man would have helped me. He looked like a nice guy."

"I would have had to kill him," he said quietly. "Do you want that?"

"You couldn't kill him!" she said, her voice rising in pitch. "You don't have the guts. Fucking coward."

The man looked at her for a moment and shook his head. "I'm sorry. Really I am. But you've got to understand—"

"I don't understand anything!" the woman shouted, the words torn from her throat. Her hands had curled into fists; tears welled up behind bruise-colored lids. She struggled out of the light jacket he had given her and threw it onto the floor, then pulled her white haltertop over her slender neck and head. She ripped at her skirt until it gave and fell around her ankles, and she stood trembling in front of him in lace bra and panties, her chest flushing red.

"Go ahead." She stared at him, her eyes wild. "Rape me if that's what you want. Come on, you son of a bitch. Get it over with, why don't you?"

"I'm not going to touch you."

"Can't get it up? Always trying to push women around when there's nothing between your legs? I know you. I know who you *are*."

"Shut up."

"Fuck you! Coward!"

The last shriek of words hung in the air and drifted away to silence. He remained still on the bed, watching her face, wondering if anyone had heard. A vein in her throat jumped. She was so thin, he thought, but beautiful. A strange thing to be thinking now but he couldn't help it. This was the first time since he had taken her that she had put up a fight, and it was about time.

"Come here," he said, and added, "please." He patted the mattress beside him and waited.

She shook her head. But then she sat. He reached into his coat pocket and withdrew the handcuffs, and she sighed as he touched her arm, letting out a single, choked sob. He closed one of the cuffs on the crossbar at the head of the bed and the other on her wrist. Then he stood up from the mattress and gathered her things from the floor. "Cover yourself," he said.

Then he went into the bathroom and closed the door, leaning his head against the slippery wood. The woman was quiet in the other room. Was he crazy, taking her like this? The thought had crept into his head lately; he had begun to think of it as a real possibility. He undressed slowly and climbed under the scalding spray, letting his head hang down, letting the needles of water wash away the dirt from his skin. Wash away the guilt.

Twenty minutes later he left the bathroom and found the woman asleep on the mattress. He stood looking down at her a moment, watching her sleep. Needle marks and bruises dotted her arm. Tears streaked her face.

Maybe he was crazy, after all. The thought did not afford him any comfort, nor did it change things much. It did not stop the images that kept churning through his head, did not stop the voices. Real or not, they were there, clamoring to be heard. They wouldn't stop until he had done what they asked him to do.

He turned out the light and quietly climbed in between the sheets on the other bed. Lying in the blackness, listening to the sound of the cars on the road, he realized he only knew her first name. *Angel.* Surely that wasn't her real name. Nothing but a stage name, like the dancers in Las Vegas used to keep the crazies out of their backyards. She knew where they were going and something of what they had to do, even if she wouldn't admit it. But that didn't make it any easier.

"I'm sorry, Angel," he whispered softly, but her breathing did not change, and he was sure she hadn't heard. He closed his eyes in the darkness, and prayed the dreams would not come again tonight.

# PART ONE:

# PAST HAUNTS

If a man dies, shall he live *again?*
All the days of my hard service I will wait,
Till my change comes.
—*Job* 14:14

*August 20th, 1726*

*My dearest Henrietta,*

*We have arrived at last, and I, exhausted from such a long and arduous journey over land and sea, nevertheless have set my pen upon the page with good speed. It is as fine a time as any to write, though Edward insists that I keep it short and attend my health; I have acquired a hacking cough, doubtless from the hold of that damned vessel and the sickness that festered like sores upon our lips. I would tell you in detail of the yellow drinking water and rotten meat, of the heat, bodies pressed all together, and the lice and rats that ran thick as cattle through the bowels of the ship; of the scurvy, typhus, and dysentery that ran rampant throughout our long journey; of the deaths of more than forty men, women, and children. But I do not have the strength for more than that now, and so let me say that it is a wonder I am still alive, and leave it at that, other than to insist you are not to worry about me. That silly charm Mr. Gatling was good enough to supply has been watching over me, I suppose—you must thank him for me again, Hennie. It has been nestled against my flesh for all these many days, and the weight of it around my neck gives me comfort. I have yet to let it leave my sight.*

*As for the journey over land, that was considerably more pleasant. Upon leaving the colony (a lively and open place, and one that will doubtless succeed), we passed along a rutted country road, moving steadily inland and to the North across wild country, guided by a friendly Indian. Many of them are friendly now; there is considerably less warfare than we had heard tell in the Motherland, although there are still groups that attack and burn villages to the ground, and murder and rape the women and children, the savages. The Indians have their own odd beliefs, as I am already learning, though quite a large number of them are being converted by the Church of Christ even as I write this. The Bible has long since been translated into their native tongue by that good Christian, Mr. Eliot, and there are native churches, though they are as yet few and far between, and are of course run by Christian white men.*

*I have the most curious story to tell you about the Indians, for something happened yesterday, just before our arrival at the site of what will be my future home (and yours, if things progress, God willing!), and I am interested to know your interpretation of it. The road we had been following had dwindled to a mere path cut through the wood, and we had lately progressed over a stretch of very rough land, hilly, with dense growth on all sides. For several furlongs we had been within earshot of the most wonderful deep-throated roar—surely the falls of which we have been told! I had been looking forward to my first glimpse of them, and the river itself, when our Indian guide abruptly stopped short and refused to go one step further along the narrow track. When asked why, he would not give a satisfactory answer—only that this was a "bad place" full of "evil spirits." He insisted that we need only follow the track upriver until we found a shallow area in which to cross over, after which the temporary dwellings built by the advance party would be found on the opposite bank.*

*We argued with him, but to no avail, and finally the three of us—Edward, Jonathan, and myself—set out along the last leg of our journey alone. The sun was still high in the sky, and the many insects and birds moving among the trees, along with the pleasant sound of the river, kept us from taking what the Indian said to heart—but I must say, Hennie, I kept one hand on the charm around my neck and the other on the knife at my side, wondering what to expect.*

*When we finally rounded the corner and set eyes on the place for the first time, I was reminded of why I made such a long and difficult journey. It is as pleasant as we have been told, the river winding through the trees before dropping abruptly over the raging falls, the land beyond flat and full of sturdy oak and pine, before the ground rises again into more mountainous territory. I have since done a bit of exploring; the only unpleasant aspect is an area of marshland downriver from the falls, which is filled with dead trees and weeds and the most abominable stench of rotting vegetation. It is this spot which I presume the Indian had been referring to as a "bad place," and on that point I am inclined to agree with him. But the bog is a good distance away from the settlement, and is of no real concern.*

*Finally, last night I did not sleep well, having the most unsettling series of dreams, for which I blame both the long journey and the incident with our Indian guide. During that period between consciousness and sleep I was filled with the strangest sense of anguish, as if I had left something behind, or had forgotten something that I must remember, and the night seemed filled with the most peculiar sounds, as if the very earth were trying to vomit up a sickness it had held for too long. When I awoke I was clutching the charm in my fist, and the engravings on its face left an impression on my palm that is still there this very moment.*

*But I worry you needlessly with these silly stories. The important thing remains that I have arrived in fairly good health, that the land is beautiful regardless of any local superstition, and that we will have a town here. Of that I have no doubt. In any case, I have run on for too long, and must attend to other things. I hope this letter finds you well (I do not know when or even if you will receive it, the post being what it is here), and be assured that I will write you again in the near future.*

*Regards,*
*Frederick*

# Chapter One

On the way to Thomaston to pick up his dead father's things, Jeboriah Taylor found himself thinking back on the events that had shaped his life. He wasn't usually one to dwell upon old memories, particularly those that involved his father. What was done was done; if you spent your life looking back, you had the tendency to keep running into walls. But tonight was different. Tonight was a celebration of sorts, a new chapter. Tonight he would finally be free.

Drinking and yelling, that's what he remembered about his daddy. That and the thing his daddy had done, the thing that nobody in this town could ever forget, no matter how hard they tried. The thing that had shaped the family's reputation in everyone's eyes forever. And all that somehow had to do with another funny thing; the confrontation he had this morning with his Gramma Ruth, who was still alive, but going senile. He could never be sure if Ruth was following things or not. She hadn't been truly herself for years. But this morning her eyes had been unusually bright, and he knew she was having one of her clear days. Jeb hadn't been sure if she even understood her son had died until then.

"You going to that prison, Jeboriah?" she'd said, when he walked through the kitchen on his way to the door.

"Later today. I gotta pick up his things."

"There's nothing of his that suits a boy like you. He's

dead, Jeboriah. I don't want his things in this house. I don't want him buried near your Momma and I don't want any service." She peered at him until he got the uncomfortable feeling she could see right through his head and glimpse what he was thinking. "I want him buried somewhere far away from here. And I want you to promise me. Promise me you won't even look at his things. Don't touch them. Just throw them away."

Jeb started to say something, but she had turned back to the stove and he could see she was already fading away, that light in her eyes a swiftly sputtering candle. Anything else he said would make little difference to her. He left her staring aimlessly into space, a smile on her face, as if she were thinking of things far away from him and her dead son.

What the hell all that had meant, he couldn't say. Maybe she hadn't been having one of her clear days after all, maybe her mind had run out on her again. But none of that really mattered anymore. Now he felt the dark all around him and the loneliness of the open road and he thought to himself, *tonight I'll finally be free of it all. Free forever.*

Route 1 wound its way along the coast, through the old sea towns and stretches of thick woods. The road was already narrow and the way the pine trees crowded the shoulder made the corners tend to sneak up on you. But Jeb Taylor drove like he might take off at any moment, lift right off the ground and into space like some nightmare ship bound for the stars. He felt a strange kinship with the darkness of space, the way he'd heard talk about the coldness up there, the distance. He felt like outrunning whatever was chasing him, but no matter how fast the car went, whatever it was kept right on behind.

The car's headlights sliced through the darkness ahead

and the '69 Chevy gobbled up asphalt and spit it out behind, dual side pipes growling like a wounded bear. Nothing like a '69 for pure, raw speed. The seats were big and slippery and the clutch was looser than a whore, but the engine was good old USA steel. Gas tank could eat a twenty quicker than you could turn around, *but ain't nobody gonna catch me out here unless he's Superman.* Jeb used to watch *Superfriends* on Saturdays, and he always thought a good double barrel in the chest would stop the Wonder Twins, and maybe Aquaman because he was such a pussy and talked to fish, but Superman could do anything. Superman was made of pure steel.

Into a straightaway the car surged again, the speedometer ticking up past eighty and still climbing as the tires scrambled for purchase. The dash lights were green and pulsed slowly as the alternator struggled along under the hood. Jeb's face seemed to pulse like a bullfrog's throat. He smelled burning oil and hot rubber, watching the road with one hand gripping the wheel, the other piloting the stereo controls.

The oldies station was playing one of his favorites by the Thunder Five:

*Good doctor-man, can ya lend me a hand*
*There's a feelin' I get and I don't understand*
*Gotta fever burnin' in my brain*
*Good doctor-man, 'fraid I'm going insane*

The song suited his mood just fine. What was it like to go crazy anyway? Was it like old Annie Arsenault out at the swap shop who sometimes forgot her own name and wandered around outside buck naked? Crazy old witch sometimes made it all the way down Route 27 to town before anyone saw her. Jeb's Gramma Ruth used to find her sitting on a bench outside the Railway Cafe wearing nothing but a straw hat, and when she tried to get her in the car old Annie Arsenault would tell her to go to hell.

*Maybe,* he thought, *your daddy could have told you something about crazy. But it's too late for that now.*

Jeb took the next corner a little too fast, and fat tires squealed on tar as the big car swung sideways into the wrong lane. He wondered for a moment as he twisted the wheel and pumped the brakes if he was going to make it. Then the car righted itself and he was left wondering whether he was actually trying to kill himself or whether he was just plain stupid. He drummed his fingers nervously on the steering wheel in time with the music. It was nerves, that was all. He had to be honest with himself, tonight of all nights; he was dreading what was ahead, what was waiting for him at the prison. Not for what his father could do to him physically, of course; it was way too late for that. Ronnie Taylor had died in his cell the night before from some kind of heart failure, and was already rotting away on a cold slab in the morgue.

No, Jeb was afraid of what other old memories might come floating to the surface. He hadn't even seen his father in ten years, never mind heard his voice. The sound of that voice wouldn't ever be able to touch him again; but he would surely see Ronnie Taylor in his dreams.

Thomaston State Prison was located just outside the town of Rockland, on a straight, dull stretch of Route 1. It looked like a factory building, and you might think it was somebody's place of business, except for the high fences and razor wire. Jeb parked and went around to the visitor's entrance, where he was met by a fat guard with a black mustache and a stain on his blue prison shirt that looked like mustard. The guard's face was greasy and his collar ringed with sweat. "About goddamn time," the fat guard said. His beady eyes blinked through pockets of fat. Jeb could see bits of white that clung to the hairs of the guard's mustache, remnants of his last meal. "Taylor, ain't it? What took you so long?"

"Sorry," Jeb muttered. He tried but could not meet the guard's stare. This was what he hated the most about himself. When it came time to stand up to people, to show them who was boss, he just couldn't do it. People took one look at him and assumed control like this guard was doing already.

*Fucking fat bastard. I oughta show you a thing or two . . .*

But he didn't say anything, just followed numbly along as the guard led him through a maze of corridors and barred doors. The doors rolled and clanged shut heavily behind them, sounding like distant thunder. They saw no one, but now and again noises floated down from the prison cells that sounded more animal than human. The corridors were thick with the smell of hot male sweat. Jeb couldn't help thinking that this was where his father had spent the last ten years of his life, caged up like something less than a man. Something to be feared. But that was part of what his father had wanted, after all; and wasn't that just a little of what he wanted too? For people to take a step back when they saw him, for the other person to look away first?

At a desk they met a second guard propped up next to a wall of television screens, his feet on the counter, hands locked behind his head. This guard was short and completely bald, his head so shiny and smooth it reflected the lights in the ceiling. "Watched you come in," he said, as the other guard disappeared into another room. "Nice wheels."

"My father's car. Restored it myself."

"Yeah?"

Jeb smiled at the man, wondering what he was thinking. *Bet you think my daddy stole it, don't you, you prick? For all I know he did. But it's mine now.*

The fat guard came back from the inner room carrying a stack of papers in one hand and a suitcase in another. "This is all Ronald's things," he said, dropping the suitcase on the floor. "There ain't a lot. Few old clothes, couple of books and girlie mags. You don't go out shopping much when you're in for murder, eh? No field trips to the mall." He grinned, then slapped the papers down on the counter. "You need to sign a few places here." He pointed with a pen. "Here and here."

"You're Ronnie Taylor's son," the bald guard said, as if he'd figured out a riddle. He took his feet off the counter and sat up. "You must be how old, eighteen, nineteen maybe? I don't remember seeing you around here."

"Me and my father aren't too close. Weren't, I mean." Jeb straightened up and handed the signed papers to the fat guard.

"Didn't like him much?" the bald guard asked, persisting.

"Ronnie was an ornery bastard," the fat guard interrupted. "Always causing an uproar around here, getting the inmates going so as we'd have to lock him up in solitary. Son of a bitch." He looked at Jeb with little squinting pig eyes. Some crumbs fell off his mustache onto his shirt. "No offense."

Jeb wanted to leave. The fat guard was blocking the door. "You said you wanted him buried, right?" the guard said. "Potter's Field, eh? No service?"

*Yeah, you fat sick blubbering pig, now get the fuck out of my way.*

He nodded. "That's right."

"Just making sure. Normally the funeral parlor has them cremated if nobody claims the body. The parlor will send you a bill for the plot."

"How much?"

"Depends." The guard paused, squinted at him as if sizing up the competition. "Costs less to cremate. What the fuck you care, anyway?"

Both guards were looking at him now. Jeb's throat felt as if it were about to close; he was starting to sweat. He looked at the floor. The corners of the room were yellow and crusted with dirt.

"Maybe you ought to talk it over with the rest of the family?"

"No. Cremate him."

The fat guard looked like he'd just won something. He led Jeb back through the dim hallways, unlocking and locking the doors as they went. Each one clanged again, and this time the sounds seemed hollow, following them as they continued to the outer doors. Jeb carried his father's suitcase in his right hand, the handle slippery under his sweating fingers. An image of the bald guard hung in his mind; watching him through the cameras, hands clutching his belly, laughing. Those damn guards had been laughing at him the whole time, but what was he going to do about it?

*If I were back there now I'd shut their mouths.* He imagined jacking the fat guard up against the wall with his forearm, holding him there while he gave the other one a look, saying, *don't fuck with me, I'll look through my father's things whenever I goddamn please.* The other one just standing white-faced, nodding yes sir, whatever you say sir.

The plastic handle of the suitcase felt as if it were on fire in his hand. He imagined something moving around inside, thumping and wriggling and bulging. Popping the latch, lifting the lid, feeling things flying out at him, liquid screams through open mouths, nightmares and memories of nightmares thrusting their cold, moist jaws into his face. And he felt that if he opened it now it would be like opening up his father's life again, ready to swallow him whole.

*Ronnie's an ornery bastard.*

*Maybe he was,* Jeb thought. *But not anymore. My daddy's dead now, and nothing else. I'm free now, you hear me?*

He left the fat guard behind and when he was out of sight of the doors, he broke into a run for the car.

# Chapter Two

Early the next morning the two strangers left the town of Holy Hill and continued on, skirting the larger cities of Columbia and Florence, following the back roads as they had for days now. Angel was a silent companion. Since the outburst at the motel it was almost as if she weren't there at all. The man felt a great breaking within him, as if the ground were caving in beneath his feet. His world had been an unsteady one for almost as long as he could remember, and it seemed that it would remain that way forever. He wondered again, as he had a thousand times before, what he really expected to accomplish. Again he came up with the same answer; he didn't know.

As they passed through Chadbourn he tried speaking to her. "You know I don't mean to hurt you."

He was sure she wouldn't reply, but after a moment, she said, "I don't know anything."

"You can trust me. I know I haven't given you much reason for it, but you can."

"Can I trust these?" She held up her arms, exposing the cruel purple bruises that ran around her tiny wrists.

"Okay," he said quietly. "I deserved that. I won't handcuff you anymore. Just don't run." It was all he could say. *Please God, don't ask for anything else.* She was so pale, so thin and fragile. It seemed impossible that she could have survived what he had put her through, *was* putting her through.

"I won't run," she said simply.

He wanted to say, *So you do understand? You know that I would do anything to stop this? That I would take myself in your place, if it would do any good?* "Are you hungry?" he asked.

"I could eat."

And so they stopped at a Burger King, and he forced himself to walk without looking at her, without touching the handcuffs in his pocket, without searching the crowd of empty faces for the one who would sense the distance between them and call the police.

For Billy Smith, the nightmares had begun one night about a year after he had been let out of jail. He was working at the time in the kitchen of a little Chinese restaurant in San Francisco. It was the third job he had held in the past four months. He was in the midst of a depression that held him in its grip like some sort of creature from the deep; a depression born out of equal parts self-pity, and self-loathing for what he had done.

He was a convict. He had been to prison, had watched what men did to each other there, primed the depths to which mankind could sink. He wondered if you could see it in his face; if there was some sort of clue to his past written in the pattern of his flesh. Yes, he had suffered, he had felt his own soul ripped away and dipped in something foul and stuffed dripping back into place; and he wondered if the smell clung to him like cigarette smoke. He watched the eyes of people passing him to see if a spark of recognition would alight on him and begin to burn.

But San Francisco swallowed thousands like him every day, and he finally realized two things. The first thing was that most people did not give a damn who he was or where he'd been. The second was that ending up alone in a city such as this one was as good as a suicide attempt. No smoking gun, but suicide all the same. Every morning he walked the short distance from the restaurant to his apartment in the lower hills, and every evening he walked home, thinking how easy it would be to simply disappear, how the world would go on without missing a beat. If he had not been born, would anything have been different here? It wasn't likely. His life was like a grain of sand against the ocean, and the tide was relentless and all-powerful.

And then he would think about the three lives that would have been saved if he had never existed. Three lives that had been worth so much more than his, an orphan child who had been cursed from the very first breath he took into his lungs.

He went on because there was nothing else to do. He thought sometimes about ending his life, but the details of the act were too much. It seemed funny to him that even in a life such as his, the will to survive was too strong to overcome. In the restaurant, he was a good worker, silent, a loner. If the others in the kitchen ever noticed the prison tattoo on his upper arm, they did not mention it. If there was something in his sweat that stunk of the hole, they did not show it. There were plenty of ex-cons working in the grimy little shops of Chinatown. Some of his co-workers were ex-cons themselves. If nothing else, there was strength in numbers.

But he was restless. Later, he would begin to understand how he had been waiting for something to happen. Each day his restlessness would increase, and he would begin to get the strangest urges, the need for movement, for escape, for confession. He shared his secrets with the voices in his head. It was as if he could hear someone whispering back but was not quite able to make out the words. These words were important, he was sure, and the fact that he could not hear them drove him crazy. If only he could understand, he would have a plan. He would have something to get him out of bed in the morning.

Finally he knew he had to move on. Down the coast, perhaps to Los Angeles or San Diego. Or maybe he would go east, yes, that seemed the thing to do. He would quit the job at the restaurant, take what little cash he had, pack up his few things and get in a car, any car, and he would drive until he found a place that felt right to him. Once there he could find a job (he wasn't picky, anything would do), a place to live, and then he would start listening for the whispers. Perhaps they would never come again.

That night he dreamed he was standing just outside a large circle of people in the darkness. A fire raged within the circle and the people were chanting in low voices. The firelight played about their features, making them seem like panes of rippling glass. They danced; their faces as they turned towards him took his breath away, as if he were looking straight through their skins and into their souls, at the animal in them. Their chanting seemed to take shape in the air around them, to become almost palpable in the smoke, to slide and slither like snakes about his ears. And yet he seemed on the verge of hearing for the first time all the secrets that had been dangling just out of his reach.

As he stood transfixed, unable to move even a single muscle, he heard a voice calling to him—*You must come, William. You must come home.*

The oddly powerful dream stayed with him the next morning as he packed his things, and kept playing through his mind even as he got into the old Volkswagen he'd bought just days before from the owner of the restaurant.

He did not usually remember his dreams for more than a few minutes, if at all. This one did not seem to be a dream at all, but a memory. He got as far as Salt Lake City without stopping, driving from dawn to dusk and into the night, and stayed in a small motel on the outskirts of the city near the great salt flats. He could smell them through the open window as he lay in his room that night and listened to the sound of rock and roll coming from the nightclub across the street. It drew him out into the night, walking across the empty parking lots, past the backs of the dark stores and rows of neat suburban houses. In Salt Lake City everything seemed so quiet and clean. He wasn't sure he liked it. The streets of San Francisco were raw and dangerous at night. But there was life on those streets; here, the world seemed like an old man drawing his last breath.

As he stood looking out across the vast white stretch of salt it began to take on features in the dark, as if a face were traced there just under the surface. He heard the whispering again, stronger now. *Dead men walking,* he thought he heard it saying. But that didn't make any sense, and he turned away. There were no faces floating in the salt flats, and no voices. He was losing his mind.

What seemed like thousands of years ago, his life had been on some sort of track, he had had a purpose. His adopted mother, who had finally lost a long bout with cancer a month before his seventeenth birthday, had always told him that the most important thing was to go to school and search out your future. Find what interests you and you'll figure the rest out later. Nobody ends up doing what they set out to do; lawyers become firefighters, singers end up running restaurants, beach bums make a million in the stock market, brokers turn into beach bums.

And alcoholics turn into killers. Education had done

nothing for him, in the end.

He returned to his empty room near the flats and that night the dreams came back with a vengeance.

He was standing on a hill, the stars peppering the sky above his head. There were great empty stretches of black on either side, making him feel as if he were standing on the deck of a boat in an endless sea. The hillside was cool beneath his bare feet and a light breeze ruffled his hair. He could smell pine needles, and the sharp, bitter smell of smoke.

Behind and below him the stretch of blackness was broken by a scattering of lights. He looked down at the roughness beneath his feet, and realized he was standing at the edge of a huge flat slab of rock jutting out into space. Below the lip of the rock the treetops swayed in the breeze.

The smell of smoke assaulted him. The heat of it against his face. And the sound of something scraping across the rock behind him.

He did not want to see what it was. Oh no, he did not.

*William.*

He turned; his mother stood there, but not the mother he remembered from his childhood. Cancer had ruined her. Her hair hung in mossy clumps against her face. Her skin was black and running with open sores. Her cold, dead eyes were covered with a yellow film. They were not his mother's eyes. The person he had called mother was long gone.

Her cracked lips opened to speak again. He screamed without sound; and behind her rose the legions of the dead, hundreds of them, ripping themselves out of the ground and pulling themselves up the hill onto the rock. Among them he saw the woman and two children he had killed, their mangled bodies and broken limbs reaching up as if in prayer. He backed away until he could feel the drop beneath his feet, and the heat of the fire burning his neck.

And the voice, always there, always the same. *Break the circle, William. You must come home.*

After Burger King they got back in the car and continued east, but the mood between them had changed. He could sense it in the way she sat in the seat, the way she watched the scenery through the window, the way her breathing had eased. It had been the first time she was out of the car with him, in sight of other people, and she hadn't run screaming for help. She knew he had a gun in the car, but he hadn't brought it into the restaurant with him and he was pretty sure she knew that too.

*You must come home.* The words tortured him, running through his mind at the strangest moments, like a record that kept skipping. What did it mean?

He glanced at Angel in the passenger seat. "You want to know why we're here," he said softly. "I'll tell you what I know, if you'll listen."

"What good will that do? Are you going to let me go? I don't think so."

He shrugged. "I can't promise you anything. All I can do is tell you my story." He glanced at her again. "I thought maybe . . . you'd understand."

"Understand what? That you're nuts?"

"That I don't have a choice."

He told her about the dreams. His life after the accident, in San Francisco, the odd sense of urgency he felt that drove him on, the whispers, and finally, the dead. And the face he began to see everywhere, starting the day after his Salt Lake City nightmare. That next morning he had driven southeast for hours, the drive passing in a frenzied blur. He could still see that little pattern of lights below him in the night from his dream, and those lights began to take shape for him, the brightest ones becoming the line of brow and nose, two of them eyes, and others tracing the cheekbones and jaw. That night he stopped in a small town outside Santa Fe and fell asleep in his car, and this time he saw the face in sharp and complete detail. A beautiful woman. Throughout the day, he kept seeing it in the strangest places; in the bathroom mirror, in the pattern of clouds overhead, among the ripples of the motel pool as he walked by. He had to find this woman, and bring her with him. That was what he had been asked to do. He had never been so sure of anything in his life.

Instead he tried to run, going back west, but the farther he got the worse the dreams became, until they were coming during waking hours and with such force he had to pull the car over to the side of the road and wait them out like a bad thunderstorm. Visions now, in broad daylight. And always her face, in the pattern of leaves beside the road, in the raindrops running down the windshield. He turned back, because the visions would drive him crazy if he did not. He began to plan. The thought of not being able to find her never entered his mind; he knew that when he got to the right place she would be there. But he must be ready. Something told him she would not come with him voluntarily.

"Finally, there you were. On the beach. I'd been looking for you so long, I could hardly believe it. But your face was perfect. I'd seen it a thousand times, I knew it by heart."

She studied him from the passenger seat, as if trying to decide how much to believe. "You said you were a dealer. I believed you."

That part had been easy. She was so desperate for a fix she would have followed him anywhere. He'd gotten her back to his car; *I could use a little now,* she'd said. *Sure,* he'd said. He'd opened the driver's side door and the chloroform was right there on the seat and no one in sight. He was fishing for something, anything to make him stop when it hit him again like a sledgehammer to the face: *dead people walking those who are born again DO IT DO IT DO IT NOW* and he moved smoothly and quickly, forcing her head into the wet cloth. She bucked and crumpled against him without a sound, and he pushed her into the car ahead of him, setting her up in the passenger seat like she was asleep. He threw the cloth with the chloroform in it on the ground, looked around and saw no one. And that was it; he was gone.

"In all that time I was looking for you, I never thought you'd be . . ."

"What?" she said. "A user? A whore?"

"No," he said. "I never thought it would be so easy."

"Sorry to disappoint you."

They were silent for a moment. "I thought about finding some other way," he said finally. "Believe me. Talking to you, trying to convince you to come with me."

"Then why didn't you?" It could have sounded accusatory, but Angel said it without any tone at all.

"Would you have come if I had?"

"No," she said. "I would have thought you were crazy."

"Do you think I'm crazy now?"

She didn't answer him. After a moment, recognition dawned. He said wonderingly, "So you're dreaming about them too."

"No!" She glanced at him sharply. "I think you're a psycho who kidnaps girls for the fun of it."

"You're scared."

"Of course I am!"

"I mean of the dreams you're having. Of what you see in them. It won't just go away. You know that, don't you? You can't just close your eyes and wish you were back on the beach. Jesus, something's *happening* to us. We have to figure out a way to work together."

"Back on the beach," she said softly. "Fuck that. I wouldn't wish that on anyone. There are all kinds of nightmares, you know." This time he was the one to sit silently, unable to respond. But something felt lighter inside him. It was a small comfort to him, to know that he was not alone. He wondered how she was taking her addiction, whether it was eating her up inside. What had she wanted out of life? How had she ended up there, at the end of the world, an addict and a prostitute?

"So where are we going, anyway?" she said. "Your own special world of dreams?" Her attempt at a smile died on her face.

"I don't know," he said. "North. Maybe way up north. When visions come while I'm awake, I know I better change direction. They haven't come in a while. I guess we're headed the right way."

"That's—"

"What? Crazy?"

This time the smile stayed. "You could say that."

They drove another mile in silence before he said, "Any family?"

"I had a brother, but he died."

"Were you close?"

"Yes."

"Do you miss him?"

"It was a long time ago."

He chose his next words carefully. "Does he . . . come to you? In your dreams?"

"I don't want to talk anymore," she said suddenly. And nothing he could do or say would draw her out again.

They stopped for the night at a Motel Six in another sleepy town, this one called Gatesville. Smith got out of the car and went in to register them as Mr. and Mrs. Simon Craig. He asked for a room with twin beds again. He had left Angel in the car alone, the cuffs off. When he returned she was still there. And he knew he had gotten through to her on some level, at least.

They found the right room and fell into the beds almost immediately. But once he was there, Smith found himself unable to sleep, his mind filled with thoughts of Angel on the beach and the things she must have made herself do to the men who came to her, filthy and violent and dangerous men. What did she think of when she took off her clothes and took them into her mouth, into herself? Did she think of home, her family, her dead brother? When they came, did she think of early sexual experiences in high school in the back seats of cars, or did she block it all out from beginning to end? And how did she feel knowing that the drug had control over her and she would do anything it took to have that feeling racing through her veins; that essentially, she was a slave?

But that hadn't changed at all, Smith thought. She was still a slave, it was just that she was chained to a different thing now, as he was. They were similar people when he thought about it. He had been chained to the bottle. Same devil, different face.

He was back on the beach again, watching her from behind the pilings of the boardwalk. The light was growing fainter by the minute as the sun began to set; it was an orange light, and the sea glowed as if it had caught fire. He saw her clearly for the first time, and she was so beautiful. Her eyes were set far apart on each side of a slender nose, her mouth full and red. He stepped out from behind the piling. The wind had grown cooler, whipping sand against his legs. The sun had almost fallen in the west, a blood-red globe hanging above a blood-red ocean.

*This isn't how it happened,* he thought to himself. *This isn't right.*

A sound behind him made him turn. A car was hurtling through a red light at the near intersection, heading straight for a blue van. A woman was driving the van and two young kids were in the back.

The van swerved and hit the brakes and began sliding sideways. Time slowed down, as if each second had become a minute, each minute an hour; the ticking of a clock was very loud in his ears. He could see the driver of the car now. The driver was drunk and wore his face.

But he already knew the end, didn't he? Watched it a thousand times or more. He had his own private seat in his own private theater. He heard a sound behind him and turned, searching for the woman on the beach. *I didn't see them, please understand.*

But the rotting thing before him was no woman. Mud and root clung to the thing's face as if it had just clawed its way out of the grave.

*Gotta take your medicine, boy,* it croaked. *Come get what's coming to you. Things gonna be a little different round here . . .*

He woke up in the dark screaming.

The lights on, they sat together on the bed. Angel was staring at the wall. He searched her eyes but could not read her expression.

The sweat was cold on his body and he hugged his knees

to his chest. The dream stayed with him, and he could not shake it. That rotting thing on the beach had been worse than the dreams of his mother and the corpses tearing themselves from the ground, worse than anything he could remember. He had been hearing the woman and two children he had killed crying in his sleep for over ten years, and lately he had been seeing them too, but the pain had never been as close as it was right now. He would get no more sleep tonight.

"My brother comes to me in my dreams," Angel said finally. "That's what you wanted to hear, isn't it? That he gets up out of the ground and he's not alive when he comes, he's dead and he's rotting and I can see it in his face, I can *smell* it."

"No," he said honestly. "That's not what I wanted to hear. That's not what I wanted to hear at all."

After a moment, she rested her hand on his arm, and they sat there until the sun came up.

Then they got back in the car and headed north.

# Chapter Three

On the way home from Mrs. Friedman's, though it was only four o'clock, Jeb Taylor thought about stopping at the local watering hole for a drink. After all, he told himself, he was almost nineteen years old, and if he wanted to stop and have a beer he ought to be able to do it. They would serve him without a fuss; his money was as good as anybody else's, and nobody much cared about the drinking age around here. To be truthful he had been thirsting for a good drink since the night before, and the only thing that had stopped him all day was the watchful eye of Mrs. Friedman herself, who came out every five minutes to check on him and make sure he was "doing things right." She would watch him work until he felt her eyes burning through the back of his neck, then finally she would sigh and go back inside, only to come back out again later to say some other meaningless thing. *I wonder what it's like to live with her,* he had thought, as he dug through the rocks and old roots in the back garden and dumped fresh manure on the soil. Mr. Friedman was a big-shot lawyer in town, and worked long hours. Jeb always figured it was a way to avoid his wife more than anything else. *Her husband probably thinks about killing himself every day of his life.*

The local watering hole was a one-room bar on Route 27 called *Johnny's*, located just beyond the town square and across from the grocery. The place used to be an old schoolhouse, and the red brick and small wooden windows had survived through several minor renovations. The owner thought the windows made the place look more distinguished, and in fact the building was listed on the historical landmark map or some such fool thing. There were four places of historical interest in White Falls; three were old houses on the square, built by founding members of the town, and the other was the schoolhouse, which had come to Johnny Berden in 1974 with a dirt-cheap price from the previous owner who eventually declared bankruptcy. The town council asked him to keep the place empty as a museum for tourists, but Johnny had laughed at them. The least he could do then, the council said, was preserve the "flavor" of the place. So Johnny put a horseshoe bar in the center of the room, a few cheap plastic booths around the edges, planted a jukebox in the corner, and hung a few pool lights from the ceiling, and *Johnny's* was born, such as it was. A lot of people still called it the schoolhouse.

Right now Jeb didn't give a damn what the place was called. He hadn't slept well last night, and today had been a long hard day digging in the dirt. It had been unusually hot for the middle of April, and so humid Jeb's shirt stuck to his shoulders with sweat. That was no job for a grown man. Now that he was turning nineteen he ought to have something better. His back had begun to ache and his knees crack a little too loud when he bent down, and for seven-fifty an hour, he thought he could find better things to do. He had begun lately to think of ways he could get out of the job and still keep gas in his car.

But now he wanted a shot of whiskey and a beer to wash it down, for starters. He couldn't remember when he'd craved a drink so bad. He'd never much cared for whiskey before, but right now it seemed like the perfect thing.

Jeb took a stool at the bar and ordered the whiskey, downed it and ordered another. *Johnny's* was empty this early in the evening and the bartender left him alone. Jeb sat and studied his hands, which were black with grime. He considered going to the bathroom to wash them and thought better of it. This kind of ground-in dirt wouldn't come out for a long time. What a lousy fucking job; Mrs. Friedman, with her shit-eating grin and hands on her hips acting like she was better than everyone else, as if just because she was paying him it gave her the right to order him around like a servant. With this kind of dirt under his fingernails he would never make it in politics. They would laugh at him when he tried to shake hands and kiss their babies. *Stupid white trash. What could you possibly do for us? And a Taylor, too. We haven't forgotten your daddy, boy, and what he did.*

Jeb sat in misery and downed his third shot. Damned if he couldn't see what they all were doing. He might not be the brightest spoke on the wheel, but damned if he didn't see how they were all shutting him out, making him into a clown, laughing at him behind his back like those two guards at the Thomaston Prison. If he could find a way to get back at them all he would do it. He would do it in a second.

He stayed at *Johnny's* for another hour and a half, and the bartender kept serving him shots, and by the time he stumbled drunkenly out to his car it was getting dark again. He was mildly surprised at that. Seemed as if he had just walked in the door a second ago, and then it had been full light. He would have to give Ruth some dinner, unless she had felt up to fixing it herself, and that hadn't happened too often lately. Jeb had begun to feel the burden of caring for his grandmother, and he didn't like it. The way he felt, his life was just getting started, and why should he waste any time farting around with someone whose life was about done? Ruth had one foot in the grave, and half the time her mind was a thousand miles away. Christ, just two days ago he had caught her mumbling to herself like she was talking to her dead husband. Told him she "had his shirts done" and if he was needing them they were in the hall closet. Crazy old bird.

He started the car and backed out of the small parking lot. By this time there were several cars parked there. He just missed clipping the bumper of a Mercedes that looked vaguely familiar, and somebody shouted at him as he drove off. He paid them no attention, speeding down past the cemetery, where his mother and grandfather were buried, past the white Catholic Church, turning along the green and turning to go up the long hill toward his grandmother's house. He passed the drug store and Thelma's Gifts and the hardware store, and all were dark, their doors shut for the night. White Falls went to bed early.

But the Taylor home was ablaze with light. Jeb parked in the driveway and stumbled up the walk, cursing Ruth who had surely left all the lights on before falling asleep in the living room chair. *Probably spooked herself, thinking dead Grandpa Norman had come back to life again.*

But when he went in she was awake and sitting in a kitchen chair. "Christ," he said. "What're you doing up?"

"Don't you swear in this house," Ruth said smartly. "I won't have it." Her eyes were especially bright, and Jeb thought for a moment she had been into the liquor cabinet, which didn't sound like such a bad idea. Wasn't much there, but a little would do just fine now. Take the edge off.

"You've been out running around," she announced.

"And in the middle of the week, too."

Ruth peered at him and he got that odd feeling like she was looking straight through his skull and reading his thoughts. "Just stopped at the store," he said sourly.

"It's eight o'clock at night and I smell whiskey. You're all dirty and sweaty. Bet you stopped in at the schoolhouse right after work, didn't you?"

"I don't have to answer to you." His words were slurring together in spite of his best efforts. He made a move as if to go upstairs. His head was pounding now, and it was either find another bottle to take the edge off or go straight to bed.

What she said next stopped him short. "Your father used to do that after a long day. Drinking whiskey at the schoolhouse."

"So what?"

Ruth suddenly seemed agitated. She cocked her head to one side as if listening. Jeb got the uncomfortable feeling he used to get around crazy Annie when he was a kid, not really sure how to react to her and always wondering what she was going to do. Because with Annie, you could never be sure what was coming; she kept you off balance.

Finally Ruth looked at him again, her eyes still holding that spark of life he recognized and was coming to hate. "What did you do with his things from the jail? Did you throw them away like I asked?"

Jeb Taylor stood in the shadows just outside the kitchen, his head a mass of pain, and considered how to answer. The suitcase was still upstairs in his closet, hidden under the clothes, and though he knew he didn't want to open it, he hadn't been able to get himself to throw the thing away yet.

He wasn't really sure what finally made him lie. "Yeah. I threw 'em in the river, Gramma. Okay? I threw 'em in the river last night."

"Did you look at them?"

"Just a bunch of clothes and some books."

"Come here." When he came, reluctantly, she reached up and patted his neck with her gnarled old lady hands. The anger welled up within him and he had the sudden urge to strike her, slap that wrinkled, sagging face, push in her eyes with his thumbs, choke her throat. He held himself tightly together and closed his eyes. She gave a great sigh, and it was as if something left her all at once, like a flock of birds had taken wing. She patted his chest. "That's good, Jeboriah."

Jeb nodded and went upstairs, leaving the crazy old woman in the kitchen. What was wrong with her, anyway? She'd really lost it this time. He'd come that close to hitting her. He balled his hands into fists, and slowly released them as the nails cut into his palms. The pain cut through his pounding head, clearing it. She would have to find her own dinner tonight. He wasn't hungry anymore.

He would throw away the suitcase tomorrow, he decided. No sense keeping it around, anyway. Or maybe he would keep it just to spite her.

The upper floor of the house was dark and he stumbled into his bedroom, too tired to wash up. He fell into bed and was asleep almost instantly.

He dreamed of circles floating in front of his face, rings of blazing light. At first he thought he was looking into the sun, but slowly the circle became clearer, until he could see the snakes wrapped around each other with their tails in their mouths.

The Mercedes Jeb Taylor had almost hit in the parking lot of *Johnny's* belonged to Pat Friedman, forty-eight years old, husband of Mrs. Julie Friedman and partner in the firm of Friedman and Soule located next to the bookstore on the square. Pat had also been the man who shouted in surprise as the big Chevy with the loud side pipes had spun out of the parking lot; he had been standing by the door to the bar as Jeb came stumbling out.

Though it had been a warm day, there was a cold wind blowing tonight. Pat stood on the front steps and stared down the road in the direction of town. In the distance he could see a glow from the lights that dotted the walkways along the square. Across the street from *Johnny's* he could see the dark windows of the town grocery and the single floodlight mounted on the corner of the roof, and behind him in the darkness he could hear the muffled voices of the falls, deep white water tumbling down the hole in the river. People came from a good distance around this time of year to see the falls and the place where the river seemed to flow uphill after the hole. Right now the water level was rising. The river would be at its greatest volume in another month, and the town of White Falls would have its festival on the green.

Pat Friedman felt the wind against his cheek, and pulled his collar up. He was not ready to go home yet. The truth was, his wife did drive him crazy (as Jeb Taylor suspected). He had married her because she was the sexiest thing he had ever seen, but he had found over the ten-plus years of their marriage that she was a flirt and a control freak. He suspected her of having an affair, maybe more than one. But he was eleven years older than she was, and a shy man around women. She had been the one to ask him out when they met. He was afraid that he wouldn't be able to find another suitable wife, and so he had given everything up to her long ago. Besides, a messy divorce in a small town would ruin his law practice.

He often wound out the hours at *Johnny's* instead of at the office. He hadn't expected to see Jeb here, though. That was certainly strange. Jeb wasn't old enough to drink yet; couldn't be much over eighteen. Pat used to see Ronnie Taylor tying one on at *Johnny's* years ago, and damned if his boy wasn't starting to look just like him. In fact, when Jeb had come stumbling out tonight and sped away in that big car, Pat had felt as if he were seeing a ghost.

Jeb hadn't looked well. That Ronnie Taylor had been a bad seed, but he *was* the boy's father. Pat hoped Jeb was taking his death okay. One of the reasons he had agreed to hire the boy in the first place was he had felt sorry for him. And Julie seemed to like him.

As he stood in the near darkness, Pat had a moment of sudden clarity, as if everything around him had come into sharp focus. He glanced at the market across the road and the light was so bright it hurt his eyes, and the sound of the falls was like the roar of a great beast breathing down his neck, and he thought, *Something's in the air tonight. Something horrible.*

He stood there frozen for a minute. A car drove by the bar, and Pat watched as its brake lights blinked once, twice as it went around the corner and out of sight.

*Silly,* he thought to himself. *It's just a cool night in April, that's all.* Julie would have told him he was drinking too much.

Pat Friedman turned quickly and returned to the warmth of the bar, and left the people of White Falls to settle in against the sudden cold and an uneasy sleep.

# Chapter Four

On the third day following Jeb's discussion with Ruth, a Friday, the strangers arrived in White Falls. Morton Kane, the high school English teacher, saw them as he was crossing the bridge to go down to Brunswick for his weekly shopping trip. A pale young woman, blond-haired, quite pretty, he thought, and a tall, intense-looking man driving a gray Volkswagen with California plates. He just caught a glimpse of them in passing, but he remembered being oddly shaken by the sight. Maybe they were tourists. He thought, *Little early for the festival, isn't it?* And then he continued on, and didn't think about them again until much later.

Just before they went past the intersection of Indian Road and continued into town, they stopped to ask directions from another local, Barbara Trask, who was out with her dog. Barbara lived near the mouth of Black Pond in a white ranch with a perfect garden and a Saint Bernard named Alaska. She was the town gossip, and so the news of the strangers spread quickly from there. By the time they had reached the town square Barbara was already on the phone with her oldest and dearest friend Myrtle Howard, who then called the doctor at the clinic, Harry Stowe, and so on. White Falls didn't get much traffic in the off-season, and there was something about the two strangers that was so odd everybody's interest was aroused right away.

They stopped in front of the drug store and went in to

ask about a place to stay. The druggist, Alan Marshal, knew of only one place currently taking visitors, and that was the Old Mill Inn. He gave the directions and they thanked him and left. *A very strange couple,* was Alan's first impression. The girl was thin and beautiful but just as quiet as a mouse. The man was tall and gaunt, with black hair and dark eyes. The eyes seemed to drill into your head like two tiny screws. The man hadn't smiled once the whole time he was in the store.

They drove past the long square and pretty, white-clapboard church and the cemetery with its rain-washed stones against the green grass, and Angel said, "I hate it. It all makes me sick."

Billy Smith didn't say anything to that, because he had been thinking the same thing. Soft green hills rose up over this town by the river, and the woods beyond the little houses were dark and thick and beautiful. But the fact that he had never been to White Falls in his life, and yet he knew what he would see here, *had seen it already,* unsettled him. It was as if he had looked at pictures of the town in somebody else's scrapbook and hadn't remembered until now.

"We could turn around and go home," he said. Home. The word felt odd in his mouth. Had he ever truly known a place he would call home? He and his mother had moved around a lot, and after her death he had kept up the tradition. After they had let him out of prison, when he had wandered from place to place getting odd jobs and saving as much money as he could, staying a month here and there before leaving again, he had thought of cities simply as places to sleep. Phoenix, Los Angeles, San Francisco. What had he been looking for? During those two years of rambling he had constantly felt as if he needed to be somewhere, hadn't he? All of it tied into his feeling that he was meant for something. Only he didn't know exactly what, or *where.*

"No, we can't. You make it seem like we have a choice. If I said let's turn around here, you'd just handcuff me to the door again. Wouldn't you?"

"I don't know," he said truthfully. He thought he probably wouldn't have the strength. But he didn't dare tell her that.

Beyond the square was the local police station, then a red-brick bar on their right, and a grocery store. Past that the road forked. As he turned right Smith could see the new school building on the left up on the hill, with its green playing fields and parking lot full of cars.

Just before they were to cross the river again, they came upon the Old Mill Inn, a three-story, rambling structure overlooking a little lake of dark water. The river quieted in the lake, gathered itself and then spilled over the dam near the old water wheel in a rush, before sliding quietly under the bridge and out of sight.

He looked it over carefully, thinking about the ghosts that must live in a place like this. Such an old building, watching people born, living seventy or eighty years, passing away. He said something to that effect, wanting to sound offhand, but somehow it came out heavy, like he had been rehearsing the lines in his head.

Angel only nodded. "It fits," she said. "It fits this town just right."

He parked the Jetta next to the only other car in the lot, a rusting old Dodge with the bumper sticker—*This car climbed Mt. Washington*—pasted to its rear end. "Last stop," he said as the motor died. Silence fell over them. "A lovely spot for a summer vacation."

"I'd rather be in Paris."

He looked at her, surprised, and saw that she was smiling at him. He felt another barrier between them break away like driftwood. As they stepped from the car and stretched their aching backs, they could hear the falls somewhere out of sight below the bridge, and it was a sound they both recognized.

*Welcome to my nightmare,* Smith thought, and went inside.

The inside of the inn was pleasant, if a little too cute. The ceilings were low, innards exposed with heavy, dark beams crossing the length of the rooms. It was necessary to walk through the gift shop to get to the lobby, and past that was the dining room. The gift shop was a small room filled with stuffed bears and crocheted wall hangings and bad seascapes on canvas. The stink of potpourri layered itself over something deeper and darker, a smell like old rotten fabric. It reminded him of the smell that sometimes came from the sea flats at low tide after the seaweed and mud had cooked under the hot sun. He remembered the great white stretches of salt in Salt Lake City. Along with that came the loneliness that had hit him then, as he walked behind the vacant stores and row houses, and he tried to shrug it off without success.

Once they passed through the gift shop they were treated to a view of the river and the lake out the dining room windows. The old water wheel sat on the water's edge, braced by a couple of posts and looking like it might decide to roll in at any moment.

The proprietor of the inn was a tall, handsome man who introduced himself as Bob Rosenberg. "What can I do for you?"

"We'd like a room," Smith said. "A suite if you have it."

"I think we can arrange that." Rosenberg smiled. "Are you vacationing here in town?"

"We'll be staying a while."

"I hope you're planning on sticking around for the festival in May. We put on a pretty good little party."

"We might be around that long."

Rosenberg went around to the back of the lobby desk and got out a ledger book. "We're about empty for the moment, so you'll have the run of the place. We don't start reserving rooms until the end of April, you understand. I'll put you in our best room. It's got a great view of the lake." Rosenberg signed them in, came back around the desk and shook both their hands, and said, "Welcome to White Falls."

After checking out their rooms (two: one decent-sized, one small, with a connecting door) they wandered down a path that led around the side of the building to the lake. Rosenberg had looked at them strangely when they told him they had no bags, but said nothing. Still, word would get around; Smith had had enough experience with small towns to know that any odd gossip would hit the grapevine, oh, say thirty seconds after it happened.

"What do you think?" he asked, when they reached the water. It was a large and heavy bowl between artificial banks, stretching out back along the river a good distance. The mill wheel loomed above them, cutting a deep swath of shade down the bank to the water's edge. The patch of shade was so dark it looked painted black, the grass around it an even brighter green. It was cool here, the spring air crisp and moist with a hint of summer.

"The rooms are nice. We'll have to move the beds."

"That's not what I meant."

Angel sighed. She plopped herself down in the grass. "A week ago I was in Miami . . ." she let her voice trail off. One hand was pulling absently at the grass, then flicking it away. *Tug, tug, flick.* She looked at him, her hand stopping in midair with a fistful of grass. The blades stuck out from between her fingers; he could see the marks at her elbow and his eyes were drawn to them helplessly.

She flicked the grass toward the water. "Look, I want you to know that I don't accept what you did. But I'm not going to fight you anymore. What you said about the dreams we've been having made some crazy kind of sense. I guess I'm crazy, too."

"Maybe we both are."

"I mean, it feels so *normal.* That's the weird thing. I guess I feel like I should be afraid of you. But I'm not."

"None of this is normal. And you probably should feel afraid. You don't really know me. It's going to take time for me to prove myself to you. But I'm going to try." He hesitated, looking at her arm again, the track marks. "Is it bad?"

But he knew the answer to that one. He knew too well. The ache of need, filling every waking hour, the constant whispering of the mind saying *just one sip, that wouldn't be so bad, no big deal, just one.*

She surprised him. "Maybe it'll hurt like hell pretty soon. But I don't want it right now. I don't know why." She flashed him a cynical smile. "Maybe I'm just lucky."

They listened to the soft rush of the water as it ran over the dam. A thin, almost invisible crack ran up from the bottom left, all the way to the top right like a dark bolt of lightning. Smith looked at the big water wheel. Close up, he could see thousands of tiny holes bored by carpenter ants. As he watched, a big black ant poked its alien head out of a hole, wriggled its antennae slowly back and forth to test the air, and then scampered down the side of the wood and disappeared into the grass.

"There's more you should know," she said, breaking the silence. "Last night after you had fallen asleep, I tried to leave. You didn't handcuff me. I got up, got dressed, even fished the car keys out of your pocket. It was easy." She shrugged. "I got as far as the car, even started it up, and then . . . I just couldn't go any farther."

"You thought about what I said?"

"I don't know. All I know is that I had to go back inside. I had the strangest feeling that if I drove out of that parking lot I would just fall off the face of the earth and disappear."

They stared at the water. Smith felt that great loneliness welling up inside again. Prisoners, both of them.

"Do you think we're ever going to figure out exactly why we're here?" she asked.

"Oh, I think so. Dress rehearsal is over. Time for the first act soon."

"So what do we do until then?"

He considered how to answer that. What should they do? *How do you prepare yourself when you don't even know what's coming?*

"I don't know," he admitted finally.

They watched the sun fall in the west, and when the last light had faded from the sky, they went inside.

# Chapter Five

The next morning, Billy Smith awoke in the hard little antique bed with a headache already beginning to gnaw at him. He glanced past the delicate lace curtains, out the window. The sun was shining brightly, already high in the sky. He could hear the river tumbling over the rocks below his window. Perfect spring day, perfect little inn, perfect little town.

He stood up, bare feet on the cold hardwood floor, and looked at himself in the full-length mirror on the back of the door. His light blue t-shirt was old and faded; prison issue. He wore it every night to remind himself how sweet it was to wake up without the taste of iron in the back of his throat, without the smell of concrete and industrial cleaner and the sound of the other inmates muttering to themselves in the dark. Ten years of that hadn't hardened him like he thought it might. Every breath of open, clean air he took into his lungs meant something to him now. Breathing was no longer an involuntary muscle spasm.

And the guilt remained, and that, perhaps, was another reason why he wore the shirt. To remind himself every morning of just who he was, and what he had done.

He took off the shirt and approached the mirror, stopped about three feet in front of it and let one finger trace the long white scar that ran from his right thigh up across his belly to just below his ribcage. A piece of the doorframe had done that to him during the accident, and just about ended his life in the process. Strange, though, he hadn't even known he was hurt until the ambulance driver grabbed him by the shoulders and made him look at himself. He felt only a cool wetness. The blood had soaked his pants all the way to his shoes.

He held his own gaze in the mirror for several moments. *Gut-check, William. Yes, you are still alive. And a goddamned handsome man, if I may say so myself.*

Not exactly true. He was too thin for his height, his skin was almost as white as the boxers he wore, and today his eyes were almost hidden inside deep pockets of tired flesh. He needed a shave; the black bristles stood out on his hollow cheeks, giving him a bit of a desperate look. But what the hell. He was right on one point; he *was* alive. And he felt a great deal better than he had the day before, even with the headache. He had slept through the night without a single nightmare. That was something to celebrate.

*How long will it last? How long before you wake up screaming again?*

The tall gaunt man in the mirror did not answer.

After he woke Angel in the other room and they had both showered, they went out in search of something to eat. The dining room downstairs wouldn't open for lunch for another twenty minutes, and so they walked slowly toward the town square, enjoying the sunshine. The air was still crisp but warm, a slight breeze drying Smith's damp hair. He had found some aspirin and crunched two of them, and his headache had eased a little. With the shower and the fresh air he felt almost human again. Now all he needed was a razor and a can of shaving cream.

They walked past the clinic and the grocery. Set back behind the grocery was the police station and volunteer fire department. Smith could see the snout of an old-fashioned pump fire truck through the open doors, candy-apple red. Someone was polishing the truck's shine with a big green cloth, nothing but the hand visible in the sunshine, sticking out from the darkness of the garage. The hand moved in big, slow circles across the red paint.

On their left was the cemetery with a pretty little iron fence around the perimeter. Long lines of white stones marched down over the hill and out of sight toward the river. The church was next, a box-like white building with a short squat steeple; as they passed it, a bell clanged somewhere inside, ringing out over the quiet road and echoing across the town square.

They found the Johnson Café within the line of storefronts along the square and grabbed a booth near a window. The café was a long, narrow place like a train car with smooth linoleum floors and water-stained wallpaper, a white Formica counter running the length of the inside wall. Quiet country music played through tinny speakers in the ceiling, the sounds of the kitchen drifting out through closed swinging doors. The place was busy, the booths along the walls crowded by couples or families with little children, the six or seven stools along the counter occupied by big men in white t-shirts and baseball caps with the same logo, a green W with a slash of white.

They sat in a booth with a scarred wooden table. Smith's hands danced across the initials carved in the wood and played restlessly with the stainless steel napkin dispenser. All activity had stopped for a beat when they first entered and though the room was now humming again, he kept catching glances from the other customers as they looked the newcomers up and down. They looked at the menus, and a minute later a middle-aged waitress with a huge orange wave of hair that crested about a foot above her head came waddling over to take their order.

A nametag pinned over her breast read *Martha.* "Busy day," Smith commented. She frowned at him over large round glasses. Her face was perfectly round as well and doughy-complexioned.

"Saturday's our busiest time. People come in before the softball games, then stop by again when they're done." She frowned again. "You ain't from around here."

"No, ma'am."

Her frown deepened. "You got folks in town?"

"Nope. Just passing through."

She directed a finger toward Angel. "This your wife?"

"I'm Billy, and this is Angel."

"Pleased to meet you," Angel said smoothly. She extended a hand.

The woman took it after a moment's hesitation. She withdrew her hand as if she'd touched something unpleasant. "Martha Johnson," she said. "Me and my husband own this place, such as it is. Don't mind all these people staring. They're just curious. We don't get new people around here too often. Least, not this time of year. Tourists ain't due for another month or more."

They ordered two cups of coffee and two plates of eggs and bacon, thanked Martha and she waddled away. The eggs came a few minutes later piled up high and steaming on white diner plates, the coffee in heavy mugs hot enough to burn their throats. They ate for a moment in silence, enjoying the simple food. Smith was surprised at his own appetite; the eggs disappeared quickly, the bacon as well, and he had waved for a refill on his coffee and looked around a bit before he spoke again. Their corner booth was a reasonable distance away from the other customers, and he thought they could talk without being overheard.

"Listen," he said finally, sitting forward in his seat. "We have to agree once and for all that we're a team. You know what I'm saying? If any of these people figure out where we really come from, what's really going on between us, it'll be all over. We have to work together."

She dragged a fork through the remains of her eggs, tracing a pattern. "They wouldn't believe it."

"There's more to it than that. Even if they don't believe all of it, they sure will call the police. I violated my parole—if they catch me, I'll go back to jail even if you *don't* press charges for kidnapping."

"Your parole?"

"I thought you understood I'd been in jail."

"You've told me a lot about your life, but not much about that. I thought it was an accident."

"I killed three people," Smith said. He said it quietly, evenly. She would never know how long it had taken him to be able to say it aloud. Such a simple little group of words, words that meant nothing much alone but together were like a five hundred-pound weight around his neck. "I was a drunk and a fool and I got behind the wheel and I killed three innocent people. I did my time and now I'm sober."

"Did you know them?"

He shook his head. "The husband came and visited me while I was in jail. I thought he would try to get his hands on me, but he didn't. He just kept asking me questions. Why did I drink that day? Why did I decide to drive home on Lakefront Avenue? Why couldn't I have gone through that intersection a few minutes earlier or a few minutes later? All the same questions I had asked myself."

"Did you give him any answers?"

"I don't know. I think he was more angry at God than anyone else. I tried to give him someone to blame, and maybe that helped, a little. I told him it was my fault. I told him to hate me. I never saw him again."

"How long were you in jail?"

"Ten years. I wanted it, I guess I would have taken more if the judge had seen fit to give it to me. Penance, or something like that."

Yes, something like that. When he was just a boy, there had been a painting hanging in the front hall. You looked at it as you came in the door—had to see it, the way it was hung, center stage. The painting was of a nun. The nun stared out at the world, stern-faced, grim, holding a prayer book in her hands. Oh, how he had hated that painting, the way it stared at him no matter where he was, the eyes seeming to follow as he walked from the front step, through the hall, and up the stairs to his room. The nun had offered her silent judgment on whatever he had done that day; *Playing in the street again, weren't you, you awful child, if your mother only knew. Lied to the teacher today? Well, may you burn in hell for it.*

He began to enter the house through the back door whenever he could. Still, he could *hear* her calling him, and he could not think straight until he had faced her, and heard what she had to say. *Stole a candy from the Watkin's cupboard, didn't you? Ungrateful child. No wonder your real parents didn't want you.*

Finally they had moved to another house halfway across the country, and the painting had been lost in the shuffle. His mother had been angry about it, she had loved that painting, and he acted as if he had, too—but secretly he was glad it was gone.

He began to drink in high school, and it had a terrible effect on him from the start. He would become angry, violent. And he would continue to drink until finally he passed out. But he could not stop. Alcohol grabbed hold of him and wouldn't let go. Finally he got himself in a fistfight and ended up in jail—this was senior year, a week before graduation—and though they didn't press charges, they gave him a good scare. As he rode home from the police station he could almost feel the nun in the painting staring at him, though she had been gone now ten years; *you were lucky this time, Billy, quit while you're ahead, or you'll burn in hell for it.*

He had quit, for a while. But after his mother died he started again, and by the time he entered college he was drinking almost every night. One DUI hadn't stopped him, neither had a series of minor fender-benders. He'd always been able to explain them away, telling himself he'd been too tired to see straight, or the road had been wet, or it was the other driver's fault.

And then the accident. He had paid for it. Even after the jail term had been served he had kept on punishing himself. And he had not had a drop to drink since. But nothing he could do would bring the children back.

Angel had asked him another question, and he had to scramble to catch up.

"I asked you what you did after you got out of prison."

"Wandered around for a while. Did some odd jobs, made some money. Enough to live on, anyway. I had a little tucked away too. Ended up in San Francisco, you know that part. And then the dreams started."

"How long ago, exactly?"

"I'm not really sure. I was restless after I left prison, and I guess they were starting even then, in a way. The real strong ones started six months ago, maybe." He took a sip from his fresh cup of coffee. "So that's *my* story, or at least most of it. What about you?"

She stiffened. "I don't want to talk about it."

"All right," he said, "that's fine with me. But I think it's important for us to know where we both stand. I think it's important for us to know *why* we're both here. What drove us to this place? Because I think you would have ended up here eventually on your own, if I hadn't gotten to you first. You understand? It's got a hold on you, the same as it does me."

Angel was silent for a long time. Then she said, in a small voice, "I come from a little town in New York. I ran away to Miami after I graduated high school because I needed a change, and I thought I could get a job singing somewhere. I was pretty good in high school, sang in the choir, even did some solo work at a coffeehouse in town. I thought that if I could just catch a break . . ." She shrugged. "Pretty stupid. Same old story, I guess. I ran out of money a year ago and then . . ." She stopped, then started again, her shoulders straightening, her voice a little stronger. "I did it for the first time about three months ago. There was a man in one of the clubs where I used to hang out, and he was always after me, and he said he'd take care of me. I needed money."

"Why didn't you go home?"

"I couldn't do that. My father would never have taken me back. You have to understand the way he is. He didn't want me to go to Miami, he wanted me to go to college. Once you defy him it's like you no longer exist. It's like you're dead."

"So the man took you in."

"I was in trouble. And he got me drugs. I wasn't feeling too good about myself and they helped for a while. Then he introduced me to a few friends of his, told me I could earn some really good money. Told me if I didn't, I'd be out on the street. Pretty soon he had me out looking for more. It seemed like it happened so fast, and I was high all the time. I wasn't myself. And then . . . and then you came." Angel's shoulders were rigid and she sat absolutely straight in her seat. She took hold of her coffee cup, took a long drink, and set it back down again. "It's not like I slept around with everybody all my life. It just . . . happened."

He watched her struggle with herself and felt helpless to do anything about it. He was in no position to judge anyone. He was not good with people, he thought, and that was the simple truth of it. Someone who was worth a damn would say a word or two to make her feel better about herself, make her feel more at ease. But everything he thought to say sounded cheap or patronizing or downright cruel in a backward sort of way, and so he kept his mouth clamped shut.

After a moment, she said, "To answer your question, I don't know if I would have come here on my own or not. After the dreams started a few weeks ago, I thought I was going crazy. I felt them pulling at me and I thought I had to do something about it. So maybe I would have come. Or maybe I'd be dead by now. The heroin helped with the dreams, you know. It made me . . . forget things, everything. Who I was."

"And your brother," Smith said, as gently as he could. "What happened to him?"

"Michael got sick when I was twelve," she said. "Leukemia. He was in his senior year of high school, I think, when they diagnosed it. He played baseball and he was very good. Everyone said he would play professionally. The college recruiters were coming to look at him, calling the house and taking him out to see their campuses. Even a few pro scouts, I remember. My father was very proud of him." She picked up her fork again and began tracing more designs in the bit of egg that remained. "Then he started complaining that he was tired all the time. We didn't think much about it, since he was training so hard every day, but it got worse, and he got very pale and started losing weight. They took him to see Dr. Lewis, and she ran a lot of tests. I remember that Michael was in and out of the hospital for a week or two, and everybody was really scared. They kept taking blood. And there were long needles, I remember that.

"He quit the baseball team just before graduation. They were going to go to the state finals, and the whole town was devastated by it. I mean, little towns like ours didn't go to the state finals too often. Without Michael they didn't have a chance. And he was well liked too, always friendly. But he just sat around his room for most of the days after that, and he wouldn't talk to me. He wouldn't talk to anyone. The whole team came to see him one day but he wouldn't even let them through the front door, and after standing out on the doorstep for a while, they left.

"The doctors started giving him chemotherapy at the hospital and his hair started falling out. It all happened so *fast.* He got really thin, I mean he was like a skeleton, and he bled so easily. He cut himself shaving once and I thought he was going to die right there, the blood just kept pouring out of him. And then he went back into the hospital again, later that summer, and they told us the cancer had spread to his brain and that he had a few weeks to live. And then he was gone."

"And you were how old, then?"

"Thirteen. He died less than a year after he was diagnosed. I didn't get to talk to him before he died. My father went to the hospital that night, and I asked him if I could go, but he said, 'Not now. It's late. You'll go tomorrow.' His words, I remember them exactly. I guess he just assumed Michael would be around in the morning." Angel sighed, saw what she was doing with the fork and her remnants of egg, and put it down carefully on her plate. "So that's it," she said. "My father didn't beat me, my mother didn't turn into an alcoholic or a religious fanatic or anything like that. They just stopped paying attention, and after a while I guess I did, too."

"So that was why you left for Miami, eventually."

"I suppose so. I told myself I wanted to be rich and famous and that I had the talent to be a singer, but I don't know if I ever really believed it. I just needed to get out." She cocked her head, looking at him the way a little dog might look at something worrisome. "It wasn't all bad, you know," she said. "I make it seem like some kind of soap opera. We had some good times together before Michael got sick. But something died with him. He was a big part of the family, so that changed things. Looking back, I guess he was the glue that held us together. My parents never really recovered. My father, especially."

"And you?"

"Oh, I don't know." She sighed again, and tucked a lock of hair behind one ear, a gesture he had come to realize meant she was feeling uncomfortable.

"Just one more thing. Did you dream about it again last night?"

"No, I don't remember anything, anyway. Did you?" He shook his head. "Maybe it's over," she said. Her voice was hopeful as she tried to make herself believe what she was saying. "Maybe we're both crazy, after all."

"Maybe."

"Listen, can we take a walk, or something? I'd like to get out of here."

He stood up and pulled a few wrinkled bills out of his pocket and laid them on the table. He was thinking about something she had said earlier, about the heroin: *It made me forget things, everything. Who I was.* And he thought, *We both have our tragedies we'd like to forget.*

But that was another thing he had been thinking about lately. They shouldn't try so hard to forget. Maybe the past was important.

They were walking past the gazebo when the old woman approached them across the square.

Her body was rail-thin and her gray dress hung off her shoulders like a burlap sack. She was moving quickly, the sunlight and shadows playing about her figure making her seem ephemeral, almost ghostlike. Smith could hear her muttering to herself as she approached. Something inside him went off like an alarm as the woman got close. He took a half step back and gripped Angel's hand. "I don't think—" he began, meaning to say, *I don't think she's quite right.* But the woman interrupted.

"He's coming!" she hissed at them. She had stopped barely three feet away, and stood with her fists clenched and the cords standing out in her neck. Her eyes were wild and rolling, her white hair a snarl about her head, and she spoke with a furious energy. "The time is close!" Spittle flew in big white flecks as she spat out the next words, as if something had curdled in her sunken mouth. Her voice had raised itself to a new level, taking on the cadence of a preacher in front of his flock. " *'And they found the stone rolled away from the tomb—'* "

"Leave them alone, Annie," a voice said from behind

them. "They don't want any of your sermons today."

They turned. The voice belonged to a man of medium height with slim shoulders, blond hair swept back from his face and parted on the side. He wore a white shirt and conservative blue-striped tie, tan Dockers, and brown penny loafers. He had an intelligent, sober face, and bright blue eyes. "Go on, Annie," he said. "You've got better things to do than this."

"I've been waiting," the old woman said. In the extremes of her dementia her age seemed to melt away, and she peered at them with the bright, focused gaze of a young girl, eyes darting from face to face as if searching for something. She nodded, her head bobbing on a long thin neck. "Yes," she said. "I've been waiting for you too, you know."

The man who had spoken took the old woman by the arm. He whispered to her quietly, gently, turning her in the other direction, and after a moment the manic gleam in her eyes slowly died. Smith thought she would start to move away, but suddenly she broke the man's grip, turned back and shuffled right up to him. He stood unable to react as she reached out to touch his cheek with a dry, wrinkled hand.

"You've come back," she whispered softly. Her touch was gentle, her voice suddenly calm. For a moment he was staring straight into her eyes, and he saw something there that shook him; it was the spark of recognition.

*"Annie,"* the man said sharply.

She turned again, her mouth moving softly, and stumbled away from them across the open stretch of fresh grass, just an old, bent woman talking to herself. Smith willed himself to relax, and let go of Angel's hand.

"Annie's harmless," the man said, after a moment. "Been like that for years, though she's usually not so vocal.

I don't know what's gotten into her. She's become sort of a fixture in town, and we let her go about more or less as she pleases. She must be near eighty years old now."

"God," Angel said. She had her arms wrapped around herself now, and she shivered. "What *happened* to her?"

"She lost her son in an accident a long time ago. The boy fell into the falls and drowned. Ever since then she hasn't been quite right. She walks around talking about the boy coming home again, returning to her."

"Her eyes—"

"Odd, aren't they?" the man agreed. "She's got a way of looking at you, that's for sure. But she doesn't mean anything by it." He extended a hand in greeting to each of them in turn. "Harry Stowe. I'm the local quack in town. Working up at the clinic this morning, thought I'd take a walk in the sunshine. Glad I did, or Annie might have run you two right out of town."

"You're very good with her," Smith said. He still felt the woman's touch on his cheek, and resisted the urge to scrub at it. *Don't fall to pieces, for Christ's sake,* he scolded himself. She was just an old, confused woman who had thought he was someone she knew. That was all.

"I've treated her at the clinic for quite a while. Surprisingly healthy. She never catches a cold, even though she walks around in her bare feet half the day." Stowe chuckled. "We used to have a problem with her wandering around town in her underwear. Thought we'd have to lock her up, but she stopped doing it after a while. Sue Hall, that's the reverend's sister, she takes care of Annie most of the time."

"Must be quite a job."

"We all keep an eye on her."

Smith nodded as if he understood. He introduced himself, and Angel as his wife, and related the vague story they had taken on as their own; a couple just passing through, looking for a change of scenery for a while. He added that they were treating it as a kind of second honeymoon, because that seemed appropriate, and tried not to meet Angel's eyes. If he looked at her he was afraid he would either give up the whole ridiculous story on the spot or burst out laughing. Either way, that would be the end of their decision to "lay low" in White Falls, for all intents and purposes.

But then again, Harry Stowe did not look like the kind of man who spread rumors around on a daily basis. His eyes were quick and sharp, and he stood with both feet planted firmly on the ground, an air of quiet authority surrounding him. He had a way of putting you immediately at ease, and Smith thought he was probably a very good doctor. *I'll bet the single ladies flock to him, and half of the married ones, too.*

"So this is your first day here in our little town," Stowe said, grinning. "Bet you've got the locals giving you the evil eye, am I right? Don't pay them any attention. Why don't you let me show you around a little bit? I can tell you some of White Falls' more colorful history."

"Oh, you don't have to—" Angel started to protest, but he held up a hand.

"The least I can do, after that incident with Annie. To show you that most of us around here are sane. More or less." He grinned again, and Smith felt a smile work its way out onto his own face. Here was a man who *knew* how to put others at ease, that much was readily apparent. He watched Angel's face as Stowe spoke, and felt a slight twinge of something—*jealousy?* he wondered. He pushed it aside.

"I've got about an hour before I should be back at the

clinic," Stowe was saying, looking at his watch. "Would you like to walk around the square? I can point out a few of the old houses. There are some good stories behind them."

They began to walk slowly together past the gazebo and under the line of trees toward the western end of the square and the hills, Stowe talking animatedly as they went. He pointed out the Thomas mansion and told them the story of the eccentric recluse who built it and kept building, walling himself in, year by year. "There were some pretty crazy stories about Frederick Thomas," Stowe said. "I've read a little about him in the town records. The people didn't like him much; they thought he was some kind of sorcerer. The way he lived probably didn't help much. I think he fed off of their paranoia and became more paranoid himself, until he was just as crazy as a shi—well, just plain nuts. Frankly, I'm surprised he kept himself alive as long as he did. Back then people didn't think twice about burning so-called witches at the stake. Or worse."

Smith studied the house and felt himself oddly drawn to the strange angles and walls that seemed to lead nowhere in particular, the brooding octagonal windows on the attic level, the right wing that hung out over the fence line on the third floor. The house seemed to watch over the square and the surrounding houses like a guard keeping an eye on a prisoner.

Stowe turned them toward the north and showed them the McDonald house, a much more manageable, pleasant-looking colonial, and the Deane house, a square, two-story box set back a bit farther from the square and surrounded by a line of hedges at least six feet high. "McDonald and Deane were the first of the white settlers to set foot on this ground," he said. "They came up from the south along the river and were attacked by some sort of Indian tribe and forced to turn back. But they remembered the place, and came back a year later with three others. Frederick Thomas was one of those later three, just a kid then, maybe eighteen or twenty. They managed to get along with the Indians, more or less, and after a while they had a neat little settlement going here. This was I guess about a hundred years before Maine became a state. By the 1800s, they were doing a pretty good trade with the other settlements downriver. They took ice from the river below the falls and sold it, and there was fishing, too. The river was well-known in those days, though I don't know if there's many fish in her now."

"Do people still live in these houses?" Angel asked.

"There's nobody in the Thomas place anymore. Henry Thomas was the last of the line, and he died about ten years ago. The other two have people in them, though those aren't the original houses. The original places burned down sometime in the 1800s, and were rebuilt on the same sites. The same families still own them, if you can believe that. Descendants, of course." He chuckled. "People born around here don't go very far, or if they do, they always seem to find their way back."

Stowe pointed a few other things out to them as they walked back down in an easterly direction. The storefronts across from them, including the Johnson Café, were built just after the turn of the century, and the gazebo went up about twenty years later. There were bands that played on the green occasionally, mostly local types, none very good. "The kids like them, though. It used to be a time for families to come out and sit down with a picnic supper, but now I'm afraid it's mostly just kids getting drunk and causing trouble. There's usually one or two fights by the end of the night, and once in a while somebody ends up in jail. Putting an end to these bands always comes up at town meetings, but they haven't gotten around to doing anything yet."

There were others out now, walking through the park-like atmosphere, enjoying the sunshine. They passed a young couple, holding hands. Stowe asked them if they'd seen the falls. They told him they hadn't, and so he took them down past the church on a nicely paved path, over the banks of a steep hill to an overlook of the river, where the water rushed through a series of deep channels and burst out over the drop, the spray reaching all the way up to them.

As they stood on the edge of it, looking down, Stowe told them the story of Annie's son Joseph, the boy who had fallen to his death in 1958, the subsequent uproar over the safety of the falls, and the argument regarding the installation of a fence around the edges. Ultimately, the town had decided that a chain-link fence would ruin the natural beauty, which was another way of saying it would scare away the tourists. Stowe told them there were still a few people that were so bitter about the decision they wouldn't attend town meetings anymore. "And Annie, she just wasn't able to handle it. Her mind went, she started predicting all kinds of things, the end of the world. Hellfire and damnation, that sort of stuff. She told everyone that her boy was coming back for her before the end, and they would go up to heaven together. It's in the Bible, you know—Armageddon?"

"The faithful will be saved," Smith said.

"Exactly. Well, she just wouldn't let up. The people felt sorry for her and a little guilty, I guess, and so they kept her out of the state institution and took care of her themselves. They still do. Sue Hall is just the latest in a long line of them to look after Annie."

The three of them stood and talked for another few minutes before Stowe glanced at his watch, apologized, and said he ought to be getting back to work.

As they walked back across the green grass, Smith thought they had found a friend in White Falls, or at least a friendly face; but later when he thought of that day, it was Annie he kept going back to, crazy Annie's savage face as she spat out her words from the Gospel According to Luke. Smith had recognized the quote from his early church school days; it recounted the occasion of Easter. *And they found the stone rolled away from the tomb, but when they went in they did not find the body.*

The resurrection. The day Christ rose from the dead.

And that other. Her touch on him, and her words; *You've come back.*

So much pain for one woman to take. Her little boy gone, just gone, and nothing had been done about it. By the time they reached the Old Mill Inn again, though the sky was warm and bright, Smith felt as if a great black shadow had fallen over the world.

# Chapter Six

Jeb Taylor was in the Friedman's back garden with the manure again, troweling it under the loose soil, pulling up tree roots near the garden's border. He had been working through the pain, concentrating on it, focusing it into a small spot in the center of his forehead where it was easier to deal with. God, what he wouldn't do for a drink right now. Take the edge off a little.

It always struck him, what people would do to have a nice garden, what they would *pay*. Here he was digging and digging and digging, and for what? For plants that would grow and flower and then wither and die in the fall. And then he, or someone else, would be back next spring to do it all over again. Turning the old dirt, mixing in the manure, peat moss, and maybe a little *Miracle-Gro*. Planting the seed, covering it all with a bit of straw for heat, watering carefully, weeding out the unwanted elements. Like a recipe from one of Ruth's old cookbooks. It seemed like such a waste of time.

In the midst of these thoughts he happened to look up at the house. What he saw there made his breath catch in his throat—Mrs. Friedman, standing at the second-floor window in nothing but a white bra and panties. When she saw him she did not move away. Her hand brushed against the lace curtain, holding it back, and he thought, *she thinks the sun's on the glass and I can't see.* She stood there for a full minute, and Jeb thought it was funny that she would think he couldn't see when the sun was shining on the front of the house and not the back, and in fact half the garden was in shadow.

He worked for the next several hours in silence as the sun crept over the rooftop and reddened his back, and then took his lunch in the shade of the oak tree just beyond the garden. All this time he didn't see Mrs. Friedman again, and by late afternoon he had forgotten the whole thing, thinking once again about what he was doing and why the hell he was doing it. Mrs. Friedman wanted a landscaped flower garden with a pebbled stream in the middle, something you saw on one of those home improvement shows. A goddamn waste of time. A manicured "small pebbled stream" belonged in L.A., Beverly Hills maybe, but not Maine. Some hot shit director or movie star with a twenty-acre estate would hire a landscaper who got paid two hundred bucks an hour to do it. Then the landscaper would hire a couple of kids to do the work and make a killing. Jeb had seen it all on *Lifestyles.* Maybe that was something he could do; move to Hollywood and work on famous people's gardens, sit back in the shade and drink whiskey from tall, cool glasses.

*They wouldn't let you in those big Hollywood gates, Jeb. They wouldn't even let you wash their dicks for them.*

True. But it would be nice to live in Hollywood and look at all the pretty girls in bikinis. He sighed, and rubbed at the small of his back where a sharp pain nagged at him. The voices had been getting louder lately, and they never had anything good to say. They'd been running around and around his head, driving him crazy, ever since the night he'd gone up to Thomaston to get the suitcase. The suitcase that was still sitting up in his closet, hidden under the pile of old t-shirts and odd socks and sweat pants.

He split a bag of cow manure down the side and mixed it with peat moss, the peat lifting dust-like in the sunshine and making him sneeze. The manure was old and dry and smelled like blood. A little of that mixture in with the fresh soil and he would have a good base. He was looking forward to the long trip down to Bath, where he would stop in at the greenery to buy the plants Mrs. Friedman wanted. He loved these trips because they always took an hour or more, and most of the time was spent on the road in his car with the windows down and the radio on. A real sense of freedom, flying down an open road in the sunshine while other people were locked up inside some stuffy office that smelled like old paint. If he hurried he could be ready to do the trip tomorrow or Monday at the very latest, and the plants could go in the ground in another week or two if the weather held.

A few minutes later he looked up to see Mrs. Friedman standing in the open doorway at the rear of the big house, hands on her hips, loose button-down shirt flapping in the slight breeze. Some of her hair had come loose from the elastic, and strands floated around her face. She pushed them back and called out to him.

"Could you come in here for a second? I've got something I need help with and I'd like to get to it today."

He slipped his shirt on and followed her inside.

"The chandelier in the dining room has burned out and I need to get the ladder from the basement," Mrs. Friedman said, as they walked through the narrow rear hall. She smelled of shampoo and something else he couldn't place. He saw her hair was still slightly damp at the center. "I'm sorry to bother you, but I can't carry it alone and we're having a dinner next Saturday for friends, and I'm just a mess running around trying to remember everything. I'd like to get this done while I'm thinking of it."

He nodded, following her through the kitchen, down into the dim basement, thinking that only rich Beverly Hills people had "a dinner for friends," and that maybe the Friedmans should move there and get the hell out of Maine. The old wooden stepladder was on its side against the stone foundation down at the end of the first chamber, between a bunch of boxes and old paint cans and storm windows. On the way over he was aware of Mrs. Friedman close behind him, the smell of her shampoo hanging in the air.

"Just take one end," she said, "and I'll take the other, if I can manage it." They lifted it awkwardly, Jeb fumbling around for a place to put his feet amid the clutter. His head kept brushing the light cord that hung down in his face, sending it flapping around. The basement was musty and smelled of varnish. It was a big basement, the kind that felt like a crypt, with exposed brick and stone, low ceilings, and interconnecting rooms that doubled back on themselves. He didn't like confined spaces. He felt trapped, like the walls were trying to close in on him.

They got the ladder to the basement steps, and it took another minute of maneuvering to work it around the support beams and up the narrow space. Jeb took the bottom end and pushed. His head throbbed, his hangover made worse by the varnish smell.

"Phew," Mrs. Friedman said when they finally had the ladder propped up against the dining room wall. She wiped her brow with a shirtsleeve. "Thank you, honey. I think you lifted most of that yourself. That would have been too much for me."

"Welcome, Mrs. Friedman."

"Please, you've been working here for weeks now. Call

me Julie, okay? I'd like that much better." She brushed his bare arm with a hand. "I don't act like a Mrs., do I? I always think of little old ladies when I hear that."

Jeb, who had thought of her as a Mrs. from the first moment he met her, said nothing.

"I don't know if I've told you what a good job you've been doing around here. Pat doesn't have the time to help out anymore, with the law practice becoming so busy. Would you like a cool drink? I think I have a soda in the kitchen . . ." She walked through an archway, and he heard a refrigerator door opening and closing, and the pop of a soda can. A moment later she returned with a glass of Coke. "There. That should help with the heat. I don't know how you stand it out there in the sun all day."

"It's only April. Wait till July." He took a long drink of the soda. It felt good on the back of his throat.

"I was wondering," Mrs. Friedman interrupted, smiling, "it's a little embarrassing really. I'm sort of afraid of heights. The ladder—if you'd help me with the bulbs . . . Please, it would only take a minute. I know, I'm just a silly old woman. Older than you, anyway." She was still smiling at him, the corners of her mouth curling up. For a crazy moment he almost believed she was going to keep smiling, her mouth getting wider and wider until she swallowed him up.

"I'm almost nineteen." As soon as he said it, he wanted to pull it back in.

"Nineteen? My, I wouldn't have guessed that. You look more like twenty-five to me. You remind me of the way Pat used to be, a long time ago."

Control was slipping away from him. Something was going on here, but it was like he had been invited to a party and not given directions. The anger welled up in him again.

"Just those two on the right side of the chandelier," she was saying as she went into the other room again. He thought she was going to leave him there to do it himself, but in a moment she swept back in carrying two boxes of light bulbs. "What do you think, sixty or hundred watt?"

"I—I don't know."

"Sixty, then. A little less light makes things so much more romantic, don't you think?"

*She's making fun of you, just like all the rest, can't you see her laughing? Don't let her laugh at you. Do something.*

"I don't know," he repeated. *Stupid.* Why couldn't he ever say what he was thinking? He put the soda down and began to set up the ladder, feeling the blood in his face and knowing he had turned beet red, hating himself for it and her for doing this to him.

She stood under the ladder as he climbed, and when she handed up the box of bulbs her hand brushed his and it seemed to him she let it linger there a few seconds longer than necessary. He remembered the glimpse of her standing in the window that morning. He hadn't had much experience with women, and he didn't know what to do with this one now. Mrs. Friedman was older than he was, but she was still attractive in a rich-bitch sort of way. She had a few wrinkles around her mouth (laugh wrinkles, Ruth used to call them), and her hair had a few streaks of gray, but she knew how to hold herself all right.

He took the box and turned to the chandelier, flustered, and as he did she kept talking below him, going on about something to do with the party and how nice the grounds looked. He screwed the dead bulbs out and replaced them with the new ones. When he glanced down he saw with a shock that Mrs. Friedman had slipped out of her button-down shirt and now wore only a white tank top. She wore no bra now. Her nipples showed through the fabric. "It's so hot in here." She sighed. "Don't you think it's hot? I just took a bath and now I feel like I need another."

"I don't know."

"Is that all you can say?" The smile had turned playful, and she made no move to cover herself, even though she was almost naked.

"I don't—" He stopped himself before he said it again. The blood had begun to thump in his ears (and somewhere else), so loud he thought for sure she could hear it too.

"Why don't you come down here before you fall." He climbed down the ladder, and she stood dizzyingly close. He could smell the shampoo again, and another smell underneath, too light for him to make out. He stared down at her breasts under the tank top, unable to help himself. "Do you like working for me, Jeb?" she said softly. Her voice was low and steady, soothing. "I love it that you're here. I get so lonely during the day, Pat's at work until all hours of the night. I never know when he'll come home. Sometimes it's not until ten or eleven o'clock." She reached out with her finger, tracing a line down his arm, across the inside of his elbow. She took his hand and placed it against her breast. "Here," she breathed softly. "That's it."

He squeezed, feeling her nipple harden against his palm. Blood thundered in his ears. She sighed again, her eyes drifting closed. A smile played about the corners of her mouth.

*Throw her down Jeb, rip her clothes off, that's what she wants you to do, put your mouth on her breasts and her stomach and let her touch you what's wrong are you gay, that's what they'll say, what she'll say they'll all laugh at you in town everybody will know you'll be the joke of the year the little stupid Taylor boy who never even had a woman can't get it up—*

Her hand had slipped to the top of his pants, it was moving lower, lower . . .

"I have to go," he managed to sputter, and then he was stumbling out of the house and into the sunshine, and the thing he felt was not sexual at all, he felt *rage,* more anger than he had ever felt in his life. She had been teasing and making fun of him like all the rest. He clenched his hands into fists and felt the nails cutting into his palms again like they had before, and this time he didn't stop until he felt blood running across his wrist.

As he was stumbling into his car she came out. "Jeb, wait." Her voice had changed. "Are you all right? I didn't mean—" Then she saw the blood on his hands, and she covered her mouth. "Oh my God."

And that was somehow worse than anything else. The look in her eyes.

He started the car and spun out of the driveway, leaving her standing there, knowing she would be back inside in an instant and on the phone to her fat ugly friends spreading the news that Jeboriah Taylor was a scared little faggot.

At *Johnny's* he sat in a corner booth with half a bottle of whiskey and went over the scene again and again in his mind. She had been up to something all right. Probably wasn't used to someone refusing her. He thought about what might have happened if he had grabbed her hard and pressed his lips against hers, and then lifted her up and carried her to the bedroom. Like a real man. Would she have gone willingly? It seemed impossible to believe, a rich woman like that willing to go to bed with him, Jeb Taylor, handyman, town idiot, son of the murderer Ronnie Taylor. He decided once again that she had been playing a game with him.

*A very dangerous game, wasn't it? Because couldn't you have kissed her anyway? There wasn't anyone else around. Couldn't you have gotten so angry that you couldn't help yourself, that you might even have—?*

He poured another shot and downed it, feeling the burn across his lips and throat, sliding down into his stomach. It lit up his entire body with tongues of fire, caressing him, easing the pain in his cut hands. He looked down at the tiny half moons of broken skin. The rage inside of him was so strong and insistent that for a moment he felt he would explode. And the voices in his head just wouldn't go away. He felt as if he were being pulled apart by something unseen and all-powerful.

*Get polluted, boy. Get shitfaced, so drunk you can't think anymore.*

He knew one thing; he had found a way to get out of that job. Or, more accurately, it had found him. He would never go back to work for Mrs. Friedman again.

Jeb Taylor sat there for the rest of the night alone, and by the time the barmaid came to get him he had finished the bottle of whiskey and had passed out with his head on the table, and finally, mercifully, the voices had stopped.

He awoke in the dark with the distinct feeling someone was watching him.

Disoriented, alcohol still running freely through his veins, he moved sluggishly across the bed and moaned. His eyes were gummy, painful pockets of flesh. How had he gotten home? He remembered *Johnny's* and the bottle of whiskey, and then nothing. His head was spinning and he felt as if he might be sick.

The room was freezing cold. He lay shivering under the sheets, and let his gaze play about the dim surroundings.

The moonlight let in through the window hardly gave him enough light. He could see only shapes in the darkness. The window was open; had he opened it before going to bed? He couldn't remember.

Jesus, it was cold.

Something was in the room with him. He did not know how he knew it, but he did. He tried desperately to clear his head, afraid now, straining to see. The dresser in the corner, as it should be; the chair next to it, clothes thrown loosely across the seat. Nothing wrong there. But still, that feeling, eyes on him . . .

The closet door was open. He sat up, his stomach turning over, his heart hammering against his ribs, and stared into the blackness of the closet. Walls running together in the dark and in the middle a black hole, and someone standing at the back, *grinning* at him. The figure looked like a man. He could just see the glint of eyes and white teeth.

"Not real," he croaked. His throat was dry and hot as a stovetop. "Drank too much, that's all. Seeing things. You're not real."

The figure did not move. Jeb Taylor sat with his back against the headboard and moaned to himself.

They considered each other.

It wanted him, he could feel it. And it looked familiar somehow. God help him, even as he sat there shaking with fear, something urged him to get up out of bed and go to it, just let it take him into the darkness.

He moaned again, the fear alive in him. With a sudden lunge that turned his stomach upside down and made his head spin, he crossed the few feet of space between his bed and the closet and slammed the door closed. He waited, but the door stayed shut and he heard nothing from inside the closet.

The thing had not spoken to him, had not even changed expression. He was going crazy.

He stood, weaving on his feet, for one long minute. Finally, unable to stand the silence and the heaviness in the air, he reached out. His hands were slick on the doorknob as he twisted and yanked the door open again.

Clothes hanging near the back, slumped like a man's shoulders, and the bit of white paper on the hanger like a slash of teeth in the dark. That was all.

*The suitcase, Jeb. Come on, old buddy. Open it up and take a peek at what's inside.*

He closed the closet door, slammed the window shut, and stumbled to the bed. His thoughts would not come together, and he was left with a blur of images in the dark empty spaces of his mind. Mrs. Friedman, leaning into him, her skin warm and smooth, as warm as the blood running down his hands. The closet door swinging slowly open like the door of a tomb, the sound of its hinges like something ripped from the ground. Blood welling up from half circles of broken flesh. And somewhere out in the dark, the body of his father, waiting for the flames.

Then the booze took hold of him again, leaving him nauseous and weak, and his head began to thump and spin, and he gladly let it take him down, into the darkness. He did not want to think about all of that, not now.

Not ever.

# Chapter Seven

As Jeb Taylor drifted off into a troubled sleep, Billy and Angel climbed into the car and drove back through the center of town, past the White Falls Church (currently filled with bowed heads and bingo boards and one soon to be discovered dead man), following the river which snaked through the darkness somewhere on their left, through the trees. The houses were close together near the road, with little screened-in porches and old vinyl chairs, flaking paint, washing lines strung out back between the pines.

The road dipped and branched off to the left where it crossed the river, and that was the way they had come into town; Route 27, running down through Bath and Brunswick and connecting onto the Maine Turnpike. The river ran along the side of the town like a moat, cutting White Falls off from the rest of the world. If the two bridges ever went out (and they were low; during the spring rains the water must almost touch the girders), the town would be, for all intents and purposes, an island.

They did not take Route 27 and instead continued on the right branch, which wound out through the trees and into a part of the town they had never seen before. Billy Smith felt like a hand had suddenly tightened its grip on his bowels. The road narrowed and began a gentle upward climb, the car's headlights cutting into the darkness and illuminating a desolate scene of alders and brush clumped close along the shoulder. They passed no other cars. When Angel turned to him her eyes looked even larger than normal, two deep pools that appeared black in the dim dashboard light. "What are we doing out here?"

"Exploring. It's what we decided to do tonight, isn't it?" What they had been *commanded* to do, he almost said, but kept his mouth shut. The less spooked they both got right now, the better.

"I—I feel like we're being watched all the time, like there's a pair of eyes out there. Someone that sees everything we do."

"We'll be fine."

"Are you sure? How can you know that?"

"We were picked, you and I. We've been brought here to do something. I don't know exactly what, but there's a reason for it, Angel. I have to believe that."

But did he, really? He was reminded of his mother's religious faith in all things destined to be, of lives that had been planned long before birth by some higher power. As much as he'd like to, he didn't believe any of that stuff. And yet here he was, driven to some unknown purpose by nightmares and voices he did not understand, driven to crimes he had not thought he'd been capable of committing.

"I find it hard to believe I've been picked for anything good."

"Come on. Kidnapping you was the best thing that ever happened to me." He tried to grin, but his facial muscles wouldn't seem to cooperate.

The darkness stretched out before them like an unexplored wilderness.

"I'm glad you're here," she said simply, and took his hand. Her touch was cool and light, so fragile, and he was reminded of how he had held her hand on the square earlier that afternoon, a gesture that had come almost without thought. When faced with something as bizarre as crazy Annie, they had quickly and easily come together, supporting each other as if they had been friends for years. It made no sense and yet it felt absolutely *right.* He felt an overwhelming surge of . . . something. He wanted to protect her, shield her from whatever they had to do.

"I feel so far away from everything," she was saying. She had turned to look out the windshield now, but her hand remained nestled in his palm. "It's almost like that other life never even happened at all. I can barely remember how I felt, what I did. Who I was."

"None of that stuff matters anymore."

"But it does, doesn't it? I mean, I have to try to understand it. Why I did what I did. I never wanted to come down and get sober because then I would realize what I was doing with those men." She shook her head. "I can't remember any faces."

"Give it time. It's barely been a week."

"That's just it." She shrugged her narrow shoulders. "It feels like forever. I don't know why, but I can hardly remember any of it."

Then something in the air seemed to change as the headlights picked up another road on their left. He slowed the car and turned into it, navigating by feel more than anything else. His heart had begun to beat faster. Angel seemed to feel something too; her hand tightened against his until he felt the little bones. It was like holding a bird in his palm. They had agreed to leave the hotel together tonight, and see what they could find, but he didn't think either of them really believed they would know where to go, or that they would find anything at all. Yet it didn't seem strange to him now that he knew exactly what to do, exactly where to turn.

Why did he feel like they were about to regret ever leaving their room, he wondered. And yet he felt compelled to continue over his own silent objections.

The new road was little more than a tunnel into the woods. It was filled with potholes and ruts and the ground seemed to catch at the car's tires so they were constantly sliding and bumping and slipping about. The headlights refused to reveal anything farther than a few feet. Above the car, the tree branches had grown in and hung down like arms, a few of them scraping the roof. Thick swarms of bugs filled the air and attacked the glass from the outside. He could hear them clicking softly as they hit. They lit up in the headlights like dust particles, forming two long narrow beams of dancing light. He had the strangest feeling, as if he had just driven out over an open drop, as if the ground beneath the car had fallen away, and they were floating through this tunnel of trees and bugs and blackness, doing a silent, weightless free-fall like a crippled satellite tumbling through space. And then a pothole cracked his teeth and brought him back to earth again.

A few hundred feet farther the car began to hitch and buck, cough, and finally it died. Smith turned the key and the starter ground but would not catch. The lonely noise was swallowed up by the thick trees.

He looked across at Angel in the dark interior and put the hazards on, listened to them clicking and saw the orange light bouncing off the trees like a neon sign, and turned them off again. "I think there's a flashlight in the glove box. You want to get it out?"

"But the bugs will eat us alive . . ."

"I don't think so." He opened the door and stepped from the car. All the bugs were gone. He thought suddenly of a corpse opening its mouth wide, bugs swarming all around, being taken in until the thing's purple skin bulged and crawled with them. He shook his head free of the image and closed his eyes tight, opened them to ordinary darkness. "It's okay," he said firmly. He clenched his hands into fists until he felt pain. "We're stuck. Might as well see what's at the end of the rainbow."

For a moment he thought she would protest, refuse to come with him. But Angel found the flashlight and handed it to him, and he flicked it on. The beam was strong and steady. He had checked the batteries three days before.

The muck was heavy and wet and sucked at their shoes. He held the flashlight in his left hand, her cool fingers in his right. They lost the car's headlights quickly and then there was only the beam of the flashlight, bouncing and wobbling and throwing shadows across their path. The night air was cool and there was no breeze. No sound, only their breathing and their shoes in the sucking mud. Tree branches hung down on either side like ghost fingers above their heads, in their hair, brushing their faces. As they walked, Smith found himself thinking of silly, pointless things, a free-for-all stream of thought that went on and on; *got to find someone to take a look at the car get it fixed and find Angel some clothes she's been wearing the same thing since (I took her) we left and I'll have to find something to give us extra money so we won't starve to death how long will they let us keep the room before they throw us out on our asses I wonder if the plugs are dirty in the car yes that's it the plugs are dirty not firing right gotta get new plugs . . .*

Then, very suddenly, the road ended in a small clearing, perhaps one hundred feet across. At the far edge the land fell off and joined a stretch of black water. He flashed the light on a broken old hand-painted *No Swimming* sign nailed to a post about ten feet in front of them. The words peeled and blistered and ran down the cracked wood; a vine had wound itself up the post and clung to the sign like a spidery brown fist.

He thought about someone sitting down on the muddy bank, taking off his shoes, peeling off shirt and pants, and diving into that black water. That sign had to be a joke. "Christ. What is this place?"

His words were too loud in the quiet of the woods. Angel didn't answer. A bitterly cold breeze touched their faces. Smith's bones ached with it. He caught a whiff of something that smelled like garbage, or worse. Angel seemed to draw into herself and become smaller in the face of it.

"This is a terrible place," she whispered. "Something happened here, but I don't want to know what." Then she stiffened, and touched his arm. She was looking to her right, and he followed her gaze with the flashlight, knowing already what he would see.

A cabin sat on the edge of the clearing, surrounded by dead brush. Its front steps had rotted and fallen in, exposing a hole like a rotten tooth. The door hung by a single hinge. A portion of roof had collapsed. The light caught a lonely crossbeam that stuck up like a broken bone. Next to the cabin was another structure, maybe a garage or storage shed, and between them was a square bit of fencing that might have been a garden at one time.

*Nothing growing there now. This place is dead.*

He stepped forward, pulling Angel along after him until he was in the center of the clearing. The grass growing up around the base of the shack rustled as the wind picked up, turning the surface of the pond into ripples of oily blackness. The flashlight beam disappeared about ten feet out over the water. The dim shape of a tire swing hung from a high tree branch, rocking in the breeze.

Rotted rubber and twine. Everything was rotting here. He could see his breath now in the freezing cold, as it was ripped away from his face by the sudden, growing wind. *Jesus,* he thought, *what's happening? What is this place?*

When the voice spoke it was like a thunderclap in his head. *Where the cancer began to feed. It all has to start somewhere, don't it? You get a couple of bad cells and they make a couple more, invite a few friends, all of a sudden you got a lump and it just grows and grows, my man, eats and eats until your legs swell up and your hair falls out and one day you look in the mirror and see a dead man looking back.*

A movement, off to his left. He swung the flashlight around at the darkness. Branches swinging back into place, as if something very large had just passed through. Something very large, indeed.

"Billy," Angel moaned. Her hand was a vice-grip around his own. The wind was whipping now, tossing the treetops about and turning the surface of the lake into froth. The tire swing was bashing itself into the tree trunk, spinning around out over the water, then in over the bank again.

He took another step forward as if hypnotized. The cabin door banged against the support post, a sound as loud as a gunshot. He swung the light on it again, caught a part of a window.

And something else, grinning back at him through the dirty glass.

It hovered there a moment, its eye sockets two empty black holes. Then it dipped out of sight.

Angel shrieked and turned to run, and he was running with her back up the narrow road, slipping and stumbling to his knees and up again, the flashlight turning everything around them into ghosts with reaching fingers. Tree branches slapped at his face, stinging his raw skin. The air was as cold as a meat locker, burning his lungs and turning his fingers to ice, the bugs were swarming all around him again, getting in his eyes, his mouth, up his nose. He heard the cabin door bang open and he thought of something coming out of it and down the steps, something with a slack, rotting face, and as he ran he could hear it coming up behind them, lurching with a heavy, lifeless tread through the darkness and the mud.

*Come out and play, Billy-boy. I've been waiting a long time for you.* A hand made of bone-fingers reaching out for his shoulder. Closer . . .

He turned wildly to face it, breath catching in his throat. The beam of the flashlight showed nothing behind him but empty road. He swung the light from one side of the road to the other, gasping, his heart hammering in his chest until he thought he might faint. Nothing. Even the bugs were gone.

He took several deep, cleansing breaths and waited for his heart to slow down.

Nothing but an abandoned cabin and a filthy pond in the middle of the woods. Somebody used to live out there and then they left, for whatever reason, perfectly rational; their grandfather died, or somebody got a promotion, or they moved to another state. That face he had seen was a reflection in the glass, the rest of it overactive imagination. Nothing more than a perfectly rational explanation.

When the voice spoke again in his head he almost screamed. *That all, Billy-boy? You don't really believe that horseshit, do you? Why are you out here in the middle of the night? Taking in the scenery? Killed the reverend tonight, by the way. Who's next? Barbara, that fat stinking bitch? Bob Rosenberg? Or is it you, Billy?*

*Stop it!* He clapped his hands to his head and pressed, hard, until the voices died away, and when he took his hands down the wind had completely disappeared and the smell with it, leaving nothing but cool dead air again. He smelled pine and the thick, earthy scent of the mud under his shoes. The trees were still.

He turned and forced himself to walk slowly back to the car.

Alone in bed an hour later, he opened his eyes wide against the darkness, and blinked until shapes began to swim into life. The light from the window was a pale silver, with barely a sliver of moon in the sky. He could see the bulky forms of the antique desk and chair in the corner, the table near his bed hunched like a three-foot troll. The shadows cast by the window frame were sketched across the wall in the form of a lopsided cross. He heard Angel shift and turn over in her bed in the other room, and thought of her lying there as he was, eyes wide, unable to sleep. He wondered what she had seen in that dusty shack window. Had it been the same dead face he saw (his mother's face, he was almost sure of it), or had it been someone else? Her brother, maybe?

He thought about a feeling that had come to him earlier as they left the inn, that he and Angel were being slowly transformed, becoming something much larger and more pure than themselves. Like being magnetized by a larger and more powerful magnet. He closed his eyes, and let himself begin to float, clearing the cobwebs away, all the trash he had accumulated over thirty-one years, going back slowly in time. Angel on the beach in Miami. A fight he had witnessed in the prison laundry. The accident and the scream of tearing metal. The first girl he ever kissed. His adopted mother's pinched face and calloused hands. The hideout he had built in the apple tree behind their house.

His childhood bedroom. He pictured a simple white dot of light in the center of his mind, a dot that grew smaller and smaller until it disappeared and everything was dark.

And then he reached. *Angel.*

For a moment, there was something. A feeling of her presence entered his mind and then fluttered away again and was gone. He caught a mixture of details; a feeling of surprise, a taste like candy apples, the color blue, the feel of a bird fluttering its wings against his skin. He tried to reach out and pull them back, but could not find them again. And as he reached he felt something else on the edge of this great black plain, something huge and viscid, open its eyes and turn to look his way.

The river ran through the dark below his window, pooling itself against the high dam, spilling over it, tumbling down through fissures of rock and spending itself over the drop of the falls. He could see the ribbon of black as it slipped silently past the long, flat fields, eddying and pooling and swirling again on its way to the pond. He was floating, riding it through the dark, coming to rest upon the slimy bank. The clearing bared itself to him like an open wound, the shack a festering sore upon its lips, and at the window of the shack some dead stinking thing crouched among the shadows.

He sat up in bed, heart hammering in his chest, and stared at the wall until the feeling began to pass. He dared not move, even to turn on the light. He sat in the darkness of the bedroom and it was hours before sleep finally took him.

# PART TWO:

# THE LEGACY

And when He stepped out on the land, there met Him a certain man from the city who had demons for a long time. And he wore no clothes, nor did he live in a house but in the tombs . . . Jesus asked him, saying, "What is your name?" And he said, "Legion . . ."

—*Luke 8: 27–30*

*October 3, 1726*

*Dear Hennie:*

*It has been a month since my last attempt at a letter, and by now you have probably imagined all manner of horrible things, but let me assure you I am alive and well and in the midst of construction on our new home, located at the end of what will be our town common. The post goes very irregularly here, as you may well have guessed, but I suppose I am still at fault for not writing you more frequently, and making more of an effort to assure that the letters reach port safely. In any case, I know that you have received word of my arrival on this continent, for Edward informs me that the ship has gone once again, and by now will have landed safely in England with a full list of the surviving passengers from our voyage. Perhaps you will be on its next voyage in the spring? If so, take care, and remember that you are strong.*

*But what of our little town, and the goings on here? We now have a series of passable roads from one end of town to the other; the ground has been cleared in preparation for our town center; and homes are already complete for two families, with three more under construction, mine being one. As I write this, the rough structure is almost complete, and I shall be able to take up residence in it in little more than a week, if things go well . . .*

*I hesitate to mention the most assuredly strange happenings that have plagued me since my arrival some two months ago.*

*But I must tell someone, and now that I am writing to you, I feel almost as if you are by my side, and are assuming that role of confidant and closest friend which you have so ably filled in the past. The cough and slight fever that followed me from the ship have long since passed, but the dreams which began that very first night have become more vivid, to the point where I often cannot tell the difference between the dream world and reality, at least until the good sun enters the sky and forces me out of bed. The dreams are not all the same, but they have the same essential qualities—that is, a sense of loss and constant anguish, and a great feeling of impatience, as if I am needed somewhere, or have some task to fulfill and have forgotten to do it. During these dreams I am confronted by all sorts of terrors, from the flames of some great burning, to my long dead friends and relatives come to life. They are always reaching for me, Hennie, as if to drag me down into the very depths of the earth with them, and it is almost as if I can feel their hands on me, the touch of their cold flesh on my own.*

*I know what you will say—I have been working too hard, and I suppose you would be right to say it. Except for a few other details, I would agree with you. But just lately the dreams have taken a most unsettling turn. I have awoken the past three nights (I am damnably sure of this, Hennie, I am fully conscious and rational) to a room so cold my breath gives off clouds of steam and the frost lines my bedclothes, with the absolute certainty that I am being watched. If you have ever had this sensation you will know what I mean—the prickling of the hairs on the back of the neck, itching of the scalp and legs, crawling skin. The sensation grows stronger with every passing second. Each time this has occurred I have raised enough courage to sit up and look about the room, and in the darkest corner at the foot of my bed I have seen a man standing absolutely still, watching me.*

*How can I relate the terror I have felt, gazing upon his*

*shadowy form? He does not move or try to speak, and yet I have the feeling he wants something from me, and that were I to give in to his wishes I would be lost forever in a hell beyond description.*

*And here is where I am sure you will judge me insane, or at least laugh out loud at my foolishness. But still, I must tell all, or be damned for it. Each time this has happened, I have become aware of a burning sensation on my chest, and have looked down to discover that Mr. Gatling's charm is red hot and glowing with a hellish fire. More than that, it is pulsing, in such a way as to render the most horrible dreams mere fairy tales in comparison; it is almost as if the thing is alive, and beating like a devil's heart against my chest. These movements repulse me, and yet I cannot bring myself to take the charm off, for reasons I do not fully understand. Perhaps it is protecting me from something, and serves as the last barrier between me and some other world (I choose to believe this, and not some of the darker ideas that have lately come into my head). I say again that I am fully conscious and rational during these moments, and that I have taken pains to assure that this is not some childish prank staged by one of my neighbors. I have all three times finally raised the courage to get out of bed and approach this creature, perhaps speak to him, and each time he has disappeared into thin air as I have advanced—but I feel him there, watching still.*

*Needless to say, this has given me the most alarming turn, and I have not been able to sleep the rest of the night. Moreover, I am unable to forget the reaction of the Indian guide upon our first approach to this place two months previous, and his insistence that we were surrounded by "evil spirits." Perhaps I should not have dismissed his warnings so easily, for tomorrow, as you well know, is All Hallows Eve, and the spirits will be out in force.*

*So, am I as mad as I fear I must be? Surely this must seem to you a bunch of foolishness, and undoubtedly you are right. But I am continually reminded through my travels that there are things in this world we cannot hope to understand, secrets deeper and darker than those kept by a rational society such as our own. I fear I may have stumbled upon one here, though what I am to do about it I haven't the faintest idea.*

*Here I have gone rambling on again, and written much more than I had thought to write—and yet I feel a bit better now, having put it all down on paper. I hope you have suffered my rantings with good humor, and still wish to correspond with such an obvious lunatic. I wonder if you could do one more thing for me, Hennie, as it would ease my heart considerably. Would you be so good as to inquire to Mr. Gatling about the charm he has given me, where he acquired it, and what sort of history it may possess? If nothing else, it should prove an interesting lesson in antiquity, for I have no doubt it is quite ancient, and genuine.*

*Yours,*
*Frederick*

# Chapter Eight

Early Sunday morning the compressor for the only cooler in White Falls suitable for bodies, located at the clinic on Route 27, sputtered, coughed, wheezed another minute, and finally died. Over the course of the day the temperature rose to over sixty-five in the small room, before dropping again that evening to forty degrees. Nobody was in the clinic on Sundays; Dr. Harry Stowe was available at his home for emergencies only.

When the doctor arrived at seven-thirty Monday morning for work, he fixed himself a cup of instant coffee and sat down with the paper, and didn't actually notice that the conditioner was down until almost nine. By that time the temperature in the small room had gone up another ten degrees and was rising fast. The sun had been up for over two hours and the outside temperature was already at seventy. Reverend Hall had been in the heat for over a day. He had gone from blue to gray, and the doctor thought that if they waited much longer he might just get up and walk out on his own.

Dr. Stowe got Sheriff Pepper on the phone and told him to come down right away, and that maybe he ought to call the reverend's sister, Susan. When they arrived the doctor pulled Pepper aside and took him into the cold storage room. "Only in my town," Sheriff Pepper muttered. "Jesus almighty, this heat. What the hell are we going to do with him?"

"The funeral's Wednesday?"

"That's right. And we can't move it up. Some relatives are coming up from Boston tomorrow night. Oh, Christ." Pepper wiped a sleeve across his sweaty forehead. "He won't keep in here until then?"

"I wouldn't risk it."

"I guess I better tell Sue." He went out into the other room, and Dr. Stowe could hear him talking quietly for a moment before Sue Hall cried out and blew her nose loudly, twice in succession. The sound was as loud as a foghorn in the quiet building.

They discussed moving a portable air conditioner into the cold storage room and setting it on high, but they didn't know if they could find a big enough one, and besides, the doctor said, it might not be cold enough to do much good. Changing the funeral plans didn't seem to be possible. They wondered aloud whether they could bring the body to the Old Mill Inn and keep the reverend in the walk-in freezer.

Finally the doctor suggested that Sue might as well go home, that they could handle things alone from now on and would call her before making any final decision. She agreed, and seemed relieved to get back into her car and drive away, still honking on her soggy handkerchief. Pepper and Stowe went back into the storage room and stood in front of the reverend, as if staring at him might jump-start their imaginations.

"Jesus," Pepper said. "I mean, excuse me, Reverend, if you're listening. But couldn't you have at least covered him up, Doc?"

"I had him covered last night, but I want to watch his color."

"Watch his color." The sheriff grunted sarcastically.

"You afraid he's going to get heat stroke or something?"

*I'm afraid he's going to start to stink,* Stowe thought, but kept his mouth shut.

They stood there for a moment. "Someplace cool," Pepper mumbled, and Dr. Stowe could almost see the wheels spinning furiously. In a moment he would be surprised if smoke didn't come pouring out the sheriff's ears. "The county morgue is an hour away, and it don't make sense to cart him out there and then back again for the funeral if we can avoid it."

"It might be the only thing to do."

"Nope." Sheriff Pepper scratched behind one ear. "They probably wouldn't get rolling until this afternoon, if then. Gotta be a better way. Say, you ever find out what killed him?"

Dr. Stowe would declare death by natural causes. He had been one of the few in town to notice the reverend's drinking practices and lousy diet, and he figured it was a sure bet the man had died of heart failure—he already knew the Reverend had heart problems. Besides, he knew that Sue Hall's wishes were for no autopsy. And there was no point in starting up gossip. He did not want people to start debating anything having to do with religion.

"Natural causes," Stowe said carefully. "God called him home."

"Hell. You don't believe that horseshit, do you?"

"I choose to in this case."

"Well," Pepper said, "maybe we ought to give the county a ring after all. They could get a medical investigator down here—"

"I really don't think that's necessary."

"Well." The sheriff chuckled. "You know what they say. The only difference between God and a doctor is that God don't think he's a doctor."

Stowe didn't laugh. "Sheriff, are you questioning my professional opinion?"

Pepper paused, looked at him, at the reverend's pale body. He shook his head. "Course not, Doc. I know you do a good job. But I thought there might be a few other people around here that could have a question or two about it."

"Are you saying they might think he was murdered?"

Pepper laughed. "No, no. Christ—" He shot a guilty look at the reverend. "Excuse me. It's been two years since there was a murder around here, and that one only happened because Jack Rice found out his wife was sleeping with that guy who lived up in the trailer park, and went nuts about it. Hit him over the head with a frying pan, wasn't it? The last real bad one we had, that must of been . . . hell. The Taylor murder. I was just out of high school back then."

Dr. Stowe remembered the Taylor case pretty well. He had just finished his internship, and had returned to White Falls that year as the school physician. He had treated Jeb Taylor for shock, and recommended a psychiatrist. The boy had been kept out of school for a few days. The murder was all the kids at the school had talked about for months. He had heard rumors about groups of them going out to the place and looking it over, searching for blood and guts and all the stuff kids loved at that age. "I don't see what that has to do—"

"Nothing," Pepper said. He hitched his pants up around his bulging stomach. "I'm just saying that murder ain't talked about much around here anymore. But I think you ought to have an explanation for the reverend's death, all the same."

"It was a heart attack," Stowe said. "No question. Honestly, with the conditioner breaking down I don't have the facilities for a proper autopsy. If we call the county coroner we'll have to wait a week for the results—"

"Sue won't like that," Pepper said. "Besides, she wants the funeral on Wednesday. Get him into the ground as soon as possible."

They finally decided to move the reverend's body to the Church basement, which was the coolest and most appropriate place they could come up with at the moment, and load it up with ice. Pepper got on the phone with his two deputies, had them bring a station wagon to the clinic, and they loaded the body into the back. Anyone passing by the church a few minutes later would have glimpsed an odd scene; four men carrying a sheeted body on a stretcher through the front doors in broad daylight. The sheet had slipped a little as they pulled the reverend from the car, and part of a rigid foot peeked out, as devoid of color now as if it had been painted white.

Bucky Tarr, the old maintenance man who mowed the town green and high school playing fields during the summers, was also the town gravedigger. In fact, he was the town gardener, firefighter, painter, sometime plumber, and occasional babysitter. His hands were long and hard and twisted with arthritis like two pieces of driftwood washed up on the beach, and his face was dark and rough as sandpaper.

Bucky had spent his whole life in White Falls. He could remember when the new high school was built (he had helped put on the roof), and when fire had taken the old Baptist church in 1981. The church had burned to the ground, despite Bucky and others' efforts to save it. That event had led to the establishment of the White Falls volunteer fire department, of which Bucky was a founding member. Bucky prided himself on being a founding member of just about every White Falls group that meant a hill of beans to anybody.

Wednesday morning, the day of the reverend's funeral, Bucky got himself out of bed early and took a gander out his bedroom window. From his house he could see the church steeple rising up like a bony finger pointing at the sky, and the belly of the river flashed through the trees. A white layer of early morning mist had settled itself like frosting over the lower points of ground. The night had stayed warm, and he saw clouds gathering on the horizon beyond the steeple. Dark purple storm clouds. *Gonna rain today,* he thought. *Been around long enough to know rain clouds when I see them.*

And he could feel them, too. As he dressed, his arthritis acted up so badly he could hardly button his shirt, and he wondered how he would possibly be able to grip the shovel hard enough to get through all that rocky Maine soil. He cursed himself for not finishing the job yesterday, but the truth of it was, he hadn't been feeling much better then. *You old coot, Bucky,* he told himself. *You ought to be retired.* It was time to find someone to help him with the difficult jobs, a young body who didn't mind getting banged up a little.

Bucky left his little three room cottage with the screened-in porch, got in his truck and drove the half mile to the cemetery, parking in the back of the church lot, out of the way. Then he took the little portable radio from its place under his feet, grabbed the old rusty shovel and pickaxe from the bed of the pickup, and trudged back around through the cemetery gates. The new grass ran in long, straight lines between the stones, freshly cut; he had mowed yesterday morning. The smell of it filled the air, along with the damp earthy smell of graves, and told him summer was coming along right soon. To his mind there wasn't a much better smell than that.

The reverend's grave had been plotted and the digging was about half completed. It was seven-thirty now; the church service was scheduled for eleven o'clock, the graveside service for twelve. That gave him about three hours to comfortably finish the job, before people started showing up. Funeral-goers did not especially like to see the gravedigger laboring away as they pulled into the church parking lot. It was a little too morbid for them.

Bucky paused long enough to turn on the radio and tune it to the seventies station; a moment later a tinny-sounding number from Gordon Lightfoot was blaring through the little speaker, loud in the early morning stillness. Bucky grinned to himself. Gordon Lightfoot was one of the good ones. Gordon Lightfoot could really let it *loose.*

Still grinning, he let himself down into the hole and went to work.

An hour later, his shirt was plastered to his chest, his back had begun to complain loudly about the stress it was under, and his hands were like two clubs. A high mound of dirt, clay, and rock rose up above him as he stood shoulder-deep in the grave. A harder rocking number was coming from the radio now, and the gravestones gave the whining guitars an odd, echoing effect, as if they were coming from more than one place at once.

Bucky swung the shovel again, hard, and felt the shock run all the way up his arms and through his shoulders. Sparks flew from the blade. He swore loudly. *Big motherfucking rock. Need the pickaxe for that one.*

He leaned on the shovel, panting, and looked up at the leaden sky. He was suddenly reminded of a dream that had been bothering him lately, where he was looking up at the stars at night from some odd position. The stars were framed by a black rectangular square. In the dream he reached out and encountered close, clammy walls on either side, and realized he was lying in an open grave. There had been some kind of horrible mistake. He was alive, but he was going to be buried. He could not move; could not cry out; a moment later the first shovelful of dirt had hit him in the face.

*Jesus, Bucky. Don't wet your diapers.* He climbed back up to ground level, glad to get out of that confined space, and looked around. Traffic was light on Route 27, most of the commuters having already left for work. For the first time that morning, it came to him that he was alone in a graveyard. This was an odd thought, considering the fact that he had spent much of his life working among the graves. But the dream had a hold on him, and he could not shake it. The radio still played, but it did not give him any comfort. Instead the music sounded like it was coming down a long dark tunnel. Or from underground. The voices were ghost images of themselves, pretty sad substitutes for human company.

The ground mist had drifted away by now, but the clouds were heavy, swollen tea bags overhead. The air was saturated; he could feel the moisture beading on his skin. He sighed heavily and went to get the pickaxe, which was leaning up against a nearby gravestone. As he grabbed the handle he happened to glance down into the fresh grave. A glint of metal, out of place among the dirt and dull chunks of rock, caught his eye.

He climbed back down to the bottom of the open grave and crouched near the odd piece of metal. He began to dig around it with his hands, and uncovered the flat side of a hinge, then a bit of splintered wood. It was another minute before he realized he was looking at the remains of an old coffin. One corner of it, actually, sticking up out of the dirt at an awkward, canted angle like a wrecked ship going down into the deep. Bucky swore to himself loudly. *Isn't this a bitch?* There wasn't supposed to be a grave *here,* for Christ's sake. This was supposed to be fresh ground.

An old grave, too, by the looks of it. The wood from the coffin was practically crumbling in his hands.

He stood again and climbed back up to ground level. What was he supposed to do now? He couldn't very well throw the old remains away, but he sure as hell didn't want to dig another hole six feet deep in this soil. *Face it, you old fart. You wouldn't be able to dig another one, not in time for the burial.* They couldn't bury the reverend on top of another coffin, could they? That seemed . . . well, wrong somehow.

*A body gets enough crowding when it's alive,* Bucky thought. *Two people shouldn't have to occupy the same space after they're dead.*

Still pondering the problem, he noticed that something was out of place among the old graves down the hill. There was a gap between two of the stones. One of them appeared to be missing.

Curious, Bucky swung the pickaxe onto his shoulder (he could not have said why he gripped it so hard; only that the emotions of his dream persisted, those feelings of being buried alive), and walked down through the newer monuments. The stones got progressively older as the ground sloped down toward the river, the oldest graves being located at the far edge of the cemetery, nearest the water. These ancient stones were so weathered as to be rendered almost unreadable. There were people with the historical society in town who had spent hours down here, trying to decipher some of the names and inscriptions on the stones. Graves had been found dating back to the early eighteenth century. The town's history was there, if you had the patience to work for it.

As he walked beyond the newer, larger monuments and down the hill, as the stones got smaller and darker, it seemed the air around him became cooler by degrees, and a chill raised the hairs on his arms to gooseflesh. He was out of sight of the road now, and the radio was nothing more than a faint hum. The feelings of his dream came back with renewed force. He felt as if he were under the ground, looking up through the layers of dirt and clay and grass with eyes that were not his own.

But that was crazy, and he was not the type to give in easily to such thoughts.

Bucky approached the gap in the line and realized what had happened. The stone was not missing; it had simply fallen over and half-buried itself in the freshly cut grass. He dropped heavily to his knees, put the pickaxe aside and lifted the stone upright, settling the base into the ground as best he could. The face of the stone was obscured by dirt and grass clippings, and mold. He scraped at the surface, wiped it with his palm as if he were trying to clear a fogged window. The stuff that came off on his hands was soggy and cold, and stained his skin a deep, dark green.

He wiped his hands on his shirt and then dug at the stone's faint letters with his fingernails, trying to clear them. Portions of the lettering were revealed, badly worn; he could just make out the last name and a date.

*Thomas*, it read. *D. 1820.*

"Jesus jumpin' Christ," Bucky said, not quite sure what made him suddenly straighten up and take a step back. He recognized the grave, sure enough. Most people in White

Falls knew about old Frederick Thomas. What he could not explain was the sudden tightening of the muscles in his back; the prickling in his scalp, and in his armpits; the way his breathing caught in his chest. The feeling of being buried six feet under, all that dirt and rock between him and fresh air.

And his unreasoning suspicion that this headstone and the rotting coffin he had just uncovered up the hill were close relations.

When Sheriff Pepper arrived fifteen minutes later, Bucky Tarr was waiting for him in the church parking lot. "Oh, Christ," the sheriff said, when Bucky told him about the surprise visitor waiting in the reverend's plot. He looked at his watch. "I honestly can't fucking *believe* this. First the cooler shuts down. Now we got a hundred people coming in just under two hours to see the man put to rest, and now we don't have anyplace to bury him?"

Bucky nodded. "Not unless we . . ." He paused. The sheriff looked at him blankly. "Move them remains," he finished.

"Where the hell are we gonna put them?"

"Seems to me," Bucky said, keeping his voice slow and even (he was still a little spooked, much to his disgust, and did not want the sheriff to see how this had gotten to him), "we might want to find out who those bones belong to. Once we put a name to them, maybe we can give them a proper burial. Somewhere down the hill, closer to the . . . you know. Friends and relatives and all."

"How are we going to figure out who it is?"

"Maybe there'll be something in the records about it. Or maybe Doc Stowe can figure it out. Dental records and such."

"Dental records that old? Fat fucking chance." Pepper scratched at his belly and spat on the ground.

Finally they walked over to the open grave and stood looking down at the hinge and rotten corner boards of the coffin, now fully exposed. Bucky had said nothing about Frederick Thomas's headstone down the hill, and didn't plan to do so. The sheriff would think he was crazy, trying to make a connection like that, and Bucky Tarr would be half-inclined to agree with him. No reason to think what he was thinking. But there were two rules in life he always tried to keep in mind. One of them was, there were things happening everyday that just couldn't be readily explained. Sometimes the answer was simple, and sometimes it wasn't, but for the most part it was easier and smarter to leave these mysteries well-enough alone.

The other, more important rule was, don't do twice what can be finished in one shot. That applied to digging graves just as well as anything else.

"Hell." Sheriff Pepper had a look of complete disbelief on his face. "This sure is a mystery. That thing looks about a hundred years old, if it's a day. Back then the cemetery ended way back down near the river. So why the hell would anyone bury a body up here on top of the hill?"

"Don't know, chief," Bucky said. "All I know is, we got one hole, and two bodies. Now, we can dig another hole, but that'll take the rest of the day. No way we'll finish in time for the service."

"You better get him out of there, then. I'll call Harry and have him bring a bodybag for the bones. We'll figure the rest out later. Try and keep this quiet for a while, will you, Bucky? We don't need people hearing about it until the service is over. When things have settled down a bit, we'll let the news out. The historical society's likely to have a field day with this one."

Bucky nodded and kept his mouth shut. It had become

the sheriff's decision now, and he was free from all responsibility, which was the way he liked it.

After Sheriff Pepper left to use the phone, Bucky Tarr went about the ugly business of disinterring the remains, and a few minutes later, the first drops of rain began to fall.

By ten o'clock, as the mourners filed slowly into the church, the rain had begun in earnest, and by ten-thirty it was coming down in a steady, solid sheet. The rain drummed on the roof, making a sound like thousands of little feet, and ordinarily that sound was a soothing one. But not at a funeral. At a funeral the sound of rain brings thoughts of mud and mildew, damp clothes and cold flesh, and all the other things a mind turns to when faced with the end of a life.

The family and a few of the closest friends were seated up front and occupied the first two pews. Sue Hall, wearing black and clutching a handkerchief which she used to dab at her eyes, and beside her, crazy Annie Arsenault, white hair carefully combed, eyes vacant; the uncle from Boston, an investment banker in an expensive black suit, with his aging wife and son; a cousin from Kennebunkport. Myrtle Howard had a place just behind Sue, along with a few of the most active church-goers.

To the right of the pulpit, on a waist-high stand, lay the mahogany coffin with the body of Reverend Hall. A wreath of brightly-colored flowers sat at the head of it, along with an arrangement of roses.

The interim preacher from the Waldoboro church led them in prayer, and then Sue herself got behind the pulpit and read from the good book until her eyes teared up. The church was standing room only. Reverend Hall had been well liked.

After the church service they all opened umbrellas, filed outside, and stood in the pouring rain while the Waldoboro preacher read the passages the family had chosen from the Bible. The rain wet the pages of the good book and made them difficult to read. The preacher sheltered them with his hands as best he could, and kept it short. Nobody had thought to set up a tent or even prop a tarp up over their heads, and most people were thoroughly soaked by the time the casket was finally lowered into the muddy hole, in spite of their umbrellas.

The big sling swung the casket some as it moved. When it passed by the edge of the hole, it bumped a chunk of dirt, or rock. "Sounded like someone moving around in there," little ten-year-old Jason Marshal would tell his friends later. "Like someone had just turned over, knocked his elbow on the lid, and gone back to sleep."

Pat Friedman noticed the sound too, and it sent a chill along his spine. He hadn't slept much the past few nights. The thoughts of his wife's late-night transgressions had begun to occupy more of his time, and he felt consumed by a fierce jealousy. She was distant, cold in bed, her mind on something (*or someone*) else. He was not the sort of man, Pat kept telling himself, to be consumed by this. He was *not.* But he kept seeing Julie in his mind, slick and naked, in bed with a stranger. In *their* bed. As hard as he stared at the image, he could not see the mystery man's face. Dark circles ringed Pat's eyes and his skin sagged with fatigue. He looked ten years older.

God, he hated funerals. Dead things rotting away in the ground. *They close you up in a box,* Pat thought, *and they lock it up tight, just in case you wake up and feel like getting out.*

As he stood there in the rain, watching the coffin disappear into the muddy hole, he was reminded of that cold night a week earlier, the night he had seen Jeb Taylor coming out of *Johnny's*, looking so much like his father it was like seeing a ghost. The feelings came back with renewed force, bringing with them a hard knot in his stomach.

*Something in the air tonight. Something horrible. Dead men are coming to life.*

Then the casket hit bottom with a solid thud and the sling was raised back out. Someone let out a sob; Pat glanced over and saw Sue Hall, her hand pressed against her mouth. The preacher closed the Bible and people began to leave, one by one, some going back into the church, some heading straight for the parking lot. Nobody spoke.

Pat Friedman remained near the grave, head bent against the rain, as the first heavy shovel of dirt was thrown in. It landed not with a patter of small stones but with a wet slap of mud on wood. The sound was a terrible one, full of the heaviness of the act. Pat thought about what might happen if the lid began to open, if a single white fingertip appeared in the crack, scratching to be let out.

Finally he turned away, but he couldn't shut out that sound of dirt hitting the casket. It followed him as he walked to his car, and as he drove home, Julie silent in the seat beside him, he fancied he still heard it, muffled by the distance but just as horrible. Each wet shovelful of mud as it slapped against wood. The sound of death.

Sometime after six o'clock, the rain stopped, and the cold closed in.

# Chapter Nine

Billy Smith and Angel were sitting in the dining room of the Old Mill Inn when the rain began to fall. Though the inn didn't usually serve a hot breakfast, Bob Rosenberg had opened the kitchen up early for them. They had the place to themselves. Smith sipped at a cup of coffee, with his Danish and part of an English muffin on a plate before him. Not particularly hungry, he watched the sky darken outside the windows, watched the bloated clouds reflected in the water of the mill pond. The water was the color of flint.

Since Saturday night, they had existed in a kind of limbo. Done some shopping for clothes and other essentials, eaten all the proper meals, explored some more of the town. Monday they had gone to look at Gedford's strawberry fields, bare but still beautiful in the bright spring sun (looking at the fields, Smith got the feeling they could almost watch the spring water flowing through their roots, the plants growing before their eyes), and had a picnic on the banks of the river. It had been pleasant but uneventful. They had not said more than a few words to each other about that night and the face in the window—and it hung in the air between them, like a great black gulf.

A great black gulf, or a line drawn in the dirt. Crossing that line meant they were fully committed; it meant anything could happen. The old rules did not apply anymore. Oh, they had talked about crossing that line before, it was true, but before Saturday they hadn't been faced with anything stronger than a few bad dreams. Now they were faced with whatever lived out there by the pond—and whatever it was, Smith had the feeling they wouldn't like it much.

"We need to talk," he said.

Angel was silent for a long time, looking out the window at the rain, her hands in her lap. One side of her face carried the color of the thunderstorm, the other plainly lit by the overhead lights. Light and dark, black and white. It was as if the storm mirrored her own struggle within, picking up her mood like some sort of lightning rod and playing it out for him to see.

"I'm scared," she said.

"So am I."

She was silent for a moment, then spoke slowly, hesitantly. "I was a goner if you hadn't come along. You asked me before if I would have come here on my own, and I said I didn't know. That . . . wasn't really true. The truth is, I don't think I would have had the chance. I think I would have killed myself. Not jumping off a bridge or blowing my brains out, not that way. I think I would have just slipped an extra hit or two into my veins one night and that would have been it. Not so bad, really, if you have to go. The truth was, I hated myself."

"And now?"

"I don't know," she said. "I feel like I've been given a second chance. Like I can live my life all over again, the way I want it—"

At the sound of those words something flashed through his mind, a memory he could not quite put his finger on. "Say that again."

She looked at him strangely. "You know. Like I've been given a chance to live my life over."

*Those who have been born again.* It was true for both of them, wasn't it? They had reached the end of their ropes in their previous lives, and had been offered a second chance, a chance to wipe the slate clean.

"Yes," he said. "That's it. That's it exactly."

"I'm a good person, Billy."

"I know you are."

"I lost sight of a lot of things, and now I'm beginning to get them back. I don't want to lose that."

Billy looked at her across the table, the contrast of bright and dark playing about her face as the rain began to fall harder, streaking the glass of the window. For a moment he might have caught a glimpse of the little girl she once was, small for her age, skin like ivory, huge blue eyes, hair in pigtails. A big gap-toothed grin. The kind of girl who could light up a room. She had changed in the short time they had been in town. He saw an inner strength that hadn't been there before, or had remained well hidden. A growing confidence in herself. And health; she practically glowed with it. *Two weeks ago she was a spaced-out junkie on a Miami beach,* he thought. *How is that possible?*

"You're not the only one who's been given a second chance by all of this," he said softly. "I feel the same way. Maybe I can't make up for what I did twelve years ago. But I can try."

Angel reached out and touched his hand, and for a moment his mind was filled with the odd, swirling images he had felt lying alone in his bed Saturday night; candy apples, the color blue, the flutter of wings. And then she withdrew her hand and the images were gone, leaving him cold and empty.

"I never really believed in evil before," she said. "I mean, most people think murderers are evil, but I bet *they* don't think they are. Maybe some of them even feel guilty but can't help themselves." She paused. "But after that night and that place . . ."

"What about a spiritual world? Goodness? Have you ever believed in that?"

"I never really did as a kid," she said. "My parents weren't religious people, so we didn't go to church. I guess I just never thought about it much."

"And now?"

"If evil can exist, there *must* be good, too," she said. "After all, something has brought us here, hasn't it?"

"God's done a lot of his own killing," Smith said. "If you believe in him, that is. Plagues, wars, all of the things he allows to happen. Do they serve some kind of higher purpose?"

"Some people might say that's the devil's work."

"According to scripture, the devil was a fallen angel."

"So what are you saying?"

"Just that it's hard for me, I guess," he replied slowly. "It's tough for me to believe." He thought about how his mother had tried desperately to grab onto something that would help her deal with her coming death. Religion, spirituality, God's greater plan, had become a central part of her life. She was certain that a lot of prayer and a flurry of good works would save her life—and failing that, save her soul. As she drifted deeper into her own world Smith found himself starting to despise it all. The church where she spent nearly every waking moment, the well-thumbed Bibles scattered around the house, the paintings on the walls. The phone calls from well-meaning church parishioners, promising to "pray for her." *And now what,* he thought. *After all that's happened to me? Does it make any difference?*

"Hard as I try," he said, "I just can't get my mind

around the idea that there's more to this world than what we see every day."

She smiled. "People have been struggling with that for a very long time."

"So what if this is all in our heads? What if we're really in some mental institution somewhere, and having some kind of delusion?"

"No," Angel said firmly. "Delusions are personal. Maybe it could be happening to one of us, but not both of us together."

He reached for his coffee, found it cold, and held the cup in his hands, staring down into the murky brown remains. Bits of black grounds floated at the top, sank, surfaced again.

"I felt it, you know," he said. "Saturday night. We went back to the inn and went to bed and I was lying there in the dark, trying to understand things, to understand what we had just seen. And I started thinking about what had happened to me in my life, good memories and bad ones, letting them play through my head, remembering. And then I just let go and . . ." He paused, unsure of exactly how to express this thing he had done. Had it been some sort of telepathy? Some kind of weird mind-link? Or simply wishful thinking?

"And I reached," he said finally. "I reached out for you in my mind. It was like I was stretching something, like I was working out the kinks in a stiff, weak muscle, and then using it to push me forward. Only I was pushing forward inside my head. My thoughts." He shrugged. "It sounds crazy, I know. But I felt something. You were there. And then you were gone, and there was . . . something else."

"Something else?"

"Yes. It was huge, that was my first impression. Larger

than I could really understand. Powerful. And . . . awake."

"That's not so crazy, is it? I mean, if this thing can talk to us, if it can make us dream what it wants us to dream, then why shouldn't we be able to—"

"No." Smith shook his head. "What I felt wasn't what's been sending us the dreams. At least I don't think so. This thing was what we've been dreaming *about.* It was about death and pain. It wanted to kill me. I felt it in my bones. It scared the shit out of me. But what scared me the most, I guess, is that it sensed me, too. It knew I was there."

"But what *was* it?"

"I don't know."

They sat in silence for a moment, considering this. They had faced great open spaces of mystery over the past few weeks, and been forced to trust in themselves and whatever had been guiding them. Smith had been able to do that mainly by keeping himself busy; physical activity, however it came, kept some of the doubts and second-guesses at bay. Until Saturday night they had not been faced with real danger (*and even then,* a voice asked him, *were you really in danger? Or were you just seeing things?*).

But it was one thing to obey what a few intense dreams and visions drove you to do. It was another to go into battle without understanding what you were up against. And that was what they were facing, if all this were true.

*It knew I was there.*

"We need to do something," Smith said. He was filled with an odd sense of urgency. Outside the sky had turned purple, and great bursts of lightning popped like flashbulbs. "We have to start somewhere, get moving. We can't just sit here."

"But what are we supposed to do?"

"There should be a library around here where we can do

some research. Right here in town, or at least nearby. The next town, maybe. I'll go ask Mr. Rosenberg about it." Smith stood up, ready to leave.

"You said you felt me, the other night," she said, stopping him. "Inside your mind. Is that really true?"

"Yes. It's true."

She got a dreamy sort of look in her eyes. "I think I felt it, too. Like one of those pushes we've been feeling, only softer. Almost like a touch, but inside my mind. Very light. I was half asleep, and by the time I woke up it was gone. I thought I was dreaming."

"So did I, at first. But it happened."

She smiled up at him. "Have you ever been in love?"

"Thought I was once. A girl in high school. It was just a crush. Why?"

"You asked me if I believed in a spiritual world. In goodness. I don't know if there is a God or not. But I think love is good. True love, I mean, the kind that doesn't ask for anything in return."

"Is there such a thing?"

"Oh, yes," she said. The dreamy look was in her eyes again, or maybe, he thought, it had never really left. "I think so. There has to be."

The White Falls library was located just past the new high school, on a stretch of empty road. Previously a private home, it had been converted to hold a few hundred novels, nonfiction confessionals, and some serious books, most of them donated by a prominent citizen several years earlier. Inside a few walls had been knocked out here and there and long, high bookshelves installed where the front hall had been. There was a pleasant reading area with a couch, table, and a couple of chairs in a room to the right of the door, another room to the left which looked to be an art gallery of sorts, and a desk with a computer terminal near the back. A set of stairs opposite the door to the right led up to a second floor; a sign on the wall read, *Private.*

All the rooms were empty except for the reading room. A girl who looked like she might be a high school student sat in a chair near the window, a book open in her lap, two more on the table. She had a freckled face and arms like matchsticks. When Smith and Angel entered she looked up at them vacantly then turned to stare out the window at the rain.

As they stood in the front hall shaking the water from their hair, a young man appeared from somewhere upstairs and came down the staircase to meet them. He was bird-like, standing five-three at the most, and kept his hands tucked nervously behind his waist. "We don't have a very large selection," he said apologetically, after they had introduced themselves. "Almost everything is privately donated. Books are constantly coming in and out of here, you know, we try to keep track of them, but the budget is limited. A few have been stolen or vandalized, I'm afraid. But the computer has a list of everything we have, more or less, and it's connected to the state system. If you can't find what you're looking for, perhaps we can locate it at another library for you."

"Actually, we're looking for something on local history," Smith said. "Anything about the town of White Falls, the people . . ."

The young man had led them down the hall as they talked, and stopped near the computer, now twisting the belly of his shirt between sweaty palms. For some reason, Smith was reminded of a mole, scurrying blindly along the ground, bumping into things, bouncing off them again before turning in another direction. "I don't know how much is in . . ." The librarian turned and punched a few buttons. "Well," he said, after a moment, "it *says* we have quite a bit. But I'll tell you—" he pointed at a reference on the screen, "—this is a book on Maine history, that might have a paragraph or two in it about this area, and this one is a paperback on Southern Maine architecture that won't have much either, and is probably missing anyway. That's the sort of book these students are always using for their papers, you know, and they're always forgetting to return them. I swear, I just don't have the time to keep sending out notices. I'm just a volunteer, you know, we don't have the resources . . ."

Smith glanced around. Angel had managed to wander off into another part of the library. *Escaped, is more like it,* he thought, and grinned. The librarian went on, his voice hushed but eager. *Not a mole, more like a terrier. One of the little ones that grab onto your trouser leg and won't let go.*

"Why don't you just point me in the right direction," Smith said. "I'll figure it out."

"Of course. Forgive me. It's so awfully quiet in here on weekdays."

Smith allowed himself to be led to a shelf of books near the front door (he thought of the librarian tugging him along with his pant leg in his teeth, and grinned again), and waited as the man pulled several books down from the racks. Among them, in fact, was the book on Southern Maine architecture, and the book on Maine history as well; that one was a grossly overwritten monster, written back to the sixties, complete with coffee-stained pages and a binding that was going to pieces.

"I would suggest," the librarian said, "that you talk to the historical society in town if you need more information.

I believe Ms. Hall is running it now. A lovely woman, such a shame about her brother. I assume you've heard about her loss. I attended the service. Such a *shame*. Reverend Hall was an absolute saint."

"You knew him well?"

"I went to church regularly. He was quite a draw, such a friendly man, and so enthusiastic. Church membership doubled under his leadership, I believe. It will be impossible to replace him." The librarian was suddenly peering at him, concern in his eyes. "Are you feeling okay?"

One of his hot, slick hands had planted itself at Billy's elbow, and the feel of it more than anything else brought him back to earth with a jerk. He had just slipped away there for a moment, back to that shack in the woods, back in the dark with the stink of it filling him, the branches moving in the dark. And that voice, the voice had said—

*Killed the reverend tonight. Who's next?*

"I'm fine," Smith said. "Just felt a little lightheaded."

"Must be the weather," the librarian said, nodding. "I get that sometimes when it's humid. Maybe you should sit down a minute . . ."

Smith assured him he would sit down until he felt better, and took the books into the reading room, needing to get away from the man and collect his thoughts. As he entered, the girl with the freckled face looked up and stared at him. "Shouldn't you be in school?" he said.

"Uh-uh." The barest shake of her head, and blank, bored eyes. "Doing a report." She nodded in the direction of the books sitting on the table. "Say, you look sick, man. You look like death warmed over."

He managed a smile, and sat down on the couch with the books. Still, he felt her eyes on him as if he were an interesting new species of insect. Opening the big, stained history book, he tried to concentrate but the words kept swimming before his eyes, the ink running together to form new words, new shapes. He blinked; a coffee stain twisted itself around a line of text and became the dead face at the shack window, leering up at him from the empty page.

*Just words, man. Just words.* The voice was so much like the girl's, he glanced up at her, startled, before he realized she hadn't spoken.

He closed the book with a snap and stood up, ignoring the girl's stare. He could hear Angel talking with the librarian somewhere in the rear of the hall, and he wandered across to the opposite room. Here the walls were covered with paintings, most of them done by local artists; bad landscapes and white frothy river scenes, the falls in the background. He noticed a few others stacked up against the wall in the corner, and flipped through them. Most were identical to those on the walls, but a few of them were quite a bit older. One near the back of the pile showed the town square in the fall or early winter, the leafless trees painted in thin spidery strokes. This was the square during its early years—the storefronts had not yet been built, and the gazebo was missing. There were great stretches of grass on either side, and a deeper patch of woods at the upper end. The roads were dirt paths, the houses small square blocks.

Except for the Thomas mansion. It was still there, looking much the same as it did today, as far as he could tell. The artist had accentuated the lunatic spread of its wings, the twists of its castle-like turrets, the strange add-on rooms like warts sprouting from its back. A hunchback peering out from behind his own spread fingers, the branches of the leafless trees reaching out toward its walls but never quite touching. A house like a troll, he thought, fascinated and yet repulsed. It drew him in a way he did not quite understand. The ground before it was empty and brown and dead. October, he thought, or early November, just before the first snowfall.

His hands were two painful cramps. Looking down, he saw he still held the book of Maine history, and had gripped it so hard his knuckles had turned white.

Later that evening, with Angel still looking over the library books in her room, Smith set out for the local bar down the road. The rain had stopped and the air had cooled enough for him to wear one of the sweatshirts they had bought a few days before. He walked with his hands thrust deep in the front pocket of the sweatshirt and let his thoughts run around in circles. Nothing came to him. There was more space out here in the open air, but not enough noise; he needed the bar. After the library, he needed to get out and find a place where there were people, lots of them, and just try and let it all go for a while. The sense of urgency that had held him earlier in the day had disappeared, replaced by a dull copper taste in his mouth, the taste of frustration, and of blood.

*But a bar? Do you think that's such a good idea? You and bars don't mix, remember?*

True; alcohol, and bars in general, with their smoky interiors and dim lights and muffled voices were seductive. Hypnotic. It had always been that way for him. But his thoughts kept returning to Angel, and that scared him more than anything else. He could not seem to keep from his mind the delicate line of her jaw, the deep, open blue of her eyes. The way she smiled at him. That was something he did not want to happen, could not afford to let happen.

Why not? She was attractive, single, friendly; he hadn't been with a woman in . . . well, a long time. And lately she seemed like she just might be interested.

He shook his head. He'd kidnapped her, for God's sake, dragged her out to this town on the edge of nowhere. It was all a psychological trap. He couldn't take advantage of her that way. He owed her that much.

The bar's parking lot was about half full, and he could hear the jukebox playing country and western music as he approached. The smell of beer and whisky hit him at the door, and his stomach did a long, lazy flip that seemed to contain equal parts nausea and aching thirst. He had forgotten how strong the pull was, and realized that he had been at least as addicted to the atmosphere as he had been to the drink, maybe more so; being able to lose yourself into another world, one where nobody knew each other, and nobody cared who your parents were, or where you came from.

*So what is this, some kind of test? See if the old drunk can resist temptation and keep the demons at bay?*

Yeah, maybe that was exactly it.

*Johnny's* was smoky and dim, the stools at the bar full of big heavy men and a few heavily made-up women past the age of forty. The booths were occupied mostly by couples or groups of three, and everywhere there were empty plastic cups and pitchers and spilled beer. Behind the bar a man filled mugs from the tap and slid them down the wood surface with a flick of the wrist, a towel slung over one shoulder. His arms were heavily muscled, his hair a deep shining black. One of the women kept bending her head toward him and laughing out loud at everything he said, as if he were the funniest man with whom she had ever had the privilege to hold a conversation. Her makeup looked to be an inch thick and cracking in places around her mouth and eyes, and she held the stub of a cigarette between her fingers.

Smith was weaving his way through the crowd when he spotted Harry Stowe sitting with a woman in one of the booths against the opposite wall. He raised a hand in greeting and Stowe waved him over. "Welcome, have a seat," Stowe said. "We were just talking about you. Myrtle Howard, meet Mr. Smith, the newcomer in town. I'm afraid I've forgotten your first name."

"Billy." Smith extended his hand. "Pleased to meet you." The woman looked up at him with big cow eyes for a moment, before taking his hand limply with her own and holding it for only a fraction of a second.

"I—I gotta go," she stammered, and he barely managed to avoid being bowled over as she stumbled past him, into the crowd. He caught a single glimpse of her as she vanished through the front door, still moving fast.

He sat down in the vacant seat. "I know I look a little under the weather, but that was ridiculous."

Stowe laughed. "Don't mind Myrtle. She's probably just nervous about meeting somebody new. Frankly, I'm glad you showed up when you did. She was beginning to drive me crazy. Can I buy you a beer?"

"A Coke, if that's okay. I don't drink the hard stuff anymore."

"Good for you," Stowe said. "A Coke sounds just right. I think I'll join you."

"You sure I didn't interrupt anything?"

"Not at all. Myrtle latched onto me the moment I came in, and I've been thinking of a nice way to get rid of her for half an hour now."

The waitress came over, a tall blonde woman with a pinched face, stuffed into a tight black halter-top. Stowe ordered two Cokes. When she had left, he said, "So what brings you out on a night like this?"

"The same thing as everybody else, I guess."

"Looking for something to fill up the dull hours?"

"That's about right."

"Well," Stowe said, "it's the only place around that's open after ten. The regulars come here religiously every night. It's no New York nightclub, but the jukebox is only a year old and the people are friendly enough."

"You've lived in New York?"

"I've been to the big cities. L.A., New York. Went to Harvard for my medical degree, and stayed in Boston for my internship and residency. But I came back here to settle down. It just seemed like the right thing to do."

"You like it here, then."

"It's more like an obsession. I guess it's the cold air and the big dark stretches of woods. It does something to you if you live here long enough. Some kind of curse—you can't ever get quite used to it, but if you're away for more than a few days you miss it so much it hurts. It's like fighting with a beautiful woman. Eventually you want to make up again, no matter how bad it was. Something always brings you back."

The Cokes arrived on a tray covered with moist, crumpled bills. Smith sipped at his, trying to get the faint taste of whiskey out of the back of his throat. "My wife and I have been doing a little research on the town today, actually," he said. "About its history. We went to the library, but there wasn't much."

"No, there wouldn't be." Stowe shook his head. "Our library tries very hard, but it just doesn't have the resources. You could try the historical society."

"Yes, the librarian said something about that. I thought I'd go there tomorrow." Suddenly, he remembered. "You were the one who mentioned Sue Hall to me, weren't you?

She takes care of that woman we met on the square."

"Annie. Yes, that's right. Sue runs the historical society, among other things. She might be able to help you. Other than that, there are a few old ladies who could tell you some interesting stories about this town. And me, of course. Is that why you've come here, to do research?"

"I thought I told you. We're just passing through."

Stowe hesitated. "Forgive me if I've overstepped my bounds. I don't mean to pry, and your business is your business. But people just don't pass through here this time of year. And you two aren't really married, are you?"

Smith looked at him. He remembered something else he had thought the first time he met Harry Stowe; a bright man. Perceptive, certainly. And a longtime local. This was his chance to learn more about the town than he could ever learn from a book. But what did he really know about Stowe? A doctor who had studied at one of the best schools in the country. A man who seemed to pride himself on his mind and the logical solution to problems. How much of their crazy story would Harry Stowe believe?

"Is it that obvious?" he said finally.

"Not really." Stowe shrugged. "But you seem like a man who could use some help. I'd like to offer you mine, if you want it."

"You don't even know me."

"Agreed. But you seem like a nice enough guy. I can usually tell about people." Stowe took a long drink of his Coke, put it down, and sighed. "Ah, caffeine. A doctor's best friend." He focused those bright, serious eyes on Smith again. "Do you want to talk about it, whatever it is?"

"Let's just say we're looking for something in town."

"Hmm." Stowe regarded him now with mixed amusement and interest. "A mystery, is it? Let's see. You're a private investigator searching for somebody's lost relative. You're a journalist on the track of a hot story. Or a jewel thief on the run from the FBI, and you want to find a good hiding place."

"None of the above."

"I give up. But until you find whatever it is you're looking for, what are you doing for money? Unless you are a jewel thief, and just lying to me?"

Now it was Smith's turn to look amused. "Good question. I brought some cash with me, but I'm going to run short soon. Frankly, I haven't given it much thought yet."

"How about coming to work for me at the clinic? I can't pay you much, and the job would be nothing fancy—helping with patients, cleaning up, answering the phone. I usually have one of the school kids in the summers to help out, but the last one I had is in college down in New York now, and nobody else has come around yet asking for the job."

"I don't know how long we're going to stay. I can't commit to much."

"You work when you can, and we'll take it a day at a time. Does that sound okay to you?"

Smith grinned. "Sounds great. I appreciate it, I really do."

"You sure you don't mind working for a few measly bucks an hour?"

"I'll take what you can give me for pay."

"My kind of employee. Maybe I can tell you some of what you want to know, too."

"There is one thing I'm curious about," Smith said carefully. "Angel and I were out driving the other day and found a place not too far from here, a dirt road that led out to a pond and a little house lot. It looked abandoned."

"You must mean the old Taylor property," Stowe said. "If you put a boat in the river in back of us and floated it downstream, you'd end up right there, in Black Pond. It's not more than two miles away as the crow flies."

"A good name for it. Does anyone live there?"

Something dark passed across Harry Stowe's face. "Not anymore. There was an unfortunate incident with the Taylors years ago. The mother was killed and the father ended up in prison for murder. There was a little boy, Jeb Taylor, he moved in with his grandmother on the hill. I treated him myself for shock, he was one of my first patients here in town." Stowe glanced around, looking up toward the bar. "Jeb's usually in here, this time of night . . . there he is. Third stool down."

Smith turned and saw a young man sitting hunched over a drink at the bar. His face was a narrow white moon under a dark slash of hair, his eyes sunken and ringed with dark circles. "Jesus, he looks like he's just a kid. Pretty bad shape, isn't he?"

"Barely eighteen, I guess, but Johnny serves him anyway. From what I hear, he's been serving him about every night for a month now. Lord knows why, except Johnny never was one to refuse a buck. If Ruth finds out, that's the boy's grandmother, there'll be hell to pay."

"He'll drink himself to death if he's not careful."

Stowe had looked away from the young man at the bar, and now focused his gaze on Smith again. His eyes were frankly curious. "Why do you say that?"

"You can see it on his face." *And I know how it is to want to lose yourself in it, to be able to lose control and blame it all on the booze. A vicious circle, where every day there is more to forget and more reason to drink. He's me, fifteen years ago.*

"Jeb's had a lot of trouble in his life," Stowe was saying.

"That whole family has. Another one of the original families still left in town, but Jeb's the youngest of them. A lot of bad blood there. Jeb's father Ronnie was some of the worst of it. He grew up in the original Taylor house in the Hills, where Jeb and his grandmother live now. I remember Ronnie, being only a couple of years younger than he was. He was a loner, didn't really get along with the other kids. He would do strange things that made the others keep out of his way. I don't think he was mentally stable, right from the beginning, and we all could sense it. You know the way kids are. He didn't have much better luck in high school, and most people just thought it was a matter of time before he ended up behind bars. But we never thought he'd do what he did."

"And what was that?"

Stowe hesitated. "Understand that when I tell you this, it's not to smear the Taylor name, or just talk for talk's sake. I get the feeling you need to hear it, though I don't know why. So I'll tell you what I know as straight and quick as I can."

"I appreciate it."

Stowe nodded. "Just before Ronnie got married he had a falling out with his father—they never really got along, as I recall, and I don't remember what started the argument that got him kicked out of the house. But Ronnie moved out, got married to the Lincoln girl from over in Damariscotta, and found a job at the paper mill. Sharon Lincoln, that was the name of the girl he married. Ronnie bought some land and built that shack by the pond you're talking about. The garden and everything else good that might have been there was Sharon's doing, I imagine. About that time I was away in school, and so I don't know much, other than what I heard second-hand from my mother's letters. She loved to write to me about the goings on in town, and the Taylors were big news, back then."

"There wasn't anything on that land before he built on it?"

"Oh, there was a natural clearing, an old foundation or something, and I think some of the kids used the pond as a swimming hole. After the house was built, the kids didn't swim there anymore. Ronnie chased them off the land. Anyway, right after they moved in, Sharon had the baby. I think she must have been pregnant before they got married, though why Ronnie would have cared is beyond me. He wasn't the type to worry about reputations. Maybe Sharon's folks pushed them into it.

"A couple of years after that, as I recall from my mother's letters, Ronnie lost his job. He'd been handling things pretty good up until then, but he was no family man. I think losing his job was the last straw for him—even with a man like Ronnie, it seems like there's always one thing he can hold onto, one thing that keeps him from going over the edge. Working at the mill wasn't anything glamorous but it kept him busy, and when he lost that, he had too much time on his hands. He started drinking. All day and half the night right here at *Johnny's* drinking whiskey, that was his new thing. People started talking about him around town. They thought he was getting into things he shouldn't, running around with some bad men. And I guess he was, because a year or so later he started buying things. Not much at first—mostly more booze, and new clothes, things like that. Then he bought a new car, and he built a garage for it next to his house. He would cruise around town in that car, showing it off."

"You think he was into drugs?"

"I don't think it was anything like that. I suspect he was

stealing things and pawning them in Portland, or someplace nearby. There was a burglary about that time here in town, the Thomas Mansion on the square was broken into and a lot of jewelry and other things were stolen. Priceless things, heirlooms, most of them never recovered. Ronnie did that, I believe. I even remember people talking to the sheriff about it, but nobody could prove anything."

"Was he ever caught?"

"Stealing things? Not that I recall. But one day soon after, this was just about the time I moved back to town, Ronnie's father fell down the stairs of the family home and broke his neck. There were a few whispers at the time that Ronnie had had something to do with it. Lord knows he didn't like his father much. But nobody really took the rumors seriously, and I guess they should have, because a couple of months later it happened."

"What did he do?"

"He took a broomstick to Sharon, the poor girl. Beat her to death."

"Jesus."

"Yeah. It was brutal. I remember it was still big news when I moved back into town, everyone was talking about it. And Jeb, the poor kid, he was getting all the stares and hearing the talk too, and probably felt like he was responsible for the whole thing. Kids are like that, you know. Taking the blame. He was always shy. Never did well in school. The teachers thought he was retarded, but I tested him once. He had an average IQ, as I recall, maybe even above average. But he was limited by his lack of social skills, and of course the people in town never gave him much of a chance. Two strikes against him every time he stepped up to the plate."

Stowe paused, and leaned forward a little. The light that

hung above the table cast deep pockets of shadow across his eyes. "There's one more thing about that story that never made the papers, something I know only because I was involved with the boy's treatment and I talked to the cops about it. I don't know if it has any significance or not, but it was strange."

"What was that?"

"The murder scene was . . . odd. The way the body had been left, and things had been arranged. Ronnie had drawn around it in blood, using the broom handle like a paintbrush. Looked like he had started in on something else, too, only he'd been interrupted when the cops came and hadn't finished it. And he had taken a knife from the kitchen, too, and he'd . . . slit her open with it. She was pregnant, Billy. Jeb was going to have a brother."

"Jesus Christ." Smith stared at him, shocked, struggling to come to terms with the sheer brutality of the act.

Stowe sat back again, and shook his head. "I could hardly believe it myself, that a man would do something like that to his wife. To his unborn child, for God's sake. But Ronnie was seriously disturbed, should have been up at the mental health place a long time ago. Who knows what kind of stuff goes through a head like that?"

"Where was Jeb all this time?"

"Apparently he had stuffed himself underneath the sofa, or his father had put him there, I don't know. He never would tell me that, said he didn't remember what had happened. The last thing he could remember was his mother getting hit, and then he blacked out. But he had her blood all over him, almost as if he had rolled in it."

Smith turned to stare again at the young man at the bar. He had not moved, and the scene was much the same, except there were now several more empty shot glasses lined up like toy soldiers on the bar's scarred surface.

His father, the town criminal, feared, hated, finally brought down into the mud of his own making. His father, the murderer. And this boy, having to take the brunt of it all, having to *watch* it happen. *No wonder he drinks,* Smith thought. But turning to alcohol when you were under stress said something about you as a person, or so he had always thought. It said you weren't strong enough to face things on your own. He had done that himself. Why that thought scared him, he wasn't sure, but it did.

But could anyone have faced what this boy faced every day, without cracking?

"Looks just like his father," Stowe said quietly. He had turned to look at the boy too, and his voice was low and distant, as if he were just realizing something. "Spitting image of Ronnie Taylor, some might say. Ronnie used to sit at that very bar, probably on that same stool, and drink all night."

"So where's Ronnie now?"

"He died just a couple of weeks ago, still in prison," Stowe said. "I've been wondering how Jeb's taking it. Doesn't look good, does it?"

Jeb Taylor had not moved, except to take a drink from his beer glass or down another shot. His shoulders were humped as if to ward off a blow. He did not look at anyone, did not say a word, even to the bartender, who occasionally glanced at him in an offhand way. Smith felt that small quick flash of fear again, racing up through his gut to tighten his scalp.

*Jesus Christ, she was pregnant. How could he have done such a thing?*

"Someone ought to do something about his drinking," Stowe said. "Ruth ought to know. I'll try to talk to her. But people around here like their privacy, and expect everyone to mind their own business. Of course, there's always the rumors running around at the same time, and everyone talking about everyone else. Gossip spreads like wildfire. You just don't tell it to people's faces."

"Sort of hypocritical, isn't it?"

"Sure," Stowe said. "But that's how small towns work." He smiled, a little wearily. "God, but I went on. I guess I just made my own contribution to the rumor mill, telling you what I did."

"You didn't say anything that wasn't true."

"I hope it helped you out in some way." Stowe studied his face. "You weren't thinking about buying into that place by Black Pond, were you?"

Smith shook his head. "It gave me a bad feeling, to tell you the truth."

"I guess I wondered whether you might be into real estate. This isn't a bad little town, and the location could be worse. Every once in a while we get some outsiders looking to make a buck."

"That's not me. But I did wonder why it'd been abandoned."

"Superstition," Stowe said. "After Ronnie was arrested the property went on the market, but it just sat there. People are afraid of the legends, the ghosts haunting a place like that."

"Every little town has its share of ghosts."

"I guess they do, at that." Stowe nodded. "There are lots of stories. I've often thought about writing up the history of the town myself. Even with all the old families and the historical society, there isn't any real White Falls history book. But I guess you found that out today, didn't you?" Stowe's face grew serious for a moment, the light twinkle in his eyes dimming as he sat forward in the pool of light. "Like I told you, Billy, I get a good feeling about you. And I don't want you to tell me anything you're not ready to say about why you're here. But I'll tell you this; there are things about this town that not many people know, things not even I know much about, and I've looked into the history a bit for my own reasons. The Taylor family is like that. Oh, I know some of it, but there's a lot I suspect nobody but Ronnie Taylor himself knew, and maybe his wife just before she died. I guess that's just as well. I talked a bit about superstition like it's a bunch of horse crap, but I guess I've got a few of my own."

Stowe smiled, finished the last of his Coke, and put a five-dollar bill on the table. "I've talked enough. I should be getting home. Got a group of high school kids coming in for spring physicals tomorrow morning. Can you make it down to the clinic around eight o'clock? I can show you some of the things you'll be doing, get you situated before the kids show up."

Smith told him that would be fine. They said goodbye, and as he walked past the bar he saw Jeb Taylor still sitting on the last stool, staring into his drink as if he saw something in there that fascinated him.

When he got back to the Old Mill Inn, shivering from the cold air, he found Angel still awake on his bed, reading through the last of the books they had gotten from the library. He told her about his job offer, and all that Stowe had told him about the Taylor family and the place by the pond, including Ronnie Taylor's possible career as the town thief, the suspicious death of Norman Taylor, and Sharon's murder.

"She was pregnant," Angel said softly. "My God. And

that little boy, having to watch it all."

"Kind of makes more sense now, doesn't it? That place out by Black Pond, falling to pieces the way it is. Who would want to live there now?"

"I don't ever want to go out there again," Angel said. "I don't ever want to *see* that place."

"I think we need to find out more about the family. What exactly happened and why. Maybe it'll help us understand why we're here."

"But maybe that doesn't have anything to do with why we're here." She sighed. "How are we supposed to figure all of this out? I spent three hours looking through every page of these books, trying to find *something* that would stand out. But there's nothing here that's any different from any other little town." She tucked a lock of hair behind one ear. She looked tousled, as if she had just gotten up from a nap, except there were bags under her eyes and her face was drawn. He looked at her, and the feelings caught him by surprise, coming up from nowhere, until he was forced to turn away with a lump in his throat. She was so beautiful sitting there, tired eyes and all, her legs tucked up under her like a little girl. She had a way of looking at you that was so direct and open, it almost seemed as if she could peer right past the bullshit and into your soul. He wanted her, and that scared him more than anything; what right did he have to feel these things? The last thing he wanted to do was hurt her, and he thought that if she saw what he was thinking, if she realized it somehow, he would do just that.

*Just forget about it and back off.*

"We should get some sleep," he said. He walked to the window and stood there, looking out into the dark. The river ran below him, he could hear it gurgling, the water swollen from the rains. In the reflection in the glass, he watched Angel uncurl herself from the bed and put her feet on the floor.

"So you sat and talked," she said. "You and Dr. Stowe."

"That's right."

"What else did he say?"

"Nothing more, other than what I told you. There was a woman there with him when I came in, Myrtle someone-or-other. Big woman, acted strange when she saw me, ended up ducking out of there. Maybe I intimidated her with my dashing good looks."

"Is she his wife?"

Smith laughed. "No, I'm pretty sure he's single. I doubt she's his type." He studied Angel more closely, wondering what she was thinking. Something welled up in him out of nowhere, and his words came out too hard and fast. "He knows we're not married. Maybe he'll take you out."

"That's not what I was thinking," she said. "I couldn't care less what Dr. Stowe thinks about me."

Smith turned around, not quite sure where that had come from, wanting to take it back. "Sorry," he said. "I didn't mean to . . . just tired, I guess. It's been a long day."

It *had* been a long day, though that wasn't the reason for the way he was feeling right now. Everything seemed to be coming down on him, all the things that had happened the past few months. He thought about Ronnie Taylor and his murdered wife and son, and the way Jeb Taylor had looked, sitting there at the bar with his shoulders set as if he were carrying a heavy load on his back. Those shot glasses lined up beside him like targets in a shooting gallery, Jeb picking them off, one by one. The taste of beer was in the back of his throat, so strong and sharp he could almost believe he was drinking again.

He could not look at her. God, he had hurt her after all,

and yet he didn't dare try and make it right. Something inside him laughed at the irony of it, the fact that his only weapon against his own loneliness, and later the isolation and brutality of prison, the hardening of his spirit and his heart, had turned against him here and left him helpless.

She sat there on the bed, not saying a word, and when he did not open his mouth again she stood up and left, closing the door to the other room and throwing the lock.

*A whisper carried softly on air; come closer. I want to kiss you.*

He was standing at the bottom of a long, gently sloping hill. It was evening, but the wind that blew in his face was warm and smelled of flowers. Reminded him of something or someone he couldn't quite remember. A dark form, bending over him in the night, rocking him to sleep.

He was looking for something missing. A part of him that had been gone for a while. He felt a little hollow without it, but the need wasn't there yet, that awful, aching need. He followed the scent like a dog, nose up, sniffing the air. It led him up the soft gentle hill. He walked with his hands in his pockets, carefree, easy. Nothing bad could come to him on a night like this. The stars were out, peppering the black sky above his head with a myriad of shapes and angles and suggestions. He touched each sparkling gem with his eyes.

The hill was getting steeper. He leaned into it, his bare toes digging into the soft ground, the grass like soft green slippers on his feet. He came up to a gnarled, stunted tree. Its bare branches reached up toward the stars like the arms of an ancient, arthritic man. He struggled, grasping at the branches for balance, but the wood shattered in his hand and went to dust. Down suddenly on his hands and knees, tottering there, pinwheeling his arms for balance, and now it was a fight to reach the top of the hill, the angle almost straight up toward the heavens.

He clawed desperately at the ground, pulling himself up. Finally, he was at the top of the hill, and he lay there for a moment on his back, gasping. The stars had disappeared into a deep grayish haze. Gravestones lined the top of the hill, fencing him in. Several of them leaned in the coarse grass like drunken old men, their faces scoured by age and weather, the dates and names a ghostly pattern lined with green moss. He imagined the bodies piled one on top of another under the grass, limbs intertwined, flesh running together, a great mass of human bedrock. He stumbled from stone to stone; here was a pretty white one with an inscription he couldn't make out, another with a tiny sculpted angel on either side, another that was almost black with dead algae. He felt the cold coming up over the hill with the fog. The cold was a bone-chilling ache that settled around his shoulders, the kind that comes after an early snowfall.

He was standing on an island rearing up out of the mist. An island of graves.

The graves were placed in giant circles, one within another. He picked his way through them, unable to keep from moving forward. Searching for something. His hips bumped a heavy stone and sent it crashing to the ground. He moved faster. That thing he was searching for was close now, he could smell it. Finally, he reached the center; a series of three gravestones placed on the middle of the hilltop, one large between two small. A bundle of what might have been roses lay rotting in the grass, the stench of them filling the air. He read the inscription on the large stone with a morbid fascination; *Here lies Amanda Potter, wife and loving mother, may she rest in peace.*

And the two smaller stones; *Judy and Todd Potter, loving children, innocent victims of a heinous crime. Murdered by William Smith in this the year of our Lord . . . May he rot in hell.*

*No,* he tried to say, Jesus, *no.* He fell back in the grass and closed his eyes, willing it all away, and then the car was coming at him again, the headlights in his face, the horn blaring and he so drunk that he couldn't see. He felt the stomach-wrenching crunch of impact, metal screaming, twisting, tearing, glass shattering over his lap as he was thrown forward into the steering wheel.

As he opened his eyes he heard a sound like fingernails scratching in the dirt. A low ripping sound joined it, like a piece of cloth torn in half. He looked down at his feet, and through the mist that now covered the ground like a thin gray blanket he saw a set of bone-white fingertips wriggling like worms below Todd Potter's gravestone. Tiny child-fingers pushing themselves upward through the dirt, tearing the sod. To his left he saw another set of fingers, and beyond that still more; all digging their way out of the grave to come for him.

He lay there as the dead climbed their way out. Two children, fresh blood on their pushed-in faces; they stood and grinned at him with bloody, toothless smiles, their limbs twisted at unnatural angles. Here and there he could see the tips of white splintered bone poking out of the skin. Todd Potter had been in the back seat and had taken the worst of the impact. His right leg had been severed at the knee. Judy, the little girl, had been in the front without a seatbelt, and she had gone through the windshield. Her face was nothing but a red pulpy mess. And Amanda Potter, wife and loving mother, had taken the hub of the steering wheel through the chest—

But when he looked to Amanda Potter's grave he saw

something else. He stared. The hawk-like, weary face of Jeb Taylor stared back at him.

The lizard eyes blinked. Jeb held up a flask. *Have a drink, my brother? Just one drink. One for the road.*

A wave of self-revulsion welled up in him even as the thirst bit at the back of his throat. How could he think of that now after all that had happened? But he was weak. Christ, so weak.

*Just reach out and take her, Billy. It's easy. Come closer. Give her a little kiss.* As he watched, Jeb Taylor's face started to run like toffee in the hot sun, the features blurring, something else coming up underneath.

He screamed.

And forced himself awake to a dark room, where everything was blessedly sane again and the only gravestones were the ones in his mind.

Angel had heard him scream and had come over from her bed in the other room, and now she sat next to him again, like she had in the Motel Six in Gatesville, while he shivered silently. The dream had been different this time. Sharper, clearer. He was afraid that soon he might not be able to tell the difference between dreams and reality.

"They're getting worse again for you," Angel said. "Aren't they?"

He nodded. Part of him felt like he was still deep in the dream, that he was being watched, that the stage had cleared and the lights had come up but the audience refused to leave.

"I haven't had one in weeks," she said, a little distantly. "I think maybe they're leaving me alone because I'm trying to let go of things myself. The things that haunt me. Maybe you should try it, too."

*Let go?* he wanted to scream. *How can I let go? I killed three people because I was a stinking, worthless drunk. And yet I've never wanted a drink as badly as I do right now.*

But he just shook his head. "I can't."

"What do you mean, you can't?"

"I mean I don't have a choice. I'm *supposed* to remember. I don't think we can change any of it. It's bigger than us, don't you understand? We're just little parts of whatever is happening in this God-forsaken place."

Her face flushed an angry red. "No. That's not true. You're saying that whatever is going to happen to us has already been decided, and I don't believe it. We have a choice, we can change things, damn it."

Somehow, he thought, the tables had turned; wasn't he the one who had taken her against her will just a few weeks ago? Wasn't he the one who had been the leader, the one who had literally forced them forward to get to this point? Christ, he had handcuffed her to the door to keep her from running, he could hardly believe he had done that to her.

But now he was drained and on the edge and he couldn't give anything more, and maybe it was only natural that she would begin to take over.

"They were—" he started, stopped, started again. "Crushed. The blood—I never saw so much blood." His stomach rolled and clenched with the memory. "I hit them in the side and the girl was thrown out the window and the boy was pinned and the mother took the steering wheel in the chest and I got out and tried to help them but it was too late. The police came and pulled them out and covered them with a sheet and I just kept puking into the bushes, blood all over me, my blood and theirs together. I kept thinking that it should be two different colors, you know?

That I had no right to have the same color blood as they had."

She sat there on the edge of the bed and stared out the window at the darkness. He didn't move, didn't even wipe the tears that wet his face. They were cool on his cheeks. Below them the river still ran, softer now, underneath a blanket of stars.

She shifted on the bed, a little closer to him. "I went out earlier to look at the stars," she said quietly, "and I walked around the square for a while in the cold. It was strange being out there alone. I hadn't really been alone since this whole thing began, you know? It gave me a chance to think. I thought about everything. I thought about why we were here. I didn't really figure anything out—at least I don't think so—but I realized that I didn't want the drugs anymore. That's strange, isn't it? I mean, only a couple of weeks ago I couldn't go a couple of days without a fix. And now . . . nothing. I felt clean, healed. New."

"It's not possible."

"I know it's not. But it's the way I feel, all the same. So I decided that it didn't matter *why* we were here, just that we *were*. The rest of it will come. That's when I realized that I had let go of my past, all of it. For good. My brother's death, my life in Miami. Everything. Those things don't matter anymore to me. They have no power over me. You have to let it go, Billy. It's not easy, I know, but you have to stop punishing yourself for something that happened years ago. Maybe that's part of this whole thing, maybe now's your chance to make up for everything. Our chance. But you have to accept what happened and don't waste another second, because another second may be all we've got."

"I wish I could," he whispered, and in that moment he meant every word. "I really wish I could."

He sat there, rigid, unable to move. Then he felt her hand on his arm, cool and smooth and soft, and when he turned to her she was crying, and the look on her face was so painful he could hardly bear to witness it.

"Why won't you let me in?" she whispered. "You talk like you want me to understand, but you don't, not really. Can't you see I don't give a damn about anybody else, that I don't care how we got here or what happened in the past? I feel like we've known each other forever, Billy. Maybe that's part of what we're going through together, but it doesn't really matter. Can't you see . . . don't you understand that I'm falling in love with you?"

He felt the muscles in his arm tense, and resisted the urge to pull away, all the time thinking, *my God, how could this happen, she's just confused, that's all . . .*

Her hand reached his face, cupped his cheek, turned it toward her gently. He felt her warm breath and then she was kissing him, the wet salty taste of her tears mixing with the softness of her lips, and she was whispering softly, "My poor, sweet Billy, stop killing yourself, let me help you let go, can't you feel that it's right, that we're meant to be together?"

And he did feel it, a great loosening within him like a dam about to burst, and that scared him more than anything else. He felt like he was losing control of the one thing that had kept him going, the anger and self-loathing that was so strong and ran so deep it had been the only thing keeping him alive. Knowing that only by remembering, playing it over and over again in his mind, would he truly pay for what had happened to those two children and their mother. *My own private hell, baby, bought and paid for.*

She kept kissing him, and the dam kept crumbling. And somewhere inside his head a voice whispered to him to stop, that it wasn't right at all, that the result of their love could only be disastrous, but as his tears mingled with hers and he felt her hot bare skin, he finally stopped listening.

# Chapter Ten

The first time was hard and hungry, too eager. But by the second time it had become the gentle love of two people who had spent a lifetime together, knew every inch of flesh and every private thought, every feeling and desire. If she had had any doubts before, they were gone now. Never had she felt this close to a person. She knew that her feelings for Billy Smith were stronger and more intense than they had any right to be. And she knew that she should hate this man, that by all rights he should be in jail for kidnapping. But for a good part of her life she had been controlled by men, by their violent acts and their sexual urges; she had made a promise to herself during the past few weeks that things would change, that no matter what else happened she would regain control of her life again. This was different, she told herself, not only because of the visions they both had shared but because he was tormented by his own demons, and because even though she had seen the way he looked at her lately, he had resisted getting physical, knowing what it would have done to her. Until finally she had made the choice, and she had made it of her own free will.

Only weeks ago she had been having sex for money, and that sex had been cold and lonely, a simple piston-like drive toward orgasm for her male partner. The faster he reached it, the better. No tenderness, no kissing, the physical feelings dulled by the heroin rushing through her veins. Many times she had felt as if she were floating somewhere above her body, as if she were watching someone else performing these acts, and other times she would let herself drift away altogether, closing her eyes as the men slammed themselves into her, thinking about hot beach sand under her feet, the waves breaking against rock, the sound of the surf. Letting herself go, finding her own private place. The man with her would speed up, looking at her closed eyes, her smile, and that was fine, because it would be over faster, and that was what she wanted.

Every once in a while, especially those last few weeks before Billy Smith came so violently into her life, these daydreams would go bad, and she would find herself watching her brother dragging himself out of the surf, and the vision would be so sharp and detailed she would be able to see every feature in his bloated face; and he would grin at her as he wriggled like a crab across the sand, his hair tangled with seaweed and crusted with salt. If she was with a man when this vision came, she would drag her nails across his back, drawing blood, and cry out. Sometimes he liked it, sometimes not, but not one of those men had realized that she was responding to something far more horrible than anything they had done. Her dead brother had come to warn her of something, but when he tried to speak that grin would resurface on his face, and he would cease to be her brother and become someone or something else.

With these visions came the sudden urge to *hurry up,* a terrible feeling that she needed to be somewhere. Only she didn't know where. At first she chalked these things up to the drugs, and if she had been strong enough to resist them she would have stopped then and there—but they had a hold on her that she could not break. And later when she began to have the visions even when she was sober and alone in her apartment, the heroin became an ally, helping to ward off the worst of the visions until her brother's bloated features became nothing more than a blur in the darkness. She took more, and still more, and yes, she was speeding headlong toward a brick wall, and she no longer cared. She would have welcomed the darkness, and the peace that came with it.

Then finally that afternoon on the beach when Billy Smith had come for her. But that no longer mattered, none of it did, not here in this cool shadowed room with the softly rushing water below their window like whispers in the dark, with his hands on her bringing out every last drop of sweat, every last tremble of her limbs.

They rolled together across the little hotel bed, the springs creaking and popping, the sheets rustling softly, twisting around their legs, forming a half-cocoon. His movements were slow again now as he slipped deeper into her, a gentle rocking of the hips as they lay side by side, as she kept her lips against the skin of his neck and whispered his name over and over like a prayer, tasting the salt of his sweat.

Later, she unwound herself from the sheets and threw her thighs up and out and let him all the way in, and still it was not enough and she pulled him closer, wrapping her legs around his waist, telling him to be quick now, gasping it out as her hands slipped down his back to his buttocks, the words catching in her throat as her body clenched and exploded and she held him so close she could hardly breathe.

Time passed, how much she did not know. They both lay there, exhausted, content, the thin moonlight through the window painting bars of shadow across their legs, the sweat drying on their skin. He lay on his back with his arm curled around her, cupping her soft breast in his hand. She snuggled in close on her side, feeling his heat, drawing her right thigh up and over his legs. Let her finger trace the long raised scar that ran across his stomach and down his hip, a ridge of hard tissue like a second backbone.

"You almost died, didn't you?"

"Yes," he said simply. "Almost."

"But you're still alive. You lived through it, and that's a gift and it should be treasured, not thrown away."

"I guess life wasn't finished with me yet."

"No," she said, "it wasn't."

He shifted, drawing her closer, and kissed her softly on the forehead. It was a sweet, unselfconscious move, and she was touched.

"You've never asked me my real name, not once. Don't you want to know?"

He seemed to think about this for a moment. "Tell me."

"Gloria Johnson."

"You're kidding."

She laughed. "I hated it as a kid. Gloria always seemed like an old person's name—I always thought of a lady with glasses on a chain around her neck and a double chin."

He smiled and kissed her again. "I think I'll stick with Angel."

The next morning when she woke up he was gone, and there was a note on the bedside table.

*Gone down to work at the clinic. Looked so sweet this morning I didn't want to wake you. Later this afternoon I'll be back, we can talk about a few things. Thanks for last night, for what you did and what you said. You did me a world of good. See you soon. Billy.*

And that was all. She didn't know what to think. Just when she thought she had him figured out, he threw her a curve.

But he had opened up to her last night and that meant something. She stood up out of the cozy bed and went to the window, clutching the sheets to her naked body for warmth. She kept getting this mental picture in her head of a road slick with oil and antifreeze, littered with broken glass and twisted metal, and Billy stumbling across the dirt shoulder holding his belly in with his hands. The children in the other car, how they must have looked to him. No wonder he had the nightmares, anyone would.

So where did that leave her? She knew she was falling in love with him, and wasn't quite sure how to handle it—it had come upon her so fast. Was it really love? She had to wonder. She knew about kidnap victims and their strange connections to their kidnappers. But she wasn't your ordinary victim. She didn't feel threatened, she was free to go any time, and she knew that he had been driven by visions that they shared. If he hadn't taken her, she might be dead by now—or she might have found her way here on her own.

Billy Smith was not exactly the type of man she had always dreamed of falling in love with, with his tall, too-thin frame and shock of unruly black hair, his dark eyes that looked like they had seen too much pain. But he had a certain charm.

Then again, so had her last real lover. In an entirely different way, of course. Billy was shy and often awkward; Rick Davenport had been smooth and self-assured.

She'd met him in Miami. When she had left home she had been little older than a schoolgirl, her head filled with vague dreams of stardom, thoughts of bright stage lights and seats filled with admiring faces, screaming fans. She hadn't had much money, but she found work in a nightclub, serving drinks, cleaning tables. The pay hadn't been much, but it had kept her alive. She found a place to live too, a little hole in the wall above a pizza parlor. While she worked, she looked in the papers for auditions. When she went to them, she found she needed a portfolio, tapes, references; most of the time they wouldn't even let her in the door, and she would go home empty-handed, curling up into a ball on the narrow bed in her single room, listening to the shouts of the cooks and the noises of the people moving below and crying herself to sleep. Sometimes she sang to herself, just to keep her voice in shape. But she knew she didn't have the money to make a demo, or even to get some decent pictures taken. And she didn't dare go home, afraid of what her father would say, afraid of admitting her mistake. Or the worst possible thing that could happen, finding out they had hardly noticed she was gone. *My brother is dead,* she had wanted to scream at them, that night before she left. *But I'm not. Don't you even care that you still have a daughter?*

Then one night as she was working at the club, Rick walked in, looking like a movie star. He started talking to her like she could be someone, told her all she needed was a break and he could get her one. She wanted to believe him, she had wanted it so much. He told her she needed a stage name, and she had thought about that one for a while, finally settling on Angel because that was what her brother had called her when she was a little girl, before he had gotten sick, when they used to play together out behind the barn in the small dirt square they used as a sandbox. One word, *Angel,* like Madonna or Cher. Rick loved the name, told her she was going to be a star. God, he was a smooth talker, so sure of himself and cocky, plenty of money in his pockets and expensive suits in his closet.

He lived in a big place just off the beach with a glass wall facing the water and a second floor that hung out over the sand. He threw parties there on Thursday nights, and that was where he had taken her for the first time, two weeks after they met. Not forced her, exactly, but she had resisted a little, enough to realize he would get rough, before she let him take her pants off. He had been gentle after the first time, and that was enough to make her think he loved her. How naive she had been! All those other women parading through the door day after day, Rick telling her that they were clients, that he "handled their careers." All of them young, beautiful, well dressed.

All of them addicts and whores.

It was how he got women to do what he wanted, by appealing to whatever it was they wanted most in life, letting them know he could get it for them, and then getting them hooked. Heroin, speed, coke. Whatever worked. And finally, controlling every aspect of their lives, their money, their apartment, their friends.

Oh, she had been so naive. The auditions had been a joke. Richard Davenport was a pimp, of course. A relatively upper class one, but a pimp, nonetheless. One of Davenport's girls could command up to a thousand a night, of which half would go to him and the other half toward the drugs she so desperately needed. And so the girl would be broke and dependent on him for everything.

Little Gloria Johnson had taken the bait, swallowed it all, hook, line, and sinker, and by the time she realized her mistake, it was too late. Rick had a way of breaking your will mentally and physically, like a cult leader who convinces his subjects that death is the only way out, making them commit suicide one by one. "This is just something temporary, on the side, for spending money," he'd told her, after the first time she had slept with "a friend of his," and accepted money afterwards, something she had thought had been a horrible mistake. He said everybody famous started out this way, it was how things worked, babe. No big deal. *Gotta pay your dues before you can make it to the big time, honey.* By that time, she had known him for six months, and the heroin already had a grip on her. She felt as if she were underwater, her lungs about to burst, and each syringe full of clear liquid was like a breath of air. But it was like coming up out of the water, taking a deep breath, and finding out the air was filled with poison gas. Either way, you were dead.

Men always wanted something from her. Richard Davenport, and those who had come after him, taking what little self-respect she had and flushing it down the toilet. Even her brother, back from the dead, haunting her sleep and then even her waking moments until she had clearly felt the edges of her own sanity, and it was like walking along the edge of a high, rocky cliff.

But no more. As she had told Billy earlier, Miami and all that went with it was behind her now, she was letting it go, and damned if Davenport would hold any power over her anymore.

She showered, dressed, and took the books back to the library, passing the clinic on her way. She considered stopping in to see what the two men were up to, and thought better of it. No sense in making the first day on the job more difficult for Billy than it needed to be, and besides, she would see him soon. Still, as she passed by, she imagined him watching her from the window and her heart began to jump and her breathing sped up. *My God, I've really got it bad.* She hadn't felt this way since high school. The feeling frightened her a little, but it excited her as well. She was alive, damn it, she was a thousand miles from Miami Beach and she was doing just fine.

At the library she handed the books to the same little man they had met yesterday. Not much sense in keeping those books around, she thought, since there wasn't much in them. The young man asked her if they had helped, and she smiled and told him they had, not wanting to seem ungrateful. Then she asked him how to get to the historical society, and he gave her directions.

When she left the library the heat hit her again, and it was like stepping into a sauna. Already it was rippling the asphalt down the road, making the new leaves droop on the trees, and here it was hardly ten o'clock in the morning. The weather over the past few days had been the strangest she had ever seen, the days so hot the tar went hot and sticky in the parking lots, the nights so cold you could see your breath. Except for yesterday, of course, when it had rained, and pretty hard, too. For some reason, thinking about the rain, she remembered the librarian talking about the reverend's funeral. Must have been a hell of a mess, the hardest part of the storm coming about the time of the graveside service. She wondered what had killed him. That night the reverend had died had been the same night . . .

But she did not want to think about that now, not yet. There would be plenty of time to worry about what that night meant. Now she wanted to think about *last* night, the way Billy had made her feel, his hands on her in the darkness of the room.

She walked with the hot sun beating down on her bare neck, feeling the air settling about her shoulders and the sweat beading on her upper lip, trying to force out the thoughts that kept creeping into her head. But they refused to leave in spite of everything she did. She kept trying to recall the way Billy's shoulders looked above her body, and kept seeing that clearing instead, the way it looked in the moonlight. The surface of the pond stretching out in the darkness like a pool of used motor oil, the ruined building canted to one side like a drunken partygoer. That woman, what had her last moments been like?

*He beat her to death with a broom handle, babe, carved her up like a Christmas turkey. Guess he wanted her to get an abortion.*

The voice in her head sounded so much like Rick Davenport she almost gasped aloud.

*That's what happens when you don't do what your man tells you to do. Shoulda stuck with me, you coulda been somebody.*

*Yeah,* she thought, *I could have been your whore. And then I could have been dead.* Davenport did not reply, and she suddenly wondered how he actually would have felt, hearing the story of Ronnie Taylor, the petty thefts, Ronnie's own father's suspicious death, and finally, his wife's murder. Would Rick say what she had just imagined he would say, or would he be shocked, as she had been; disgusted, horrified? It was hard to believe anyone could shrug off a story like that. *Even a snake like Rick would have to feel some kind of disgust for a man like Ronnie Taylor. Maybe he would even be afraid of him, if they ran into each other on some lonely street corner at night.*

But that was stupid, of course. Ronnie Taylor was dead, he would never be running into anyone again, and Rick had never been afraid of anything in his life, as far as she knew.

Still, it held a certain morbid fascination for her, this idea of the two of them, side by side. Running a mental hand over each like a farmer checking a team of horses, considering the teeth, the muscles of the thigh, the temperament. On the one hand, Richard Davenport was one of the most frightening and ruthless men she had ever met. His good looks, his self-confidence and arrogance made him even more dangerous, because they were deceptive. Morality was a matter of convenience.

*But he never took a broom handle and beat someone to death,* she thought, *never took a knife to a pregnant woman's stomach. At least as far as I know.* Ronnie Taylor had done that to his wife, and right in front of his young son. Dear God, what could make someone do such a thing?

And that, of course, was one of the reasons she was on her way to the historical society right now. To try to find out.

The historical society (also the swap shop, recycling center, and private residence of Miss Susan Hall) was located past the grammar school, along the gentle upsweep of Route 17 as it led out of town and up into the north hills. It was a rust-colored ranch with a circular driveway and a wooden sign out front. Near a small wooden shed behind the house were tables heaped high with all kinds of junk, littering the small open space beside several large metal bins. Behind the shed rose the edges of the north woods, a dense tangle that stretched unbroken for almost fifteen miles.

Angel walked across the gravel drive and climbed the front steps slowly in the heat. She hesitated a moment, not really knowing why, only that she had been walking now for twenty minutes and though the sweat dampened her shirt and the sun made her squint, she did not feel all that bad. The sun felt good, actually, and the walk had given her more of a workout than she would have thought, considering the distance.

And maybe there was a part of her that insisted she really didn't want to know anything more about Ronnie Taylor after all.

She reached out and rang the doorbell. There were two narrow sidelights on either side of the white door, but the curtains were drawn and it was impossible to see if anyone was home. A small hand-painted sign read *Welcome.* She waited, rang the doorbell again, waited some more, rapped on the door with her knuckles. Nothing.

Just as she was about to give up, a chunky middle-aged woman in a pair of corduroys and a sleeveless blouse came around the corner of the house. She wore large glasses in rose-colored frames, and her straw-colored hair was pulled back and fastened with a barrette. She carried a hardcover book under one arm, and wore a pair of yellow rubber kitchen gloves.

"Just now heard the bell," the woman explained, a little out of breath. "Was going through the boxes."

"Boxes?"

"The swap shop? Miss Simpson left quite a load this morning, most of which ought to go to the dump. You're welcome to have a look, though—never know what you'll find. One person's trash is another's treasure." She raised a hand to shield her eyes, noticed the gloves and hastily pulled them off, as if she had been caught in some kind of indecency. "Come on around back if you'd like a look."

"Actually, I wanted to see the records. For the town? I was doing some research on town history, and the young man at the library said I might find something here, that I ought to ask for Miss Hall . . ."

"Oh, silly me. I . . . haven't been feeling myself." The woman stepped forward, shifted the book to her other arm, and introduced herself as the one and only Sue Hall. "We don't get many people here for the historical society," she explained, shaking Angel's hand in a grip that was soft and moist. "Most people just come by to drop off their junk, or their bottles and cans for recycling. We're one of the most advanced recycling towns in Maine, you know."

"That's very impressive."

"We do our best." Sue Hall blinked behind large round lenses. "It's Angel, isn't it? I don't mean to pry, but aren't you the one who's staying at Bob's place, the Old Mill? With that young man, what is his name . . ."

"Billy Smith."

"Of course, Mr. Smith. You're married, then."

Angel nodded, beginning to feel distinctly uncomfortable about that little untruth. She remembered that Sue Hall was some sort of relation to the reverend, and wondered if she should offer her condolences.

But Sue Hall was already opening the front door and inviting her in. She swept down the hall that ran from front to back of the house, showing Angel into the first large room on their left, a room with fake wood paneling, a dark carpet worn thin in spots, and prints of fishing boats on the walls. The wall directly opposite the door was occupied by a gigantic map of the town, hand-drawn and accurate right down to the streetlights along the square. A line of glass display cases were situated below it, and at the end crouched an old copy machine with a handwritten sign over it that read *ten cents a copy, on your honor please.*

In the other corner sat a microfiche machine with a printer, and above it ran several long shelves with various bound books and pamphlets. There were zoning maps, lists of historical sights, some of the original documents from the 1700s (these were kept in a separate room, and could be viewed upon request), and minutes from every town meeting since the turn of the century. They had every issue of the White Falls *Gazette* on film, dating from 1950 when the paper began, Sue Hall explained. Before that there had been a one-page flyer announcing the town news, and that was on film too, back to 1860. She had done all of that herself, she said, and indexed some of it by subject as well, to make finding things a little easier. Her own little contribution to the town. "It's a shame we don't get more of the kids interested in history these days, but they just want to go to their rock and roll concerts and drive their cars up to Augusta, looking for trouble."

She showed Angel how to work the microfiche machine and asked her if she were looking for anything in particular. Angel shrugged noncommittally, and said she was simply a history buff and interested in the town, hoping that would satisfy Sue Hall. The woman brightened, smiling as if she had finally found a kindred soul. "I'll just be out back with the boxes. You yell if you need anything."

Taking a guess at the exact date of the Taylor tragedy from what Billy had told her, Angel got down the volume of the *Gazette* marked July 1980–June 1985, settled into the chair in front of the machine and started going through the entries. She scanned through pages filled with engagement notices, wedding invitations, old letters to the editor, articles about the high school sports teams, town meetings, local celebrities, obituaries. She watched five years of life in White Falls flash before her eyes, and got an idea of how the past forty years had been, or a hundred and forty for that matter; slow to change, people playing the same games over and over as children were born, grew up, got married, had children of their own. The black and white newspaper photos of smiling young people and middle-aged housewives and old men all blended together into one face, the face of a history that probably was not much different from the one told in the records of her own home town. An article about the White Falls basketball team winning the state class-D championship in 1982, with a picture of the team; a clipping announcing the engagement of Miss Anita Simpson to Mr. Jody Falcino; a notice about the 1983 White Falls Festival.

Then she found the article about the break-in, dated January 16th, 1984.

*The home of Mr. Henry Thomas, noted poet, collector, and descendent of one of the original settlers of White Falls, was burglarized yesterday. Several hundred dollars worth of damage was caused to the home, and valuables were taken. The break-in took place while Mr. Thomas was away on vacation, and no suspects have been identified. The local police have refused to comment at this point, saying only that they are "investigating the incident" and will be following up several leads.*

*Among the items taken were a jewelry box containing an estimated several thousand dollars worth of precious stones; four oil paintings, of undetermined value; silver that Mr. Thomas describes as having "been in the family for generations"; and several historic artifacts, at least one of which has been traced back hundreds of years and may have come over on the Mayflower (see related article, pg. A12). Mr. Thomas has promised to keep the name of the thief a secret and pay whatever sum is demanded for the safe return of the artifacts, which he describes as being "extremely delicate and of great personal value."*

That was Ronnie Taylor's handiwork, of course. She

didn't know how she knew it, but she did. *Call it intuition.*

Except it was more than that, wasn't it? She was on the right track, and something was pushing her forward, wanting her to keep going, to *see.*

She hit the print button, waited impatiently for the paper to curl out of the machine, and then scanned down to the related article.

## PRICELESS AMULET A KEY TO OUR PAST

*One of the artifacts stolen from the private collection of Mr. Henry Thomas on Wednesday is not only a priceless work of art, it is also the stuff of legend. This exquisitely crafted piece, in the form of an amulet worn about the neck, can be traced back to Mr. Frederick Thomas, a relation of Henry Thomas and one of the original settlers of White Falls, and beyond. Attempts have been made to date it, according to Mr. Thomas, but were "ineffective in determining the exact age of [the amulet] . . . we know that it is genuine, and that it is one of the oldest artifacts ever found in this area."*

*The amulet was discovered in 1957 in a secret hiding place in the basement of the Thomas family home, along with a few other valuables, and Mr. Thomas added it to his already extensive private collection. Anthropologists have discovered historic writings about the piece from as far away as Paris, France. "One like it was apparently owned by Louis XIV during the Age of Kings," says Dr. David Rutherford, a former Professor of Anthropology at Harvard University who now resides in Brunswick, Maine. "Evidently, the Sun King was quite attached to the piece though no records have survived to document how he acquired it."*

*The amulet was supposed to have brought the wearer great power and wealth, Dr. Rutherford says. "But according to the church it was also very dangerous . . . there are several records of its being destroyed, both after Louis XIV's death, and later . . . it kept turning up again in England."*

*Mr. Thomas has described the loss of the piece as "tragic . . . like losing a bit of history." He has issued a substantial reward for its safe return.*

Angel hit "print" again, scanned through the last few pages on the machine and found nothing of interest, and continued through three more issues, looking for suspicious deaths. Finally, in the February 1985 edition of the *Gazette*, she found the death notice of Mr. Norman Taylor, sixty-one years of age. She read it quickly, feeling her heartbeat speed up again. The article stated that Mr. Taylor died in his home; the death was described as an unfortunate accident.

A few issues later the murder of Sharon Taylor was plastered across the front page. The article did not discuss the gory details but the point was clear. The woman had been beaten to death by a blunt instrument in her home while her child watched.

*No need to fuck around, is there, babe? Those are the facts. Sharon dies, life goes on.*

Except her husband had done it. The same man who had lost his job and turned into a mean drunk, and finally a thief. The same man who had probably pushed his own father down a flight of stairs.

Next to the article about Sharon's murder was a blurred photograph of Ronnie Taylor. The black and white photo showed a man with straight black hair, a hawk nose, and thin lips. The look of a man who had worked hard for a living.

But it was the eyes that fascinated her. Even in the grainy newsprint they held a strange sort of power. Set back in his head, beady and heartless. The eyes of a predator. And yet she recognized something in them; something horrible, and yet strangely hypnotic and familiar. She pictured Ronnie Taylor watching the broom handle come up and down, again and again, watching with the cold mindlessness of a lizard as his wife's skull cracked and her jaw shattered.

She flipped back to the article about the break-in, read it again. Read the follow-up article, then printed more copies of all of them. A feeling of dread was growing in the pit of her stomach and it felt razor-sharp. There was something at her fingertips that might explain everything. But what was it?

*Why don't you ask me, babe? Haven't I always helped you out in the past? You wanted to line us up like a couple of used cars, see which one could whip the other. Which one's got the bigger engine? Now you got a case of the chills. Let me tell you something, honey. I can tell you about evil. This one, you don't want to check under the hood.*

A noise from behind her. She jumped, whirled around in her chair.

Annie Arsenault stood in the doorway, her wild white hair floating around her skull. She wore a yellow nightgown that hung oddly on her emaciated frame, giving her body the appearance of being not entirely solid. Angel rose from her chair, her mind whirling, shifting gears. Since that day on the square she had been dreading another encounter with this woman. She did not do well with people who were mentally unbalanced; they frightened her, especially the loud ones.

But Annie was not the same woman she had been on the square. There was something in her eyes now that hadn't seemed to be there before. Annie took several shuffling steps forward, stopped, and cocked her head to one side. *She looks like a bird, hopping along on the grass. Just before it pounces on a worm.*

"So you have finally come," Annie said, her voice high and thin and sharp. "I have been waiting for a very long time."

"Excuse me?" Angel took half a step back, felt the table against her thighs, and stopped.

"You want to know more about the Taylor family. You understand nothing yet. But I will tell you what I know." Annie extended a long, bone thin arm as if to touch her. Her skin was translucent, blue veins crisscrossing just under the surface. "Come along with me."

"Where are we going?"

"Come." Angel found herself following the old woman against her better judgment. They left the records room and passed through the dark hallway, Annie moving quickly and almost silently across the carpeting. Past another closed door on their left, photographs on the wall, a long, narrow table. At the end of the hall on the right an open door led down into darkness. Annie paused at the top of a flight of steps, and began to descend.

Angel went to the open door, hesitated, and took a deep breath, looking down. From the bottom of the stairs came the flickering glow of candlelight. Annie was no longer in sight. A faint, mossy smell came drifting up to her from the cave-like depths, the smell of old leaves after a rain.

She took the stairs cautiously, feeling her way with her hands against the close walls on either side. At the bottom the space opened up and she found herself in a dimly lit, furnished basement apartment.

Furnished, in a way. She felt like she had just stepped back a hundred years in time. The floor was bare, cold stone. Along both walls ran high shelves filled with hundreds of books. Further along the books gave way to dusty jars containing things she could not bring herself to look at too closely; vague, foggy shapes that suggested old lab specimens swimming in formaldehyde.

The flickering light came from a pair of candelabras placed on a solid wooden table at the far end of the room. To one side, thrown in like an afterthought, was a narrow bed. The arrangements of the little furniture in the room implied some sort of ritual space in the center.

Annie stood swaying over an open book on the table. She was muttering softly, and the sound sent an icy chill down Angel's spine. What had she gotten herself into, going down into the basement of a crazy old woman mad with grief over the loss of her son these past forty years or more?

Annie turned around, her hair lit in a fiery halo by the candlelight, the outline of her scarecrow body now plainly visible through the thin material of the nightgown. She seemed to float several inches off the floor. "A crazy old woman, out of her head with grief. I suppose that's what they've been feeding you, these people that *watch over me.* I should be grateful that I didn't end up in a home." Her mouth was lost among the shadows that held her face. "They see what they want to see, as you do. And they are holding the secrets of this town very deep within themselves. It would not do them good to have those secrets come out."

"I don't understand."

"And yet you come here looking for answers to bad dreams and night sweats. Your loved ones come back to you in your dreams, eh? Back from the dead? But they are not as they were, they are something else, something evil."

Out of the corner of her eye Angel saw something move in one of the jars, twitch once and be still. A trick of the light. It had to be.

The old woman took a shuffling step forward, deepening the shadows across her face. "All your life, everything in its place, everything rational. Science is your religion, seeking to explain the world and everything in it, and by doing so, closing doors on other worlds. But now you have come looking for answers. Seeking out the reason for the unexplained urges you have felt, the needs that have begun to consume you. The world is not as you have known it. There are other worlds. There are things . . ." She paused, cocked her head as if listening. "Even now, they are looking for you."

"Who?"

The woman shrugged. "The dead."

Angel took a deep breath, the fear making her shudder. And then suddenly it became clear to her. *Of course.* "You lost your son in the falls long ago. It's a terrible thing. None of us could have handled—"

"You want to see, and yet you are blind!" the old woman said. Her wrinkled face seemed to dart out of the darkness, like a snake about to strike. "This town and everyone in it is sick. You and Billy Smith are a part of it, as you have always been. Only now are you beginning to feel that sickness, but it has always been there. It will get worse, until you are both dragged down into the darkness with the rest of us. A darkness of the spirit. Pure evil. That's difficult for you to understand, isn't it? You're raised to think there's a reason for everyone's actions, no matter how vile. But I am telling you now that there are higher powers at work within human beings, and larger things at stake than you can know."

*No.* Annie Arsenault was obviously a very old, very confused woman. The drowning of her young son had unbalanced a mind that was perhaps already on the edge, sent it tumbling down into a world of magic and sorcery and witchcraft. A world that did not exist.

And yet, hadn't she opened her mind to just this sort of possibility? Hadn't she slowly been convinced, by the vivid dreams, and the coming of Billy Smith, and finally that horrible place below the falls, that there were things she didn't understand? Unseen powers that could, and did, affect her life?

"Why didn't you tell us this before? If all this is true, why did you wait so long?"

Annie's face seemed to crumple. She turned away to face the jars, and seemed to search for something within them. "I am not so strong anymore," she said softly. "I am in great danger even talking to you now. They would take me if they could."

"Who?"

"The dead," she said again, simply. "They are restless, don't you see? They are watching us, even now."

A whisper of breeze from some unseen crack in the walls made the candles flicker, throwing moving shadows about the bookshelves and dusty old jars. Things moved and slithered about in the darkness. Angel suddenly felt as if she were standing on the edge of a hole so deep and wide she could not see the bottom. An image of her brother's face came to mind, not the way he looked when he was alive, but the way he looked in her dreams, the disease rampant in him, bloated and purple with seawater, his flesh slowly sliding away from his skull. His mouth a deep round hole, lipless, opening to speak, his jaws grinding with sand, and then . . . nothing.

"I'm sorry," she said, "I . . . I don't . . ."

Annie Arsenault was at her side in a flash, holding her in a grip that was surprisingly strong. Her flesh was dry and cool. The old woman led her over to the narrow bed and sat her down on it, then busied herself for several moments among the strange bottles and jars, moving from the desk to the shelves and back again. A moment later she returned with a small clay cup. "Drink this," she said. "It will help."

The liquid inside the cup was black and smelled faintly earthy like a strong tea. It was not an unpleasant smell; after a moment Angel closed her eyes and drank it down, and to her surprise the taste was quite sweet and spicy. *Apple cider,* she thought, *it tastes like warm apple cider . . .*

The old woman had pulled the chair from the desk over to the side of the bed, and now she sat perched on it. Angel felt a momentary dizziness, a smooth and powerful rushing sensation in her head, and then everything became curiously clear and sharp. She began to see more details in the room, as if the candles had gotten brighter, and her mind focused all at once. It was as if her insides had been given a thorough cleaning, top to bottom. She began to pick up faint signals from the woman across from her; not quite thoughts, but subtle images and shapes.

"Better?"

"Yes. It's as if I can tell what you're thinking."

Annie nodded, seemingly pleased. "It is one of the effects of the drink. We all have the ability, but in most it has been repressed to the point of uselessness." She nodded again. "In you that ability is strong, as it is in your . . . friend. You only need to learn how to draw it out."

"How do you know all this, Annie? Who *are* you?"

"You were right in one way about my son. His death changed me, made me see things in a new light. He had been taken by something I could not hope to overcome, that much I already knew. I felt it strongly. But what could I do? I turned to the church, and then when that did not comfort me enough, I studied my mother's books. I taught myself how to contact the dead. These are disappearing arts, scorned by modern society, just as hundreds of years ago they were feared. Years ago, one of my relations was hung for her beliefs. Now, I am simply ignored. Which is better? In the end, there is no difference; nobody listens."

*I didn't listen,* Angel thought, and suddenly she felt shameful and so very, very ignorant. All these things that had been happening to her, all the conversations between Billy and herself, how they had promised each other they would believe, and fight, when what they were really doing was engaging in disbelief. Constantly questioning, wondering, skeptical. *Who says there aren't such things as ghosts?* she wondered now. *Or demons, or witches, or any of those things we laugh at these days? Maybe they've just been waiting silently, patiently, for their time to come.*

She was picking up stronger signals from the old woman now; satisfaction, acceptance, relief. Annie Arsenault seemed to understand the change of heart in her young guest. She smiled, nodded. "When I contacted them, I found them to be different than I had thought . . . hungry. But once I had made contact, I could not turn them away. I have been haunted by them ever since." She shrugged. "Most are harmless, some are not. One, in particular, is very powerful. And he has found you. You have to understand. This place, it attracts them. The ground is ripe for it. And when they find a focal point, a way to get at the outside world . . ." She shrugged. "They will not stop."

"What can I do?" Angel whispered. "You must tell me why I've been brought to this place."

"That is not an easy thing to see or explain. There is a great division inside of you, and inside the man as well—a struggle for control. Your coming has been planned for a very long time; and yet, up until a few weeks ago I was not sure whether you would come at all. There are things that even my books do not explain, and things that are better left a mystery."

"But you said you would tell me what you know."

"You visited the place below the falls?"

"Yes."

"And it frightened you? Sickened you?"

"That's right."

"That is where the ground is at its worst. Terrible things have happened there, bloody things, but even before these things it was evil. The ground seeks them out and calls to them, the sick, the weak, and makes their sins fester and grow."

"You're talking about the murder," Angel said. "Ronnie Taylor murdering his wife."

The old woman stood up abruptly, moving toward the table. She picked up the book, studied it for a moment, and placed it gently on the table again. Next to it was a small flat dish, covered with a scattering of small bones. She scooped these up and tossed them down again, staring for a long time at the pattern they made on the white surface of the dish.

When she turned back and approached the bed her eyes were burning with intensity. "Ronnie Taylor was one of the most vulnerable, always searching for something to believe in. He fell into the hands of something he did not understand—and being feeble-minded, did not have the strength to fight it. *But he was not himself.* That you must understand, above all else. The dead had taken him."

"Possession?"

"In a way. They controlled him, in an effort to get what they wanted."

"And what do they want?"

"What they have always wanted," the old woman said simply. "Life."

*Life?* It seemed such an obvious thing, and yet it was horrible to imagine; what did that say about the afterlife? That the dead spent eternity wishing they could return? "I can't believe that," she said. "I won't believe it."

"Then you are lost." Annie sat down again in the chair, heavily, her age returning all at once. "We are all lost."

"Someone told me recently that the future has been set, and that we are here only to carry out the plan. But I don't believe it. If that's true, then there's no real sense going on, is there? I see myself changing things every day, altering what could have happened, changing a possible future into something new and different."

"Do you?" The old woman seemed genuinely surprised. "Or are you willing to see that as part of the plan, as you call it? How do you know you weren't supposed to change these things, that it was all preordained? And yet no one can see the future. We can only predict, and that is not always right. Little more than guesswork." Annie smiled again, but this time it was a tired smile, creasing her face and bringing dead white spots to her cheeks. "Remember the past, Gloria Johnson. That is written in stone. Do not try so hard to forget, and you will do well."

"You—how do you know my name?"

Annie shrugged. "There are things you would know about me, if you looked in the right places."

For a moment, Angel let the thoughts come. But as she did, she felt a great rush of things crowding hungrily at her, and she tightened up to shut them out because of the way it made her feel. Dirty, violated. Like she was losing control.

Annie had reached out and touched her arm. "What I have seen is not clear. You and your friend will each have to make a choice, and from these choices you will either save us, or destroy us. You will not understand what that choice is, or the role you are to play, until the end. You must trust your instincts when the time comes. It may be very painful for you, *but you must do it.* Do you understand?"

"What else?"

"The boy, Ronnie's son. Jeboriah Taylor. Even now he is succumbing to temptation. Do not let him make your choice for you. He will have his own struggle and his own demons. Much rests on the actions he takes, but not everything."

"And Billy?"

"Ah, yes." The old woman paused, looked away, as if studying something far out of sight. "You and he are close, eh? You have a special bond. William Smith has his own past to confront. He will come to understand things that will make him scream—but I do not think they will break him. He is stronger than he thinks."

When she turned to look at Angel again, her eyes were softer, filled with something like compassion. "The past is a long, flowing river. Things may be swept up and carried far downstream, and surface again in the future. Too many people forget their history, and don't know what to do when they face it again. You need to look into the past for the answers you seek, before they come looking for you."

"If I knew what those mistakes were—"

"I am a weak woman, old, brittle. Perhaps once I would

have been able to uncover it all." She shrugged. "I will tell you this. The dead are dangerous. They are hungry, and they are reaching out for us. Do you understand? One of them has found a way to return to this world. A portal. You must find it and destroy it, or the dead will rise and claim us. This town and everyone in it will be lost. We will see hell on earth."

And that was all. No matter what she said, she could not get Annie to speak again. The light had died in her eyes, and she seemed to withdraw into herself, once again becoming that crazy old woman who had approached them on the square. Or at least appearing to; Angel was not so sure it wasn't all an act, put on to fool a disbelieving world.

*The dead are reaching out for us.* When she climbed the stairs again, coming back up into the light, Angel remembered that phrase, and it kept repeating over and over again in her head.

*We will see hell on earth.*

She didn't know what it meant, but it frightened her, more than anything else she had ever heard. She thought of dead flesh in the moonlight, swollen fingers groping across a black screen, and shivered.

# Chapter Eleven

In the stifling heat of mid-afternoon, Harry Stowe climbed the front steps of the Taylor house and paused by the door. All was quiet inside, and he wondered again, as he had a hundred times during the past few hours, whether he was doing the right thing. Surely Ruth had to be told of her grandson's drinking. But was it his place to tell her? He wasn't sure.

Harry Stowe did not consider himself one to meddle in other people's business if he could help it—though, come to think of it, that was just what he had done with Billy Smith. *That was a special case,* he told himself. *Anyone could see that man needed help.*

But what kind of help did he need? A job, certainly, and that Harry had given him. The morning's work—Billy's first on the job—had gone extremely well. Billy had a way with the high school kids, seemed able to talk to them better than Harry could, maybe because Billy seemed a little shy and awkward himself and could relate to them. They had spent the morning getting him acquainted with the clinic, then the kids had come in for their spring physicals, and suddenly it had been lunchtime. After that they had spent some time catching up on the paperwork. Yes, it had gone just fine.

*Okay, so he had needed a job. What else?*

That was an interesting question. Billy Smith was an odd

duck, one of those people who always seemed to be hiding something deep inside. His eyes were deep and there was pain in them, so much so that Harry had found himself about to ask the same question time and time again; he had stopped himself before the words could come out. Billy would tell him about it when the time was right.

*He needs a friend.*

Okay, that could be done. And Harry Stowe was damn well going to do it. He wasn't sure why he felt so strongly, but he knew in his heart that Billy Smith was a decent man. He didn't have these kinds of hunches too often, but when he did he was always right. And right now that was good enough for him.

That left only one other thing bothering him, besides his coming meeting with Ruth Taylor; the matter of the unidentified bones that had disappeared this morning from the clinic's walk-in cooler. He had excavated the male remains from the unmarked grave with help from Bucky Tarr, and they had managed to get them out of the way in time for the reverend's burial service, and also managed to move them, more or less intact, from the coffin to the clinic. He wasn't sure he agreed with the sheriff's decision to move them in the first place (disturbing a grave, even an old and unmarked one, was never a good thing to do), but he hadn't said a word about it. He had found that dealings with Sheriff Pepper were best kept as short and painless as possible.

He had spent the next few days studying the bones and immediately made some odd discoveries. For one thing, unless he and Bucky Tarr had somehow disturbed the remains in the process of moving them (and he didn't think they had), the bones just hadn't been lying right in the grave. Either this mystery man had been beheaded and not put back together properly, or there had been some vandalism. As far as he could tell from the way the bones lay, the head had been turned around to face backwards in the coffin, and the hands had been severed and placed at the dead man's feet.

*So what? Maybe he was a thief, or a murderer. Maybe he sinned against the church. Maybe he asked to be buried that way. They had all sorts of strange rituals in those days.*

And yet, as he worked on them again yesterday and tried to get a fix on their age, alone in the empty, spacious cooler room, the strangest feeling had come over him. As if he were being watched. That was silly, of course. There was no one else in the building but him.

*That's how demons broke the necks of witches, you know, when they had used up their usefulness. Turned their heads completely around. And when they were found that way the people didn't burn the bodies, they cut off the witches' heads and kept them facedown in the coffin and buried them in an unmarked grave. It was supposed to keep them in the ground, where they belonged.* He didn't know where he had picked up that charming little bit of folklore. Read it in a book somewhere, he figured, though he couldn't remember exactly where. It didn't really matter; he didn't believe in that sort of crap. Of course, back then the people did believe in it, so maybe the mystery man in question had been accused of witchcraft. It was a place to start.

In all other matters he had been progressing quite quickly. He had pinned down the age of the male remains as somewhere around two hundred-fifty years (give or take thirty or forty), and the age at the time of death in the nineties or even a bit higher, which was extremely unusual for that time period. There was also evidence of slight deformities of the feet and hands. He thought that if he plowed through any town records remaining from the 1700s, he had a pretty good chance of putting a nametag on the unfortunate skeleton.

And then the "unfortunate skeleton" had up and walked away. Harry had gone into work early this morning, intent on cleaning things up a bit for Billy's arrival, and when he checked the cooler the bones were gone. Who would go to the trouble of stealing two hundred-fifty year old bones, he had no idea. Must have been some kind of nut who had gotten wind of the gruesome discovery. In any case, it raised a whole other can of worms; he would have to notify the sheriff of the theft, and forms would have to be filled out, etcetera, etcetera.

But now on to the business at hand, which he simply could not put off any longer. He took a deep breath, reached out and rang the doorbell.

A long, empty silence greeted him from inside. *Okay, so nobody's home. Fine. You didn't really want to do this anyway.*

He rang the bell again. This time there was a series of thumps, a crash, and a muffled oath from somewhere upstairs. More thumps, someone coming heavily and awkwardly down the stairs. The door opened a crack and Jeb Taylor blinked out at him through a pair of red-rimmed eyes. "Yeah?"

Stowe cleared his throat. "Is Ruth at home, Jeb? I wondered if I could speak with her."

There was a moment of silence, as Jeb regarded him with what could only be called suspicious eyes. "She's pretty out of it today, Doc. I . . . I don't know if she wants to see anyone."

"I'd like to talk with her just the same. Can you tell her I'm here?"

Jeb shrugged and disappeared, leaving Stowe standing on the doorstep. He waited. A minute passed, then another.

Finally Jeb reappeared and motioned him inside without a word. They passed through a darkened hall, past stairs leading up into the gloom. The house smelled stale. Dust lay over everything.

Ruth was in the living room, wearing a knitted red sweater and heavy skirt in spite of the heat, sitting in a chair near one of the only open, unshuttered windows. Sunlight drifted across a face that was empty and slack. He moved across the open floor as Jeb banged heavily back up the stairs behind him, leaving the two of them alone.

"Ruth? It's Doctor Stowe, Ruth, Harry Stowe."

Slowly her head turned to track him, but the eyes remained blank. "Norman? That you?"

He hesitated. "No, Ruth," he said, crouching by her side, gently taking her hand in his. "Not this time, honey. Norman's gone out for a while."

"Oh, yes." She sighed, seemingly relieved. "Would you like some tea?"

"Fine. I'll make us some."

"In the kitchen . . ."

He moved across the thin patch of sunlight and the faded red rug, past a series of boxes full of books by the bookcase, through an archway and into the dark kitchen. Fumbled around a moment in the gloom, found the lights, switched them on. Another minute or so to find the tea in the lower cupboard, and then he put the pot on to boil. Only then did he allow himself to get angry. The kitchen sink was filled with dirty dishes. The house was a shambles, dirty, depressing. The house needed light, fresh air, a new attitude, and Ruth needed care. Obviously, Jeb Taylor was in no shape to watch after her; he couldn't even watch after himself.

The water hissed, rolled inside the kettle, finally began

to shriek. He filled two cups, added some milk from the fridge, and carried them into the other room. Ruth hadn't moved, and so he pulled a small table and a chair over next to her and sat down, wondering what to say. He couldn't tell her what he had planned to tell her about Jeb, at least not while she was in her present state. What could she possibly do about it anyway? "Honey," he said, "I've brought you some tea . . ."

This time when she turned to look at him her eyes were more focused. "I could have gotten that myself. Don't you feel like you have to wait on me, Harry Stowe."

He smiled. "Good to see you, Ruth."

"Did you put milk in it?"

"I did."

She picked up the cup in slightly shaky hands, took a sip and put it back down. "Don't trust myself anymore. Likely to spill it right down my front."

"You look good, Ruth."

"Oh, don't lie to me. I know how I look. Like an old woman." She frowned, a little of the vagueness coming over her again. "I just can't seem to keep my mind on things. The sun is so nice here, isn't it?"

"It's a good spot. But you ought to open this place up a bit. Have some fresh air."

"Jeboriah likes it dark." An odd expression flitted across her face, as if she had just tasted something bitter and was not quite sure whether to swallow or spit it out. "Dark is the way he lives. Always been that way. Like his father."

"That's one of the reasons I came, Ruth," Stowe said. "I'm worried about him. He's been . . . drinking a bit. Down at the old schoolhouse."

"Jeboriah doesn't drink," she said sharply. "He knows better."

"I'm afraid it's true. I saw him there just last night. Looked like he'd been at it for a while."

"Is it the whiskey?"

"I think it is."

This time the expression on her face was of fear; she seemed to sink deeper into the chair. "He's found it," she whispered. "I can't fight it, Lord, not again, I won't—"

"I just want him to be careful," Stowe said, as gently as he could. "Believe me, I don't mean to hurt you with this or get Jeb into trouble. That's the last thing I want to do. I would have talked to him about it directly, but I didn't feel it was right without your permission. This is your business, and Jeb is a special case."

She kept muttering to herself, and he feared he had lost her. When the words finally trailed away and she took up her cup, her hands were shaking more violently. A bit of the tea slopped over the edge onto her wrist, and she gasped, before seeming to come to herself again. "Jeboriah's a good boy," she said.

"I know he is, Ruth—"

"I won't hear it!" she shrieked, her mouth opening and closing like a fish out of water. "I won't!" Her hand, which had been holding the cup of tea, jerked to the right, sending milky brown liquid splashing across the tabletop and onto the rug. Stowe moved to take the cup from her, but she held it in a grip so strong her bony knuckles had turned white. Little drops of tea were splattering across her wine-colored sweater and the back of her hand, blending with her mottled skin. Her breath was coming in shallow, rattling gasps.

"Take it easy, now," he said, wishing he had brought in a sedative. He wondered what kind of doctor would come in here and drop such a load on an old, feeble woman. How had he so badly underestimated things?

Just as he was thinking about bringing her into the clinic, her breathing began to ease and her grip on the teacup loosened until finally he was able to take it from her. She stared out into space, cocking her head as if listening to someone, then nodding. "Yes, Dear . . ."

He felt a chill in spite of himself. Fear was a funny thing, creeping up on you when you least expected it. He had seen plenty of people in various stages of senility, and many of them spoke to dead relatives or friends or even pets, but somehow with the dark, quiet house settling heavily around him, and the way she said it, as if her dead husband were hovering right here over his shoulder . . .

He touched her hand and then went quickly out to the car to get his bag, and as he passed the dark stairs to the second floor on his way back inside he stopped suddenly. Jeb Taylor was standing on the top step, unmoving, his face obscured by shadows. "How long has she been like this?" Stowe said angrily. "You should have called me."

He continued through the house without waiting for a reply, back into the living room where Ruth sat, muttering to herself. He prepared a light sedative. When he took her hand her flesh was cold and moist.

After the injection she seemed to quiet a bit more, her mouth moving now without speech, her eyes gaining that loose, vacant look they had held when he had first arrived. He grabbed some paper towels from the kitchen and mopped up the tea as best he could. As he was scrubbing uselessly at the rug he heard the front door slam and a car start in the drive, and then gravel thrown up by spinning tires.

There was no way to know how much of their earlier conversation Jeb had overheard. But did it really matter?

After all, Jeb needed to know people were worried about him. Stowe didn't want to be the bad guy here, but something had to be done. The boy was on the edge of something very bad, he could sense it. A feeling of unease came over him, all the more unsettling because he couldn't get a handle on it. The feeling of a train coming at him down the tracks, a long way from him yet, but coming fast.

And then there was Ruth. Giving up on the rug, he moved to the chair next to her, and sat holding her hand. She gave no sign that she had felt his touch, and continued to move her mouth noiselessly, pleading with a man who had been dead ten years or more. *True love never dies.*

But was that an expression of love passing across her face just now, or fear?

He sat with her quietly in the patch of afternoon sun, wondering what in the world he ought to do.

When Jeb Taylor arrived at *Johnny's*, the bar was almost empty. He took a seat and ordered a double shot of whiskey, then ordered another. His brain was on fire. *How dare he come into my house and stick his fucking nose into my business?*

*People been doing that all your life. Saying they know what's best for you, thinking they can control you. Passing it off as neighborly concern, when it's just plain arrogance.* How many times had he heard somebody telling him what to do, how to live his life? The doc had no right. He would drink if he wanted to drink. After all, he was over eighteen now, he was a man.

He'd downed four shots before he knew what was happening, and his head began to buzz comfortably. Stowe was an idiot, and Ruth was half-dead, and he didn't give a damn about either one of them. He'd been spending most of his time lately at the bar or holed up in his room. Closet door shut tight, chair pushed up against the handle, no way anything could get at him from there, no sir. Not that there was anything in there anyway.

As he felt more comfortably stoned, his mind drifted back to the week before. He saw Mrs. Friedman standing in front of him in her white tank top, and this time instead of running he tore the shirt off her, then unzipped himself and let her drop to her knees, her eyes growing wide as she took in the full length of him. “Fucking old bitch,” he said to the mostly empty room, ignoring the stare from the bartender. The truth was he couldn’t seem to get his mind off her. It was driving him crazy. Had she really wanted him?

Nobody had ever liked him before. No girls had flashed their little bitch glances at him from across the room or handed him their panties in the back of his car. No guys had asked him to go out drinking or shoot some baskets or grab a movie. He had always been alone.

For a moment he actually considered getting his ass up and going down to the clinic to see the doc, crazy as it sounded. There had to be some pills he could take, something to stop this maddening chatter in his head. But what would he say, anyway? *Excuse me, Doc, I was wondering—I think maybe I’m losing my mind. Do you think you could give me something? Maybe I could pick it up at the drugstore on my way back home?*

He stayed at the bar and continued to drink, imagining his skin turning blue and then black, his hair falling out and dissolving, his eyebrows and fingernails too. Finally his teeth would become as loose as kernels of old corn and pop out, one by one. An hour later his bladder was screaming at him. He got up and steadied himself against the wall until a wave of dizziness passed, then shuffled down to the bathroom. Standing at the urinal he had a sudden, brilliant idea. Struck him like a bolt of lightning from the sky. Heat lightning. Mrs. Friedman was driving him crazy, wasn't she? And that was her fault, wasn't it? Yes. She had been the one coming on to him.

*The chandelier in the dining room has burned out and I need to get the ladder from the basement. We're having a dinner for friends.*

That dinner was tonight. Slowly the idea took on shape. Oh, it was perfect. Just perfect. That burning heat in his stomach flared up again, the blood pumping. Thrilled, he finished relieving himself, shook, and went back down the hall to the door.

In the parking lot, he slipped behind the wheel. As the sun set he felt the first touches of another cold night in the air. It was incredible how fast the temperature dropped these days; one minute he would be sweating his balls off, the next his teeth would be chattering. *Should have brought a jacket,* he thought. But maybe he wouldn't even notice the cold. He would be having too much fun.

At the edge of the lot he hesitated. The Friedman house was just a mile or two up the road, but the setting sun was still lightening the sky and he wanted a little more darkness for this one. He drove to the grocery store for a six-pack of Budweiser, loitered for a few minutes until the clerk told him to leave, then drove back past his house, past the Friedman's (he could just see the circular drive from Route 117, and it was empty), and parked up the road on an old logging track he used to walk down when he was a kid. The ground was freezing up again, and he knew he wouldn't have any trouble getting out of there later even though the mud was thick. Then he took the beer and crossed over the road to the woods, and from there worked his way down until he could see the lights of the Friedman's big house. The whiskey he had swallowed at *Johnny's* kept him warm and made his head thump pleasantly. He was surprised that he had been able to keep the liquor down, but it had been getting easier lately.

*Yes sir, Jeb my boy, you're a man now. Got a man's drinking habits and a man's constitution to go along with 'em. I'm proud of you, son, real proud.*

That voice had sounded like his father; in fact, come to think of it, quite a few of the voices he had been hearing lately sounded like his father. He wondered why he would hear that voice now, after all these years, but the answer, he decided, was simple. His father had just died and things were fresh in his mind.

And the suitcase.

*Go home and open it, Jeb. Forget about this goddamned kid prank. There's better things to do than this silly crap you got your mind set on. Go straight home and open up that suitcase and I'll tell you about 'em.*

Jeb Taylor shook his head hard from side to side like a dog trying to lose a few fleas. He popped the top on one of the cold beers, took a long swig, and felt better. That was just what he needed. Now he could think straight. Mrs. Friedman's breasts were in his mind again, sliding nicely against their cloth harness. Just out of reach.

He skirted the back of the storage shed where they kept the weed-eater and the mower, grass seed, bags of manure and other things, and slipped around the edge of the property to the rear of the house. Across the dark lawn he could see the outline of the garden, and above it, rising like the mast of a ship, the oak tree. Beyond that he could see the house and the lights on the first and second floor.

Feeling that tingle of anticipation below his gut, he

downed the beer, tossed the can aside, and hooked the empty plastic circle in the six-pack around his right hand. He sprinted across the soggy ground, stumbled, fell heavily to his knees a few feet before the tree, and crawled the rest of the way, feeling the icy cold of the muddy ground soak through his pants. *Jesus, what a shitty lawn,* he thought, *who the fuck takes care of this place?* And laughed out loud. A couple of hard kicks dug up the lawn even more. Satisfied for now with the mess he had made, he turned back to the job at hand. The first branch of the tree hung down about a foot over his head, a good, solid-looking one. He reached up, hooked his arms around it and struggled awkwardly up the tree trunk, his feet in their muddy Converse high-tops slipping and sliding against bark. The six-pack of beer kept bumping him in the head, but he wasn't going to throw that away, no sir.

The rest of the way up was easy. The oak was a perfect climber, branches large and flat and spaced just about right, *even for a drunk like me.* Whenever he slipped the branches seemed to catch him like gentle arms. When he reached the level of the window, he propped himself up with his back against the trunk and his legs hanging down and opened another can of beer. The can exploded in his hand, sending froth down over his arm and legs, and he guzzled it eagerly like a newborn at his mother's tit.

Finally he turned to the window, and wished he had brought a pair of binoculars with him. The distance from the tree to the house was about fifty feet, just enough to frustrate him a little. But otherwise, the view he had was perfect. The window was actually a few inches lower than where he sat, and he could look directly into the Friedman's bedroom.

The bed was against the right wall, instead of the left one

like he remembered. He could just see the foot of it and a black dress draped over the side. A large round mirror hung on the wall across from the window, above a wooden table and chair. A few odds and ends sat on the tabletop. This was where Mrs. Friedman would sit after her bath to comb out her hair and put on makeup, perfume, earrings. Staring at herself in the mirror, making herself look pretty for him. *That's right, for me, not that big fat balding piece of shit she calls her husband, the guy who slinks around at night alone instead of fucking her.*

He sat in the tree, playing out his fantasy. Mrs. Friedman coming to meet him at the door after a long day in the office, meeting him with hugs and kisses and wearing a long flowing red slip with a slit up the side. *Welcome home, darling. I've cooked a big dinner for us. But first, I just can't wait. I've missed you.*

Taking him by the hand and leading him upstairs—

And then it happened. By God, he had timed it just right. Out she came from the bathroom, her hair wet and shining, her skin glowing in the yellow light of the bedroom, and, sweet Jesus, she was completely naked. He could see her big, soft breasts and dark nipples as she turned for a moment toward the window, her slightly rounded belly. She paused as if posing for him, and he wished again for a pair of binoculars, so he could see her better.

Then he saw her turn and face someone who had come into the bedroom, and a moment later Pat Friedman walked past the window.

That ruined everything. Jeb swore under his breath, and continued to watch as Mrs. Friedman sat down at her vanity table and picked up the hairbrush. But now he had a queasy feeling in his stomach. Pat Friedman, the town lawyer, a little chubby, thinning gray hair. He was the real husband in our little drama, wasn't he?

Even if he was a spineless piece of shit.

It looked like they were arguing. Mrs. Friedman put the brush down hard on the table and when he put his hand on her shoulder she shrugged it away and stood up, walking out of sight. A moment later she came back into the picture wearing black panties and carrying a bra, which she hooked her arms through and fastened in back. Finally she picked up the dress from the bed and stepped into it.

Jeb cracked another beer and let the foam run this time. His good mood had vanished suddenly, replaced with dark storm clouds in his head. Nothing seemed to make sense to him anymore, and he wondered when this slow unraveling had begun to happen. Had it begun the other day, when Mrs. Friedman had asked him to help with the ladder? Had it begun just a few nights ago (seemed like a year ago now) when he had stopped in at *Johnny's* for a beer after work? Had it begun before that, with the trip up to the State Prison?

Or had it really begun years ago, one afternoon when he was seven years old, when the blood wouldn't come out of his hair and his world seemed to come crashing down?

Here he was, an eighteen-year-old man, nineteen in July, sitting up in a fucking oak tree playing peeping Tom, drunk on beer and whiskey. Living with his grandmother, too scared to tell the old bitch to lay off, too lazy to take care of her when she needed it. The people of White Falls might have thought him slow, or ignorant, or "disadvantaged," or whatever the hell they called it these days, but Jeb Taylor knew the truth. He was smart enough, and always had been. Maybe even smarter than most folks in his own way. He just couldn't relate to people. Even way back in school, when little boys were supposed to be making friends, he was the one sitting in the lunchroom corner alone. Hearing the voices of the other children, in their childish way, relentless; Dickey Pritchard and Marcy Stone were the worst, big mean Dickey Pritchard, who now worked for his father at the garage across from the high school, calling him "daddy's boy" and "dummy" and "retard." Marcy Stone passing him notes and then laughing in his face with her girlfriends when he got up the courage to go over and talk to her. Name-calling on the playground at recess, nobody letting "the stupid kid" play because he couldn't learn the game. When the teacher called on him in class for the answer, he couldn't open his mouth to tell her. He would just sit there like a *dummy, yes, just what they called me, a dummy,* until she sighed and shook her head and called on someone else.

Sometimes she'd pull him aside after class, and ask him why he wouldn't say anything during the studies, and he'd just shake his head. What could he say? *I just watched my daddy beat my mommy over the head with a broom until he cracked her skull, Miss Hennin, and the other boys won't let up on me, calling me names, and the girls too, telling me my daddy's a killer, telling me he's going to hell. Don't feel much like talking right now, Miss Hennin.* No. Better just to keep his mouth shut. After a while, she stopped asking. And life went on.

Jeb looked down through a fog of booze and realized he had finished the whole six-pack and was left holding the plastic husk. His right leg had fallen asleep and he moved it carefully, feeling the pins and needles start up. The bark of the tree was so cold against his back he was afraid he was frozen to it and someone would have to climb up with a spatula to get him off. That would be quite a scene, now, wouldn't it? Half the town gathered around on the Friedman's lawn to see the dumb kid who'd stuck himself to the oak tree, trying to catch a glimpse of a little pussy.

He looked over at the dark bedroom window. Where the hell had they gone?

Jeb unwound his arms from the tree branch and climbed back down until he was standing on the ground again. Beer cans, some whole, some crushed in a way he couldn't remember doing, littered the frosted grass around him.

He felt like he had been cheated out of something and it left a sour taste in his mouth. He looked around. For a moment he expected to see, lurching toward him through the darkness, the townspeople of White Falls; not whole and healthy but walking corpses, hands out and hungry. Dickey Pritchard and Marcy Stone leading the others. *Come here, Taylor boy. We've got something for you, dummy. We don't tolerate your kind around here.*

He blinked. Nothing there but a half-finished garden and a bunch of his own tracks in the mud.

He worked his way over nearer the house. All the lights were burning on the first floor now. He caught a glimpse of movement in the living room, slipped a little closer, a little closer, until he was right up against the wall and an open window. He could hear voices inside.

"I don't understand why you don't just call him," Pat Friedman was saying. "If somebody doesn't show up for work, isn't that what you do?"

"I just don't think I should. I don't want to bother him. Maybe he's sick. Lots of people are coming down with colds right now. He'll call me when he's ready."

"But we *pay* him to come to work. I mean, he does work for us, doesn't he?"

"Don't be an ass."

"An *ass?* I'm sorry, I wasn't aware I was being an *ass.* I thought I was pointing out an obvious answer to the problem. People just don't do what he did. I mean, if they want to keep their job, they show up for work when they're supposed to. He's only been working here for a few weeks, for Christ's sake. I hired him because I thought it might help him get straightened out. But I am so sick of everyone walking on eggshells around that kid—"

"First of all, he's *not* a kid, he's eighteen years old. And if people walk on eggshells around him, maybe it's because his father just fucking died—"

"Oh, come off it. He hasn't seen his father in ten fucking years."

"You know, sometimes you are the most insensitive pig—"

The doorbell rang. "Jesus . . . okay. I want this to end, right now . . ." They moved away and Jeb couldn't hear any more.

He stumbled away from the wall. A cold feeling gathered in the center of his body and sat there, weighing him down. All this time he had been fantasizing about Mrs. Friedman, but he'd never really thought—couldn't imagine that they would actually talk about him. Not like that. As if he were some kind of . . . mental patient.

He heard more voices at the front door, muffled greetings. He could hear more cars crunching along the gravel drive. Someone was going to see him out here. He had to move.

He trudged off through the cold and the quickly hardening mud to the road, walking right up the yellow line until he reached the logging track and his car. He had come to watch Mrs. Friedman get dressed and to tear up the garden a little and get revenge for whatever slight he felt had been given him. But now he felt like an outsider, a loser—worse, the crazy kid who needed handouts and special favors. When had he ever had any friends? Could he count Dick Pritchard, the boy who called him "retard?" Or Marcy Stone, the girl who had passed him a note saying, *I like you. Do you like me?* And then laughed out loud and said, "not!" when he came up to her, stuttering and red-faced?

Maybe he could count Mrs. Friedman. Julie. But the way she had talked about him just now, it was like she felt sorry for him. He didn't need anyone's charity, not for a job, and not for . . . whatever she thought she had been doing the other day. Would she really have done anything with him that afternoon? Or was she just trying to make him feel more comfortable, less like a freak? The more he thought about it, the more he wondered. Hell, maybe she was making fun of him like all the rest. Had a good laugh after he left. Probably told all her friends.

He got in the car and started it up, spinning the tires and spraying frozen mud up into the floorboards. The big car slid, caught itself, squealed out onto solid tar. He leaned over and switched on the radio. There was something rolling around on the floor under his feet, and he reached down and picked it up; a bottle of whiskey with a couple of swallows left in the bottom. He twisted the top, tossed it aside and drank the fiery liquid in one long gulp.

When he got home, the house was dark. He parked in his usual spot near the front door and stumbled through the hall to the stairs, not wanting to turn on the lights. His head was spinning again, and something was at work on him, an eagerness that hadn't been there before. *Do it,* a voice whispered, and this time it was his voice, only his, echoing through the dark chambers of his mind.

He climbed the stairs quickly, holding onto the railing for support, and now he let his thoughts drift back to his father for the first time in years, allowing himself free rein. His father who had worked for a living until the mill shut down; coming home with the stink of sulfur and wood in his hair, swinging his empty lunch pail. To Jeb he had been the largest, strongest man alive, capable of anything. And later, his father stumbling in during the early morning hours, his voice loud in the quiet house. Still the biggest man in the world, as dangerous now as a cornered animal. Telling his mother to "shut the fuck up and let him alone," he was only out doing what men do; Jeb knew where he had been, oh yes, he'd been out at the old schoolhouse drinking that drink that lingered on his breath, that sweet-sour smell that remained on his clothes and in his car. And hadn't Jeb wanted to be like his father when he grew up? Hadn't he admired his father, the way Ronnie Taylor took control and didn't let his wife "push him around" like so many other wives pushed around their husbands?

In his room he paused, pale moonlight filtering through the window. The closet door was open a crack. Had he left it like that? He couldn't seem to remember.

Blackness inside. Jeb Taylor stood in a moment of sober clarity and looked at the closet door. As he stood there wide-eyed, the door swung outward on its own until it hit the wall with a quiet thump.

*Come on inside, Jeboriah.* This time it was his father again, speaking to him, standing back in the dark. *I been waiting for you.*

He moved to the open doorway and kneeled in the blackness. His mind was completely empty now, except for the hunger that ate at his insides like acid. He was unaware that he was grinning. The effect was like skin stretched tight over an empty skull.

*Hurry boy, hurry . . .*

Jeb reached into the shadows, felt under the pile of clothes and drew out the suitcase. It was an ordinary case, brown pebbled cover, not real leather of course, they couldn't have afforded that; two latches, one on either side, and a combination lock in the center with the numbers all lined up zeros. Cheap lock, easy to break, all he needed was a screwdriver.

But it wouldn't be locked, would it? Of course not.

He unsnapped the latches, one by one, and it swung open easily, as if there was something inside pushing to get out. He stared down at the contents of the case, a lump in his throat. An old sports almanac and a couple of girly magazines from the '70s, a picture in a cheap silver frame (of him as a boy, he saw with dull surprise), clothes underneath, a pair of faded corduroys that smelled like dust, a black leather jacket he remembered his father used to wear when he went out driving or down to *Johnny's* in the evening, a heavy blue work shirt. When he pulled out the shirt he almost tossed it aside before his fingers brushed the pocket and he felt something cold and hard.

His heart thumped crazily in his chest. Something wrapped in a yellowed piece of newspaper, a round, clumsily fashioned piece of stone. Its weight was more than seemed possible, considering the size of it. The weight was perfectly balanced, drawing it evenly down toward the floor.

He stared at it. Two serpents wrapped around each other with their tails in their mouths, fascinating yet somehow repulsive. The eyes were drawn to them, the way they circled without end, and oh, you could lose yourself in those two twisting shapes, and if you stared hard enough they almost seemed to move, to slither across the cold stone, to open their fanged and bloody mouths . . .

Now something else spoke up in his mind, something new, a desperate sounding voice full of fear. This voice was sober and small and urgent. *This is your last chance,* it said. *If you surrender to it, there's no turning back. It will sit for a while and brood, and you'll hardly notice that it's there, but soon you won't be yourself anymore, no more Jeb Taylor, not really, you might think you control it for a while but one day it will wake up and eat you ALIVE—*

But that voice was weak. He had nothing to look forward to as Jeb Taylor. When had he ever been himself, anyway? Hadn't he been meant for this all along, hadn't he felt as if he were just going through life's motions, waiting for something else? He sensed something larger just around the corner. Revenge. Control. Power.

The hole in the amulet was strung through with some kind of braided rope, cool and slick to the touch. Jeb slipped the cold heavy stone up and over his head, feeling the steady pull as it settled around his neck. He opened his shirt to let it in and when it touched his skin, *oh Jesus, Jesus God,* the stone seemed to jump and pulse like a living thing. He looked into the dark closet and saw hands raised and clenched, holding something out over fire and dripping blood, dark hooded figures swaying in the light of the dancing flames. Chanting seemed to fill the darkness and throb in rhythm with the light. The flash of a silver blade whistling down through air. A dark man standing at the edges of the fire, arms crossed, watching.

Sudden, searing heat, and the thing wriggled against his skin. Unable to help himself, he cried out and made as if to tear it away. Then he stopped, because the amulet was cold and the room was dark and normal again.

Breathing hard, Jeb Taylor kneeled at the mouth of his open closet, his hand poised to rip the amulet off and throw it across the room. But it was nothing but cold hard stone, a little heavy, maybe, but just a piece of rock, and he was fine, he was cool, he was smooth, he was slow and in control.

Something caught his eye. He reached down to smooth the yellow newspaper from 1986 on the threadbare rug. Handwriting there, on a blank part of the page. The writing was old and faded, but he could read it clearly in the light of the window.

> so you finally got here boy well it's about fucking time. like i said i been waiting a while. i got a lot of plans for you boy and ain't they good, and you can have all you want too. just wait a little longer and I'll show you. ain't we gonna have some fun.
>
> welcome to the party, boy. welcome to the party.
>
> your pop ronnie.

Jeb stood up and swayed in the gray moonlight. The amulet swung against his chest. His head was full and fuzzy again and he felt the booze deadening his limbs. Had he really cried out? It seemed that he had. He listened for a long time, straining to hear around the thump and swish of the blood in his veins, waiting to hear footsteps in the hall and Gramma Ruth's voice. But the house was quiet as a tomb.

Something else, half-buried under the frenzied mess he had made, pulling clothes out of the suitcase. A bit of white sticking out. He kneeled again, pawed at the jacket, shirt, uncovering whatever it was he had seen.

A pile of bones and a skull, staring back at him with empty eye sockets.

* * * * *

Across town, Annie Arsenault came wide-awake in the pitch black of her basement room, her heart thudding in her chest. For a moment the fiery red eyes continued to stare down at her from the depths of her dream, and then they faded away, leaving the acid taste of fear in her mouth. She knew what that dream meant.

She did something she hadn't done in years. She got up out of bed and knelt in the darkness, ignoring the ache in her old bones and the mossy scents of her dusty jars and ancient books, and she prayed for strength to a Christian God she no longer really believed in, prayed for the soul of a town she had lived in since birth. The only home she had ever known.

Her prayers would go unanswered.

# PART THREE:

# BLOODSTONE

"Father, if it is Your will, take this cup away from Me . . . And being in agony, He prayed more earnestly. Then His sweat became like great drops of blood falling down to the ground.

*—Luke 22:42–44*

From the diary entry of Mr. Frederick Thomas:

*April 30th, 1727*

*It is near the end of the month of April, the spring rains are upon us, and I am all but lost. Dear God (dare I mention that name?), how can I record all that has happened these past few months? And yet I feel that I must, or risk the last vestiges of my own sanity . . .*

*Oh, Hennie, how I wish that I had confided in you and sent those letters, and that you were here now as you had planned to be. But I did not want to worry you, and I feared you would think me insane, reading what I had written about ghosts and corpses and dark men coming in the dead hours of the night, and charms (or damned things, as they should rightly be called) coming to life and pulsing like the bloody heart of a demon. If only I were insane! But insanity is a mere refuge the mind takes when confronted with things such as I have seen, I am convinced of that, and it cannot be called up at will. How I have tried to lose myself in these thoughts, and let myself believe that I am in the grip of a brain-fever that has held sway ever since I stepped off that ship almost a full year ago. And yet in my heart I cannot believe it to be true; the work continues around me, and every day there is a new wonder to appreciate in town, a town office and meeting house and the beginnings of industry, and in all other aspects life goes on.*

*It is light now, and the horrible dark dreams have left me, and so I must try to relate what has happened as best I can, in order to complete a record, if only for the benefit of others after I am gone. It must be done now, for I fear that by nightfall I will no longer be able to resist and will be taken once and for all, as the new month of May begins the Roman celebration of*

*Lemuria, the festival of the unhappy dead. It is this which I am afraid the creatures have been waiting for since All Hallows Eve, and my heart speeds with dread to think of what may come of all of it.*

*Where to begin? I suppose I must start by accounting my own investigations, which began near the end of October and ended only a few short days ago, in the muck of that damned place below the falls. After the series of unsettling dreams about the man who had appeared in my chambers, and the odd reactions of my charm to his unholy presence, I began to search for any possible explanations that might be found, all the while dreading the coming of night and the dreams which accompanied it, which were becoming progressively wilder and more vivid. I sent a man whom I trusted to the colony in search of books on the occult, but I was hesitant to explain myself fully to him, in light of the recent incidents at Salem and the tendencies of the people to condemn one another at the mere mention of witchcraft and the black arts. Nevertheless, I felt I must do something, and so I sent him with enough money and a silly little story about research and the writing of a book of my own. He returned with more than I had hoped for, saying that he had encountered a man (or, more properly, a man had encountered him) the very first night in town, who had bought him a drink, and had offered to sell any number of books on that subject, of those that he had available to him. This mysterious man, whom my messenger described as having strangely hypnotic features and an unsettling way about him, had been out walking late, supposedly in search of good wine and conversation.*

*The coincidence is more than suspicious, and the books offered were all kinds of rare and ancient texts. Can there be any doubt, knowing what I know now, who this man was, and what he was (and is) after? Or that he was a man at all? I shudder to think of it.*

*In these dark books I found more than explanations; I found my worst fears confirmed. They describe all manner of wicked rituals and gibbering demons, as well as the necessary articles required to call them to life. What this cursed charm around my neck embodies can no longer be in doubt, for it is ancient, the very essence of all that is evil in this world! And yet, God forgive me, I do not have the strength to take it off, for it has a hold on me I cannot break. In the dead of night I have heard the most seductive whispers, and promises of what I may become and may hope to command, and I am weak, and so very small in the face of such things.*

*And yet it is worse by the day, and I do not know what to do about it. How am I to feel upon waking in the midnight of my own private rooms, with this thing wriggling against my neck and a series of unknown and unthinkable words upon my lips? Or worse, coming to my senses and finding myself out of my bed, dirt caked upon my naked feet and blood on my hands, with no idea where I have been or what I have been doing?*

*Still, I continued to read the devilish books through the long cold winter, gaining a kind of morbid fascination and satisfaction from them, and when I encountered a man from Salem, who had recently passed through our village in search of work during the first thaw, I interrogated him for hours without thought of the consequences, consumed with the need to know everything about those brutal trials several decades previous, and all that surrounded them. He did not know much, only that many men and women had died, and that it all seemed a lot of craziness to him. I passed my eagerness off with a general reference to research and the writing of my own book on the subject, but still he looked at me strangely, and I was glad when he left town without mentioning our conversation to anyone.*

*Since that time, I have begun awakening in odd places as I have said, after having had those terrible dreams, with no idea how I arrived there, but only with the most burning feeling of impatience and need. The last and most horrible of these places I have visited three nights in a row now; I have come to my senses standing in the freezing cold in my undergarments, my legs buried almost to the knees in filthy black mud, looking out over the darkest stretch of foul water one can imagine. It was only after considerable distress and reflection that first night that I came to realize I was in the midst of the boggy land below the falls. How I had arrived there in my sleep, through the dense tangle of brush and fallen trees, I cannot guess, but always when I awake I am filled with a hunger that no amount of food and drink will satisfy.*

*This very moment I remain alone in my new home, as the rains beat against the roof, and I feel the hunger for it growing once again in my belly, urging me to leave this place and go out into the weather to find . . . what? What is calling to me down there, and why am I unable to resist the temptation to discover it? This I cannot hope to know, though I sense that the very ground there is rotten. I have felt places such as this before, though I have never given them much thought.*

*But now, I wonder. Are there truly evil places, as there are evil people? Places that, through some obscure coincidence of time and space, act as a kind of unholy magnet, drawing into themselves the blackest thoughts and deeds of mankind? I cannot hope to know the truth, or perhaps I fear to know it; but this I do know, that I must somehow find the strength to fight away this demon, and I must find a way to get word to you, my Hennie, and keep you from coming to this place.*

*If you do, the good Lord help us, if you do I do not know but of what hell will come.*

# Chapter Twelve

In the early hours of the following Tuesday morning Billy Smith came quickly and gaspingly awake from another vivid dream. He and Angel were being chased down a dark passage by something monstrous. He looked back; the creature was snapping at their heels, the hair of its long, ugly snout stained red with blood, round yellow eyes shining like two lamps in the darkness. They rounded a corner, and in front of them the ground gave a sudden, violent heave. For a moment he thought of lava forcing itself through subterranean cracks, spewing forth a geyser that would consume them. Then he saw the skeletal hands, reaching, bodies pulling themselves up out of the black earth. Thousands of them; one stepping forward, cleaner and more whole than the rest, his face wasted by some pestilence, eyes like a hawk, hooded and yet familiar.

When he turned to Angel, her mouth was hanging open in an expression of surprise and puzzlement. She frowned, and then lifted up her shirt with one hand. Surprise turned to pain, her lips making a round, red "oh" as her chest split and opened wide. He caught a glimpse of something that wriggled and twisted and turned.

That was when he woke up, clutching the sheets in tight, sweaty palms. He glanced across the bed to where Angel slept on her side, her back to him. He could see her soft, round hips and the curve of her shoulder, and just the top of her head where it protruded from under the blankets. She was sleeping peacefully, thank God. He wanted to hold her in his arms again, feel her touch. But he would not wake her.

Silently, patiently, he waited for the dawn.

That night they sat again at a corner table in the dining room of the Old Mill Inn. There were three other patrons for dinner, all of them far enough away to be out of earshot. "So now what," Angel said, reaching across the table and taking his hand. "You've got yourself a job, and I'm running around talking to crazy old women and researching old books. Neither of us knows what the hell is really going on. We're not any closer to figuring things out than when we got here, are we?"

He shook his head. He wasn't so sure about that. She had told him about her trip to the historical society when he returned from work Thursday night, told him everything Annie had said in great detail. He remembered the way the old woman had looked at him that day on the square; something in her gaze had made him stop short. *The look of recognition.* It was as if she had been waiting for him, all this time. What was it she had said? *You have come back.*

"Annie knows more than she told you. She's got to. I mean, who better to figure out voices and demons and the occult than a witch? If that's what she is."

"She certainly thinks so. I'm telling you, she had me believing it too."

"All right. Let's say then, for argument's sake, that she does have some inside knowledge on why we were both brought here. What exactly did she say to you? Maybe we're missing something."

"She knew why I was there. Knew about the dreams

we've been having. She wanted to tell me about the Taylor family."

"So whatever is happening to us involves the Taylors too. We had a good idea about that already. What else?"

"She said the town was sick. Under the control of something she described as 'pure evil.' Or maybe someone. She said we were a part of it. And she was scared too."

"Of what?"

"The dead. She said they were watching us, reaching out for us. And she said that we would have a choice to make, and that it wouldn't be clear until the end what we would need to do." Angel shook her head. "I don't know. Remembering it all now, it seems crazy. But I know that when I was in that basement with her I believed every word."

Smith had read the old newspaper articles Angel brought him from her visit to the historical society. *The break-in at the old mansion in the square. The death of Norman Taylor, and the murder of Sharon.* He had stared at the grainy newsprint photograph of Ronnie Taylor for a very long time, finding something that intrigued him, though he wasn't sure just what. A look about those eyes, such power and malice in them, visible even through the camera lens and across the thousands of hours that had passed since the photo was taken.

And somewhere close by, Ronnie's firstborn son. On the edge of something that could tear him apart. Such rage inside of him, surely. Billy could almost feel it himself, a burning, twisting fist in the guts. Such pain.

He and Angel had made love every night, and sometimes in the mornings, their bodies held tight and close. He felt that heavy knot inside loosening still more, the dam cracking, getting ready to give way and unleash a flood of forgotten feelings and banished thoughts. It had been so long since he had allowed himself to be truly vulnerable to someone else, and he wondered what would happen when the knot slipped its final coil; if the wave, when it came, would be so strong it would sweep him away. Yet he wanted it. Never had he wanted anything so badly. He had been alone too long.

After a half-day of work at the clinic, Smith had returned to the empty hotel room and got out the old newspaper articles again. Angel had been feeling a little under the weather, and was sleeping in the adjoining room (she had been sleeping a lot the past few days, seemingly able to leave everything behind, finding escape in a world without dreams. In a way, he envied her). He reread the articles. More and more his eyes were drawn to the one about the burglary of the Thomas place, and the related story of the amulet.

The professor quoted in the story caught his attention. He placed a call to information, asking for the number for Professor David Rutherford. It was a long shot, to say the least; the article quoting Rutherford was written years ago. He might have an unlisted number, moved, or even died.

But he got lucky. A moment later the operator said "thank you" and he heard the electronic voice giving him a number.

Dr. Rutherford answered on the third ring. Smith introduced himself, heard a moment's questioning pause, and wondered where to begin. He couldn't tell the doctor anything over the phone. Hell, he didn't even know what he wanted to say yet. He made up something about doing research for a book, and asked to meet with the doctor that afternoon. To his surprise, Rutherford readily agreed.

After he hung up, he peeked into the adjoining room. Angel had not stirred. Deciding to let her sleep, he climbed into the car, rolled down the windows to get a breeze, and headed for Brunswick alone.

Dr. David Rutherford lived in a sprawling three-story Colonial off Main Street. It seemed that Rutherford was something of a local celebrity. Grew up in Brunswick, taught at Harvard for twenty years, published numerous articles and three fairly well-known books on ancient cultures. Still lectured occasionally at Bowdoin College, which was located just a mile down the street.

Rutherford was not at all what Smith expected. He was a tall, well-built man with long, curly hair pulled back into a ponytail that lay like a fat gray snake on his shoulder. He sported a thick mustache and came to the door in a pair of Levi's and a plaid shirt. He showed Smith into a large, high-ceilinged living room. They sat in comfortable, overstuffed chairs. One wall of the room was lined with leather-bound books on mahogany shelves. Dr. Rutherford caught him looking. "Those are the boring ones. I keep everything interesting under lock and key." He smiled, and the expression brought life to his face and softened his eyes so that he looked much younger. "I've gathered a pretty substantial collection over the years. A lot of them belonged to my father, actually; he worked at B.I.W. down the road, but he was a closet reader. I guess it rubbed off." He settled deeper into his chair. "So, Mr. Smith. What can I do for you?"

"I'm afraid I lied to you over the phone," Smith said. This was the hard part, he thought; how to tell a former Harvard professor that his dreams were being haunted by the walking dead, without being laughed at, or worse, being thrown out on his ear. He wished he had a drink now; his throat ached for the burn. And then quickly wished it away; *never, never again.*

"I told you I was writing a book. I'm not."

"I see." Apparently Dr. Rutherford was not the questioning type. He sat back and waited.

"The real truth . . . the real truth is a bit more complicated."

Rutherford smiled again. "I took a look out the window when you drove up. California plates? That's quite a trip. It would be a shame if you came all this way just to lie to me."

Smith took the articles out of his pocket and handed the first of them to the older man. "Do you remember this robbery?"

Rutherford studied the article and nodded. "Yes, I do. Henry Thomas had a beautiful collection, the Louis XIV amulet being the best among them. I did some research for him when he first discovered it in the basement of the family home, as I recall. I tried hard to get him to donate it to a museum where it could be better tested and protected, but he refused. Thomas was something of an eccentric."

"The newspaper articles say that its origins were never accurately traced."

"Well, that true, to a point." Rutherford was nodding again. "Although I have seen similar designs before. I wouldn't want to swear it in court, but if it's genuine, I now believe that amulet was Egyptian."

"That makes it what, three, four thousand years old? How could it possibly have survived to make it over here?"

"No real mystery. There are plenty of relics from that period in museums all over the world. The ancient Egyptians were an extremely successful culture. I don't have the slightest idea how something like that got into the basement of a resident of Maine in the twentieth century. But I suppose anything's possible."

"Do you know anything more about it? What it was used for, that sort of thing?"

"That amulet was used mainly for burial purposes, placed around the neck of the dead man to assist him in the afterlife. That particular amulet was quite rare." Rutherford frowned. "Now, really, I must ask—what's this all about?"

Smith handed him the article about Norman Taylor's death, and finally, the murder of Sharon Taylor. The older man read them in silence, then looked at him curiously.

"Sorry, I don't see the connection."

"A lot of people believe Ronnie Taylor was the one responsible for the break-in at the home of Henry Thomas."

"And where is this Ronnie Taylor now?"

"He died in prison a couple of weeks ago. Ronnie murdered at least one and possibly two people soon after he stole that amulet. People noticed a change in him, the way he acted, the way he carried himself. Let's say it was a psychological affect. He believed in what the amulet could do, and it gave him the courage to start acting out. Asserting his control."

"That's a possibility," the older man said, nodding. "I have heard of these relics being used in black mass ceremonies, devil worship, that sort of thing. And they still haven't found the piece?"

"No. But I believe it's still around. It's a pretty safe bet that Ronnie's son may have possession of it. He's been acting very odd lately, under a lot of stress. Isn't it possible that Ronnie might have passed these beliefs down to his son, along with the amulet? And that his son might try to follow in his footsteps?"

"If he was sufficiently unbalanced, I suppose it's possible." But the man was frowning again. "Forgive me, but I have to ask—why come to me?"

"I work at the clinic in White Falls, with Dr. Stowe.

We're trying to help Jeb Taylor cope with his father's death, get back on his feet. But he's resisting. I thought that if I learned more about his history, and this amulet, I might be able to understand where the pathology is coming from."

"I see." Rutherford stood up. "Would you like some coffee? I had just made a pot." He disappeared into the kitchen, returning a minute later with two cups. When they had settled back into their chairs again, he took a long sip, closed his eyes, and then put the cup down on a nearby end table. "I'm not a stupid man, Mr. Smith. If that's your real name. Your car has California plates, yet you talk about having a job at a local clinic. What's more, you claim to have traveled all the way up to see me just to help out a local boy with whom you have no ties. And you come here with a story about a very valuable piece of history that's difficult to believe, to say the least. If I wasn't such a trusting soul, I'd say you were looking to profit."

"I'm not after any money."

"That may be. But you're after something."

"All right. Let's just say that I'm a mystery buff. Something strange is going on, and I'm interested in finding out the truth. The fact that I'm from California, that part's true. My wife and I were running away from some bad memories. We figured we'd start fresh, about as far away from the past as we could get. The part about the job at the clinic, that's true too. I happened to meet a guy who wanted to help me out, and I'm grateful for that. Now I want to return the favor. Helping him with this kid would go a long way toward making it right."

Rutherford studied his face, took another sip of coffee. "Okay. I guess that'll have to do." He put the coffee down. "So you want to know more about what you think this kid has found." He got up, wandered to the bookshelves, but did not seem to find what he wanted there. He disappeared into another room, returning a moment later with another leather-bound book. "Here's a picture of what I believe is a similar piece."

Smith found himself staring down at a photograph of a very old, chipped circle of stone. The figures on the stone looked to be some kind of dragons or large serpents, intertwined around a large open eye made of some kind of gem. Next to the photo was a reference: *Ceremonial amulet of the Middle Kingdom.*

"The Egyptians believed in an underworld," Rutherford explained, settling back in his chair. "The spirits of the dead were taken there and were ruled by several deities. Apparently, this amulet represented one of them, or one of the smaller demons that populated this place. The amulet could be placed around the dead man's neck to assist him in the underworld journey. Also, wearing the amulet could give a living person certain defenses by becoming a focal point; that is, the demon would become more interested in the stone than the person, and perhaps inhabit it for a certain length of time. In this way the person could harness some of the powers of the demon. Of course, the demons were fickle, and didn't always stay put."

"You're talking about possession."

"In a sense."

"So if Ronnie believed the amulet—"

"He would have to be educated in the ways of the Egyptians. This sort of stuff isn't common knowledge."

"But he could read," Smith continued doggedly. "He could have done the research."

"There are some decent books on the subject."

"Okay. What else? You talked about the powers of the demon."

"Yes," Rutherford said. "Each of them could possess the living, and command the spirits in the second realm. Then they had individual specialties, which could be called upon in certain places and situations. According to the old texts, this one could raise the dead."

"How?"

"By letting their spirits return to this world. The Egyptians believed in many places these spirits surrounded us, but they could not always make contact. In the right hands, and with the proper rituals . . . this amulet opened the door."

"What kind of door?"

"A door to the afterlife. But their idea of the afterlife wasn't exactly the same as ours. For them, the dead could be a great deal more frightening—and dangerous."

Smith stared down at the image captured on film. Just an old stone, chipped and worn, the carvings barely recognizable. So many years had passed since this thing had any practical use, and yet there was something compelling about it, the very simplicity of shape, of form. The serpents, writhing around the middle eye, dizzied him. Suddenly his dreams rushed at him with almost palpable force; the living dead, clawing up out of soft, black-colored earth, hunger on their moss-covered faces. He saw a circle of blood like an open eye, and within it a struggling human form.

*Dead men walking those who have reached the end and been born again . . .*

"Are you all right?" Rutherford was up out of his chair, a look of concern on his face. He had taken the book from Smith's cramping fingers and placed it aside. "You look like you've seen a ghost. Excuse the expression."

*Jesus Christ.* "Sorry." He rubbed at his face with a hand, found his fingers trembling. "I'm fine. Just a little tired, that's all."

But the chill that had prickled the hair of his neck and turned the backs of his arms to gooseflesh would not leave him. Looking up at the older man's face, searching his features for warmth and understanding, he saw instead the shadowy afterimage of the amulet, two serpents intertwined, floating softly in darkness.

"The ancient Egyptians believed in other realms beyond ours, other worlds—not all that different from Christian beliefs, in some ways. There are theories that say the Christian religion is simply an offshoot of a much older one. But in one important way they differ. To Egyptians, the dead would not always stay dead. If they did not make the journey to the next world, they could be stuck in limbo. And they would try to get back. It kept the Egyptians more honest, I suppose. After all, if you felt that anything you ever did to anyone might return to haunt you, even long after that person's death, you'd be pretty careful not to wrong anybody. Don't you think?"

"I suppose so."

Rutherford returned to his chair, picked up his coffee cup. "I have an appointment in town in half an hour. Have I given you enough to think about?"

Smith nodded. He extended his hand; Rutherford shook it. His grip was cool and dry. "Thank you," Smith said. "You been very helpful."

"I wish you luck." Rutherford held his hand a moment longer, then released it. "In finding whatever it is you're looking for."

He returned to the hotel that Tuesday evening in a mood of quiet contemplation. The idea of underworld spirits, possession, demons and charms, black masses, all of it began to fill his head like an ancient voice that would not stop its ravings and let him think for himself. A world so very different from the modern one, beliefs that had supposedly died out hundreds of years ago. Beliefs that should have been banished with the coming of Christ. And yet, some of the Bible's teachings he found no less unbelievable; Christ healing the crippled, the blind, then rising from the dead. Why were people so eager to believe those stories, waiting patiently for the second coming of the savior, the afterlife, the resurrection, all the while denying the existence of a devil?

And below all that, another voice, like a chant, the voice from his dreams. *You must come, William. Break the circle. You must come home.*

Coming home. The idea of it was almost enough to make him laugh. His adopted mother was dead and gone, and he had never met his real parents. His life had, for almost as long as he could remember, consisted of running from place to place.

Had he been chasing something, or had something been chasing him?

When he opened the door to their hotel suite, everything was quiet. He slipped softly into the next room where Angel waited, her breathing deep and even in the stillness. How he envied her ability to sleep now, letting everything dissolve itself in blessed darkness. How he wished he could lie down beside her and sleep too. But he knew that as soon as he closed his eyes the images would come again, and he would wake up screaming.

He touched her face and her eyes opened dreamily, a smile working at the corners of her mouth. She half turned to him, her arms coming up at him out of the warmth of the blankets (so stifling in the room; how could she stand it?) like the gesture of a child wanting to be held. He pulled off his shoes and climbed into bed with her, and she enfolded him, drew him into her little cocoon under the sheets. Soon, he knew, he would be struggling against the heat, but now he welcomed it, stretching his aching muscles, feeling them relax. "The middle of the afternoon," he teased, "the height of laziness. Are you *ever* going to get out of bed?"

She nuzzled his ear, still half asleep. Murmured. *I love you.* Had she said it out loud, or had he imagined it? Settled into him, her shape reworking itself around his. Her breath warm against his neck. Soon he could feel her breathing deepen and even out again.

He held her close, feeling that constant struggle going on within him. The dam gaining one more crack. He wanted to take her away from here, just gather her up and run, get as far away as possible. Forget all of this madness, and try to live their lives together in peace.

When the heat under the blankets had become unbearable he managed to extract himself from her arms. Still she slept, as if gathering strength for battle. Which was what he should be doing; that was what was coming, wasn't it? The old woman had said as much. Besides, he could feel it, the way you could feel electricity in the wires when you put your hand against a telephone pole. A deep and terrible thrumming beneath his feet.

He put his shoes on and walked down through the inn, back out into the sunshine that came more slanted now as evening wound into night. The air was heavy, the roads still, the parking lot of the inn almost empty. Directly across from him was the entrance to the scenic turn-out above the falls. He crossed the road and wandered across the dusty surface of the dirt track. The dirt road widened into a small parking lot, and a guardrail ran along the edge of the steep drop. He could hear the water roaring through the narrow chute, boiling out over the drop, the spray reaching his face like mist as the river crashed into the deep pool below. He listened as the muffled roar grew louder, watching the river on his left as it spilled over the dam, flowed swiftly under the bridge and down between the deepening banks, getting narrower and faster, more purposeful as it sped toward the drop. He imagined how it must have been for Annie Arsenault's boy, the one who had fallen to his death so many years ago. Joseph would have stood here for a moment in the middle of an empty parking lot, a little tow-headed boy, his gaze wide and curious, a bit frightened, his heart beating heavy and fast.

*Don't play near the falls, honey. They're dangerous for little boys like you.*

*I'm not little, Mama!*

Taking a small step closer. The roaring coming louder now; the voice more insistent. Catching just a glimpse of white froth, imagining an animal caged down there, furious and bloodthirsty, leaping at the steep sides, snarling, jaws flecked with foam. Another step taking him to the rail, and then he was ducking under it, standing on the edge of the cliff, his small chubby legs trembling at the sight; not the river pouring from a rocky spout, but a great dark shape throwing itself against the sides of the cliff, foam flying from its ragged jaws, eyes like two silver moons. The head rolling up on a thick neck, catching sight of him; grinning! And then the leap, huge, dark haunches tensed for the spring upward, even as it came for him, the dripping teeth shifting until they became a dark wall of water smashing into his feet.

Smith came to and found himself standing on the edge of the drop. What had he meant to do, throw himself off?

The water twisted and churned below his feet, the spray wetting his hair, his face, turning the last of the dying sunlight into a thousand shimmering colors before his eyes. Below the boiling pool the river ran swiftly away again through a deep channel gouged into the earth, a dark ribbon flowing past the Gedford's fields and through the thickening alders and cattails, until it reached the pond and beyond that, the bog. The river, running with the blood of the land, the falls its beating heart.

He shivered. The drop here was merciless; if the boy had survived the fall, the water would have dragged him under and spun him about like a whirlpool, battering him against the rocks before it carried him away to oblivion. Or perhaps it had sucked him down and kept him there below the boiling currents; perhaps he was there still.

A gust of wind blew more spray into his face, and for a moment it almost did seem as if the water had reared up and grabbed at him. He took half a step back to more solid ground. But another little voice in the back of his mind was saying *wouldn't be so bad, champ, just a quick unpleasant minute, a couple of bruises, and then it's all over, all of it . . .*

He thought about Angel. Was he really going to try to love her, and if so, could he do it and remain here, in the middle of something so foul he could almost smell it on the air? On the other hand, if they tried to run, would they ever be able to live with themselves? Assuming they could get away at all, would their lives slowly turn sour, all the purpose bleeding away until they were left with two empty husks?

*I could love her. I could.* She was everything he was not; passionate and warm, open, at peace with herself now, after those difficult years since her brother's death and in Miami. He was falling in love with her for all those reasons, and yet there was something else between them, something darker and less definable and even more intense, something that would frighten him if he dared to confront it. Perhaps it was the way they had met, the promise of violence during those first days. He didn't know. But he felt as if he had known her forever, and that she was as much a part of him as his own conscience.

*The taste of candy apples. The color blue. The fluttering of wings.*

Yes, that was close to the way he felt about her, the essence of her. But they were feelings that could not really be expressed by words.

In the fading light of late afternoon his thoughts turned again to that thick, high wall he had built up around his heart, and he wondered if the wall, or at least its foundation, had been laid not during his time in prison, but during his very first few years, when he had been told of his adoption; growing up without a father, losing his adopted mother in his late teens, never feeling entirely safe in the world. It was true that he had always felt something was missing in his life. He had needed an escape, something that would banish those thoughts that always seemed to come to him in the dead of night, the feeling that he was doomed from the very beginning, and that he would not live to see another day. For the first time in years, he wondered about his natural parents, who they were, where they were, whether they were still alive, or dead and buried. If he knew, would it make a difference?

A chill had entered the air, the promise of another cold night. He backed farther away from the edge until he felt the guardrail against his legs. No, they could not run from this. *He* could not. Hadn't he already decided? Perhaps he had decided the night he had stood at the edge of the salt flats in Salt Lake City. Or even farther back. Every particle of his being told him that he needed to confront his fears or risk losing something more important than his sanity. He began to understand how the most dedicated priests must feel, giving up the most intimate parts of life, taking vows of poverty, chastity, assuming the burdens of others, all for the love of something greater than themselves.

What was it Annie had said about him? He tried to remember the way Angel had related it; *He will come to understand things that will make him scream—but I do not think they will break him. He is stronger than he thinks.*

That feeling of dread. A battle he could not win. And an odd sense of loss, as if he were mourning in advance; later, there would not be time.

Billy Smith turned and slowly made his way back to the inn, his back bent as if to ward off a blow.

# Chapter Thirteen

At six o'clock, people gathered at the high school for the town meeting, which was held in the Henry Thomas Memorial Auditorium. The parking lot slowly filled with cars; a couple of BMWs and Mercedes Benzes, but most of them ten-year-old Dodges and Fords and Chevrolets with the mufflers rusting out and the motors skipping a beat or two.

Pat Friedman wasted little time getting inside, for the temperature had dropped below fifty degrees again and would go much lower before morning. The whole town seemed to be going crazy lately. This week had brought even hotter days and colder nights. Early Monday afternoon the temperature had crept up over ninety, another record, and by Monday night it had plummeted to twelve degrees above zero. It was as though some crazy obsessive-compulsive upstairs had his finger on the thermostat, *turn it up, turn it down, up, down,* and so on, each time gaining a little more momentum; as if someone was trying to wreak havoc, fray nerves, shorten tempers and generally turn people inside out. Sooner or later it was inevitable that cracks would start showing up.

The building was warm and bright. He followed the hallway past the classrooms and the brown lockers and bright arts and crafts that peppered the walls and sat down in the auditorium, which was already half-full of noisy people. Everyone knew about his wife and the handyman, he thought sickly. She was fucking that little shit, it was obvious to Pat now, and the fact that he had been blind to it before made him burn inside. That disastrous party. People had been staring at him all night, it was painfully obvious. He was the laughingstock of White Falls already.

He watched the people coming in, waiting to see if anyone stared at him or pointed and said something to their friends. But no one seemed to notice him and after a while he was able to relax. An hour later he was listening to the town treasurer drone on and on about the festival budget, hardly paying attention. He had something else on his mind, something that had been taking up more and more of his attention lately; that little shit Jeb Taylor, and the strange . . .

*Visions? Dreams?*

Whatever they were. He had them at all different times of the day and night. It didn't matter if he was at work, or eating supper, or in bed. Once he had seen a flash of blinding light and when he had come to, he was in his car and on the wrong side of the road headed for a tree. Jesus, that had given him a scare. He wondered if he was breaking under the stress, or if it was something even worse than that, like cancer or a brain tumor. He looked at himself every day in the mirror and wondered, *Is this the day? Is this the day I'm going to drop dead?* Morbid, he knew. But he was a different man than he had been just a few short days ago. That man had been getting fat and comfortable and a little lazy within the easy routines of his life. This one was struggling just to hang on as the world tilted and whirled.

The real reason he had come to the meeting was to talk to Sheriff Pepper. He had heard there had been some vandalism at the church yesterday and had sensed some sort of connection with that little pissant. He wasn't sure what, but he knew he had to pursue it, had to trust his instincts.

Pat Friedman had come close to the breaking point last night. He had had the same dream he had been having for the past three nights, the one where the things came up out of the ground, only this time when he had turned to run he looked back over his shoulder and saw something that stopped him short; one of *them* stood over a fallen woman, bludgeoning her, swinging something again and again with horrible force on the woman's arms, shoulders, head. He could hear bones snapping, cracking ribs, and the thing didn't stop, just kept swinging with machine-like precision, the blows raining down. Unable to help himself, he had turned back, drawn by the horror of it, wanting a closer look, *closer, closer,* and then the thing had turned around and hissed at him, bloody weapon raised for another strike. Its features were twisted into a snarl of rage and hatred, hardly human, but recognizable nonetheless.

He had been staring into his own face.

Even now, sitting in this large room with a hundred people talking at once, it gave him the chills. He looked around the room, searching for old Ruth Taylor or maybe Jeb himself, but he didn't see either one. The next half-hour passed in a dim blur, the room too warm, the flashes of people's faces like pale ghosts, the noise a thundering din that threatened to send him over the edge. But finally the meeting was over and he was left wondering why he had come. *Could have spoken to the sheriff some other time, maybe gone down to the station tomorrow.*

Somebody was saying something to him. Myrtle from the office, standing in the aisle, staring. She leaned in close, and he could see the beginnings of black stubble on her upper lip (*time for a wax, Myrtle honey,* he thought, and pressed a hand to his mouth to suppress a grin).

"Excuse me?"

"I was just saying you look a little ill. Do you feel all right?"

He nodded, told her he had a headache and excused himself, just catching a glimpse of Sheriff Pepper as he disappeared through the auditorium doors. Pat fought his way through the groups of people lingering in the aisles, until he caught up with the sheriff at the front doors.

He must have seemed like a maniac, because when he put a hand on Pepper's shoulder the man turned and took a step back, a look of surprise on his face.

"I wonder if I could talk with you a minute."

"Well." The sheriff scratched his head. "I've got to get back to the station . . ."

"I heard about the vandalism at the church. Horrible business."

"Is that what you wanted to talk about?"

"I thought maybe I could help, you know, take up the case for the town. I've got some pro-bono hours I could give you—"

"That's mighty kind of you to offer, but I don't know that we'll be making any arrests right away. Probably a couple of kids that did it. Maybe even an animal. The point is, there aren't too many leads to follow." Sheriff Pepper looked at him strangely again, as if he half-expected Pat to start slobbering at the mouth, maybe grow a couple of fangs.

"I'd be happy to start a search party, organize a neighborhood watch—"

"Do you feel okay, Pat? I mean you look a little tired."

*Everybody's asking me that lately. Just shut up and mind your own business, shut up, shut UP—*

"I just hate to hear about our pretty church being the object of such awful . . . pranks." Pat forced another smile and felt his jaw pop as the muscles tightened. "What exactly happened anyway?"

"Well, a basement window was broken, for one," Pepper said. He hitched at his belt. "And a few gravestones got knocked over. All in a line from front to back, like something big and clumsy jumped the fence and ran right on through. That's why I thought maybe an animal done it." His face got suddenly hard, his eyes faraway, and his hand touched the butt of his gun in an unconscious motion. "I got a few ideas about that. That fucking Trask's dog . . . excuse the language."

Pat didn't notice. He was too busy thinking about what the sheriff had said. *Pushed a few gravestones over.* He felt a trickle of sweat run down his side. He licked his lips. "Were any of the graves . . . violated? Dug up?"

Pepper's eyes snapped back and he frowned. "That's kind of a strange question."

"I heard of it happening before. In this kind of case." The sweat was pouring off him now, though he suddenly felt cold as ice. He continued to flash his painted-on smile.

"No, I didn't see anything like that."

"Are you *sure?*"

"I told you, didn't I?" Sheriff Pepper showed the first signs of annoyance. "You sure you're all right, Pat? You're looking kind a green around the gills. Don't know what the hell's happening in this town lately. Christ, Jack Perot was almost killed the other day when Hank Gunderson just about run him over. Jack started swearing, Hank stopped that goddamn truck and started right in swinging. Jack had a black eye and a chipped front tooth by the time someone pulled him off. But hell, that was nothing compared to the brawl out at Indian Road Trailer Heaven . . ."

"I'm fine, sheriff." Pat made a move toward the front doors, the painted-on smile still plastered to his face, and Pepper touched his arm, stopping him.

"Listen, let me give you a little advice. I appreciate you wanting to help and all, but let me do my job. Like I said, I've got a few ideas of my own about what happened at the church."

*Oh I don't think you have the faintest idea,* Pat thought, *not the faintest.* The world tipped crazily for a moment, came back the other way, and settled again. He thought of Jeb Taylor in his house, on his bed, making love to his wife.

He swallowed hard. Whatever it was that seemed suddenly caught in his throat went down, a little. He spoke over it, and to him, his voice sounded quite normal. "Yes. You're absolutely right. I'm sorry for bothering you."

"No problem. Get some sleep, okay?"

Pat nodded, pulled his collar up over his cheeks and stepped out into the cold, leaving Sheriff Pepper standing at the school doors, shaking his head and staring after him.

Jeb Taylor was not, in fact, at the Friedman's house with Julie (though another man still was, and having a fine time of it, too). Jeb Taylor was at *Johnny's*, having a drink. Actually, he was having several. Drinking with an old friend.

Just a few minutes ago, as Pat Friedman was standing in the school lobby talking with Sheriff Pepper, Ronnie Taylor had walked into the old schoolhouse, sat down on the next stool and said hello to his son.

Jeb had changed into the black leather jacket he had found in his father's suitcase. Since he had been at *Johnny's*, he had been drinking whiskey and beer and anything else he could get his hands on. Anything to get that image out of his head, what he had just seen. Julie Friedman naked and sweaty, clinging to another man's shoulders.

After the Friedman's party he had lapsed into an alcoholic coma, a paralysis of voluntary thought, spending the next day and night drinking and as close to the edge as he had ever been, not wanting to think about what that *thing* had done when it touched his skin. That *burrowing.* The next morning had found him at a crossroads; lying in bed, fiercely hung over, he had known that one more false step would send him into a downward spiral from which he would never be able to recover. And what frightened him the most was that he knew he wasn't strong enough to resist.

But yesterday, it had gotten better. He had somehow stayed away from *Johnny's* and the whiskey and kept himself busy with other things, and slowly his head began to clear. He had worked on his car, which was in dire need of a carburetor cleaning and an oil change, and when Ruth had come tottering out the back door of the house to ask him if he would help her "find her tea," he had gone willingly, for reasons he did not entirely understand. He had thought she was having one of her spells, but after he got out the teabags and put the water on the stove, she touched his arm and her eyes were bright and wet. "I've been praying for you, boy," she said. "I don't know what kind of trouble you got yourself into, but I've been praying real hard."

He surprised himself again by smiling at her and patting her hand. "That's awful good of you, Gramma," he said. And meant it. She hadn't asked him about his job or pressed him about his drinking, or even mentioned the doctor's visit. He had a glimpse of something better in his life, a goodness that most people take for granted.

That had kept him off the bottle another night.

This morning, he had left the house early and took the newly-tuned car out on the open road, whipping up Route 27 to Route 1 and up the coast, touring through the small towns that all began to look the same after a while; railroad tracks and trailers, junkyards filled with the ghosts of old Gremlins and AMC Chargers, 7-Elevens, Mom and Pop stores, Shell gas stations, old brick buildings along the water filled with pizza joints and hardware stores and gift shops. He rolled the windows down and let the wind tear through the car's heated interior, roaring through Camden and Lincolnville and Belfast, Searsport and Stockton Springs, feeling like he was on the run, a man being chased by something large and mean. That brought back memories of his wild trip down from Thomaston with his father's things on the seat next to him, and thinking of that left a sour taste in his mouth.

By the time he had returned, though, the sour taste was washed away and he was ready for something more. He had started wondering if maybe Mrs. Friedman hadn't been making fun after all. Maybe he should have given her more of a chance to explain. Before he lost his nerve, he drove straight home and dressed in the best clothes he owned; a dark blue sweater and gray slacks, something Ruth had bought for him at the K-Mart in Brunswick for his seventeenth birthday. Then he went down to the store just before it closed and bought a red rose from Thelma, who reminded him of the town meeting tonight. Pat Friedman would be at that meeting, he thought. Which meant maybe Julie would be home alone. It was more than he could hope for.

He forced himself to wait half an hour until six-thirty.

Then he got back in the car and drove back up the road to the logging track, feeling remarkably sharp and sober, the voices that had been clamoring in his head the past few weeks blessedly silent. He parked, crept back along the road and then around the storage shed, carrying the rose in one sweaty fist.

Pat usually kept his car in the drive. The driveway was empty. He ran a hand through his hair, straightened his sweater across his middle and wished he had thought of ironing his pants. Too late. This was the best he could do. If she didn't take him now, she never would. Stepping up to the front door, he raised his fist to knock, and hesitated. *Just because Pat's car isn't in the drive, doesn't mean he's not home. Car could be in the shop or something, getting some work done. Maybe he put it in the garage tonight. Maybe he left it at the office and she gave him a ride home from work so they could go to the meeting together.*

He went around back again, this time closer to the house so he could see through the windows. Nobody in the kitchen; but there was a light on in there, just visible as dusk began to fall. Encouraged, he crept along past the dining room where he had replaced the bulbs in the chandelier (empty), to the spacious, elegant living room. Lights on in there, too. He stopped and looked in.

At first the room appeared to be empty. Clothes strewn across the floor. Then a naked foot threw itself up over the back of the couch, seemed to clutch and dig at the soft cushion, a woman's foot and ankle. He could see the couch rocking back and forth.

And then they sat up. Jeb recoiled; the rose crushed in a tightening grip, the stink of it filling his nostrils. He moaned, as if in pain, watching Julie Friedman, naked, eyes closed and head thrown back, mouth open, and another man bouncing her in his lap. He could not take his eyes away from the scene through the window, the two of them, joined together below the waist. Silently, like two partners in dance, the man bent over her as she arched backward and he took a nipple between his lips.

*She was just playing with you, you fool. Just for laughs. You really think she'd be interested in a little shit like Jeb Taylor? It was never you, not like that. Stupid ugly little freak . . .*

He lurched away backwards through the yard, stumbled once and went down into the dirt. Somewhere inside he knew how crazy it all was, that there had really been nothing between them but a little flirting. But to him, this was more than just some horny housewife playing games; this was the end of his last chance. Worse, it had been the last thing between him and something horrible he could not name. He felt himself tumbling, end over end, down that deep, dark, bottomless hole.

*Get ahold of yourself, son.*

The words had been spoken against his ear. He whirled, no one in sight, of course. The wide, open yard was criss-crossed with shadows. Sniffling, he wiped the back of his hand across his face, smudging it with dirt. The sun had dipped below the horizon, and a faint, cool breeze had sprung up, rustling the new leaves in the oak tree. There was a chill entering the air as the suffocating heat of the day disappeared by degrees. He looked back at the house. It was quiet, the lights beginning to glow behind glass as night crept in. They were still in the living room. Julie had changed position, and now the unknown man thrust into her from behind. Both of them seemed to be laughing.

*She'll pay, son. She'll pay soon enough. They all will. Didn't I tell you your time was gonna come?*

Slowly, he became aware of heat against his chest as

the cold breeze tugged at his clothing. He yanked down the v-neck of his sweater and exposed the amulet. It glowed a hot, blood red against his skin. He stared at it dumbly for a moment before understanding dawned.

Jeb Taylor was never meant to be normal; that much was obvious. He had another calling.

He was struggling now to keep his eyes in focus. The bar was almost empty, most of the people of White Falls still at the town meeting; Jeff McDonald, the town drunk (*the* other *town drunk,* Jeb thought, correcting himself with a bitter grin; *you could give him a run for his money*), occupied a booth in the far corner, and he was drooling over a *Jugs* magazine and eating pretzels from a small wooden bowl. Every once in a while he would look up, take a pull from a can of Black Label, and stare at the silent television screen above the bar with vacuous eyes, as if he were playing out a scene in his head. Something by the Eagles played quietly in the background.

And that was when his father walked in. Ronnie Taylor looked good, a little pale, but not at all dead. His hair was thick and black, swept back from his smooth forehead, his deeply hooded eyes sparkling like the depths of some moonlit pool, his cheeks glassy and white, almost transparent. "You look real sharp," Jeb said. It was the best he could come up with under the circumstances, and seemed oddly appropriate. "What took you so long?"

His father did not answer at once. Johnny the bartender (who had just now returned from the town meeting) looked up, said, "Hmm?" and, getting no response, moved away. He did not seem at all concerned that a dead man was sitting in his bar. After a moment he disappeared into a back room.

Ronnie Taylor was grinning. Even his teeth glowed white, like those toothpaste commercials where everyone ran around looking like they had bars of soap crammed in their mouths. "I had a long ways to come, boy. You don't just pick yourself up off a slab and walk out. You got to pay your bills."

Jeb thought about this as hard as he possibly could. He pictured his dead father under a sheet, suddenly sitting up in a roomful of corpses, paying his bills, and saying *adios*. Wandering over to a bored-looking teenage girl behind a counter snapping gum, saying, "Check, please."

He looked around the bar to see if anyone else was watching them. But Johnny was still in the back room, and Jeff McDonald had put his head down on the table next to the magazine and was snoring lightly.

Something still wasn't making sense. "But they burned you. I told them to. Cre-mated." He had trouble saying the word.

"There's ways to get out of that," Ronnie said vaguely. "I'll show you sometime." He pointed to the whiskey bottle. "You gonna offer me a drink?"

Jeb reached over the bar and found a glass. He poured a drink for his dead father. Very, very carefully, his eyes squinted in concentration. It wouldn't do to spill any of it, no sir. His daddy would be pissed off. Might even get out the belt. Jeb could remember the shine of the metal buckle as it whistled through the air. He shivered.

"So are you a ghost, or what?"

Ronnie clapped him on the back. "Son," he said, "I'm whatever you want me to be. Now you gonna give me that drink?"

Jeb slid the glass down the bar. "That's it," Ronnie said when he had wrapped his fingers around it. "Oh, yes. It *has* been a while." His fingernails were clean and very white, like his teeth. He grinned, drool running down his fine smooth chin, and raised the glass to his mouth.

Jeb watched his father close his eyes in appreciation as the amber liquid disappeared. He could see it running down his father's throat, a darker color below his pearl-white skin. Ronnie Taylor's Adam's apple bobbed up and down as he swallowed. It was a fine Adam's apple. Manly looking. As the whiskey went down, Ronnie's cheeks gained some color, his fingernails began to glow pink.

"Why, I do believe you're getting a hard-on just looking at me," Ronnie said. He put the empty glass down on the bar and wiped his mouth with the back of his hand. Jeb remembered him doing that a long time ago at the kitchen table, and it was then that he knew for certain that this was his father after all.

"I knew you'd come," he said, unable to keep the trembling excitement out of his voice. "I waited and I waited and sometimes it was hard but I knew you'd come back for me. We're family, right?"

"Got that right. And family got to stick together. Bartender!"

Jeb looked up and saw with surprise that a new man stood behind the bar, a man in a dark suit with a face that would not come into focus. *You're not Johnny.*

"Course not," the man said cheerfully. "Johnny brought me up from Alabama. What'll you have?"

Ronnie grinned again. "Good to see you again, Mart."

"You too, Ronnie. Whiskey?"

"You bet. And one for my son."

"You sure he's old enough?"

Jeb looked at Mart fearfully, but a moment later the dark man laughed. "Just gettin' a rise out of Ronnie, kid. Don't you worry. I know how old you are. Just old enough, right?" He winked, and poured two more shots of whiskey.

They drank together. After a while Jeb noticed that the bar had gotten noisier. He looked around, and saw that Jeff McDonald had disappeared and been replaced by laughing couples and workmen and young teenagers and college kids with long hair, some of them drinking and talking, a few dancing near the jukebox. He didn't recognize any of them, and that was strange, because he thought he knew most of Johnny's customers. A couple of the college kids wore little round sunglasses, even though it was dark in the bar.

*The bar.* He saw with amazement that *Johnny's* looked practically brand new. Well, not quite *new,* but better than it used to look, anyway. The paint that had been chipped and faded a moment ago was now bright and fresh. The cheap plastic booths with the gray electrical tape over the rips had magically healed and shone under the soft lights. And the counter itself was dark, polished wood. He began to feel just a little bit afraid, as if all along he'd known it was just a dream he was having, but now it seemed to be getting out of control and outrunning him.

Jeb leaned over, forced his eyes to focus, and took Mart the bartender by the wrist. The man's skin was cold and dry and very smooth. "What day is it?"

"Why, it's Tuesday, son," Mart said, still smiling genially as if this sort of thing happened all the time. *People coming up out of nowhere, bars healing themselves, happens everyday down South. Where you been?*

Tuesday, of course. That was fine. But still: "What *year?*"

"Ronnie, I do believe your boy's gone out to pasture," Mart said. Then he looked at Jeb, and it seemed that his smile faltered, just a little, and his eyes went hard. For a moment, just a moment, they seemed to glow with a red fire. “1985, son. The year is 1985.”

“Oh,” Jeb said. He was currently having trouble making his mind work the way he wanted; the connections wouldn’t come. The year wasn’t quite right, but it *was* still a dream, wasn’t it? And yet it continued to go on and on and it seemed as if someone else was pulling the strings, and he began to think that deciding it was all a dream might be a very, very bad idea.

Mart’s skin felt like scales. Jeb released his grip and sank back on his seat. “The bar,” he muttered. “Looks like new.”

“Ain’t it beautiful, though?” Ronnie said. There were three empty glasses in front of him now, and he knocked back another. “Come on, boy, keep up. You don’t want ’em saying that the Taylor kid’s a pussy, do you?”

Jeb picked up his glass and drank the fiery liquid because damned if it wasn’t easier to just go along and not *rock the boat,* and a little while later he began feeling pretty good in spite of himself, pretty laid back and cool. Drinking with his father, just like he’d always wanted. The bar was practically new, so what? Why did that have to matter?

Mart poured him another drink. “On the house. We like the looks of you in here, son. You belong here. Just like your daddy. His daddy before him, in fact. Long, full line. Good blood.”

Jeb smiled. That was true enough. He’d been waiting almost twenty years for someone to say he belonged. The amulet throbbed against his chest and there was no pain this time, just the slightest heat on his skin. Like standing a little too close to the fire, that was all.

The party went on around him, and people kept coming up to Ronnie and clapping him on the back, telling him how much they appreciated everything he'd done. When Jeb looked at his father, he began to see what he could become if he set his mind to it. "Power," he whispered, dry-mouthed. It filled him until he thought he would burst; how had he ever lived without such a thing as this? Such a feeling of utter strength and control, as if nothing and no one on earth could touch him. He was a God.

Like father, like son.

*Take your dreams by the balls, boy. Live forever.*

"We're gonna have some fun," Ronnie Taylor said. His little hooded reptile eyes gleamed like two coals; for a moment, there seemed to be someone else standing just over his shoulder, hundreds of dim, ghostly shapes filling the bar. "I'm talking *revenge,* son. We're gonna bring this town to its knees. I got things to show you you won't believe, and after we get done with them, I got something else. A surprise."

"A surprise," Jeb echoed. The amulet was pulsing, throbbing like a blood-filled heart, burning him. The pain was delicious. He could do anything, anything he wanted.

He wanted to tear White Falls apart.

"In time, boy," Ronnie croaked. "First we gotta rattle a few cages. Take care of some old business."

Jeb Taylor grinned. He could hardly wait.

Harry Stowe sat bolt upright in bed, the sheets damp with his sweat, a scream lodged in his throat. He looked around his empty bedroom. The nightlight he had used ever since he was a child (one of his cowardly secrets, being afraid of the dark) did not press the blackness back during these early morning hours, but only blunted it, throwing monstrous, misshapen shadows upon the walls, turning his ordinary pine dresser into a crouching demon, his racks of clothes in his open closet into rows of bony shoulders.

He had dreamed of Ruth Taylor. The dream would not remain with him, however, leaving behind only its handprints; a vague feeling of dread, guilt hanging like a heavy cross around his neck. A sense of frustration over the fleeting glimpses the dream left him was enough to keep his heart beating hard and fast but not enough to remember. Flashes of blood splashed against a wall, someone tumbling . . .

He had been feeling guilty ever since his visit to the Taylor home. Yet he had done nothing, unsure of what he should do, knowing he would need permission from next of kin to put her into some kind of home and also knowing somehow that the boy would never permit it. And he couldn't see Ruth in a retirement home, one of those musty little rooms with their double beds and flowered curtains and get-well cards tacked to the wall.

He had a professional responsibility, didn't he? It wasn't like him, such an unreasonable hesitation to do what was right.

And now, this feeling of unnamed dread coming over him at the end of a moonless night. Sleep bringing his subconscious to light, he supposed. Or to dark, for that was more appropriate.

He got up out of bed and went to the window, shivering in the cold. A heavy frost lined the edges of the glass. The lawn outside was dark and still, covered in a fine, swirling mist; he stood, motionless, watching the horizon. Dawn, just touching the edges of the night sky. Still early. She would be asleep, along with the rest of the town.

It was crazy, what he was thinking.

*Hurry, please, she's in trouble. Please hurry.*

He stood and watched the sky lighten by degrees, but the

thought would not leave him, along with that one vivid image from the dream; a splash of blood against a white wall.

He dressed quickly, not knowing why, and as he left the house the feeling of dread and urgency grew until he was running for the car.

Ruth sat up in the gray light and still silence of early dawn and felt disoriented for a moment before she realized she was in the living room, and not in her big soft bed. *Fell asleep downstairs again, you foolish old lady,* she chided herself. *Right here in this chair.* But the truth was, she didn't remember how she got here, what day it was, or whether she had been dreaming when she saw Jeb come in through the rear door and stumble up the stairs to bed. It had *seemed* real enough; and then the faint light had caught him as he closed the door, and that had given her a scare. For just a second she had thought her dead son was home again after all these years.

She worried about her grandson, when she felt up to worrying. Her mind worked every once in a while; she could almost feel it cranking up like somebody had clipped a set of jumper cables to her ears and turned on the juice. She knew Jeb spent these nights drinking, she wasn't a complete fool. Yes, Jeb was drinking, and he wasn't working anymore, she didn't think, though whether he had quit or been fired was a mystery to her. But he was a stubborn boy, like his daddy. Nothing she said or did would change that.

Now something had gotten her up; a noise somewhere deep in the house. Shivering in the cold, she stood and fumbled her way to the foot of the stairs and peered up into the darkness. The early dawn light hadn't yet penetrated the upstairs corners, and the hallway that led to the three bedrooms was alive with shadows. She fancied she saw things moving in the inky blackness, shapes that twisted and turned and would not remain still. *Never liked shadows much,* she thought. *At least, not since Norman died.*

That got her thinking about her husband, and she looked around to see if he was standing with his arms crossed the way he did and shaking his head at her silliness. But the house was empty. Her mind had started buzzing again, like it sometimes did, and it was so loud she couldn't remember what she was looking for. Ronnie, that was it. Ronnie had come home—

*You crazy woman. Ronnie's long dead. That was your grandson, Jeboriah.*

Oh, yes. She remembered now. Norman had set her straight.

A noise like a cracking board. There was one that did that, at the door to Jeb's bedroom. If you stepped on it just right, it went off like a gunshot. She took one step up and held onto the railing. "Jeboriah?"

At first she thought she had imagined the sound. Then he materialized out of the blackness, the white vertical slash of his t-shirt seeming to float five feet from the floor, his open leather jacket blending with the background. She couldn't see his face. The dark hid it well. Was that a shadow moving behind him, or something else . . . ?

"Jeboriah? Something wrong?"

"Come up here a minute," he said softly. "I think Norman's had an accident."

"Norman?" *Oh my lord.* Confusion washed over her and she hurried up the steps, one hand pressed to her mouth, filled with that image of her husband crumpled awkwardly at the bottom of the staircase. *He's fallen again.*

No. That was years ago. She paused halfway up, something in her raising an alarm. She couldn't see his face. But the way he stood, the jacket he wore . . .

Her voice trembled. "Ronnie?"

"Please. It's Norman, Gramma. He's hurt bad. You've got to hurry."

The pain in his voice was unmistakable, and she went to it without thinking, a mother's instinct, as pure and mindless as the sun's heat. At the top of the stairs she paused and he stepped out into the gray light that filtered in through one of the bedrooms. *Jeboriah,* she thought immediately. It was his face, long and pale, full-lipped like his mother. And yet his eyes, hooded, burning from a well of shadows. His eyes told her something else. What was it in those eyes, some sort of glint that hadn't been there before?

A scream died in the back of her throat. Ruth Taylor took a trembling step back, felt the awful lurch and emptiness of the drop, and teetered. Her two gnarled hands came up, grasping. They scrabbled across the cool leather jacket and brushed his shirt, and she felt the smooth round stone of the amulet, and it was warm, *Lord, like the body of some living creature sucking on him.* Her fingertips tingled. He had let her hands touch it. He wanted her to *know.*

And then she was twisting backward over the drop. She felt an odd, dreamlike sensation of flight before her hip connected with the third riser from the top and she heard the bone snap. The pain was immediate and terrible.

Then her head struck the wall and mercifully, she felt nothing else.

When Harry Stowe pulled up outside the Taylor house, dawn was lightening the treetops and sending bright prisms of color through the morning frost. The clock on his dash read 7:05 a.m. As he stepped from the car the air was crisp, light, with a touch of warmth already beginning to seep in from the sun.

Jeb Taylor's big Chevy was parked sideways across the lawn, a series of tire marks dug deep into the grass marking its passage. Harry touched his hand to the hood. Not quite cool. He walked quickly to the front door, paused one last time with his finger on the bell. Jesus, what the hell was he doing? Getting hysterical over a dream? He would wake up the whole house, and he wasn't on the best of terms with them already. *What ever happened to that logical even-headedness of yours? You're acting like, well, like . . .*

*Ruth.*

He stepped away from the door, the thought of her starting something clamoring within him again. An insistent voice, urgent, frightened. He stepped through the wet grass and looked in the kitchen window, cupping his hands to the glass. It was empty and dark inside.

He went around the side of the house, his shoes soaked through now (grass was getting long, nobody had done any mowing here this spring), and looked through a side window. From here he could see Ruth's favorite chair, the little table where she had spilled the tea. The chair was empty, the table bare. He squinted. And if he looked at just the right angle, through the living room to the front hall, he could see what looked like a body, crumpled at the foot of the stairs.

Everything else fading from his mind, he hurried back around the house to the front door, rapping loudly on it before he remembered the bell. He could hear the chimes echoing loudly in the bowels of the place. He rang the bell again, rapped hard on the door, finally twisted the handle. It was unlocked. The door swung open.

He paused briefly on the step in spite of himself. This

was what he wanted, wasn't it? He could check on her in bed, didn't even have to wake her up. But the fact of the open door, such a subtle, innocent thing, told him something was wrong. People locked their doors at night around here, as they did most places. Not because of the threat of crime, but because some deep, instinctual warning light blinked on and said, *You're sleeping. Anything can happen.*

He did not want to go in there.

*Jesus, make up your fucking mind, will you?* Over the past few days he had had all sorts of wild notions, crazy ideas that would never have crossed his mind a year, even a month ago. *Bones getting up and walking out by themselves. Visions in the middle of the night. Jesus Christ.*

Angry again, he gathered his loose shirt around himself and stepped into the dark front hall, an odd sense of finality settling across his shoulders, as if he had walked into a jail cell, and the door had rattled shut and locked behind him.

He saw her immediately. She had come to rest draped over the bottom riser of the stairs, just out of the light from the open door, her head bent sharply up to the right and backward, her hips turned at an unnatural angle. Even from here he could see her open, glassy stare. He went to her quickly, a moan dying in the back of his throat, and touched the side of her neck, feeling for the jugular. No pulse. The back of her head was pushed in, thin white hair matted and bloody. He looked up past her body to the red-streaked mark on the wall, and his dream came crashing back to him like a wave; tumbling, her head hitting the plaster with a sickening crunch, a splash of blood, her hip snapping like dry kindling. Just the way her husband had died, ten years before.

He raised his gaze to the top of the steps and his eyes

locked with sudden shock on the thing that had been Jeboriah Taylor.

Glittering, feverish eyes set deep in hollow sockets, behind heavy brows, searching him out, pinning him with their fury; yellow skin, a wound for a nose, pale, lipless mouth spread in a lunatic's grin. He heard the deep, rasping breaths in the silence of the house, and then the stink hit him in the face like an open-handed slap. A smell like a rotting sewer.

*Oh my sweet Jesus.* He backed away, mindless now, the fear like bile in his throat. He could not take his eyes from the creature at the top of the stairs.

The thing chuckled, a deep, bone-jarring sound. A long, slow line of spittle dripped from the corner of its mouth and spun itself to the floor. It grinned at him.

This was not Jeb. It could not be, and yet, the slump of his shoulders, the way he stood, hip cocked, head forward on a thin neck. Harry thought of the frightened little boy so many years ago who had acted like a dog that had been kicked too many times. He felt himself gasping for air, his chest heaving, hands out, as if in supplication. *You cannot be Jeb Taylor.*

His back touched the edge of the open front door. It hadn't closed on him after all. He was free.

Harry Stowe turned and ran, shirt flapping, out into the cheery bright spring morning.

# Chapter Fourteen

On Wednesday morning Billy Smith dressed in silence and walked the short distance down the road to the clinic. Angel had not stirred when he got up. He was starting to worry about her. She slept so soundly and so long he wondered if it could be good for her, and he began to think that perhaps she was having more problems than he thought. When she was awake she complained of nausea and exhaustion, and lightheadedness; he thought she might be running a fever, but couldn't be sure. The extreme temperature shifts couldn't be doing anyone any good. Maybe she had caught a cold, or the flu.

All those thoughts disappeared, however, when he opened the door to the clinic and his gaze fell upon Harry Stowe.

Harry was sitting on the yellow couch in the front room. His clothes (long casual shirt over what looked like a pajama top, faded slacks), were rumpled, his eyes bloodshot. His normally combed-back hair tumbled across his brow in a disorganized wave. When he heard the door open, Harry's eyes came up slowly, but his gaze showed little change.

"Jesus, Harry. What happened?"

"Ruth Taylor is dead," Stowe said quietly. "I think Jeb killed her." His voice was like the rest of him, wavering, uncertain. Gone was the old confidence Smith had come to recognize. Harry looked like a soldier who had seen enemy fire for the first time, and watched his brother go down.

Smith sat beside him, aware of an underlying sense of destiny, of something coming to an end. "Tell me."

Stowe did, in halting, broken sentences, often seeming to lose the thread of speech before picking it up again. When he told of finding Ruth's body, and then tried to describe the thing he had seen on the stairs, his speech became even more difficult. He had seen Jeb, he said, but it wasn't Jeb; he didn't know how else to explain it. Some kind of apparition . . . "I don't expect you to believe me," he said, when he had finished. "Hell, I don't know if I believe it myself."

"I believe you." When Harry looked up with blank surprise, he said, "You're not the type to get hysterical, are you?"

Stowe blinked at him, then nodded. "I called Sheriff Pepper. Did that much at least. But I couldn't go back to that house, not after . . ."

"What did the sheriff say?"

"Called me back a half-hour later. Said he'd found Ruth's body, all right, but Jeb had been asleep upstairs, never heard a thing. Seemed pretty shook up when he heard the news, the sheriff said. I asked him if Jeb . . . looked all right. He said, sure. A little hung over, and upset, that was all. Hell, I don't know." He shrugged, looking miserable. "Maybe I'm going crazy."

"I don't think so."

"Or maybe I just haven't been getting enough sleep. I've been having these . . . dreams." Stowe waved an arm in front of his face, as if trying to wipe something away. "No. That's why I went there in the first place. I'd *dreamed* it, Billy. I watched her die. And Jeb did it. He pushed her, or at least he made it happen. But there's no evidence, no reason to suspect it. I just can't go accusing him of things like that without proof. What am I supposed to say? I saw it in a dream?"

"No," Billy said. "I suppose not."

"It's only a matter of time before Pepper starts asking questions. Why the hell would I go there at seven in the morning? Why didn't I hang around when I found the body, try to do something for her? Things like that. Before long people are going to hear about it. They'll be looking at me like I'm nuts, avoiding me, or even worse, thinking I had something to do with it."

"It wasn't your fault."

"But it was, don't you see? I should have helped her. Anyway, there's more."

"What else?"

"Pat Friedman killed his wife last night. Pepper told me about it on the phone. That's why he's not here yet, he had to clean up that mess. I guess he came home from work and caught her fucking Bob Rosenberg on their living room couch, took a shotgun, let loose with both barrels. Bob got out, he's pretty shaken up, says that Pat was just out of his mind. Couldn't talk any sense into him."

"Jesus Christ."

"Yeah." Stowe wiped his hand across his stubbled face. "What's happening to this town? It's like everyone's suddenly going crazy all at once."

"Maybe, maybe not."

"I know one thing. I can't keep seeing patients in my state of mind. I'll go crazy then too, if I'm not already."

"I don't think it will come to that."

"What do you mean?"

They looked at each other. "Maybe it's time I do a little talking of my own," Smith said.

* * * * *

He told everything; the dreams, his first violent encounter with Angel on the beach, their visit to the old Taylor property, Annie's advice, his discussion with Dr. Rutherford. He showed Harry the articles about the break-in and the amulet, which were still in his pocket from the day before.

When he had finished, well over an hour had passed. Harry Stowe was shaking his head. "If I hadn't seen . . . I mean . . ."

"I know. That's why I waited to tell you everything."

"I keep thinking I hallucinated it," Stowe said, a little distantly. "But Goddammit, I know the difference. It was real. And his laugh . . . that wasn't Jeb Taylor."

"No," Smith said. "You're right on that one."

"So you've been having these nightmares for how long?"

"The really bad ones, for six months, maybe a year. But now I'm beginning to wonder if I didn't always know about this place, somehow."

"So that's your secret," Stowe said. Listening to Billy's story had seemed to clear his own head, and now he smiled tiredly. "All this time I thought you were a jewel thief on the run from the feds."

"Don't I wish. Then I wouldn't have to work in a dump like this."

They both laughed a little. "We both belong in the nuthouse," Stowe said finally. He ran a hand through his rats' nest of hair. "Jesus, I mean, demons and possession and witches? I went to medical school, for Chrissake. I'm supposed to diagnose delusional thinking, not contribute to it."

"So does that mean you don't believe me?"

"No," he said. His voice held a hint of sadness now, but it had regained some of its strength. "To tell you the truth, I've often felt something in this town wasn't right. But that didn't keep me from coming back here. It . . . drew me back, I think. I've always felt it was like that."

They were both silent a moment. "So, assuming I do believe all of this," Stowe said, "and I guess I don't have a choice, unless I decide we're both crazy—what do we do next?"

"Keep a close eye on Jeb Taylor, for one. We have to find out more about what's happening to him."

Stowe was shaking his head again. "I guess we have nothing to lose by checking things out. Demons. Jesus Christ." But his eyes had regained that haunted look, and now they held the sober glint of fear.

A few minutes later, Sheriff Pepper pulled up outside the clinic and began asking questions. The first were directed at Harry Stowe. What were you doing up at the Taylor place at seven in the morning? Did someone call you? Hear a noise, somebody screaming? What did it look like happened to her? Stowe handled these without much trouble, saying nothing about his suspicions of murder. Then the questions became more difficult. *Why didn't you stay there with the body? Wake up Jeb? Call the police from there?* Stowe did not answer these with as much confidence, and Smith saw the sheriff keep glancing at him, annoyed. Finally he asked what Billy had to do with the whole thing. Smith told him he was just coming into work for the day and ran into Harry, that was all.

Then the deputy had come into the clinic with Julie Friedman's body, and that had ended their discussion abruptly. Harry took his medical bag and wheeled the body into the other room, and Smith busied himself with some paperwork that needed to be done, trying to keep his mind off of what had occurred.

An hour later Harry returned, looking gray-faced, his shirt spotted with blood. "Lord," he said, collapsing into a chair. "She was shot point-blank in the chest. I've never seen such a mess." He rubbed at his stubbled face. "You don't want to see what a shotgun does to a body. Excuse me." He disappeared into the bathroom, and there was silence, then the sounds of retching. He came back a few minutes later, his face pale and wet. Dark circles ringed his eyes. "Sorry. Guess I'm having a bad day."

"You're not the only one."

"No. Julie Friedman had a pretty shitty day too, didn't she?" He shook his head. "My God, I mean, Pat? He's a damn good lawyer. He's the First Selectman."

"Would there be any connection between the Friedmans and Jeb Taylor?"

Harry Stowe looked at him with sudden understanding. "He was their handyman. Jesus, you think he had something to do with it?"

"I don't know."

"I should have never let that boy out of my sight." Harry shrugged. "Maybe we should talk to him. Just go to the house and let him know what we suspect, and see what happens."

"Something tells me that's not a good idea."

"What else can we do? Tell Pepper?"

"You said yourself the police would never believe you. We have no evidence. At least, nothing that doesn't sound crazy."

"We've got to do *something*."

That was how they ended up hunkered down in Billy

Smith's car outside the Taylor home, waiting for Jeb to emerge.

They had pulled off the road at a decent place, with a clear view of the Taylor house, and were using Stowe's binoculars to keep watch. Smith had started the engine as daylight bled from the sky, and turned on the heater. Ten minutes later Jeb stepped through his front door.

They both sat in silence for a moment, concealed from view by a row of bushes, Stowe watching Jeb's legs in the dim light as he went around to his car.

"How does he look?"

"Human," he said dryly. "Better move before he sees us."

Smith pulled out into the road and turned on the headlights, cruising slowly up the hill and by the driveway. They caught a glimpse of taillights flashing once, twice. Smith went up the road a few hundred feet, turned around, and headed back.

The big Chevy was headed down the hill, into town. Jeb drove slowly past the lighted storefronts, turned left on 27, and then pulled into the parking lot of *Johnny's*. Smith drove past, made a U-turn and headed back. When they arrived at the parking lot a second time, Jeb was already inside. They followed him in, saw that he had taken up his customary spot at the end of the bar, and took a booth nearby, thinking they would be there for the night.

But Jeb stayed at the bar only long enough to down two shots of whiskey. Then he left on foot across the square. After a moment's hesitation, they decided that Billy would follow, while Stowe remained in the parking lot to watch the car.

Smith grabbed the flashlight from his glove compartment and set off, trying to keep a good distance in order to keep from being seen. But Jeb never looked back. By the time they passed the gazebo, the last of the sunset had faded and the evening cold had set in. The streetlamps painted hard yellow circles in fifty-foot intervals along the edge of the square, but the light did not reach its center. A bitter wind ripped through the trees and cut through Smith's thin cotton shirt. The air burned his lungs and turned his breath to clouds of steam, raised gooseflesh on his arms. He moved forward through the dark, keeping the flashlight off as the leaves rustled above his head. Jeb's back was an indistinct blob a hundred feet in front of him. A minute later, he realized where they were going.

Jeb Taylor was headed straight for the Thomas mansion.

A thrill ran through him, and he remembered two moments with such complete recall it was as if he were reliving each; the afternoon on the square when he had seen the Thomas mansion for the first time, and later, at the White Falls library, when he had found the painting of the place in winter, leaves off the trees, empty branches reaching into a slate-gray sky. The mansion had seemed to be a living, breathing presence, gazing down upon the town like an angry god, its odd twisting towers and labyrinth of rooms turning stone and wood and brick into flesh.

Now, the house held the same presence. It was a darker shape among shadows, a squatting many-limbed beast.

Jeb paused at the gate, and looked around before quickly scaling the short iron fence and dropping into the long grass on the other side. Smith waited until the boy had blended with the deeper shadows that blanketed the walls of the house, and then darted forward in a half-crouch. He heard the tinkling of glass and a door opening somewhere to the left. Then he was over the gate and running across the long soft grass toward the place where Jeb had disappeared.

About twenty feet from the front door the left wing of the house took a sudden turn inward, forming a brick and stone patio. A window set into a side door had been shattered. No sign of Jeb. But as he crouched against the wall, he could hear someone moving inside. A thud and a muffled crash, as if something had been knocked to the floor. He hesitated. The noises quieted. *Don't lose him, damn it.* He ran across the open space to the door and slipped inside.

Utter darkness enveloped him with ice-cold hands. A musty smell like rotten cloth hung in the air. He paused, waiting for his eyes to adjust. Nothing but blackness inches from his face.

He shuffled ahead and heard muffled footsteps deep within the bowels of the house. He stumbled, struck something heavy and hard with his hip and spun away, fighting the panic that rose in the back of his throat. For the first time, he wished he had brought a gun. Any kind of weapon. The old musty smell deepened until the stench filled his nostrils. He banged his foot, turned again, stumbled forward and something caught him at the waist, flipping him onto his face. The cold wood floor hit him like a slap and he lay there absolutely still, breathing in the dust that had settled on the floorboards.

He struggled to calm himself. What had Harry told him about this house? The last Thomas had died almost a decade ago, soon after the amulet had been stolen, and his will had specified that the house remain untouched. The town had wanted to turn it into a historical landmark, but there was enough money to pay the taxes and the house had remained empty for years now.

The heaviness of the house wrapped itself around him.

He coughed and blinked as the dust swirled against his face like the wings of tiny moths. Smothering silence returned his greeting. Had Jeb heard him fall? He listened, but there were no answering footsteps, no shouts or cursed words. Maybe he could chance the flashlight now. He drew it from his pocket, cupped his palms around the bulb, and flicked it on. The beam glowed a soft red through his flesh, giving his hands a bloody, raw look. He stood up carefully and let a single ray of light escape. It illuminated a room filled with the ghostly shapes of furniture under white sheets.

He was standing between a dining room and a kitchen. Dust was everywhere, coating the floor, the sheets, the walls, swirling lazily in the air. An intricate glass chandelier hung over the dining room table. On the dark, paneled walls were expensive-looking landscapes and portraits of stiff-jawed men and women in period clothing. Against the wall, on top of a cabinet filled with china, sat the marble bust of a man with blank white eyes.

Directly ahead of him, leading through an archway and into the dark, was a line of footprints.

As he passed through the archway and found himself in an empty hall, the echoes began. It seemed just right to call them that; what other word would better describe the voices that seemed to float and hiss and careen all around him, fading in and out like a badly tuned radio?

There was carpeting here. The hall had low ceilings and the same dark-paneled walls. Paintings draped and festooned with cobwebs hung neatly on each side. It seemed to stretch the full length of the house. A tunnel leading through the heart of this monstrous building, icy cold and empty and running with tainted blood.

(. . . *saw him dancing in the dining room* . . .)

(. . . *such a lovely house* . . .)

Smith cupped his hand over the light. Blackness surrounded him once again. He felt like he was standing backstage in a theater, listening to the whispers of a nervous cast before opening night.

(. . . *I really have to go* . . .)

(. . . *Frederick* . . . *we mustn't* . . .)

His heartbeat sped up another notch, and he felt the panic edging in again through the heavy dark. Not Frederick Thomas, the man who had built this horrible house; he was dead, long dead.

*Don't listen to them, William. They can't hurt you.*

*Angel!* His mind went instantly out to her, and he caught himself feeling in the dark for her hand. But it was not quite her voice; feminine, yes, but older. The voice was calm and yet firm.

*You must not listen to them. Just mental footprints, echoes of things that happened a long time ago.*

He probed, reaching out tentatively, and felt her open her mind to him willingly, allowing him to see everything, her life spread out and frozen before his eyes like a photograph. He saw her childhood, Joseph's death through her eyes, her long years of waiting. Waiting for him. Annie.

*Never mind that now. You must go forward to find the answers. Follow Jeb's track, and soon you will know everything. What you have always wanted to know. Who you are.*

He shook his head. *No.* But his mind was filled with fire, his palms wet with sweat. Her words remained with him.

*Help me, Annie.*

No answer this time. He probed for her again and touched only emptiness. He wondered if she had ever been there at all.

The voices returned.

(. . . *do you love me* . . .)

(. . . *no, Frederick, please* . . .)

They had become more insistent, pleading with him, or with someone else long dead. He closed his mind to them. He could not afford to listen to this house's ghosts. He had a feeling that if he let them in he could drift here forever, slowly becoming one of the ghosts himself as he mindlessly wandered these deserted rooms, searching for something he no longer knew how to find.

As he followed the prints a cobweb brushed his face, and he wiped it away, only to feel a plump wriggling body on his skin. The spider, big as a bumblebee, ran down his arm and dropped to the floor. He kept going, past rooms filled with dusty, white shapes, furniture and sculptures and other unknown things hidden under sheets. Mirrors with delicately carved frames next to shelves of books. The house would be a goldmine for antique dealers. All these old treasures slowly rotting away in the dampness. Why would Henry Thomas have wanted such a thing to happen?

*Maybe he knew things about this house other people didn't. Things that he decided should remain hidden.*

The footprints ended at a half-open door on the left side of the hall. He pushed the door open, revealing what must have been the Thomas study. The chamber was empty. Lines of books on mahogany shelves, a heavy, ancient grandfather clock, its striker long silent, an old rolltop desk, a cabinet filled with sculptures and vases and figurines, a big stone fireplace taking up the middle of a wall. The rug under his feet looked Persian and had once been expensive, though now it was covered with dust and had begun to rot through in places. Above the desk hung a portrait of a man dressed in a black coat. His skull-like face held a long prominent nose and thin hard mouth, and yet there was something familiar in his eyes, staring out from beneath hooded brows.

The sound of something heavy being dropped came from somewhere close. He jerked the flashlight away from the painting to another closed door across the room. He crossed the moth-eaten rug, swung the door open and found himself at the top of a staircase leading down into blackness. A damp, moldy smell wafted up at him.

*You're not really thinking of going down there, are you?*

He waited another minute, perfectly still, listening for more sounds, but heard nothing. He took a step down onto the staircase, dust wafting up into the beam of his light. Then another. He pointed the flashlight down into the depths. The darkness ate up the light greedily. He went down.

At the bottom of the steps he found a vast chamber with a stone floor. The coldness from the square stones radiated up through the soles of his shoes. When he lifted the flashlight he could see a wall about thirty feet ahead of him, made of dark, packed earth and crossed with wooden beams. The air was wet; in many spots, chunks of wood from the beams had rotted or been gnawed away. Somewhere nearby he heard water dripping.

The chamber contained nothing but stone and dirt and wooden beams. He played the light slowly along each wall, looking for the entrance to another chamber. The dirt walls were unbroken. He turned and flashed the light behind the stairs, but that space was empty.

He felt a cold draft touch his skin and flicked the light upward. High over his head were more heavy beams. He thought about them rotting through and giving way under the weight of the old house, burying him forever under thousands of pounds of stone and brick and wood. How would it feel to be buried alive?

The house seemed to be coming to life again overhead. He heard creakings, scratchings in the walls. A thump. The sound of footsteps, echoes of voices raised in anger and fear.

(*No, Frederick, keep away from me . . . I won't have . . . we can't . . .*)

Shrieks. More sounds. Running footsteps. A grandfather clock, chiming deep in the bowels of the house. He imagined the dusty old striker starting to swing, slowly at first, then gaining speed.

He stumbled for the stairs, the flashlight beam bobbing across empty space. Silence moved in again at the voices' passing, such complete silence that it was a sound in and of itself. He played the light around the chamber and found it still empty.

The house creaked once, settled, and was still.

*Oh my sweet Jesus.* He stood on shaky legs, realized he had forgotten to breathe, and took in lungfuls of the moist, moldy air. Jeb Taylor was gone. How he had disappeared was a mystery, but he was gone all the same. *The house swallowed him up.*

Somewhere far away, someone seemed to sigh, as if in answer.

As he passed through the study again an unnamed thought made him pause. The house remained silent and still, as if waiting for him to leave. The room was empty, and yet . . . something was there. His eyes returned to the cracked painting that hung over the ancient desk. The old man's eyes were black except for the glint of light in his pupils, which gave him the eerie appearance of life. Staring down at him. Watching.

That face. Where had he seen it?

He shined the light on the grandfather clock and found it silent and still. Even the striker was dusty; a cobweb stretched across its insides. It had not run in ten years.

Standing in the dark room, he found himself drifting back to the day before, the falls crashing beneath his feet at the spot of Joseph Arsenault's tragic death. The constant noise of the water pulling him closer, like a whisper in the dark, *come to me, come to me . . .* His earlier feelings of loss and despair washed over him, along with the inevitable and relentless movement of time holding him helpless in its grip like an animal caught in the headlights.

*If you persist, you will lose everything. You will never be the same.*

The answers were here, all he wanted and more. He could feel them at his fingertips. He walked over to the desk and ran his finger along it, drawing a line in the thick dust. He rattled the top, and found it locked.

There would be a key, of course.

Full of a mindless, still growing need, he searched the room. A minute later the beam of the flashlight uncovered the key near the back of the mantle above the fireplace. He fitted it into the lock on the desk and heard it slide home with a distinct click. He rolled the top of the desk back on its frame.

Papers. Piles of them on the desk's surface, shoved into cubbyholes. He grabbed some, found them to be yellow and crumbling in his hands. He unfolded them carefully, focusing the flashlight by holding it in his teeth. They were letters done in a spidery script, dated 1726, and addressed to a name he could not make out. He read from the first: *Darling Henrietta: We have arrived at last . . .*

Billy set it gently on the desk and picked up a leather-bound diary, rotting in his hands, as old as the letters and inscribed with the same spidery script. He opened it, causing a small trickle of powdery dust to fall from the binding onto the desktop. On the inside cover, in fading ink, was written the name *Frederick Thomas*.

He put the diary down, his heart beating thickly in his throat. Thomas had written these probably at this very desk, hundreds of years ago. That they were genuine, he did not doubt; what they contained he could only guess.

More papers in another cubbyhole, the pages newer and whiter than the others. He pulled them free and smoothed them on the surface of the desk with a trembling hand. Stationery. At the top, above an address, was stamped the name *Henry Thomas* in bold, dark type. The first few pages were full of notes.

> *Made an exciting discovery this morning in the cellar, a secret place that has remained undisturbed for centuries. An artifact in there, I can only guess at its origins but it is genuine (Roman? Assyrian?). With it I have found these letters from Frederick, addressed to Henrietta, and a diary. Perhaps with these I will finally be able to unlock the mysteries of my strange ancestor! As for the piece of stone, it is surely priceless . . .*

The amulet. Henry had brought it up into the light, and there it had waited until Ronnie Taylor came along and set it free.

The notes went on, scrawled with a familiar, heavy hand. Henry had been interested in genealogy. The pages were covered with names, along with references to places in Europe and America. The notes were apparently written as Henry read successive pages of Frederick's old diary.

Finally, on the fourth page of notes, Henry had evidently read something that shook him badly.

*I now have to assume that my ancestor was insane. He is no longer himself—I had thought I had come to know the real Frederick Thomas over these past few days, but now I feel like a stranger has written these pages. He tells of the amulet doing crazy things, and speaks of demons, of death as being only an illusion . . . His writing has turned cold. What he has done to Henrietta, his own sister, in the name of the devil! The things these walls have seen, if he is telling the truth. It sickens me. Do I really have his blood running in my veins?*

The next three pages of notes were connected. Evidently Henry Thomas had done a lot more research on family history. The pages contained an intricate diagram of the Thomas family tree, beginning with Frederick and Henrietta, his sister.

Henrietta had borne him three children.

*Dear God.* Those voices he had heard, those echoes. Frederick had brought his own sister here from England and had kept her as his mistress. He had done unspeakable things in this house, all in the name of . . . what?

The three children, all healthy, had all grown into adulthood and had children of their own. One of them, a male, carried on the Thomas name; the two women took the names of their husbands. The lines continued, mingling with the blood of the town until it seemed each and every resident had a drop of Thomas blood in their veins.

Finally, at the bottom of the third page, he saw something that chilled his own blood. One of the last spaces on the tree was blank, and circled in red ink.

*Thirteenth generation male child, born to Elizabeth Price, May 1, 1963. Given up for adoption. Name and address unknown.*

His own birthdate.

Billy Smith felt a great weight pressing down on him from above that threatened to crush him into dust. Time passing slowly from generation to generation, tainted blood mingling, purifying, thickening, echoes of the past haunting each successive member of the Thomas family as they sat here at this very desk, writing first by the flicker of candle-light, then kerosene lamp, then finally electricity, the coming of the modern age brightening every shadowed corner of the room.

But there were shadows here still.

He moaned; his throat was full of sand. But he had already guessed, hadn't he? Somewhere deep down, he had known that the secret he held inside could destroy him. The strange words Annie had spoken to him, that first day on the square; *I have seen your face.* He realized why the man in the painting above the desk had looked familiar to him. The face was his own.

Still, there was more, and this last bit threatened to push him over the edge and send him careening down that deep, dark hole in his mind. After she had given up her first child for adoption, Elizabeth Price had eventually married the child's father, and become Elizabeth Johnson. They had two more children. One of them was a boy named Michael.

The other, a girl named Gloria.

Billy Smith stared down at the bright red circle of ink. Like blood.

Gloria Johnson. Angel.

*She is my sister.*

The flashlight clattered to the floor; he barely heard it.

He was still sitting there in the dark when the police cruiser pulled up outside.

# Chapter Fifteen

The next morning dawned frosty and gray, the heat that had plagued the little town during the last few weeks holding off in favor of a continuing, bone-chilling cold. In the middle of the last-minute plans for the next day's festival, the church found itself having to begin preparations for two hasty funerals, keeping old Bucky Tarr busy; but when the time finally rolled around to have them (both that same afternoon, one after another), the turnout was surprisingly small. The Friedman service drew a few close friends and several curious onlookers, wondering if the killer would be there (he wasn't). But Ruth Taylor's service was attended by less than ten souls, Jeb Taylor among those conspicuously absent. Perhaps had he been there, he would have been surprised that his grandmother had so few remaining friends. In fact, the majority of those who ordinarily would have come and were not otherwise occupied with the festival preparations had simply stayed home. Most people in White Falls were feeling a bit under the weather today, so to speak. They passed it off in various ways; some decided they had caught one of those nasty spring colds, and one or two decided they felt too depressed. A few claimed to be hung over.

In spite of whatever excuses they were telling themselves, the real reason was the same for all. An odd, vague sense of unease had come over everyone. Had he been asked, old Bucky Tarr might have said a goose had walked over his grave. The people of White Falls were battening down the hatches, preparing for a storm.

At nine that morning, Angel called the clinic and asked to meet with Harry Stowe as soon as possible.

"I'm glad you called," he said, when she had arrived. "I was going to get in touch with you."

"He won't see me," Angel explained, her voice uncertain, the confusion and pain plainly visible on her face. She had had a rough night, waking up at some point to find her pillow wet with tears, and left with only the sense that she had been dreaming of something; of what, exactly, she could not recall. She had reached out for Billy in the dark and found his side of the bed cold and empty, and had been filled with a sense of dread. He hadn't returned, and at seven-thirty the telephone rang, the voice on the other end telling her he had been arrested.

"I went to the jail but they said he wanted to be alone. Please, Dr. Stowe—"

"Call me Harry," Stowe said gently. "I think we've reached a first name basis, don't you?"

"You've got to help me. You've got to talk to him and find out what's happened. The sheriff wouldn't tell me anything."

"Billy won't see me either," Stowe said. "I've tried."

"What's wrong with him? I don't know what the hell to do."

Stowe guided her to the yellow couch and sat her down. "Hold on. I'll get you some water."

"Coffee?"

"Sure, if you'd like."

She looked at him gratefully, aware of how exhausted

she must look, how completely out of touch. She had been sleeping for almost two days straight; how could she still be tired? But there was a fog on her brain that refused to lift no matter how long she remained in bed.

Harry had returned with the coffee. "What's wrong with me?" she said. "I feel like I've been drugged."

He handed it to her in a white Styrofoam cup. "Billy mentioned you were feeling a little sick. Maybe I ought to have a look at you."

"When was the last time you talked with him? Yesterday at work? What did he say?"

"I was with him last night. At least, for the beginning of it."

*"What?"*

"Later," Harry promised. "We've got lots to talk about, I think. Maybe we can help each other. But first, let's see if we can find out if there's anything wrong with you physically."

She protested, but he took her by the hand and led her into the other room, where he made her sit up on the table, his manner turning professional. Took her blood pressure, temperature, looked in her eyes and ears. Listened to her heartbeat. Frowned. "Dizziness?"

"Yes."

"Nausea?"

"Some. I threw up yesterday, but today I kept down a little food." This was exaggerating things; she hadn't been able to eat more than a bagel and fruit juice in three days.

"So you're feeling weak, generally out of it. Mood swings?"

"I suppose, if you call sleeping half the day away a mood swing."

"I do, if it's not your normal routine." Harry frowned

again, turned and rummaged about in a drawer. He turned back to her with a needle, pricked her finger and took a little blood. Then he held up a small container. "I'll need a urine sample."

"Harry—"

He held up a hand. "First things first. You do this and we'll talk. If half of what Billy told me is true, you're going to need your strength."

He took her samples into the cluttered, windowless lab room next door to run the tests, and when he returned to wait out the results, they talked. He told her about finding Ruth's body and his encounter with Jeb Taylor. He told her about Julie Friedman's murder and about their final decision to follow Jeb that night. When he learned of the arrest, Harry said, he had spent the early morning hours talking to the sheriff, trying to get Billy released (he was unable to get Sheriff Pepper to budge an inch—Billy had been caught breaking and entering, and would spend the night in jail, end of story), and then spent another two hours looking for Jeb. No dice. The big Chevy was still in the parking lot of *Johnny's*, and the Taylor home was locked up and dark. The boy had disappeared.

"We've got to see the sheriff again," Angel said desperately. "Maybe both of us together will do more good. I don't care how, we've got to get Billy out—"

"The sheriff can't keep him there forever," Stowe said. "But we'll need a lawyer."

"There's no time! Can't you feel it building? Whatever is going to happen is going to happen *soon*—"

"Calm down, now," Harry said, laying a hand on her arm. "Save your strength. You won't do anybody any good like this, least of all yourself."

She took a deep breath and let it out slowly. Her stomach lurched, and for a moment she thought she might be sick. Another deep breath and the feeling passed.

"Why won't he talk to us, Harry? Why is he shutting me out?"

"I don't know." Stowe frowned. "Something happened in that house, that seems clear enough. Something that shook him up pretty bad. Bad enough to make him change his mind about a lot of things, I guess, or at least make him think it all through again."

"It's driving us apart," she said dully. "Whatever controls this town. Dividing us, making us weaker. Together, we have a chance. One on one, we're as good as dead."

"Now, don't go jumping to conclusions. We need to keep our heads here, and take things one at a time. We've got to get Billy out of jail, I agree with you there. And we need to find Jeb Taylor and make sure he doesn't hurt himself or anybody else. Then we can sit down and reassess this thing—"

She cut him off, her eyes searching his face. "Wait a minute. I get it. You don't really believe all this, do you?"

He hesitated. "It's just . . . you have to admit, in the cold hard light of day, some of it seems a little . . . farfetched."

"I need to know," she said curtly. "I need to know if you're with me. It's all or nothing. I can't afford to trust someone who thinks I'm a lunatic."

"Okay, okay. I'm sorry, and you're right. You'll have to give me some time to adjust, that's all. You just don't throw away thirty years of rationality training in a day."

"I don't think we have a choice. Don't waver on me now. Please. I need you. Billy needs you."

"Right." He sighed. "I've got to check those tests. I'll be right back."

When the door had closed, she slapped her hand against the table in frustration. *Damn it!* She needed him to help her; she would never be able to get Billy out alone. But she didn't know if she could afford to trust someone who had doubts, not now. Time was too short. She could feel it running out on them like sand slipping through her fingers.

And there were other reasons for her anger. She felt left out. What had she been doing these past few days? Sleeping like a baby, while Billy ran around risking his life, chasing a monster who had already killed at least one, maybe two people. All her conscious thoughts about taking control of her life, not letting others make decisions for her, learning to fight, and then as soon as things got a little rough she took to bed like an invalid.

She could not afford to let that happen anymore. *Face the facts, babe. You have responsibilities, to this town, to the people in it, and most of all to yourself, because you made some promises you have to keep, as crazy as they might seem. If you don't, you'll never be able to live with yourself. Besides, you may be the only one left that can stop this from happening.*

Stop what? That was the question. For all their digging, she and Billy had come up with very little in the way of guidance. A couple of frightening experiences, a few teasing words from an old woman who was generally regarded as being several cans short of a six-pack. Suddenly she felt very much as if they had both been lulled to sleep, albeit in different ways, conned into playing along ever since that first day they had driven into town. Maybe she'd had the wrong idea after all. Maybe they couldn't change the future.

*What am I supposed to do? Will you tell me that, please?*

No answer.

A moment later the door opened, and Stowe walked back in and dropped the bombshell she realized she had been waiting for all along.

"I've got the results."

"So, what do I have?" she asked. She could not read the expression on his face. "A cold? Stomach virus?"

"I don't know how to say this."

"What? Am I going to die, or something?"

"Oh, I don't think so."

"Well?"

He took her by the hand. "You're pregnant," he said.

# Chapter Sixteen

Despite the depressed mood of most of the people in town, an admirable effort was made to get the festival off on time. The square was a bustle of activity for most of the day, with Sue Hall presiding. The lawn had been mowed, its edges carefully groomed by Bucky Tarr and his volunteer crew. Booths were constructed and set in place for the selling of pies and cookies and other baked goods supplied by the church board. Various machines for cotton candy and popcorn were delivered and waiting at the town office, and there were a few games for the kids, ring toss and darts. There were balloons and flags of all shapes and colors flying from shop windows, the porches of houses, the gazebo was draped with streamers, and a makeshift sound system was put into place. The maypole rose out of the ground nearby. Colored lights were installed in the lamps along the square and a modest fireworks display was put in place, ready to go off over the river when dusk fell on the following day.

Up at the high school the gymnasium was being prepared for the traditional evening dance, sponsored by the church singles group. The dance had been moved from the gazebo area, where it had been held in years past, to the school, due to the anticipated cold weather during the later hours.

The volunteers were subdued and went about their business quickly, without the usual excited chatter that marked the day before the yearly event. There were fewer tourists than usual this year, but nobody really seemed to notice. They stepped across the cold, moist ground like they were stepping across hot coals, a few of them wincing in an unconscious gesture of disgust, as if something had moved unexpectedly under their feet. The air was heavy and crackling with electricity, and though the weather report had not said anything about showers, people kept glancing up at the sky. In the distance they could hear the falls, and the sound, normally cheerful, now brought a chill to their raw bodies.

By late afternoon the roar had grown to an unnaturally high pitch, and some trick of the wind occasionally made it seem as if the water was muttering to itself. People had stopped looking up at the sky by then. The patterns in the clouds made them feel uneasy.

At first she had been stunned by the news, then angry; why now, why this way? She had always wanted to have a child someday, but she wanted it to be a planned pregnancy, she wanted to be married. But the more she thought about it the better she felt. They were in love, weren't they? That was the important thing. She felt the new life growing within her, a life dependent on her love and protection, and a new and welcome emotion overwhelmed her. She did want to have his child. It was right, after all; she felt it in her heart.

But what would Billy say? Would he be happy (she wanted him to be; oh, how she wanted it), or would he turn his back on her?

He would have to see her now.

They arrived at the police station and asked the deputy at the front desk to see the sheriff. A moment later Pepper came out from in back, adjusting his belt over his sagging stomach, wiping his hands on the shirt of his uniform and leaving dark streaks. His usually pink face was pale, and his eyes looked tired.

"Hello, Doc, Ma'am. What can I do you for?"

Stowe stepped forward. "You know damn well what I want."

Pepper shrugged. "I told you, Harry, I won't release him on bail until I talk to the judge, and that I won't do until Monday morning. He's a flight risk. Sorry, but that's the way it is."

"You can't hold him."

"I can, and I will. We caught him in the act, Harry, and I've got a witness to the whole thing. Myrtle spied him climbing the fence."

"Jesus Christ, Claude—"

"Look, I've got to get down to the square, there's a million things to look after today. My advice to you is, get him a good lawyer."

"I'm his wife," Angel said, cutting in and stepping forward. "I want to see him."

Pepper shook his head. "He's refused all visitors, like I told you before. I can't force him to talk to anybody."

She stepped past his large bulk, going for the door to the back, and he grabbed her arm. She wrenched free. "I'm going to see him, Sheriff. If you want to stop me, you're going to have to arrest me."

For a moment, she thought he might do it. Then he sighed, waved his hand, and said, "Five minutes. That's all. And Harry stays here."

She found him in the last of three cells, lying on his bed. He did not move when she stopped in front of his barred door. The change in him was dramatic. He looked wasted, beaten. His clothes were rumpled, his hair oily and limp, his face an eggshell white except for two dark circles under his eyes.

Had he started drinking again? Was that it? For the first time, she acknowledged her fear of what might happen if he did start again, but she did not let the fear take her over.

She called out his name. He did not move, did not even look at her. "Go away." His voice was flat and empty.

"I won't," she said. "Not until you tell me what's happened."

"I want to be alone."

She felt tears welling up in her eyes and angrily brushed them away with her fingertips. "Damn it, I want to help you. I thought we were in this together. Why are you shutting me out?"

This time he turned his head, and the haunted look in his eyes almost broke her heart; so full of sadness and pain. "You don't understand anything. We were wrong to come here. We were wrong about everything."

"No," she said. "Not all of it. We weren't wrong about you and me. I love you. I want to be with you." *Say it, go ahead. I'm pregnant, Billy.*

But she could not. He turned away and smiled, but there was no humor in his expression. She recoiled from it as if she had been struck. How could she tell him about the baby now?

"Just go. Run, get as far away as you can. It used us, understand? We're just a couple of pawns in a very old, very sick game. The only thing you can do is get out of here before it's too late."

"I won't leave you," she said. The tears were running down her face now, and she couldn't stop them. "I don't care what you say. I won't."

"Please." He turned to her again, and she saw he was close to tears himself. "You're making things worse."

She stepped up to the bars, closed her eyes and before she realized what she meant to do, she was opening herself up like a flower, searching for him, feeling something flex and reach out from inside her mind. The slightest bit of resistance, as if she had placed her hand against a pool of warm water, and then . . .

She had not known for sure if she could do it. She had not tried before, other than that brief moment at Annie's the previous week. But he was there, and she knew it was him like she knew the lines of her own face. For a moment she felt his naked surprise at her entry, a wave of quick, half-formed thoughts leaping out at her, and then a glimmer of something horrible held deep down that was tearing him up inside.

It was as if a door had slammed shut, pushing her back, and she found herself inside her own mind again, bruised and aching. She winced.

"Don't *ever* do that." He was sitting up and staring at her, the black pouches under his eyes like bruises from a beating. "Believe me. You won't like what you see."

She turned from him, sobbing, her earlier determination seeping from her like blood from a wound. She could not tell him, not like this; he was not himself.

Or was this the real Billy Smith? Had she been just fooling herself, thinking she had come to know him?

High in the western hills, Jeb Taylor stood on the Rock as dusk fell over the town. From here, the lights in the houses along the square looked like a ring of fire, burning faintly against the coming of the night. A breeze sprang up, ruffling his hair and bringing color to his cheeks. The words to a familiar song came to him; *Goddamn, doctor man, 'fraid I'm going insane . . .*

Insanity no longer bothered him. Now, he embraced the true meaning in it. Not a loss of control, no; a release, a freedom from the chains of the mind. Insanity was only a name given to something ordinary people could not understand. The power was like a drug, like electricity, he could feel it thrumming in his veins. He owned this town. It was his to do with as he pleased. This was his destiny. This was what he had been waiting for all those lonely years, the power to rule the world and then bring about its destruction.

Somewhere deep inside, a very small, very weak voice tried to raise a final protest. *It's not really you they want, don't you see, they're going to throw you away when they're done, what do you have to offer them?*

But it was much too late for that. He laughed at the voice, ridiculed it. Of course they wanted him. It had been him all along. His father told him so.

*Didn't I tell you, boy? You'll have your revenge. Gonna give you a little taste now, whet your appetite. Then we got work to do before I introduce you to the boss. You ready?*

Yes. The amulet pulsed softly against his skin, slowly, then faster. He raised his arms high over his head, and screamed it into the wind. He was ready, all right.

He had been waiting for a very long time.

Thunder rumbled. All through town, restless bodies tossed and turned in their beds. Sheriff Pepper dreamed of monstrous, slobbering beasts with red eyes and yellow teeth, chained to walking corpses with rotting faces. Myrtle Howard, finishing her copy of *Love Music* and turning out the light, found herself staring up at the pale white ceiling, wondering about drug addicts and demon cults and what they did to women they found alone in bed at night. Harry Stowe could not sleep either; in the faint glow of his nightlight his guilt returned, and he thought of Ruth Taylor lying at the foot of the stairs, her eyes not glazed and sightless, but clear and bright, and fixing him with an accusing stare.

At the jail, two people in separate cells rode the backs of their shame through the night, each of them hearing the soft, seductive whispers of absent lovers, their dreams filled with fire and flood and murder—until one was awakened by his lover coming home. And at the Old Mill Inn, a lonely woman in an empty bed held a pillow to her chest, and dreamed of a man with a ruined face, bending to kiss her lips.

Across the square an unnatural light flickered at the windows of the Thomas mansion. Sounds emanated from within; low, rhythmic chants, the words guttural and possessed with a deep and heady power. The sound joined the rolls of thunder from the sky, separated, joined again.

As the thunder lulled and the voices ceased abruptly, the grandfather clock in the empty study sprang to life. Dusty gears clicked together, whirred, ending a decade of silence. The heavy pendulum began to swing behind the foggy glass. The clock chimed once, twice, three times, four. All the way through twelve.

The minute hand fell into place with a soft click. Midnight. May first.

# Chapter Seventeen

Dick Pritchard stood within the bright well of light inside his father's garage and swore audibly to himself. A car was up on the lift above him, its back tires hanging down just over his head. A long, thin ribbon of black oil still dribbled from the pan and into a bucket below. He had misjudged the distance and oil had splattered across the concrete floor. Now he would have to clean that up too. He still had to dump the old oil, put new oil in, and get the car down off the lift. Add scrubbing the floor to the list, or his father would have his ass. He would never get the fuck out of here, not early enough to get laid, anyway. His girlfriend's parents were still strict enough not to let him come over after eleven, and it was close to ten now.

He kicked at the full bucket, sending more oil slopping over the side onto his foot. His father had no right making him work late like this. Dick stepped over to the workbench at the back and took another beer from the half-empty case, popping the top and downing a third of it in one big gulp. His father was down at *Johnny's*, keeping his fat, greasy ass warm and toasty, throwing a few back with some friends, getting ready for a hell of a party tomorrow. And here he was, alone in this shitty shop and freezing his tail off.

A noise came from somewhere out back. The repair shop included two gas pumps and a junkyard, filled with rusted hunks of Chevys, Fords, and other monsters of American steel (his father wouldn't let a foreign-made car within fifty feet of his garage, and that went for the junkyard, too). The yard was fenced in and lighted, but occasionally some punk would try to cop a free hubcap by climbing the chain-link, or maybe two or three of them would sneak in with a sledgehammer and smash some glass, just for jollies.

Now it sounded like one of them was at it again. Dick waited, listening. A sound like a body falling to the ground, then the scrape of metal against metal. He finished his beer, tossed it with the rest of the dead soldiers (there were quite a few of them now), then stepped out into the cold air and looked around. This promised to be interesting; it was just what he needed tonight, a good ass-whipping. Beat the piss out of someone . . .

The floodlights in the junkyard went out. "Son of a bitch." He stood with only the light of the open garage bay at his back, his shadow stretching out on the ground in front of him. His breath puffed out in front of his face. Impossible to see anything now; the lights over the gas pumps had been turned off two hours ago. He went back inside, checked the breakers and clicked them a few times without success. Some kind of power surge had blown the bulbs. Probably the cold weather. Even with the beer starting to go to his head, he could still feel the cold numbing his hands and face. His nipples felt like hard little pebbles under his work shirt.

"Okay, you fuck," he muttered. "You asked for it." Grabbing the big, heavy-duty flashlight from the workbench, he set off on the sloping dirt path that led around the back of the garage to the junkyard gate. As he walked, he whistled softly to himself, slapping the heavy end of the light against his palm. *Gonna beat some ass tonight.* It had been a while since he had been in a good fight, and he looked forward to it the way some people looked forward to a night on the town.

He reached the fence. It was dark back here behind the garage. He clicked the flashlight on and played it along the gate. The padlock was secure, the gate closed, which didn't mean a thing, except that the little son of a bitch had balls enough to climb the eight-foot high chain-link and drop over.

He let the light play slowly among the rusted hunks of cars, some of them piled two and three deep. The light slipped across shining metal, old rubber, and bits of broken glass. Nothing moved. "Coming in, you pricks," he said loudly. "Ready or not." Taking the ring of keys from his belt, he sprung the lock, then pushed the gate back. A hanging, rusted edge scraped along the frost-covered ground, making a sound like cloth tearing.

As he stood there at the mouth of the junkyard, he felt the first hint of fear, like fingers lightly touching the back of his neck. Something was not quite right here, though for the life of him he could not understand what.

"You hear me, you little fucks? I know you're in there and I'm going to bust your skulls if you don't come out right now."

Movement near the back, just beyond his light, as if someone had darted between two of the older cars. He stepped forward, shining the beam on the spot; a Chevy hot rod and an ancient Dodge truck, thrust up at an angle, its empty headlight sockets staring back at him and trailing two fists of wires like optical nerves. The Dodge's engine was exposed, dull, gray steel thick with grease. The hood was yanked askew and hanging like a flap of skin.

He walked slowly up the narrow aisle in the center of the yard, the bodies of abandoned cars looming over him on either side, most of them stripped of anything useful long ago; cloth ripped, stuffing spilling out, pieces of metal and shards of broken glass protruding like broken bones, hinges sticking out into empty space. They threw misshapen shadows all around him, shadows that were constantly changing as he moved the beam of the flashlight back and forth, stretching and bulging and running from him like living things, until he was no longer sure whether the movements he saw among the narrow rows were real or imagined. Glass crunched under his boots as he walked, and once he kicked an empty bottle that skittered up ahead of him and rebounded off a piece of sheet metal with a dull thud.

Halfway up the aisle the stink hit him, and he stopped for a moment, wondering at the strength of it. Something must have crawled in here and died, a woodchuck or maybe a stray cat. But the smell wasn't quite the same. Not like rotting meat, more like a sewer. Or like he'd stepped in a big pile of dog shit.

The fear came back again, stronger now, like someone had gripped his balls in a vice. His stomach ached with it, and he knew right then that something very bad was going to happen.

Movement at the end of the aisle. He flicked the light up. A very tall man dressed in a long, black coat stood with his back against the chain-link fence, head down, greasy black hair hanging in his face and arms sticking straight out from his sides.

No, not standing; Dick moved the light down, feeling the muscles in his throat contract with fear. There was a good two feet between the man's shoes and the ground.

"You," Dick said, as loudly as he could. Sudden, unreasoning terror made his voice shake. He had forgotten all about his recent desire to fight. "Get down from there, okay? I mean, right now."

The creature lifted its head slowly and fixed him with its fiery gaze. Deep-set eyes burned like two embers in a dead face, the flesh around them yellow and split and running with pus. Dick felt his bladder let go in a warm gush, and he smelled the sharp, fresh scent of his own urine mixing with the smell of shit. All at once he realized two things. He was in the presence of something that no longer belonged to the human race.

And he was not going to leave the junkyard alive.

"Oh," he muttered. "Oh, God—"

Slowly, pinned with the beam of his flashlight, it began to descend, its eyes never leaving his face. An inch, two inches, until finally it was standing on the ground. It lowered its arms to its sides, then took a step forward. Dick stared. Something familiar . . .

*Jeb?* This couldn't possibly be the same spineless twit he went to high school with, could it? He opened his mouth, tried to speak, swallowed, and tried again. What came out was nothing more than a high squeak.

*"On your knees, boy."*

The voice was impossible to resist. He stumbled backward and fell heavily in the dirt, a shard of glass cutting deep into the meat of his thigh. He raised himself enough to kneel, the ground growing moist with his own blood and urine. He had dropped the flashlight, but he was not even offered the simple blessing of darkness; the light had rolled and come to a stop against a flat tire, still pointing straight ahead.

Laughter. The thing was chuckling. The sound was not human, not coming from such a monstrosity as this.

"Jeb," he said, pleading now, his words thick and heavy

in his throat. "That's you, ain't it, buddy?"

"An eye for an eye," the thing rasped. "*Dickie for Dickie.* Time to get what's coming to you. Things gonna be a little different around here."

It stepped closer. Dick recoiled, trying to scramble backwards; the creature raised its arms, and a deep growling sound came from somewhere near the entrance to the junkyard, behind Dick Pritchard's back. He froze, trembling at the promise of blood in that sound. He did not want to see what was making it.

Then the thing in the black coat stepped forward and reached out and he was gagging as the cold, stinking flesh pressed against his face.

He beat at its legs, tried to turn his face away. A hand curled itself around his head, as strong as iron, pushing him forward in a terrible vice-like grip. He began to pray, tears running down his face as his throat stretched, jaws opening past the breaking point, tissue ripping, salty blood wetting his tongue. *Oh God, please, anything, just let me die.*

Then the real pain began.

Pat Friedman came awake with a gasp, and sat up on a damp corner of his narrow bed. He remained still for a minute, confused by the bars on the door; for a moment he had thought, oh, he had thought . . .

What? That he was back in his home, with his wife sleeping peacefully beside him? That would never be again, never, because he had done something so horrible—

*She was a bitch, a no-good slut, you did what you had to do Pat a man's gotta take control of his life you know . . .*

Pat Friedman moaned, cradling his head in his hands. He was dirty and his face and hands were still flecked with dried blood. He had refused a shower, refused to let them touch him for anything. He would not wash off that blood because it belonged to her. It was all he had left.

What had he done? Oh, what had he done?

He had been dreaming the same dream that had haunted him the past few weeks, the one where the things clawed their way out of the dirt and came for him, tipping gravestones into the grass, their footsteps heavy and relentless. Now, he understood what that dream meant. It meant death, and guilt, and payback. *Payback's a bitch, and when it finally comes, you better look out because it's gonna hurt like hell.*

He knew he was going crazy because his thoughts did not make sense anymore, and he could not seem to concentrate on anything for very long. Those recent visions of death and decay had become so vivid he could hardly tell the difference between them and reality. And he had killed his wife, murdered her in cold blood. That fact did not escape him. He remembered the moment too well, the blood seeming to explode from her chest as the shotgun did its dirty work. Was that the act of a sane man? No, of course not. Sane men got angry and then worked their problems out. They sat down and had a beer and talked about it, and maybe if things had gone too far, and too many feelings had been hurt, they got a divorce.

They most certainly did not take a shotgun and blow their wife's guts out through her back.

He whimpered softly to himself, pulling at his snarled hair and rocking slowly back and forth. Lightning flashed, lighting up the cell through the window and throwing the shadows of the bars across the empty hallway, and a moment later thunder cracked overhead, so close it shook the concrete walls. A storm was coming soon, and from the sound, it would be a bad one. When he was a boy and the thunder was particularly loud, his mother had always said that God was rearranging the furniture in his living room.

Pat waited. He rocked, pulled. Clumps of hair fell to his lap. Light rain began to patter on the roof, sounding like hundreds of tiny rat feet skittering across a wood floor. Usually he liked the rain, found it soothing, but now the sound made him shiver. It reminded him of the day of the reverend's funeral, when he had stood on the edge of the grave as the rest of the mourners filed away and listened to the slap of mud as each heavy shovelful was thrown onto the waiting coffin. He thought of his wife lying in the cold ground, under six feet of sodden earth, and tears ran down his blood-smeared cheeks. He saw now that none of it had been her fault; he had been inattentive, fat and lazy. What else could she do? He had driven her into the arms of another man.

He held his hands in front of his face. Blood under his fingernails. He used to get that when she had her period and he touched her down there. He thought about making love to her, holding her close in their warm bed, feeling her breath on his neck. Once, during their first year together, they had been shopping at the mall in Portland, going through the racks in a clothing store, and she had begun to hold up short dresses and strike seductive poses, flirting like a schoolgirl; and then she had glanced around and grabbed him by the hand, leading him into the dressing room, into a private stall. He had taken her up against the thin plywood wall, other customers just a few feet away, and she had tried to keep quiet, really tried, but it had been so hot and so good and finally she was gasping his name, over and over, into the hollow of his neck. Afterward, she told him she loved him, and that he could try on clothes with her anytime.

Back then it had been so pure and so strong. Oh, God, after all that had happened, he still loved her. He would do anything to have her back again. *Please,* he thought, *my wife. I'm sorry, baby. I'm so sorry. Please come back to me.*

A noise, somewhere out of sight. Like a door opening and closing.

Pat sat up straight on his narrow bunk and stared out beyond the bars, into the hallway. But the noise did not come again. Lightning popped three times in quick succession, illuminating everything with white, blazing light; thunder rumbled and split the sky directly overhead. He blinked, trying to chase away the ghost-figures that blazed across his sight. He realized that the hairs on his arms were standing straight up. A trick of the storm, the electricity in the air.

His mind began to gibber at him again. The ache of his guilt was almost too much to bear. He broke down and sobbed, pulling at his hair again. He would pray, yes, that was what he would do. Pray for God to bring her back to him.

The rain began to fall harder, drumming on the roof. Lightning crashed, thunder rolled through the heavens. In the black and white flashes of the silent jail, he thought he saw a shadow moving across the far wall. Was that the soft tread of bare feet on the tiled floor?

Pat stared at his hands again. Blood under his nails. He would not look up, did not dare. Was he afraid that she would not come, or afraid she would?

The soft, lurching steps ceased abruptly. There was a faint, rotten smell on the air, drifting through the cramped cell to caress his face with ice-cold, filthy hands. He stared at the blood caking his fingers, clenching them, unclenching. He felt the hair on his scalp begin to rise.

*Oh, my love, my darling. Have you come? Have you really come back for me?*

He looked up. Someone was standing just outside the cell door, motionless. It was too dark to see clearly, but his eyes followed the slope of shoulder, the gentle curve of hips, the meat of the calf. A woman, surely.

He rose from the bed, whispered her name.

The figure did not move. He blinked, no longer sure whether he was seeing a person standing there, or a shadow. Less than ten feet separated them, but the darkness was thick now, no moonlight through the windows, and the storm rocking the ground outside did not cooperate with a bolt of lightning. He took a single step forward, and then was overcome with sudden doubt; this could not be. He had watched her die. She could not be alive for him, or anyone else. Things had long since passed the point of no return.

And if that was so, then who had come back to claim him?

He blinked again and rubbed a hand across his eyes, but the figure did not disappear as he thought it would. Something was dripping softly and steadily onto the floor. He took a half-step in retreat, felt the iron side of the bunk against the back of his legs, and finally lightning came jagged across the angry sky, shedding light through the window and across the small cell. For a moment he was able to see everything. He bit back a scream.

Julie Friedman stood there in the hallway of the jail. In the flesh. Only a glimpse, but her image was burned into his mind forever; he felt himself frantically scrambling to re-sculpt her in his head, plumping those sunken cheeks, scrubbing the mossy growth from her white skin, restoring color to her gray, lifeless lips. *Yes, yes.* His wife, whole and new, offering him a loving smile. She had forgiven him.

For a moment he had it in his slippery grasp, and then the image dissolved back into the nightmare of his dead wife as the lightning flashed again. Thunder shook the jail to its foundation.

She was dressed in her favorite sundress, the one they had buried her in yesterday afternoon. The dress had ripped down the front, exposing the bloody hole in her chest where the shotgun had done its work. Her breasts were two raw and mangled humps of meat, the skin around them burned black by the heat of the blast. Her hair was plastered to her skull, water running off it onto the floor in muddy streams; she had mud on her face, on her hands and bare feet. Her fingers were white nubs of bone, the nails torn off, flesh rubbed raw where she had clawed at the wood coffin.

The lightning faded and there was blessed darkness again. She raised her arms to him through the bars. A soft, guttural sound escaped her lips that sounded like "come." Something slid wetly down her ruined front, and landed on the floor with a soft plop.

Pat Friedman opened his mouth to scream. All at once something snapped as the connections broke. The lights went out inside his head as if he had blown a mental fuse. It was no longer difficult to re-sculpt his image of her; but not entirely satisfied, he went further. There were no bars separating them, no jail cell, no storm. His wife was whole and alive again. He was floating somewhere in the middle of a warm, soft cloud, nothing to worry about, nothing to fear. After all, she loved him, didn't she? Everyone had their little arguments, but things always worked out in the end.

*Abandon ship. All hands on deck.* He smiled vacantly, dreamily, nodding to himself, but as he went to meet her embrace, he was irritated to find that something had made him pause. One last sliver of doubt; somebody trying to flick the breakers back on up there, which was not a good idea, no sir . . .

He cocked his head. "It won't hurt?" he whispered. His throat felt raw.

She did not answer him. Of course she wouldn't; he did not deserve an answer. He had been a bad boy, but she was willing to forgive him everything. He could see it in her loving gaze. That was all that was important.

He smiled. She held out her arms again on the other side of the door, and he stepped into them, wrapping his hands around her slimy waist, closing his eyes, kissing her cold, slippery lips through the bars. *My love.*

He let her take him down into that blessed darkness.

# PART FOUR: THE FESTIVAL OF THE DEAD

They found the stone rolled away from the tomb. Then they went in and did not find the body... as they were afraid and bowed *their* faces to the earth, they said to them, "Why do you seek the living among the dead?"

—*Luke 24:2–5*

From the diary entry of Mr. Frederick Thomas (undated):

*I am lost.*

*This thing that has hold of me will never rest. I understand that all too well now. It is after something I cannot hope to know, but I must try to hold it at bay, if for no other reason than to spare others' suffering. For I have no doubt that suffering will come, more than I might imagine now. And yet the sound of its voice is like honey, its seduction all-powerful. Promises too dark and wonderful to speak aloud are but an arm's length away.*

*There is something I must mention. Just two nights past, I discovered a most disturbing and yet fascinating passage in a rare dark book called* Necronomicon, *and another in a book with the title which, translated from the Latin, means* Book of the Worm. *According to these two volumes, there exists the possibility of certain black miracles that must remain unnamed, even here. These passages are written in the old tongue, and are cryptic and quite puzzling, but they raise the strangest thrill in me, which I am unable to explain. The rituals described may only be performed on the first of May, when according to the books the spirits will be restless, and moving about when things are set in motion.*

*I am horrified by what these rituals suggest, and yet the ideas will not leave my conscious thoughts. For who, faced with the possibility, would not want to live forever?*

*And yet my head is filled with the most confusing din. So I remain, unable to act, unable even to move from my place at my desk. There are terrible noises in the walls and below the floor, scratchings and ominous thuds, that no rat or even squirrel would make; sounds that send a chill down my spine, and bring to mind horrible thoughts. I wonder what sorts of things I have been doing all those hours when I had thought I was tucked safely in my bed.*

*That is all. Now I must rest, while the daylight, such as it is, still graces the window of my study, and the dark man is at bay. I write all this not to prove my own sanity, but to provide a record in case it is needed. Also, perhaps, to cleanse my own mind of the burdens it has found too heavy to carry in silence.*

*If someday you read this, Hennie, I can only hope it is not too late for you to run from me, for I have had premonitions of a terrible sort. And yet still I cannot bring myself to warn you, for as I have said I am weak, and no match for the powers of darkness.*

*The devil has found me. I pray only for an end to this sudden and horrible madness. May God save my soul.*

# Chapter Eighteen

During the early morning hours the storm began to ease somewhat, and Angel slept more peacefully, her horribly vivid dreams fading into the blurred edges of her subconscious. When she awoke her nausea had eased, and she began to wonder how much of it had been the pregnancy, and how much could be attributable to the town itself infecting her with its sickness like a person passing along a communicable disease. Perhaps it was her newfound sensitivities, but she felt the sickness in the air today, so thick she could smell it, a subtle yet rancid odor, like curdling milk or something similar.

Her thoughts turned back to Billy, and she realized that they had never really left him all through that long night. His rejection of her the day before had not weakened her resolve to have this child she carried in her womb, or to break through the barrier he had erected; on the contrary, she was more determined now than ever to discover his secret, and what it meant. That glimpse she had received when she thrust herself inside his mind, the pain he was struggling to contain, made her love him all the more. He was a mystery; the more of him she thought she understood, the more there was to know.

As she lay in bed and listened to the wind and rain that was still falling steadily outside her window, she had an idea. It was so simple she wondered how she hadn't thought of it before. She would go talk to Annie. Annie would help her. Annie would know what to do about Billy.

She dressed hurriedly, pulling on a pair of jeans and a gray sweatshirt, and then she went downstairs to look for a phone book. The lobby was empty, as were the gift shop and dining room, which was not really surprising. But there was something odd about that emptiness. The smell was stronger down here. Some food had gone bad, probably in the kitchen. *The cook left the milk out,* she thought, *or maybe he forgot some hamburger on the sideboard . . .*

She felt herself being drawn to the big dining room windows as the entire inn rocked from a sudden gust of wind. She crossed the floor between tables set for dinner, deep red tablecloths, white folded napkins, candles in glass bowls. Beneath the tables the dark, wine-colored rug showed the fresh, clean lines of yesterday's vacuuming. The room seemed twice as large with nobody in it, and she suddenly felt very lonely.

When she got to the window she paused, then put her hands on the rain-streaked glass. The lake was swollen to nearly twice its normal size. Water had climbed the banks of grass, submerging the spot where she and Billy had sat and talked that first day; the old mill wheel was leaning and on the verge of being pulled in, and if that happened it would surely go over the dam and smash on the rocks below.

The dam itself looked pitifully small to be holding back such a large body of water. She could hear the river rumbling, the vibration coming up through her feet. It rushed over the little spillway, crashing onto rock and muddy earth, sweeping under the bridge (the water was almost touching the lowest beams, she noticed), and disappearing beyond her sight. The currents in the water were hypnotic; along the banks of the swollen pond, they seemed to flow back upon themselves, moving upstream, before swirling and mingling again in hundreds of little whirlpools. A branch as thick as her thigh floated by, turned lazily in the currents, and snagged itself on the bank.

Finally she pulled herself away with an almost physical wrench. She moved back through the empty dining room, went beyond it, and found a telephone book under the reception desk. The chair was empty, and nothing about it suggested that anyone had been there since late the night before. No half-full cups of coffee, no opened newspaper. *Someone should be here by now . . .*

She looked up the number for the historical society, dialed, and listened to the phone ringing distantly in her ear, once, twice, three times, four. She glanced at the clock on the wall. Past nine-thirty. Sue Hall should be up and open for business. Maybe the historical society had closed down for the festival.

So they had gone out. But something nagged at her. This was not the day to be out running around; obviously, all the planned events on the square would have to be canceled. The rain showed no signs of letting up.

She stood behind the big wood desk and stared at the entrance to the gift shop, and beyond that, the door to outside. Something was not right. She could not put her finger on it, but that feeling of expectancy was growing. She felt as if the very walls had eyes. They were all watching her, peering out from the shadows. She realized she was holding her breath, and let it out slowly between clenched teeth. Around her, the stillness seemed to buzz with an underlying tension. She felt as if she were the only person left alive in the entire world. Stepping out from behind the desk, she fumbled in the pocket of her jeans for the car keys. She didn't want to stay in this empty tomb of a place more than a second longer.

The gift shop was dark, and she paused at the door before going through. No sound or movement came from within. The racks of clothes and shelves of odds and ends were staying put. Feeling a little silly, she took a deep breath and hurried past them, keeping her eyes straight ahead, and when she reached the front door she ducked her head and kept on going, out into the storm.

The wind caught her immediately, and for a moment she thought she might actually leave the ground; her oversized sweater billowed out like a parachute and she fell forward and almost stumbled over the curb. The rain lashed at her tender skin. The storm had gotten worse, and now it seemed to be howling in frustration, perhaps over its failure to pick her up and send her tumbling like a leaf across the asphalt.

Inside the car, she wiped her hand through her wet hair and dried her face with a sleeve, shivering. Her clothes had soaked through to the skin almost instantly. Rain drummed on the metal roof, sounding like a thousand little hammers. Gusts of wind rocked the car on its springs, whistled through tiny cracks, wrenched at the doors. She put the key in the ignition, turned it, pumped the gas. Nothing happened. *Oh, shit.* She slammed her palms against the wheel, pumped the gas again, and turned the key once more. A dry, empty click met her efforts. Then she looked down and saw the gear lever had been left in drive. She shifted to park and this time the engine ground and caught.

The rain came so hard and fast now the wipers were all but useless. Water pounded off the pavement in front of her car, ran down the asphalt in rivers. She passed the high school parking lot, which looked strangely empty, and Pritchard's garage, which looked closed. A minute later she pulled into the circular driveway of the historical society and parked up close to the steps. The wooden sign on the front lawn was swinging crazily back and forth on its short chain, every few moments bashing itself against one of the support posts with a dull thudding sound.

She peered at the house through the passenger side window. It was dark, but the sign on the door said *Open*, and so she readied herself for the dash through the rain and stepped quickly from the car.

Silence met her inside, as the wind slammed the door shut at her back. There was a light on in the kitchen to her right; but the hallway was dark, and there was no light coming from the room at the end where she had used the microfilm machine the week before.

That smell again. Something rotten. Maybe the sewers were backed up? The wind shook the panes of glass in the two narrow windows that flanked the door, battered itself against the roof. Again, she had the feeling that something was not quite right here. Too quiet, for one . . .

"Ms. Hall? Annie?" Her voice intruded on the silence, tried to force it back unsuccessfully. In the kitchen the refrigerator kicked on, causing her to jump slightly.

*Relax, you silly bitch. Don't get your panties in a bunch. They're just downstairs, or maybe out back at the swap shop, getting things under cover and fastened down for the storm.*

She stepped forward, feeling that familiar nervous itch at the back of her neck and uncomfortable prickling under her arms. She moved quietly across the hall rug and paused at the archway to the kitchen. It was empty, but the smell was even stronger in here.

*Little town like this wouldn't have a sewer system, most likely. At least if it did, this house wouldn't be on it.*

That was probably true. So what was that smell?

She found herself staring down at the linoleum floor. A line of muddy footprints led from the edge of the hall carpet, through the kitchen, and disappeared through a door in the back. Somebody had come through here not long ago, and hadn't bothered to wipe off on the welcome mat.

*But these aren't ordinary footprints, are they, sweetheart? This particular person wasn't wearing shoes. Which means they were walking around out there in the freezing cold, in the middle of the storm, in bare feet. Now, who would do a crazy thing like that?*

She knew where that smell was coming from. She knew who had walked through this brightly lit kitchen.

Reverend Hall had come home.

*That's crazy. He's dead and buried.*

But she knew. Her dreams rushed back into her mind, the dreams she had almost managed to wipe from her consciousness over the past few days; her brother's bloated, purple face. Annie's warning about the dead.

*One of them has found a way to return to this world, a window. You must find it and shut it, or the dead will rise again.*

Here were the answers that had been there all along, waiting to be seen, or, more likely, hidden purposefully from her until just this moment; and they pushed at her, wanting to be understood, refusing to be ignored. Her lust for heroin fading so easily, for one. Did she really believe that was all her doing, that simply by letting go of the past she could loosen the physical hold the drug had on her?

*Are you blind, woman? What makes you think that you have been drawn here by something good? Who said that it wasn't all part of the plan for you to be standing here this very moment?*

Oh God, the smell. There was a dead man in this house. She stepped back from the kitchen (so very normal and plain-looking in the bright lights, so *sane*) until she felt her shoulder blades touch the wall. The refrigerator kicked off, and now there was nothing but the howling of the storm outside. She stood frozen, the fear alive in her, confused and struggling to come up with an answer to silence the doubts that had suddenly gained such a strong voice. Then she had it.

*Annie did. Annie said my future wasn't yet written.*

Annie. The thought of the old woman gave her fresh confidence. She glanced back down the gloomy hall, but the door to the basement room was closed. Taking a deep breath, she began to edge very slowly toward it, keeping her back to the wall, her eyes watching for any movement.

*A dead man in this house.*

Horrible images sprang unbidden into her head; imagining what he would look like after a week in the ground, the parasites already at work on him in the coffin, flesh beginning to puff, run, and dissolve. She reached the records room. Risking a quick glance inside, she saw the vague bulk of the microfilm machine and the long glass display case against the wall. The room appeared to be empty. She passed by quickly, and felt the comforting press of the wall again at her back. Then she was facing the closed basement door. She reached across, turned the handle and pulled it open.

The faint, flickering glow of candlelight filtered up from below.

She leaned over the top step and whispered Annie's name. A faint breath of air touched her face, cold and moist and full of the mossy smells she remembered. There was no answering voice, but the stink of decay was not as strong down here, and that decided her. She started down, gripping onto the rail, remembering the last time she had been here, holding tight to the memory. The old woman with the bright, knowing eyes, her hair like a halo of white around her wrinkled face. *Annie, please. Help me.*

She reached the bottom. The basement room was lit by a single candle, placed in the center of the desk at the far end. A sensation of movement made her glance to the left, and now she could see things wriggling in the milky yellow jars on the shelves, suspended in the cloudy fluid like amniotic sacs. She had time to wonder what they might be, and then her gaze fell upon the bed against the wall.

Annie lay on her back, silent and still. Something was wrong with her, with the way she lay with her hair covering her face. Angel hurried forward, and then stopped, her hand creeping to her mouth. The old woman's head had been turned completely around. "Oh, Annie," she whispered hoarsely. She touched the old woman's arm; the skin was still warm under her fingers.

The last of her confidence dissolved, leaving her weak and shaking with fear. The candle flickered, and for a single, horrible moment she thought it would go out and leave her in darkness. It did not, but she felt as if she were being watched, the sensation so strong it started the itch in her scalp again. The smell returned, stronger than before, and she whirled in all directions, fighting panic. Shadows, rippling against the walls, but nothing solid, no lurking, nightmare figure from the grave waiting to lunge at her. She wished for a weapon, anything heavy to hold in her hand. But there were only books and those jars—

*There is no one else in this room, damn it!*

But there was. The air had changed; the temperature had plummeted. She could feel eyes on her. She looked up into the darkness.

A man was hovering flat against the ceiling over her head. A grin played about the corners of his ravaged mouth.

A small, helpless noise escaped her lips. The candle suddenly flared, illuminating him clearly. His grin widened, his features bubbling, running into themselves, a hundred faces moving behind whatever was left of Jeboriah Taylor.

Sheriff Claude Pepper drove through the gloomy streets at a crawl, the rain that lashed at the windshield keeping him from moving any faster. He was irritated, hungry, tired, and shaky. His headlights were on, as was the spotlight on the top of his car, and still he had to lean forward against the wheel and peer out through the frantically sweeping wipers to see anything.

*Wasn't supposed to rain like this, for Chrissake. Weather service said it would be hot and sunny. Clear skies for a week.* Which was why they had gone to all the trouble of setting up the festival outside. The storm had come out of nowhere and surprised them all.

He jumped, his heart skipping a beat, as a trail of something slippery and red slapped wetly against the windshield and then slid up and over the roof; it took a moment before he realized that the fabric was part of a festival banner that had graced the top of the gazebo. He drove slowly past the storefronts and stared miserably out at the destruction on the square. The booths that still stood were leaning one way or another, signs had been ripped out of the ground and tossed fifty feet, bits of red and white and blue paper decorated the limbs of the trees. The maypole had been flipped up and thrown like a javelin, imbedding itself in the gazebo steps, where it quivered in the hurricane wind. There would be no festival today.

But that was the least of his worries. Foremost on his

mind was the fact that everyone in town had apparently gone bonkers all at once. First it was Pat Friedman, shooting his wife the way he did, which was the craziest thing that had happened in years. But apparently that was just an opening act. During the past several hours he had received no less than twenty calls from frightened residents, reporting to have seen some sort of creatures walking in the streets. The first calls had come to his home during the early hours, plucking him from a restless sleep, and they continued, unabated, for the rest of the morning. A few of them had whispered urgently into the phones (their voices full of hysterical fear), saying that they had barricaded themselves in some back room, insisting that their dead relatives had come back to claim them. He had tried to calm these callers as best he could, and had promised to send someone; then he had gotten both his deputies out of bed and handed them the job. After all, what were deputies for?

Except neither of them had reported in, and soon after that a phone line had gone down somewhere, and he didn't know whether they'd both driven to Brunswick for doughnuts and coffee, or whether he was dealing with the end of the world here.

Before he left the house, he'd taken his lucky Smith and Wesson out of the safe and loaded it, the first time he'd done that in over a year. He didn't really know why, only that he had started feeling a general nervousness about the whole situation and it bothered him. He was not really one to go along with gut instinct, but here it was, and shouting quite loudly to be heard. *A cop's gotta feel things,* his father had always said. *You develop a kind of radar for trouble.* Until now, he hadn't really understood what his daddy meant.

He continued up the square, not sure what he was looking for, but needing to have a look all the same. There were no other cars on the road. Most of the houses he had passed were dark and hostile, shades pulled or curtains drawn. Were there people in them, cowering behind overturned couches, behind locked doors, gripping the barrels of shotguns? Worse, had his deputies knocked on a couple of those doors, invited themselves in, and gotten their heads blown off by itchy trigger fingers? The thought brought a feeling of sick dread to his empty stomach.

As he passed the end of the green he spotted someone walking along the upper side of the road that ringed the square, a vague shape in the blowing sheet of rain, dressed in what appeared to be a nightshirt or something similar.

In this weather? *Jesus, Mary, and Joseph.* The whole world had gone crazy.

He backed the car up and swung it around. The figure continued walking slowly away from him along the edge of the road. As he got closer he trained the spotlight on it. A woman, and a big one, by the look of her. Naked under the nightdress, too, the white fabric clung to her back, exposing her flabby buttocks and thighs. There was something wrong with her, that much was apparent. She walked with a stumbling, lurching gait, her arms down at her bulging sides.

He honked the horn, but got no response. *Jesus,* he thought suddenly, *that looks like Barbara Trask.* The thought of dealing with her craziness did not particularly appeal to him, but she was obviously in serious trouble. He honked again, stopped the car just behind her, settled his hat firmly on his head and stepped out into the storm.

It was not as bad as it could be here, with the trees sheltering the worst of it. Still, he gasped as the needle-like, blowing raindrops whipped his bare skin. The wind tried to snatch his hat from his head and he slapped a hand on it to hold it down.

Barbara had continued moving slowly away from him, and he shouted her name, but she did not change direction or indicate that she had heard him. He approached her and put a hand on her ice-cold shoulder. Just before he turned her to face him, something in his stomach did a lazy, backward flip. *Something is very wrong.*

The first thing he saw as she turned was her staring, unfocused eyes that seemed to look right through him. Then he glanced down, and stumbled back away from her, feeling his stomach trying to heave up whatever food he had left from dinner the night before. He tried to regain his balance, lost the battle and ended up on his rear in the cold rain, with the taste of bitter stomach acid in his mouth.

Something had torn out her throat. Her head lolled on her ruined neck. Blood still oozed from the ragged wound, but the rain washed it away as quickly as it came, leaving the meaty flesh clean and exposed.

His stomach heaved again, hugely, and he gagged and spat onto the ground. As if in answer, a piece of paper flipped through the air and landed on the pavement at his feet; *Don't miss the festivities!* it said. The print was starting to bleed down the page in streaks of red. *Join us on the square . . .*

He spat on the paper and wiped the rain from his face, struggling for control. Barbara had crossed the road and was moving toward the Thomas mansion. He watched her, fear and nausea making him weak-kneed. *She's dead,* he thought, *Jesus, she was mangled, nothing could live through that—*

*She's not dead for Chrissake, she's in shock, now get off your big fat ass and do something!*

He heaved himself to his feet. He knew what had made that wound. That was a dog bite. The worst he'd ever seen, but a dog had done it, all right. She had reported her dog missing yesterday morning, but they hadn't been able to find it (*serves her right,* he had thought at the time, hearing the news); today, she must have spotted it, tried to chase it down and been attacked.

*Can't trust a dog,* he heard his father saying, *you could have one for ten years and then one day they'll turn on you just as quick as you please. Wild animals, pure and simple.*

Maybe it had gone rabid. He would have to find it and kill it. Surprisingly, the thought gave him no real pleasure. He felt only disgust and a rolling, queasy sort of fear. But now he had to chase down Barbara Trask or she would bleed to death.

He crossed the road after her. Barbara had passed the gate to the mansion and was now almost to the side door, moving with the same slow, lurching steps as before. Strange, the way she moved. He remembered the fearful voices on the other end of the phone this morning.

*She's in shock, that's all, you've seen it before. She needs blankets and medical attention, fast.* He passed through the gate and up the walk just as she disappeared inside the house. He stopped in front of the open door. Dark in there. Something told him to stay outside. He pulled his weapon, checked it, and then stepped into the darkness. "Barbara?"

He had time to see a pair of glowing, hellish eyes coming at him, and then he was hit in the chest by a huge, twisting bundle of fur. It knocked him back against the frame of the door, jaws snapping, its powerful neck pressing forward. He wedged his forearm in between its teeth, felt them crunch down on skin and bone, the blood running hot and wet down his arm. He raised the Smith and Wesson from his side, pressed it into soft, yielding flesh, and pulled the trigger.

The report was muffled, but he felt the big body jerk in his arms. For a moment the jaws tightened even further and he screamed with the pain, squeezing the trigger again, then once more. This time, the dog went limp, and he let it fall to the floor with a heavy thump.

*Oh, God. Motherfucking Christ.* The vicious son of a bitch had been right here, all along. Which was probably why Barbara had come here in the first place, still trying to rescue the same goddamn mutt that had ripped out her throat. His arm throbbed with pain, and the smell of the gun was strong, momentarily overpowering the other, more disturbing stink he had noticed the second he stepped into the house. The wind plucked at his back through the open door.

*Fucking hellhound.* He kicked at the body at his feet, put another bullet in it for good measure, then stepped over it, cradling his hurt arm against his chest. If it had rabies, he would have to get a shot, and he hated needles. Now he knew why he didn't like dogs. His father had been right. You couldn't trust them.

"Barbara!" he shouted, into the silence of the house. No answer. *Crazy woman,* he thought, *gonna wander around in here until she passes out. I'll be lucky to find her in time . . .*

He heard a scratching noise behind him.

He whirled. The dog had dragged itself to its feet and was standing in the dim light of the open door. It was braced with its paws set widely apart and its head hanging low; but it was standing. It was alive.

*No. Not alive.* It had taken four shots to the chest. Even as he raised the gun again, that fact pressed down on him and weakened his grip. The damage done had to have been fatal. And it was not breathing. He could see that from where he stood.

He fired. The bullet ripped a chunk of flesh from the dog's right shoulder. It staggered, then came at him. He fired again, and again, muttering to himself as the hammer fell on an empty chamber and the dog kept coming.

He kept pulling the trigger of his lucky Smith and Wesson, hearing the clicks. He stumbled backwards, over a piece of furniture; the creature was upon him, snapping, ripping, tearing. He put up a hand weakly, felt it seized in an iron grip, and then the teeth were at his throat.

*Dear God,* he thought, and a moment's grace let him wonder if this was the end, after all.

Then he thought nothing more.

# Chapter Nineteen

There were limits, Billy Smith told himself within the confines of that cold, empty jail cell, to what a mind could take. And there were checks and balances, a cosmic scale. If something especially good happened, then something equally bad would return the favor, and vice versa. It was a theory that had been with him all his life, and though he supposed it wasn't the best way to live, always looking over your shoulder if you were happy, it had served him well when things had gone sour; he always had something to hope for.

But now hope eluded him. The theory simply did not hold any water. He had suffered much, and just when he thought he had a chance at happiness again, he discovered that someone had played a cruel joke. There were no limits after all, this joker said with a smile and a shake of the head. You just roll the dice, buddy, and whatever comes up, you get. But it's house rules here, and house dice too, and guess what, they're loaded. Nothing we can do about that, sorry.

Last night, the dreams had been the worst he could remember. He dreamed of death coming home, in the flesh. One long, continuous dream that was so clear and vivid it might have been real.

As the sky in the east began to turn the color of lead with the approaching dawn, the dead of White Falls clawed their way out. They pushed up through layers of heavy earth, their bony hands grasping the sides of muddy graves like misshapen children fighting their way from the womb. They returned to their husbands, their wives, their lovers, their children, seeking life that they had given freely, and now wanted back. They came in waves, stumbling through empty, rain-washed streets, mouths gaping, blind and hungry and united by a single voice; *return what is mine.*

He watched it all happen. And then, just as he thought it could not get any worse, he had been granted a look from the other side.

The world went dark. Color bled out of it like a shirt running in the wash. His limbs grew cold and lost all feeling. He began to float within himself as the ground faded away beneath his feet. He was offered a glimpse of the void beyond; blackness there, emptiness, horrible, maddening, endless space without light or warmth or taste or smell. He heard the noiseless screams of the walking dead, and screamed with them, suddenly filled with a mindless hunger. Life had been cruelly snatched from his grasp; he wanted it back. *He wanted it back.*

When he awoke, sobbing, the hunger was still very much with him, its bitter taste lining the inside of his mouth like the morning after an especially rough bender. The jail cell in which he lay was cold and gray, full of the stench of stale human sweat. He had gained a new perspective. His body was a frail shell made up of dead and dying cells, a mortal thing that would fail soon enough and leave him floating in the horrible emptiness of the void. No amount of human company would ease this pain. If he looked into human faces, searching for understanding, he would see instead the number of years they had left, months, days. Perhaps he would even be able to see them slowly dying, hair turning gray, skin wrinkling and sagging by degrees as the structures underneath dried up and cracked and dissolved.

*And there's more to this game, pal. We ain't done with you yet.* He felt as if a great battle was being waged for his soul, but he had no weapons with which to fight. The dream and the hunger had revived the thirst again, and now it raged on. His throat ached for the burn, his fingers longed to feel the cool smooth glass of the bottle.

*Roll the dice. Sometimes the dice go sour. Sorry, nothing we can do about that. House rules.*

He sat in the empty cell, his head cradled in his hands, and wondered. His life seemed to lay itself out for inspection. He realized that everything that had happened, everything he had done, had been leading him to this place. His adoption, his adopted mother's death, his drinking, the accident, his isolation, his guilt and obsession. And then the dreams, providing the final push. Perhaps they were some kind of trace memory, living on in brain cells inherited from Frederick Thomas, operating instinctively to carry out the man's poisonous plan, like a homing pigeon returning to the nest, bringing its cargo to the required drop spot without the slightest conscious intention of doing so.

If so, he had been a fool. They had all been pawns in the hands of a man who had been dead over one hundred and fifty years. The dreams hadn't come to warn him at all; they had come to bring him home. He had found his way home, all right. But first he had gone and collected his long-lost sister, kidnapped her, and locked her in handcuffs until she agreed to go along with his crazy scheme. They had managed to fall in love, which perhaps was more of the game; then, finally, he had driven her away when he needed her most.

*Had no choice there, though, did you, pal? Not if you wanted to hang on to what's left of your sanity.* True. He could not face her and tell the truth. He did not want to hurt her that way. Why not keep the secret and hold it deep inside where it couldn't do any more real damage? Besides, something told him that the best thing she could do now was leave, take the car and run, as far away from him and this town as she could get.

Except it wasn't going to work out that way, and he knew it. The game wasn't over yet.

A door opened somewhere near the front of the building. Up to this point, he hadn't really thought why the deputies hadn't shown up with his breakfast; now, almost despite himself, he felt his stomach growling. *Bodily functions don't care much about all that self-pitying romantic bullshit,* he told himself grimly. *They just go about their business. You ought to take a lesson from them.*

Another door opened, closer this time. He heard footsteps, which stopped abruptly nearby; a muffled oath and a long moment of silence; then the steps resumed, and Harry Stowe appeared outside his door. Stowe's hair was plastered wetly to his scalp and his face was grim.

"He's taken her," Stowe said. He held a ring of keys in his hand. "There's no time for your bullshit. We have to go."

Harry Stowe had arrived at work as usual that morning, planning to take a half-day. He hadn't slept well, but that was to be expected. He couldn't let that interfere with his life. He still had a job to do. Jackie Marshal was coming in for a check-up; Lester Pritchard wanted some painkillers for his tooth. But when the time rolled around for his first appointment, Jackie Marshal never showed. Lester Pritchard didn't come in either, but by that time, Stowe had begun to get an uneasy, burning sensation in his gut. He tried the

Marshal house, and got no answer. Same at the Pritchard garage. Finally, he tried the police station, and when the phone continued to ring emptily against his ear, that nervous feeling turned itself up a notch. Not sure why, he dialed the number for the Old Mill Inn. No answer there, either.

*You didn't listen to her, did you? She told you that time was running out.*

He picked up the phone again, but this time the line was dead. The wind must have taken it down somewhere. He climbed into the car and drove down the street through the rain, and when he saw her car was gone from the Old Mill parking lot the nervous feeling upgraded itself to serious fear. He thought about Jeb Taylor, the way the boy had looked on the stairs the morning he had found Ruth's body. Jeb Taylor was no longer himself. Something had taken hold of him. Had it infected everyone else in town as well?

He was driving past the high school when he spotted Angel's car parked in front of Sue Hall's place. He got out into the rain and stood hunched at the door, ringing the bell again and again. No answer. Finally he returned to the car to figure out what to do next, and that's when he spotted Jeb's car parked in back, partially concealed by the garage.

Did Jeb have Angel? There was no real reason to think so, and yet the feeling would not leave him. Time was running out.

Filled with a sudden fear he turned around and drove to the police station. When he got there he found the door wrenched open and the front room empty. It smelled strange in here, a smell he recognized but couldn't quite place. A line of muddy footprints led beyond the door into the back.

He grabbed the ring of keys from a hook behind the desk

and followed the footprints, not sure what he would see. Pat Friedman's cell was empty. Bits of blood, bone, and matted hair clung to several of the bars. *Almost as if he squeezed right through. But that would shatter his skull . . .*

He wiped the unsettling image from his mind. When he stopped in front of the next cell, Billy Smith was already staring up at him from the cot along the wall. He looked terrible. Huge dark circles ringed his eyes, and his usually intense features had gained another dimension, producing the haunted, skeletal look Stowe had seen only a few times before in his worst patients. People who had witnessed a great tragedy, or were told they had a month to live.

"Ironic," Smith said. "That I end up in here again, after all that's happened. Locked up in another cell. I guess it's where I belong."

In answer, Stowe fumbled through the ring of keys. They made a faint jingling sound as they tumbled together. He tried one, then another. The third one threw the bolts, and he slid open the cell door. "Not anymore," he said. "Now, let's go."

"Where?"

Stowe paused. Jesus, he was acting like a lunatic. "I'm not sure," he admitted. "But Angel's gone. We have to find her."

"I told her to get away from this place," Smith said. He didn't wait for a reply. His face seemed to waver a moment, though it was hard to tell whether he was distressed, relieved, or a little of both.

"She didn't run because she's pregnant," Stowe said bluntly. "I tested her myself."

"Oh, my God."

"She wanted to tell you . . ."

Smith wasn't listening. Sudden understanding washed

over his face. "He wants the child," he whispered. "That's what he's always wanted."

"Who?"

As if in answer, Smith closed his eyes. His body went rigid, then relaxed. He sat there for a minute, perfectly still, slumped against the wall. Expressions played about his face, not quite his own and yet strangely familiar. Then he opened his eyes.

"I know where she is," he said.

His mind flexed and reached and then joined, two becoming one, two halves of the same mind. A feeling of completion, unity, satisfaction. Her essence flowed within him, the wings fluttering in his hands, the taste of candy apples filling his mouth, the color blue washing over his sight like ocean water.

Then the fear began. He was seeing through her eyes, feeling her emotions. She was scared all right, and confused, like a bird cupped in a giant hand, heart beating like a jackhammer. *Dark now and dead so many dead his face oh his face . . .*

A jumble of images, flipping by so fast. Memory. An empty house, a dark hallway, a set of stairs leading down. Darkness, fear growing, gaining a voice. *We have been waiting for you.* A face leering out of the dark overhead, a demon's face, twisting and churning, liquid features. Touched by ice-cold hands; darkness and confusion; then the cold wet rain, moving through the gates and up to the door of a monstrous house, and through, and more darkness.

Then he felt her pause, questioning, and he knew she had felt him. He withdrew carefully, slowly, before she could sense anything else. He was open and vulnerable now; she could read him too easily. He did not want her to discover his secret.

When he returned to himself and opened his eyes, the sudden emptiness made him gasp. He felt incomplete, torn in two. He had never fully realized how close two people could be, sharing the same breath, the same blood, the same mind. He had never been a hardcore drug user, alcohol had always been enough for him. Only once had he tried anything stronger, and that was during his freshman year in college, when he had dropped a single hit of acid. Now he was reminded of that feeling, a disassociation that brought on a whole new perception of the world. It was as if someone had opened the door to another dimension and given him a peek before slamming it rudely in his face.

Harry Stowe was staring at him with a mixture of wonder and apprehension, and he realized he must have spoken. "Where?" Stowe asked. "Where are they?"

The last image remained with him. The black gates, the narrow walk, the huge house looming over them. "The Thomas mansion," he said. "At least, that's where they were. I don't know how long ago. It felt like a memory."

"You were with her just now, weren't you? I could see it in your face, some of her expressions . . . eerie." He shook his head. "Like there were two of you."

"We're connected, somehow." He waved his hand. Suddenly he felt almost helplessly angry. All the pieces had fallen into place. *A child.* The fruit of their passion growing even now inside her. The product of years of crossbreeding the damned, incest upon incest. New life tainted with old blood, pure blood. That was what Frederick Thomas was after, all along, why he had reached across the years and dragged them thousands of miles to this town.

New life.

Harry had crossed the small cell and was holding his arm, lifting him to his feet. "He'll kill her," Smith whispered. "When he's gotten what he wants."

"Then let's get going."

He was muttering to himself now; his dream of the night before had snuck stealthily back into his head. Not exactly the dream, but the feelings it had invoked. He remembered the awful emptiness of that place, the way his body felt after he awoke, a frail shell, already dying.

*New life.*

Harry stood firmly, holding both his arms now and keeping him upright, looking into his face. He could see every pore in Harry's skin, dead cells clinging to them in a dull-gray film of biological waste. Dead hair and nails, dead eyes. Decay, happening even as he watched.

Harry was talking to him. "I don't know what's happened to you over the past few days," he said, "what's made you lose your faith. But you have a chance to help her now. Help all of us. But we have to move."

"You might not like what you see. What we find out there."

"I can handle it," Harry said. The hard glint was back in his eyes. "I can handle whatever that bastard throws at us."

*Maybe so,* Billy Smith thought. *But can I?*

They returned to the front room of the empty police station. Several rifles stood behind glass on a rack on the back wall. Stowe broke the glass and reached through.

There were blue raincoats in the closet. Some sort of automatic pistol lay in the top right-hand drawer of the front desk, unloaded, along with a pair of handcuffs. Smith pocketed them both. It took them a few minutes to find the ammunition, but they finally located it in the locked bottom drawer of the file cabinet. Three boxes of shells for the rifles (they emptied these into their pockets) and two clips for the handgun. Then Smith went through the desk again, looking for a flashlight. The Thomas place would be dark. Finally, he found a heavy-duty model with a steel grip winking at him from the back of the middle drawer.

The wind screeched and battered them as they climbed into Stowe's Volvo. Little raging rivers ran down the pavement, carrying leaves and twigs and bits of trash. They could see part of the square between the backs of houses, and even through the blowing rain the destruction was clearly visible. Bits of color clung to the treetops, pieces of tattered decorations. The booths were nothing more than shattered boards sticking up from the ground.

They made it out of the parking lot. On the way past the church cemetery, Stowe suddenly clamped both feet down on the brake pedal. The big car came to a shuddering, sliding stop in the middle of the road.

"Holy fuck," Stowe said in awe. The cemetery looked like a battlefield. The ground had erupted, spilling mud and hunks of sod everywhere. Stones had been tipped up and overturned, and now lay every which way in the grass like broken teeth. Empty graves loomed here and there like black, open sores in the earth. The cemetery gate swung back and forth in the storm, making a cracking sound like a bone breaking as it clipped the posts and rebounded, again and again.

The windshield wipers whined. At the far end of their line of sight, where the church building met the cemetery plots, there was movement, barely visible through the sheet of rain. Something gray and naked and obscenely human slipped around the corner of the building and disappeared.

* * * * *

They drove on, skirting the edge of the ravaged square, and pulled up in front of the Thomas mansion. It crouched among the trees like a huge and twisted animal ready to spring. Most of the upper windows were shuttered, but one on the right was bare, and gave him the unsettling feeling that the house was winking at them.

Stowe was pulling the rifle out of the back seat and popping shells into it, one by one. "Used to go deer hunting with my uncle up in the hills when I was a kid. Never killed anything before. Once I had one in my sights, and I froze up. Just froze up. Damn thing looked at me, turned tail, and hopped away." He gave Smith a look that was almost a grimace. "Sorry, I was rambling. I do that when I'm nervous."

"Harry—"

"What are we hunting? Can you tell me that? Anything that can be killed?"

The question seemed to hang in the air. *We both know damn well what we're hunting,* he thought, but didn't say it. Finally, he shrugged. "We'll know when we see it."

Stowe was looking at him again. "Those graves," he said. "Nobody dug them up, did they?"

"Not exactly."

"Oh, hell. Night of the living dead." He sighed and wiped a hand across his face. "I told you I can handle it."

Smith was thinking about the child again. His child. Nothing more than a collection of cells at this point, clinging to the wall of her womb. But Frederick Thomas was reaching out from the void even now, with the help of Jeb Taylor, wanting to claim those cells for himself, wanting to create . . . what? A lifeless husk to inhabit? A walking, breathing vehicle for another soul? And if he succeeded, what would he bring with him into the world? Such a resurrection surely had a price.

Stowe had opened the door, and the cold wet rain blowing across the car and into his face brought him back. Smith pulled the gun from his pocket and slapped a clip into the butt, the way he'd seen it done. The back of his throat itched for a drink. He shut it out of his mind and stepped out of the car. He had to act now, or the town and everyone in it would be lost. And he knew Angel would not survive whatever was supposed to happen. He would be responsible for her death, above all others. His sister. A surge of conflicting emotion washed over him. God, he still loved her, still wanted desperately to be with her. He couldn't shut the feelings off like that, no matter how hard he tried.

They crossed in front of the car and trotted up the walk. Rain dripped down around his ears, into the collar of the slicker. It slid like cold hands down his back to his waist. He stared at the house. The anger was growing, and now the fear came too, and he welcomed it. Fear, he could handle. Fear was natural.

The door was wide open, the same side door he had entered a few evenings before in pursuit of Jeb Taylor. Beyond it, darkness beckoned. Smith wrestled the big silver flashlight out of his pocket and switched it on.

Inside the smell hit him at once. He played the light around the floor and saw a number of muddy, incoherent tracks leading off in the direction of the hall. There were signs of a struggle; bloody splashes on the white sheets.

Then the light fell upon the body hanging beneath the arch. It was a young man in greasy overalls, tall and well built. His hands had been nailed to the frame on each side of the arch, and he hung crucified, his body slumped forward, his legs splayed wide apart and bent at odd angles below the knee, his feet nailed to the floor. Blood ran down the overalls in a dark, dripping stain, and pooled on the floor below his crotch. There was something else odd about the body, but it took him a second to realize what it was. The boy's head had been turned around to face backwards.

He heard a sharp intake of breath from behind him, and then Harry hurried forward. But there was nothing that could be done to save this patient. Harry touched the head, turning it back towards the light. It wobbled loosely on its stalk of a neck, and Smith felt a greasy sickness in his belly. "Broken," Harry said. "Arms and legs, too." His voice held the barest tremor. "It's Dick Pritchard, Lester's boy. About Jeb's age. One of the ones who picked on him when they were kids. Poor son of a bitch."

"We'll have to get him down," Smith said. "We have to go through." He set the handgun and flashlight on the sheet-covered table, moved forward and grasped the cold, dead flesh of the boy's right arm, as Harry grabbed the left. "Pull," he said. There was a terrible, wet, tearing sound as the nails jerked through flesh, and then they lowered the body gently to the floor. As it fell forward, the nails came free from the boy's feet, leaving two small, nearly bloodless holes.

"That was bad," Smith said. He wiped his mouth with the back of his hand, feeling his belly begin to churn again. *Only the beginning,* he thought, *if you can't stand up to this much, then you might as well go home.* There were worse things ahead. The back of his throat began to itch again, as if in reply.

Just as they reached the study the voices began again. At first they were nothing more than a whisper, almost inaudible over the muffled howl of the wind. Then they gained strength like a radio tuning itself in, floating through the cavernous rooms, echoes drifting down across the years.

"Do you hear that?" Stowe asked. He had stopped dead in his tracks at the study door, listening.

"I hear them," Smith said grimly. "Don't pay any attention."

But it was difficult. The voices had taken a distinctively nasty turn. They ranted and raved incoherently. There were screams of pain, a woman sobbing. Sounds of a struggle; the screams began again. Another voice, male, spoke in a tongue Smith had never heard before. The words were guttural, corrupt, obscene.

The footprints led to the basement door. Smith shined the light down the first few steps. "This may be the end of the line," he said. "I was in this cellar the last time, and it doesn't seem to have any way out."

The voices went on, ranting louder now. They looked at each other. There didn't seem to be anything else to say. Smith began down the steps, the gun and flashlight held out against the dark, one in each hand.

When he reached the cold stone floor he swept the light along the walls and was relieved to find the carved earth chamber empty once again. He let out a deep breath. The heavy, rotten beams seemed to breathe with him, and he thought, quite clearly, *if this house is alive, I am standing in its lungs.*

"Jeb Taylor disappeared down here once before," he said. "There must be another way out. We have to find it."

They began to search the big, empty room. The voices continued above them, muffled now like the storm, shrieks of agony, screams of rage and violence, and then the shrieks slowly dissolving into a woman's racking sobs. *You bastard,* Smith thought as he worked his way around the room, searching for cracks in the solid earthen walls. *You raped her. Raped your own sister.* Henrietta had had three children by him. Had the rape happened again, and again? Or had she finally given in, her spirit broken, willing to submit if only to avoid the physical pain Frederick inflicted?

The majority of muddy tracks seemed to congregate in one corner of the room, and that was where they finally found what they were looking for. A corner of one of the big stone slabs was a little out of place, and when they tried to lift it they found it was just a thin, flat piece of rock that concealed an old rotten trapdoor underneath. They raised the heavy trapdoor together, with some difficulty, the edges of the wood crumbling in their hands and making it almost impossible to gain a solid grip.

Below it, a square, black hole, descending deeper into the earth. From this rose a stench that made all the others pale in comparison. Stowe stumbled away from it, holding a hand across his nose and mouth. "My God," he breathed softly, through his fingers.

The flashlight revealed the remains of a wooden ladder clinging to one side of the hole, its rungs streaked with fresh blood. Smith put the gun in his pocket and stepped down on the first rung carefully, feeling the spongy wood give under his shoes, and then lowered himself to the next. Incredibly, the wood held. He felt dirt pressing in close on all sides, and kept going, knowing that to stop would be to give in to claustrophobia.

Thankfully, the ladder was no more than six or seven feet long. From the bottom rung there was another drop of a few feet, and then he was standing on the packed earth floor of a narrow, black tunnel, perhaps three yards across at its widest point. He flashed the light around and saw crumbling wooden beams bracing the low ceiling at intermittent intervals. Dirty water dripped down the walls. A faint breath of noxious air touched his face, and was gone.

His hackles rose. He drew the gun. There was a cracking sound, a muffled curse, and Harry Stowe dropped on all fours beside him, the rifle clattering to the earth. "That last rung gave on me—" he began, and then looked up. "Incredible," he whispered, gaining his feet and staring down the empty tunnel. "How long has this been here, do you think?"

Billy Smith wasn't listening. He had gotten a sudden clear picture in his head of oily black water stretching out below a midnight sky. It was as if he had been holding a pair of binoculars before his eyes and someone had just adjusted the focus, so that the two blurred images joined and became one. The Thomas mansion was only a diseased limb; it was in another place where the sickness had begun, and where, God-willing, it would end. A place where dead gray trees rose like ghosts through the mist.

He remembered the white face of a ghoul, grinning at them through dirty glass.

"Frederick built it," he said. "It leads to the old Taylor property on Black Pond."

They had been moving along in tense silence for perhaps five minutes. The tunnel sloped gently downward for the first hundred feet or so, then leveled off. The earth was soggy and ice-cold under their shoes. The flashlight danced along length after length of dark walls and darker wooden beams that were thicker than his chest. Here and there a minor cave-in had spilled a mound of dirt from the ceiling and they stepped over these carefully, as if avoiding something that might eat the shoes right off their feet.

The tunnel took many small twists and turns, but it always seemed to return to the same general direction. There was only one place where they could possibly end up. All this time, he had believed that the evil in Ronnie Taylor had been responsible for that sour spot of earth below the falls. He realized now that it had been the other way around. Ronnie Taylor had picked the wrong place to build his house, that was all, and over the months the ground had taken its toll on him, and the amulet had done the rest.

But who the hell had dug this tunnel? In the years before machinery it seemed impossible that something like this could have been created. Frederick had had help, of course. But he wouldn't have been able to turn to the local villagers. Smith didn't want to think of what kind of help he might have received.

The flashlight flickered and he froze, holding his breath. Something had moved up ahead in the darkness. Terror washed over him now, making his legs tremble and his bladder ache. *"Billy,"* Stowe hissed. He was pointing to a point about thirty feet ahead, where the tunnel took a sudden turn to the right. Smith flattened himself against the wall, and slapped the flashlight against his forearm. It flickered again, and then came on strong. He raised the beam of light.

Sheriff Claude Pepper was coming steadily toward them out of the shadows. Something had been chewing on his face and throat; the front of his uniform was soaked with blood. One ear was gone, the other hanging by a ribbon of flesh. The fingers of his right hand had been bitten off at the first knuckle, and the mangled stumps wriggled in the air in front of him like fat bloody worms. It took Smith a moment to realize the odd swishing sound came from the sheriff's two pant legs rubbing together.

A small, trapped noise escaped his mouth. He raised the handgun and tried to pull the trigger, but the gun would not fire. The beam of the flashlight bobbed in his hand and threw monstrous shadows across the walls.

A shot rang out just behind him, deafening in the close confines of the tunnel. Dirt showered down upon his head. The sheriff stumbled back a few steps, and kept going. Stowe's bullet had taken him in his fleshy stomach; a quarter-sized hole showed near his belt.

The rifle roared again. This time Pepper's head jerked back on his neck, and he paused, not ten feet away. One hand went to his ruined face, exploring the contours of it as if for the first time. Stowe pulled the trigger once more, and a hole appeared in the back of the hand. The big man twitched like a puppet on strings, dropped heavily to his knees, and then fell face first into the cold black mud.

"There," Stowe said quietly. His voice was cracking. "There, you bastard."

Smith looked at him. Stowe was gripping the rifle too hard; his face was flushed, his hair hung wetly across his forehead, and his eyes were hidden in two circles of shadow. Caught in the strange, yellow beam of the flashlight, he looked like a madman.

"Harry . . ." he said. Stowe jerked his head around and stared at him. His mouth was a thin white line. "Thanks," Smith finished simply. His legs felt rubbery. Stowe kept staring at him a moment, then he nodded and took a deep, rattling breath.

"Safety," he said. "Turn off the fucking safety."

Smith turned the handgun over and found the red button on its side. He felt like he was going to be sick.

At their feet, Pepper's huge body twitched in the mud, like a landed fish.

They moved on. Twice more, they ran into roadblocks.

The first, a big, white ghostly creature who turned out to be a very dead Barbara Trask in a nightdress, had almost gotten her hands on them. She had been waiting around another sharp bend in the tunnel, and although mangled as badly as the sheriff in other ways (her neck was a mess of tangled, red flesh), her face was mostly intact, which made it more difficult to shoot. Smith froze up, finger on the trigger, and her eyes fixed on him. He saw the lust there, as bright and naked as the full moon. He had time to wonder what might happen if she touched him, and then Stowe came to his rescue again, pressing the barrel of his rifle against the side of her head and pulling the trigger, splattering most of her brains against one of the wooden tunnel beams and dropping her, twitching, at his feet. Stowe looked whiter after that, and his hands trembled like a drunk's after a hard night. But he did not falter.

Then, just as they turned to continue, the huge dog came at them out of the dark, and this time Billy Smith did not hesitate. He fired five times into the dog's snarling face. Blood and brain and shards of bone flew up in a bright red cloud, and when it was done, the dog was on the ground next to its owner. The top of its head was gone, but it kept trying to gain its feet. Smith was reminded of a turtle flipped over onto its back. He steeled his stomach, walked up, placed a foot on the big dog's neck (even now it tried to snap weakly at him), and emptied the magazine into its skull.

Finally only the tips of its paws moved, scraping uselessly against the thick mud. It looked like a dog trying to run in its sleep. Except this dog wore nothing but a red pulpy mess above its shoulders. *Oh Jesus,* he thought dully, looking at the paws twitch. His throat felt thick and swollen. *I'm not going to make it.*

Then Stowe's hand was on his shoulder. He did not say a word; the look in his eyes was enough.

They went on. A few minutes later the tunnel began to rise, and the mud was not as thick under their feet. They began to hear the thunder again, a distant booming sound like artillery. As Smith walked, each step seemed to increase the load he carried around his shoulders, and the terrible doubts and depression that had plagued him since that morning kept creeping back at him. Doubts, he realized, that had never really left; he had simply allowed the urgency in Harry Stowe and his own anger at being played for a fool to carry him through so far. His mind returned to the night he and Angel had investigated the Taylor property for the first time, the way the trees had moved with the passing of something gigantic and dark, and he remembered the way he had turned tail and run like a frightened child from the puffy white face of his dead mother in the dirty window.

He thought of Angel. For a moment, that great shining dam inside his soul groaned under the weight of his guilt, and almost gave way. Why was he here? Was there nothing more to it than an ancient curse, was he doomed from the very beginning, as he had often thought? And if so, would he have a chance to look the darkness in the eye before it sent him tumbling into the void?

*Does the devil know who made him? Where he came from? Or is he just like us, constantly questioning his existence, the reason for it all, the meaning?*

Light, up ahead. The tunnel was coming to an end. Above their heads they could hear the thundering voice of the unknown.

The tunnel ended abruptly at another ladder. This one was fashioned out of newer wood; it looked as if it would hold their weight easily. Gray, lifeless light filtered down through cracks in the trapdoor above. Smith looked up into the narrow shaft, water dripping onto his face. He listened. All sound had ceased, except the rain and the whistling wind.

"Well?" Harry Stowe whispered. Stowe's voice did not seem to belong to him. It was high and tight and shaking. But his eyes were still bright and sane, and he stood with both feet braced and ready. He had not hesitated for a single moment. Not when it counted. Smith felt an almost overwhelming gratitude. He hadn't had to carry the burden alone, after all. *Without you, I'd be dead right now,* he thought. *I'd go into battle with you anytime, my friend.*

"Go to her," Stowe said. "I'll watch your back."

Smith closed his eyes, and willed himself to relax, letting that hand inside his mind flex its psychic fingers and come to life. He would have to be careful this time, he knew. There were dangers within this realm as well, false steps that could mean death, if he began to feel around in the wrong place. The darkness was close.

Reaching, he pushed out gently—

—and joined. This time, entering her mind was as easy and smooth as listening to his own thoughts. He almost cried out with joy. So shallow to think that the only closeness between a man and woman came from the physical act. That was simply one way of sharing a *mind* together, and even then, even during the best of it, the touch was just the barest brushing of mental fingertips. Not like this. Never like this.

There was no fear this time, no conscious thought. She was asleep, or out cold, and dreaming. Her (their) dreams were unfocused, flowing flowerbeds of color. They floated as one through plains of soft white and green and blue smoke, pale shadow shapes slipping close, then away again like little birds. He heard their wings beating, felt their caresses upon his face. Warmth flowed through his limbs, tears ran freely down his face, and the burdens began to lift, he was growing lighter, lighter still, ah, Jesus, the beauty of it . . .

He was being shaken, hard. *"Billy!"* someone said against his ear. He came partway back, jolted out of the dream. Cold gray light filtered through his closed lids. He tried to brush the hands away and found them pulling at him again. "Billy, come on, not now, oh, Christ . . ."

Harry. He opened his eyes and found himself standing in the tunnel again. Real tears flowed down his cheeks. They were cold against his skin.

Harry Stowe was staring anxiously into his face. "Don't," Smith muttered absently. "Don't do that. Don't take me out."

*"Where is she?"*

"I don't know. She was asleep." She was still there; he could feel the dreams playing in the back of his own mind. There was a faint, sweet taste in his mouth, the taste of candy apples. He had the odd, disjointed feeling of being in two places at once. The connection between them had been stretched thin, but not broken.

He wanted only to return to the dream. Reality was so hard.

"You want to help her, don't you?" Stowe shook him again. "He'll murder her when he's done. You told me that yourself. Do you want to be a part of it? *Do* you?"

Smith winced. *No. Please don't ask me to leave her, though. Please don't ask me that.*

Stowe simply pushed him toward the ladder. The rough wood against his hands brought him back a little farther, and he began to climb. The gun was gone; he thought he remembered stuffing it into his pocket.

He reached the trapdoor. The water was dripping faster now, running through the cracks in the wood. He reached up, pushed and felt it give. Colors were still blooming in front of his eyes, greens and soft reds and blues. It was like looking through colored glasses at a dead winter world. Inside was where you wanted to be, inside, where it was warm and you could smell wood from a fire and your feet were stuffed into a pair of soft, comfortable slippers.

Stowe was hitting his legs from below the ladder. He looked up. The trapdoor was open. Had he done that? He couldn't quite remember. He climbed the last two rungs, grabbed the edges of the frame and lifted himself over.

And stepped into Ronnie Taylor's domain.

He was standing in the middle of a ruined room. The roof was sagging and there was an open hole above his head, bare and broken rafters pointing up into a splintered gray sky. Rain slashed into his upturned face. There was a gaping hole just to the left of where he stood, where the floorboards had rotted and fallen in. The walls had crumbled in places, plaster giving way to glimpses of the wooden frame and the world outside.

This had been the kitchen in the old Taylor home; the ends of rusted, broken pipes stuck out from the wall below a shattered window, and in the corner sat part of a chipped porcelain sink, half full of brown water. Through the remains of the window he could see the rippling water of the pond and the tire swing flipping crazily in the wind.

He turned toward the door, which now hung crookedly on its hinges. The next room was more or less intact. The floor was solid, the roof and walls closed. This was where it had happened; Ronnie raising the broom handle again and again, bringing it down in a vicious, slashing arc, turning his wife's face into something unrecognizable, blood thrown in wide, splattering half-moons across the floor, the sofa, the walls. Then taking the knife up from the kitchen and going after the baby in her womb.

Or had that happened first? Had he tried to take the baby from her and failed, and only then taken up the broom handle in a frenzy of rage? Had he realized, too late, that his blood was not quite pure enough? That he was not the one they wanted, after all?

Smith blinked. Rainwater ran freely down his face and mixed with his tears. His nightmarish vision faded slowly, and the woman with the bloody, beaten face changed, but did not disappear.

Angel was lying on her back in the middle of the floor. Someone had drawn a circle around her body with red paint. No, blood; of course it would be blood. She was still whole, thank God, and alive. There was a pile of white bones near her head. He stared, not quite sure what he was seeing. The bones were *wriggling* like grubs. Frederick's remains, even now trying to come to life.

Then he knew what was meant to happen, and he recoiled from it as if struck. Jeb would butcher her, as his father had done to his mother years ago, and this time, Frederick and the thing that had taken him long ago would get what they wanted.

Stowe had come up the ladder behind him, and he went forward quickly toward the next room where Angel lay, skirting the edges of the places where the floor had fallen in. *No,* Smith thought dully, watching him go. He wanted to cry out, but his voice had left him. *That's what he wants, he wants to separate us.*

But it was too late. As Stowe knelt beside Angel's body,

knocking the bones away with a cry of disgust, the crooked door picked itself up and slammed shut with a bang, cutting them off. Smith jumped; the noise and sudden movement seemed to break the spell that had fallen over him. He ran forward across the spongy floorboards and threw himself against the door, battering it with his fists. He could hear Stowe shouting on the other side. But the door would not budge.

"What's happening!" he screamed. He could feel the ground thrumming under his feet, as if the very earth was coming alive. A great gust of wind shook the little shack. For a moment he thought it might go right over and sink into the foul black mud, burying them all forever.

Then the voice spoke up in his mind, dark and dripping with a naked lust that made him shriek with fear. *So you've finally come. Welcome. Welcome to the void.*

# Chapter Twenty

Angel was drifting through a pleasant warm fog. Somewhere along the line (time had no meaning here in this perfect place), someone had taken her hand, and they drifted together for a while, and that was nice. She felt as if she knew this hand, like it belonged to someone she had been waiting to come for a long time. At first she thought it was her brother's hand, but he had died years ago. He was gone forever. For a moment the familiar ache of the loss passed through her, and then it faded away.

The hand pulled away. She reached for it but she couldn't catch it again. This was troubling; it was like having an itch on your back in that spot you couldn't quite reach.

Then someone was shaking her. She heard a voice calling her name. The fog was replaced by the feeling of cold, hard boards against her back. She opened her eyes. Harry Stowe was slapping her cheeks lightly. "There you are," he said, when she looked up at him in confusion. "Thank God. I was beginning to think we were too late."

Everything came crashing back at once. Annie, dead, and that thing coming down at her from the ceiling . . . she shook her head. The hand in her mind was still there. But she had lost its grip, and now she could not find it again. It was an odd sensation. Voices, echoing through her head, none of them making any sense.

She tried to gain her feet. Pain ripped through her stomach, and she cried out in surprise.

"You have to keep still—"

"Billy!" Something was happening to him; she felt for the hand again, but it eluded her. Damn it, she could not see!

"We can't do anything now," Stowe said. "The door's stuck. He's on his own."

Then she cried out again, because she could see how vulnerable he was, how his guilt would open the crack and let the darkness in. Jeb Taylor had been only a diversion, a plaything, something that could be used and then thrown away.

*Oh, Billy,* she thought. *It's you they want, don't you see? It was you all along. It has to be you.*

The voice, booming through his skull, struck him dumb. *We've been waiting for you,* the voice said. *We're all here. Jeb and his father and a good many others. Aren't you going to come and say hello?*

He was filled with a mindless, seething rage. He whirled around and saw Jeb Taylor hanging there like a huge black vulture against the ruined wall, his long coat billowing in the wind. Jeb's face was a constantly changing canvas, a boiling, seething ruin in which different features surfaced and then disappeared.

*Will you come into the void with us?*

No!

*But you must. There is no other place to go. The void is all there is.*

His mind rebelled against the idea. Death, with all its mystery, could not end in something so terrible, so empty. *That's not true. You lie.*

The thing in the dark coat raised a bony finger. *Look, then. Look upon them, and see.*

Helpless, he looked. Through the broken window, and at intervals where the walls had rotted through to outside, he could see the corpses gathering at the edges of the clearing. They were in all stages of decay, some of them mostly whole, a few no more than bones and tattered flesh. Skulls gleamed whitely through the slashing rain as they stumbled blindly closer. *Oh, dear God,* he thought. *Please. I can't fight them all.*

*They smell the fresh life here, and they come.* The creature against the wall was grinning at him, its features congealing. Red, burning eyes regarded him with all the coldness of a reptile. He knew he was seeing Frederick, not the man in the painting that hung in the Thomas study, but the way he was now, after the evil had turned him. *The woman and children you killed. Did you think that was an accident? Nothing is an accident. You are meant for this. Search yourself. You have always been meant for this.*

He did search himself, and hated what he saw. The weakness, the fatal flaw that had always been there, waiting to take him down. As Jeb Taylor's weakness had taken him. *We are connected,* Smith thought. *I could have been him; I was him, years ago, and only a freak accident was enough to sober me up and stop me from killing myself.* The line between good and evil was so fine it sometimes blurred or disappeared completely. *One day you look down and realize you've stepped over it somewhere and you can't get back.*

Had he crossed that line between good and evil long ago? Had the dice been loaded from the very beginning? *Sorry, house rules. Now roll.*

He looked back at the thing against the wall. It was holding out a small silver flask. *Take it, Billy. Bring us new life, and join us forever. We'll even let you come out once in a while.*

Ah, God, the thirst. It ripped at him, cutting him to the bone, leaving him defenseless. Suddenly he couldn't think of anything else. Offering him sleep, precious sleep. He reached for the flask. As his hand closed over it, something rippled and changed and he was holding the handle of a long, curved knife.

"That's right," the Jeb-creature said eagerly. "Go on. Do it, and you will forget everything. You'll finally have peace."

Billy Smith thought of the three lives he had taken so cruelly, lives that were worth so much more than his could ever be. Children who would never see another day, never see their own children's faces. Were they in the void, too? It couldn't be. He would not believe that. The guilt was so heavy he thought he might break. Here was his chance to settle his own private score. Words came back to him, words he had heard from the very beginning, and had not made sense to him, until now. *Those who have reached the end and been born again.* That was him, wasn't it? He had reached the end a long time ago.

Now, he was being offered a chance to make up for what he had done by making the ultimate sacrifice, and through that, only through that, could he be reborn.

"Go on," the thing said. *That's what you were meant to do what are you waiting for go and DO IT—*

In this last moment, full of wonder, he knew; the void was not all there was, because there was goodness in the world too, there was love, and the devil was a liar. *It's not about forgetting, Angel,* he thought triumphantly, *my sweet, sweet Angel. It's about remembering the past, remembering all of it, because only through that can we learn to do what's right.*

He held the blade high above with both hands, letting

the rain wash it clean, and then he brought it down, plunging it handle-deep into his own belly.

Something shrieked inside his skull. He sat down hard on the wet floor, his legs folding underneath him. Through a dull haze of pain he heard the door to the other room burst open, and then he saw the Jeb-creature coming at him from the wall, a great, swooping monster, its features contorted into a grimace of anger and pain.

As it reached for the handle of the knife, trying to pull it from him, and as the dam finally let go somewhere deep inside, Billy Smith did the last thing he could do.

He reached into the pocket of his jacket, pulled out the police handcuffs from the station, and slapped one side on himself and the other onto Jeb Taylor's wrist.

The thing screamed. It thrashed wildly against the cuffs, trying in vain to get free. Smith felt his own arm being yanked almost out of his socket. But the cuffs held firm. The dam had been ripped away now, his soul was bare, and the feelings came pouring out of him, making him gasp, bringing the tears again. The dam, releasing the flood that he always knew would carry him away.

A great, dull roar had come up over the sound of the howling wind, a roar growing louder by the second. He got a sudden clear picture of the lake next to the Old Mill Inn, swollen and massive, thousands upon thousands of gallons of water held back by a single stretch of cracked concrete. He saw the concrete crumbling, bits of mortar falling into the stream, the stream growing stronger, faster, until the barrier gave way all at once and the water thundered down the deep riverbed, swelling and engulfing the falls, boiling through the flat stretch of land, a huge wave of water erasing everything in its path.

*Okay,* he thought, letting the pain slowly take him into

its arms. *If there's something good out there somewhere, listen up. I've done my part, now you do yours. Show me I was right, after all.*

She had gained her feet in spite of the pain in her belly, and Stowe was standing with his arm around her for support, when the door suddenly flew open and crashed against the wall. At the same moment, she felt the hand inside her mind suddenly clench itself into a fist. She screamed; it seemed that something screamed with her.

Stowe still had her around the waist, and they both went to the door and stared in horror at the monster shackled inside the next room. It was a writhing, shrieking insanity, a great, black, long-limbed creature with the face of a nightmare. Like a badger with its foot caught in a trap, it threw itself mindlessly against the ends of the cuffs, half-dragging Billy Smith along as it tried to make its way across the sagging floor toward them. Smith wrapped an arm around one of the supports in the wall, and they fought against each other.

She tried to go to him, but Harry Stowe's grip tightened around her waist, holding her back. She fought him; for a moment, there were two raving creatures in the room. Then she saw the handle of the knife sticking out from Smith's stomach, and she saw the blood.

She felt again for his hand inside her mind. It was there, waiting for her, and she grasped it as tightly as she could. Warmth flooded through her aching body.

*I'm sorry. I did what I had to do.*

A sob caught in her throat. *Oh, Billy. Please don't leave me.*

*You have to go now. Run. Don't worry about me. I've always known it would come to this. But you were right, you know. There is goodness, after all.*

A picture of a wave filled her mind, a great and shining wall of water so tall it eclipsed the sky. At the same time she heard a low rumbling in the distance. She tried to look inside him then, tried to see the terrible thing he had been hiding from her, but it was gone, washed away by the flood. All she felt was love, so strong and so pure it drove the breath from her lungs.

She looked at him with wonder, and that was when the demon thing showed its face. For a single moment she got the impression of a many-limbed beast, much larger than the little room they were in, its tentacles stretched across miles of open land, saucers like suction cups digging into the earth, a beaked maw like an octopus that snapped and lunged at them. It was a thing of pure hatred, pure evil, and she took an instinctive, half step back. But it could not reach them, and she finally understood. It was held captive by the same thing that gave it power; as long as the amulet still hung around Jeb Taylor's neck, it could not escape his flesh and blood. Billy Smith had won.

The roar was getting louder. The floor had begun to shake beneath her feet. *Run, now. The flood is coming.*

The hand inside her mind seemed to flex again, offer a final, gentle caress, and then it was gone.

# Chapter Twenty One

She was never sure later exactly how the end went. She remembered a gentle, warm fog dropping over her mind again. Harry was there. Somehow he guided her gently across the room as the roaring reached a thunderous pitch and a huge and blinding flash of lightning split the sky above their heads. Then they were climbing down into the earth. She felt something give deep inside, and then a warm, heavy flow of blood was running down her leg. She thought; *I've lost the baby.* Strangely, the thought did not depress her. The baby was never hers, not in the way it should have been. That much she understood.

Then the darkness descended as Stowe pulled the trapdoor shut, and they began to fumble their way forward in the dim beam of the flashlight, away from the nightmare, away from the man she loved.

Above them, the flood shook the earth.

It thundered through the steep, narrow passage where the dam had been, carrying sticks and sludge and rocks and pieces of concrete, slabs of earth and sod, uprooting everything in its path. When it reached the upper bridge, the structure groaned under the sudden pressure, girders snapping like guitar strings. The water roared on, shooting out over the falls as if expelled from a gaping mouth, erasing and overflowing the churning pool below. Three houses that had been built too close to the river, houses that had seen their basements flooded many times and their foundations weakened by the moist air, were swept away as the wave passed. Boards, pieces of furniture, and other things too shattered to be recognizable joined the deluge. The great wave carved the deep banks of the river even deeper as it rumbled along its path of destruction.

At Billy Smith's side, the creature had become silent. It, too, was listening, as if aware of its own fate. The hellish light in its eyes slowly died, and it seemed for a moment as if Jeb had returned. He seemed bewildered, as if waking up from a long, dreamless sleep.

The water reached the clearing and seemed to rear up a moment, like a huge dark stallion pawing the air. Then it fell. The corpses, still standing in a circle around the broken shack, were swept away and torn apart by the flood. The rope of the old tire swing snapped, and then the tree it had been tied to swayed and came crashing down.

The wave lifted the shack, but even before that Billy Smith had felt himself begin to drift. The light overhead faded away. Tears still flowed unchecked down his pale cheeks. But he had been washed clean, and for the first time in as long as he could remember, he was free.

Something was calling him. The place that opened up before his eyes was not empty at all, it was not dark and cold and lifeless. There were people there he recognized, whole and happy to see him, and as he moved closer and the water swept him away, he knew that this was the way it was supposed to be.

Finally, and for the first time in his life, he was going home.

# Epilogue

"I am the resurrection and the life. He who believes in Me, though he may die, he shall live. And whoever lives and believes in Me shall never die."

*—John 11:25*

From the May second edition of the *Portland Press Herald*:

*BIZARRE STORM ROCKS SMALL TOWN*

*WHITE FALLS—The strange weather patterns that had plagued the small Maine town of White Falls for over two weeks came to a tragic end yesterday, the day the town was to hold its traditional May festival.*

*Experts are at a loss to explain the powerful storm front that developed over the course of several hours, caused extensive damage and claimed the lives of over 50 residents. In a prepared statement, a representative from the weather observatory claimed that the storm had raised a type of tornado, caused by the extreme variations in the temperature of several storm fronts in the area.*

*During the course of the storm the mill dam, a fixture in town for over 100 years, gave way under the tremendous water pressure, spilling what amounted to a small tidal wave down a mile of riverfront property. Both town bridges were damaged, and three houses were lost to the flood.*

*"There was no warning," claimed a survivor. "One day we're told the sky's going to clear, and the next thing we know all hell breaks loose."*

*The bizarre story does not end there, claim those who have witnessed the tragedy. For reasons yet to be brought to light, the town cemetery was vandalized during the storm. Many remains are now missing and presumed stolen. Several survivors reported seeing things that "defy description." One unidentified man, after barricading himself inside his house during the storm, took pot shots at state police from a second floor window, screaming incoherently and holding them at bay for over three hours. Psychiatrists called in to assist on the case referred to these incidents as stress related, and declined to go into any further detail as to what witnesses claimed to have seen . . .*

From the diary of Gloria Johnson:

*It's been two days since it happened, and Harry has left me alone in this ugly little hospital room for the first time. I have settled down with a pen and a pad of paper in my lap because I feel that I have to write it all down or go crazy. But nothing comes. So I sit here, holding this pen in my hand like an idiot who doesn't have a clue what it's for, and I cry like a baby. All I feel is emptiness, as if a part of me has been taken away, a part that I don't know how to live without. How can I write anything down when such a vital part of me is gone? I don't know where to begin. There's too much unfinished business.*

*So I guess maybe I should try to finish it first, and go on from there. I'm going to make this a letter, because that's what I need it to be. We have some unfinished business, Billy Smith. Are you out there somewhere, watching me? Are you taking this down?*

*Ever since we met I felt like you were a part of my destiny. Even during those first few days, when I was scared and angry, I knew that you had come to me for a reason. There were the dreams, of course, but what I felt went deeper than that. I had the feeling you had come to save me. Isn't that funny? I mean, we didn't exactly meet under the best of circumstances, did we? But my life was a mess. Anyone could have seen that. I had gotten myself in over my head in Miami, and I didn't know how to get out before I drowned. You saved me from that, even if you did have your own reasons.*

*I'm in some pain. Harry says I had a spontaneous miscarriage, caused by the stress of what happened. He says there will be no lingering effects, and I should be able to have children again when I'm ready. I told him I was glad, because I didn't want him to worry too much about me.*

*But inside I'm dying, Billy. I try to make sense of your death and I can't do it—not because I don't know what you did for me, what you did for all of us, but because it seems so damned unfair. I'm selfish, and I don't care. I need you with me.*

On the third night following the flood, Gloria Johnson had a dream. She was standing on the edge of a beach, and the surf was washing softly against a stretch of white sand. The sun was shining brightly, but the light did not seem to warm her, and as she watched the unbroken line of blue water against the lighter blue horizon she felt something familiar suddenly touch her face. She shivered and turned, but saw nothing, and yet the touch was still there, inside her mind.

When she turned back toward the water, her brother Michael was standing at the edge of the surf, looking back at her. He was whole and healthy, and smiling in that teasing way he did when she had done something especially crazy or silly, and she felt a sudden gentle twist of her heart.

As she watched him, the touch inside her mind changed. Michael changed. One moment it was her big brother, smiling at her, and the next she found herself staring into the pale, shadowy face of Billy Smith. Her heart twisted itself tighter in her chest. Billy wore Michael's same teasing, lopsided grin. He raised a single white hand and waved.

*I'll always be here, Angel,* he said. *Remember. I'm a part of you, a special part, and that can never be taken away. We're the same, you and I.*

She raised a hand in return, and watched in silence as he slowly made his way into the surf and disappeared. But she felt him there still, and it was as if something missing had finally been returned to her.

When she woke up her pillow was wet, but the tears seemed to have lost some of their bitterness, and when she slept again, she slept peacefully.

From the diary of Gloria Johnson:

*Yesterday morning, three days after I left the hospital, I drove back to town. It was a beautiful day. Reminded me of the first morning after Billy and I came here, the day we met Annie and Harry Stowe . . .*

She crossed the bridge into town, seeing the damage for the first time since that day, seeing it in the bright and hopeful spring sunlight of mid-May. Harry had told her some of what was going on, but until now she hadn't been back. She hadn't known if she would ever come back.

On her right the river now flowed unbroken, swelling slightly through what was left of the mill lake. The Old Mill Inn leaned dangerously toward the water, and she knew that they were going to just let it go. Bob Rosenberg had been one of the people who had disappeared that hateful day, and no one had come forward to run the inn in his absence. Worse than that, nobody seemed to care.

On her left after she crossed the bridge, uprooted trees stuck up here and there like hands coming up out of the earth. Giants buried in the barren soil, unable to free themselves. Most of the debris from the flood still spread itself across the open stretch of road leading down to the scenic turnout. A telephone pole had gone down, and it had been propped up but not yet replaced. The clinic was still open, although Harry hadn't gone back to work and swore that he never would. Not there, he said. The town had gone sour for him, as she supposed it had for many of them.

She turned and drove past *Johnny's* and the grocery, and beyond them, the cemetery. That, at least, had been cleaned up, the graves filled in, though many of them probably contained nothing more than dirt and empty coffins now. The Portland paper had carried a single follow-up story about what they called a "senseless act of vandalism"; they claimed that most of the bodies had been dug up by a still unidentified person or persons and then left for the river to sweep away. The bog below Black Pond was reputed to be a gruesome display of partially decomposed body parts, some of which had been disposed of, some which would never be recovered. Billy's and Jeb's bodies had not yet been found, as far as she knew. Maybe they never would be.

Someone stood out near the gazebo on the square, which had been one of the few things left whole by the storm. The figure held a big green trash bag and slowly bent to pick things up and stuff them inside. Beyond that was the Thomas mansion, and though she couldn't see much more than an occasional glimpse through the trees, she knew it was still there, as it had stood for over two hundred years, empty and cold and silent. *Have they found the passage yet?* she wondered. And if so, had they found Sheriff Pepper and Barbara Trask? That would surely raise some interesting questions. There were bullet holes in them, after all.

*They won't find a thing,* she thought suddenly. *Because*

*somehow those bodies disappeared too. I don't know how, but they did.*

The thought brought a chill to her, though it had been warm enough to drive with the windows down most of the way from Portland.

She kept going past the town office, turned onto Indian Road, but it wasn't until she was almost there that she realized where she was going.

Yellow police tape had been stretched across the beginning of the narrow dirt track that led down to the old Taylor property. She pulled over to the side of the road, turned off the engine, and got out to walk. She had her own demons to face.

*The track was much as I remembered it, tree branches hanging down on all sides, mud under my feet, only a lot of trucks had been down here since it happened, and the ground was even more rutted than before. And it was cold in there out of the sun. I started getting a little scared, which is natural I guess, after what we went through. Except I began to get that funny feeling again, and this is what really made me nervous, that feeling of being watched, as if something big and ugly was hunched down in the bushes. I felt it coming up through my feet, too, as if the ground itself was crying out at a high pitch I couldn't quite hear.*

*That's when I began to wonder if it was really over, if it ever could be over. Maybe the land is spoiled, and maybe this is the most rotten spot, like the dark bruise in an apple that's been sitting around awhile. I thought about what Annie said, about certain places calling out the sick, the weak, and making them fester. I almost turned back, but I forced myself to keep going because I knew that if I didn't face it now, I never would, and it would keep haunting me for the rest of my life.*

*When I reached the clearing I knew that something was there. It shouldn't have been anything but a bare patch of ground by an ugly little pond, but it was more than that.*

*The clearing was empty, the shack and the old shed washed away, just a sunken hole in the ground left to mark where they had stood. I could see a few boards sticking up out of the brush at the far end, but that was all.*

*Then I heard something calling to me, and I knew. It didn't speak, exactly, not in the way people do, but it called just the same.*

*I walked across the clearing to the spot where those boards were sticking up, and there it was, lying in the dirt like the world's biggest jewel. I say that because it was sparkling, as if it had caught the sunlight and held it inside.*

*I picked it up before I knew what I was doing. It seemed much heavier than it should be. The carvings were fascinating. The two serpents with their tails in their mouths, and the red eye in the center, which was the part that seemed to sparkle, almost as if it were a real eye, watching you, letting you know it was awake and knew exactly what was happening. Clever. It felt nice in my hand, a little warmed by the sun.*

*And then it jumped. My God, it wriggled against my skin like it was alive and trying to burrow inside me. I grabbed one of the boards and laid it flat on the ground, and then I put the amulet down on it. There was a good-sized rock nearby, and I picked that up and brought it down with everything I had. I swung that rock again and again, until my shoulder started to ache, and it felt like Billy was there with me, watching. Maybe he took a few swings himself.*

*Then when I was done, I took the pieces in my hand and I threw them as far as I could into the pond. When they hit the water they didn't make a sound or even a splash. They just disappeared.*

*I think I found that window you told me about, Annie. The one between the worlds. And I think maybe I closed it, once and for all.*

Two weeks later, Gloria Johnson made the drive up from Portland again, where she had taken a motel room. She parked on the square and hiked into the hills, above what remained of White Falls. There, by the big slab of rock overlooking the valley, she found a good spot. The ground here was dry and soft and full of pine needles and rich soil.

She did what she had been wanting to do for a while now. She built a marker for Billy Smith.

It took her an hour to collect the rocks, and close to another hour to get them the way she wanted. Then she knelt in the good, soft ground. She did not speak and did not pray, only waited, and remembered.

A cool breeze blew in across the pines, bringing their fresh clean scent. A squirrel began to chatter in the trees, angry at whatever had interrupted its daily routine; after a few moments, it ran farther up the trunk and then jumped to another, moving steadily away, and before long she couldn't hear it anymore.

"Billy," she said softly. "This is a good spot, isn't it? The one you would have wanted?"

She waited, feeling a few hot tears work their way out and burn her cheeks. But no answer came. She thought she felt him there, or maybe it was just the wind and the smell of the pines and the way the ground felt against her knees. Maybe it was just the feeling of a good clean spring morning.

She thought of him every day, and every day it seemed he got just a little farther away from her. At first she had tried to hang on, tried so hard, and then she realized that it wasn't what he would have wanted. He would have wanted her to live her life and make it a special one. *Remember the past,* she could almost hear him saying, *learn from it, but don't live in it. There's a difference.* She understood his strength, his sacrifice, that by taking that final secret to the grave with him, he had spared her an unnecessary agony. *He is stronger than he thinks,* Annie had said, and she was right. He had given her her life back. She remembered a question he had asked her; *Do you believe in goodness?* She had thought on that one quite a bit lately, and wondered if perhaps it didn't rest within each and every human soul, in small sacrifices and small events.

Harry was still visiting her every day, and was helping her find a job in Portland. He was a good man, kind and attentive, and she thought eventually he might ask her to dinner, and eventually she might even accept. But that was a long way from now. Right now even thinking about it made her feel like a traitor.

*Billy,* she thought. *I miss you so much. It's so hard.*

She stayed there for a while, and finally the squirrel came back. It sat in a tree above her head and chattered at her, and she decided that she was being asked to leave. Her time was up. It wasn't really a place for humans, after all.

As she started down the trail she looked back, and for a moment she could see Billy standing there. He looked the way he had looked in her dream, smiling gently, hand raised in greeting. Or perhaps it was farewell.

Then he was gone, and she made her way back down the trail to her car, tired but no longer quite so empty.

She was healing.

# About the Author

Nate Kenyon grew up in a small town in Maine with dark nights and long winters to feed his interest in writing. His stories have appeared in various magazines and in the horror anthology *Terminal Frights*. Kenyon lives in a recently-restored 1840s Greek Revival home in the Boston area with his wife Nicole and their three children: Emily, Harrison, and Abbey. Their ferocious cat, which terrorizes neighborhood dogs, comes and goes as he pleases. Visit Nate Kenyon online at www.natekenyon.com.